MÉLISA RYUN

Published in the United States by Create Mode Media, LLC. All rights reserved. Printed in USA. First edition 2025. Cover design by Lisa Kubja.

Create Mode Media LLC
7925 W. Russell Road #401103
Las Vegas, NV 89140
eBook Edition ISBN-13: 9781947775169
Paperback Edition ISBN-13: 9781947775176

For permission requests contact:
info@melisaryun.com
www.melisaryun.com

TRIGGER WARNING: This book contains explicit sexual content, a toxic parent, death of a loved one (mentioned), bullying, gaslighting, and body shaming.

ALSO BY MÉLISA RYUN

HOT MESS SUMMER SERIES

Italy Can Bite Me

Hawaii Can Suck It

Mexico Can Choke On It

THE DENTON SISTERS SERIES

The Love Startup

a Raunchy, Geeky RomCom

STAND-ALONE TITLES

Fake It 'Til You Sleigh It

a Holiday Romantic Comedy

Live From New York... It's Love

Short Story

DEDICATION

To the chaos agents, the rule breakers, the ones told they're 'too much.' Your fire isn't a flaw, it's the spark the world needs. Keep burning bright.

CHAPTER ONE

PETRA

THANK FUCK IT'S FRIDAY.

This is the kind of day that dry-humps your dignity, kicks you in the emotional shin, and then farts in your face for an extra layer of humiliation.

I've got a whopping forty-five minutes to snag some lunch and FaceTime my best friends. It marks the first time all week I don't want to stab something. And honestly? I'm clinging to it like a life raft made of melted mozzarella and juicy gossip.

I'm in the driver's seat of my car, twisted into a reverse down dog position. My butt's smashed against the steering wheel, and my face is practically kissing the passenger seat floor. I'm not proud *(but also not ashamed)* as I dig through God knows what, now touching some kind of sticky goo. Is that a smooshed fry? Melted gum? All I know is, it's nasty.

I've survived twenty-five years on this flaming hell rock, but hands down... this week takes the crown for the worst ever. I knew it'd feel shitty—selling my soul to my perfectionist older brother to work in his corporate empire—but throw in zero sleep, a gas tank thirstier than I am, and an outfit still soggy from my building's broken-ass dryer? And yeah...

Today sucks ass. And not in the fun, consensual way.

My jet-black hair falls into my eyes as I shove aside a tower of coffee cups—growing steadily since my last "I'll clean my car next weekend, I swear" promise. And then—a quarter!

"Score one for Petra Brinkman! This day is looking up."

I peel off the melted orange Starburst that has fused to the metal then exit my car—a mid-2000s black Lexus LS 400. Sounds classy, but one look at the mismatched silver panel and... not so much. The thing is a piece of crap with rust spots, duct tape, and graffiti, more like a rolling middle finger than a car. My brother Gavin says it's why people think I sell meth. *Whatever*. It's paid for and it runs... most of the time.

Oh, and the trunk? Um, that's a massive dick. Some genius from my sketchy neighborhood in Hollywood spray-painted a huge penis with the words: CHOKE ON IT.

All right, fine, it was me. I thought it was hilarious.

It started as a joke, but now it's my anti-theft system and life philosophy. No one's gonna grand theft auto this busted chariot—they're too scared it'll explode or stall. But the joke's on them. Still a Lexus, baby. Suck it, trust fund kids.

Here in Beverly Hills, my beat-up ride is the equivalent of arriving at the Met Gala in a garbage bag and Crocs. I'm wedged like an unwelcome thought between luxury vehicles. To my left? A pearl-white Bentley that probably gets exfoliated and waxed daily. To my right? A Maserati that runs on the tears of the working class. Every car parked on this street is a trophy wife on wheels, not a hint of bird poop in sight.

I tap my steering wheel. "Don't sweat it, girl. You belong here just as much as they do. Sure, your A/C is wheezing its final confession, but that's our business. No one's gonna treat us like some hot mess cousin with trust issues and a tattoo obsession."

I flip down my sun visor, the mirror panel hanging by one stubborn hinge. My reflection stares back, unimpressed.

"Let's not look like a total disaster," I mutter, digging into my bag for my lipstick. I swipe it on, pressing my lips together in a practiced move.

Sexpot Red. Wet n' Wild. $1.99 at any drugstore. I've been wearing this color since high school. It's less *fashion statement* and more *warning label*. The kind of red that says, *I came here to ruin your day.*

My full lips—the only feature I inherited from my father besides his uncanny ability to disappoint—bloom crimson against my pale skin.

Ah, crap. I spot some mascara flakes under my hazel-green eyes and gently rub them away.

My winged eyeliner? Still sharp enough to kill a man.

This midnight hair of mine is caught in that in-between style—half waves, half straight. I tuck a piece behind my ear, revealing the tiny broken heart tattoo hidden there: a quiet reminder of the first and last time I wore my heart on my sleeve.

Time for a wardrobe adjustment.

"Sorry, ladies," I say, kicking off the heels I found at a consignment shop. When you're living on mac and cheese, thrifting is essential. They're not actual Louboutins, but a clever touch of red nail polish on the soles passes them off as "Faux-boutins."

The scuffs at the toes tell the truth.

Reaching into the back seat *(and nearly dislocating my shoulder)*, I grab my combat boots. "Come to mama," I grunt, hauling them onto my lap.

These babies have stomped through protests, bar fights, and a blind date so terrible it deserves its own standup routine. The leather's all cracked, the strings frayed, but they feel like home. I jam my feet in—laces be damned—wiggle my toes, and breathe easier.

I grab my worn black leather jacket off the seat, slip it on, and step out of the car. Even if life is crap and I'm forced to wear a pencil skirt and blouse for work, in my real life—the one that matters—I can still look badass.

BAM! The door slams shut with a kick *(it needs the encouragement)*. The loud bang echoes across the hushed promenade. Two women clutch their designer handbags and give me a *please-don't-mug-me* expression.

Good.

Let them worry. I'm not here to blend in.

I strut toward the meter, my personal soundtrack blaring in my head—"Bad Reputation" by Joan Jett, obviously—my anthem since before I wore a bra.

Beverly Hills is like the ultimate rich girl's Instagram feed—flawless, filtered, and fake as hell. Pretentious designer labels. Botoxed smiles. Entitled, holier-than-thou attitudes. Royalty in their own minds. The trees are trimmed to perfection, the trash bins smell of eucalyptus, and even the pigeons may have had a little nip and tuck.

I should know. I grew up here.

I jam my quarter into the parking meter, but it bounces back as if it's allergic to poor people.

"Come on." I try again, wiggling it, but the slot is clearly jammed. "Take my money, you greedy little troll!"

I yank out my debit card and tap it against the reader. It blinks. Then nothing.

"Are you fucking kidding me?"

I tap it again.

Again.

Nothing. No mocking beep. No error message. *Shit!*

"Screw it. The Beverly Hills meter mafia doesn't scare me."

I cram my card back into my wallet, where it lounges in sad solidarity with my maxed-out Visa and an expired condom. I mutter a final curse at the meter. I now have forty minutes to inhale my lunch and talk to my besties. Then it's back to the hellscape that is my brother's office.

I step into California Pizza Kitchen and inhale. The holy trinity: dough, cheese, and overpriced IPA.

Edison bulbs dangle like they're trying to look edgy, abstract art vomits color across the walls, and the crowd is peak LA—assistants power-lunching and tourists who wandered in thinking this is where the celebrities eat. *Amateurs.* The real power players are three streets over, drinking liquid gold and eating endangered species off the backs of unpaid interns.

The bar's got a few open seats left, so I slide onto a high-top stool, the leather still warm from someone else's ass.

The hot bartender's rocking a man-bun, sleeve tattoos, and a face that says, *I may have been an actor in that biker show you didn't see.* He slides me a menu.

"Don't need it. Whatever IPA is on draft. BBQ chicken pizza. Extra cilantro. No judgment."

"Why would I judge a woman who knows what she wants?"

"You say that to all the overworked assistants or just the ones in combat boots?"

He grins. "Only the ones who might bite."

I like him immediately.

As he walks off to place my order, I tap the green *Call* button on my contact labeled: CPK FOREVER.

The name's a tribute to our college obsession with California Pizza Kitchen. Also, our initials: Cam, Petra, Katie.

Camila Morales and Katie Crawford.

My ride-or-dies since freshman year of college.

The people in my life who accept me exactly as I am. The *me* who went through a devastating heartbreak and ugly-cried so hard in a bathtub, they both climbed in and hugged me fully clothed.

In my experience, finding friends like that is a fucking miracle, so I cherish the hell out of them.

Katie's face pops into frame, her blonde hair in perfect waves—despite what looks like a very bumpy bus ride.

"You survived your first week and didn't burn the place down!"

"The day's not over yet." I smirk.

The bartender slides me a beer, and I raise it in a silent toast then take a swig.

"Can we backtrack to the decision where you spontaneously flew to Italy and I wasn't invited to be your morally corrupt plus-one?"

"Trust me, Spontaneous Katie is having major regrets. This trip is a disaster. My tour guide keeps changing the itinerary for 'authentic moments' and 'true Italian experiences.'"

She flips the camera to the window, and there it is—the Italian countryside in all its dreamy, rolling glory, blurring past.

"I'm on a bus headed to Tuscany today," she continues, her voice rising over the background noise. "The windows are smudged, it smells like someone died in here, and the guy behind me is eating tuna."

"Hold up—pan back to the front of the bus."

"Why?"

"Because I wanna see this menace who dares to disrespect your schedule. And maybe judge how tight his pants are."

Katie rotates her phone with an exasperated sigh. The Italian Stallion turns toward the camera as if he *knows* he's being watched. *Holy mother of thirst traps.* He's gesturing passionately about something, his smile flashing white against olive skin, and my God he has perfectly tousled dark hair.

"That's Matteo. The bane of my itinerary's existence."

"You don't have to like the guy to have sex with him."

Katie's cheeks flush pink. "No thanks. I'm here to see art and architecture, not hook up with some wannabe Casanova who's got a different tourist warming his sheets in every city."

"That just means he's had plenty of practice. Experience is never a bad thing when it comes to orgasms."

"Oh my God, Petra!"

Cam's face pops up on screen, splitting our call into thirds. Her rich chestnut hair is yanked back in a messy ponytail, secured with one of her signature scrunchies. Behind her... *Is that a palm tree? Indoors? And why are there vines all over the ceiling?*

"*¡Ay, Dios mío!* I am so sorry I totally lost track of time filming," she says.

"Um... Cam?" I blink. "Are you calling us from inside a sex-themed Rainforest Cafe?"

She exhales like a woman who's aged ten years in two days. "Yeah. No. Kinda. This room has no walls. None. What it *does* have is ambient jungle sounds, a spinning bed, and a scent that makes me feel like I'm being seduced by a piña colada."

Katie squints. "Wait—is that a *sex swing*?"

"Don't ask," Cam mutters. "If I had known fake-dating my boss included sharing a bed in the Love Den, I never would've gotten on the plane to Hawaii."

Poor Cam. Two years as the videographer for Reece Dare, the internet's favorite daredevil-turned-lifestyle-brand, and all she has to show for it is an impressive collection of stress headaches. The guy is YouTube-famous for jumping off buildings and eating ghost peppers, but from what Cam tells us, he's a brooding asshole with control issues and no amount of washboard abs can make up for his personality.

"Catch me up! Have you handed out any well-deserved smack-downs at work yet?" Cam asks.

"There's been violence, but not the kind I prefer. Monday, I drenched the quarterly reports in coffee. Tuesday, I broke the printer twice and caused a system meltdown trying to hide it. Wednesday, I called a board member *Dick* instead of *Ronald*. Thursday, I answered my brother's phone with, *Broken Bottle. Drink responsibly, tip recklessly,* because my brain was stuck in bartending mode."

Cam is cry-laughing. Katie looks like she's buffering.

"You're both thinking it, so I'll just say it. I am thriving." I wink.

Katie takes a steadying breath. "I could make you a binder to keep your tasks more organized. Step-by-step procedures—"

"No thanks," I say, cutting her off. "I'm sticking with my proven strategy of not writing shit down and seeing what happens. The deal

I made with my brother is to work for him this summer to get my college money. He never said I had to be *good* at it."

"So you're still working the bartending gig?" Cam asks.

"I'm broke AF, so yeah, but only weekends now. Gotta make rent on my shithole apartment." I flash them a devilish grin. "Unless I wanna take my landlord up on his oh-so-generous offer to swap sex for rent."

"You're joking, right?" Katie asks. "Please be joking."

"Relax, I'm kidding. The guy's a fossil who reeks of mothballs and Fritos. But seriously, the stack of unpaid bills on my counter is starting to resemble a freaking Jenga tower."

Cam's eyes flicker with concern, and I can already tell what's coming before she opens her mouth. "Sooo... can we ask about the Bryce situation? Have you seen him?"

There it is. The B-word. The name that makes my stomach do this annoying flip-flop.

Bryce Sterling.

He's the reason I dropped out of UCLA senior year.

Why I didn't graduate with my friends.

And he's why I bought a one-way ticket to Europe and tried to eat, hike, and slut my way into forgetting him.

Spoiler: didn't work.

"Haven't seen him. He's been in New York all week on business."

Both of their faces soften immediately, and I hate it. They're the only two people on this planet who know the truth about Bryce Sterling—my brother's best friend. Co-CEO of the company I now work for.

They're painfully aware that I've been obsessed with him since I was fifteen years old.

Fifteen. That brutal age where hormones take over your brain and you think any guy who looks your way is your soulmate. But with Bryce, it wasn't just another teenage crush… it was an all-consuming romantic freefall.

Guys like Bryce don't choose girls like me. He comes from old money, and I'm counting quarters to avoid parking tickets.

My heart's been stuck on him for a decade, and he's clueless. Or maybe he knows and only plays dumb to save me the humiliation. That night at my high school graduation party—when I kissed him and he fled—it's in the past.

"I've moved on. Grown up. End of story."

My besties' faces are unconvinced.

"No, I'm dead serious. This summer I'm getting my shit in gear, not crushing on a guy who sees me as his best friend's chaotic little sister."

And reality check: Bryce is taken. He's been living with his girlfriend for two years—a blonde socialite, exactly the type you'd expect. He'll be putting a ring on it any day now, just like my brother did with his fiancée Fiona. Soon they'll all be hanging out in the Hamptons, chatting about stock portfolios and Ivy League preschools.

Whereas my bankrupt ass had to swallow my pride and beg my brother for cash to return to college. I'm sick of mixing drinks and making bad decisions. Gavin is always trying to play the dad role, and this time he came up with a plan to prove to my family—and myself—that for once, I can actually finish something I start.

Translation: prove I'm not a screw-up.

My phone buzzes like a pissed-off hornet, lighting up with a text from my Bossy McBrotherface.

Gavin: *They moved up the Public Relations IPO strategy meeting. It's in 30 minutes. I need that slide deck NOW!*

Shit. That's on my laptop.... in pieces. I don't want to say "corporate espionage," but I may have lost interest halfway through figuring out how PowerPoint animations work. And then, I may or may not have accidentally deleted half the transitions.

More vibrations from my phone.

Gavin: *PETRA. SLIDES. WHERE ARE THEY?*

I'm typing some BS about the slides being "almost done" when the hot bartender arrives with a heavenly BBQ chicken pizza. The tangy sauce and melted cheese make my stomach growl loud enough to turn heads.

"Can I get it to go?" I say, already grabbing my stuff. "And the bill. It's a corporate emergency, which apparently is a real thing and not just something people say to sound important."

I turn back to my phone, where Katie and Cam are still waiting.

"Bro dropped another all-caps text, and in Gavin-speak, that means someone's about to get canned or killed or both. Miss you, love you, bye."

"Good luck!" they chorus as I end the call.

With incredible speed, both a pizza box and the bill materialize. I tap my card to the reader and pray to the Bank Account Gods. *BEEP!* Transaction approved. A fucking miracle.

Quickly, I check my banking app balance. $35.62.

Great. I'm one splurge away from selling my kidney in some shady back alley.

I grab my pizza box, back away from the bar, and I see it: his number scrawled on the side in black Sharpie, complete with a little smiley face.

"Has that ever worked?" I ask.

He leans against the bar, muscles flexing casually. "Call me later, and I'll let you know."

"Fair warning—I'm the red flag people warn their friends about."

I hip-check CPK's door open, pizza box in one hand and phone in the other. I'm ready to dash to my car when I see a familiar figure sitting on a nearby bench. His faded Army jacket and worn boots clash with the perfectly manicured shrubs around him. Wispy silver hair catches the sunlight—longer since the last time I saw him.

"Well, if it isn't my favorite sidewalk philosopher," I say, changing course toward him. "I haven't seen you in the neighborhood lately."

Between his calloused fingers, I spot the worn-out cover of *The Great Gatsby*—because Jim might be homeless, but his taste in literature is top-notch.

"Thought I'd come see how the other half lives. Maybe absorb some wealth through proximity."

"Careful—these people don't do outsiders. Linger too long, and they'll call security on you for blinking too loud."

I study him.

"You eaten yet?"

"Nah. Just feasting on the ambiance."

Before I can stop myself, I'm thrusting the pizza box at him. "Here."

"That's your lunch, kid. I may not have a roof, but I don't need your charity."

"It's not charity if it's friendship."

His fingers curl around the box. "You spoil me."

"So... you go to Legal Aid yet?" I ask, not staring at him. That's the trick. Don't look too hard, or he'll shut down.

"Not yet. But I will."

"I'm holding you to that, Jim. They owe you. And not the 'thanks for your service' bumper sticker bullshit kind of owe. The actual benefits kind."

Jim cracks the faintest smile. "When you're a big-shot lawyer, I expect you to sue the pants off every last one of them. Pro bono, of course."

"Obviously."

His words are a shot of adrenaline to my heart. Everyone thinks I'm crawling back to finish my art degree. But Jim knows the truth. That my dream, which low-key terrifies me, is to go to law school. I wanna fight for the little guys, the ones who get stepped on, ignored, and shoved aside. Everyday people who need a voice and a good lawyer.

But for now, I'm tucking that little secret away, safe and sound, in case I crash and burn.

My phone buzzes another screaming text from my brother. "Oh shit! I gotta go. The rat race owns me now."

"Give 'em hell."

"I will!"

I rush toward my car, mentally calculating how many traffic laws I can violate and still maintain plausible deniability. And then, lo and behold, "Let's Fuck With Petra Day" kicks into high gear.

A parking enforcement officer.

Standing by my car.

Writing a ticket.

"No, no, no—I'm here! It's fine!"

The officer—built like a garden gnome—doesn't even look up, tapping away on his little ticket-spitting machine.

"Tears don't work on me, sweetheart. Ask my ex-wife."

"I wasn't going to cry."

"Smart. Flirting and bribery won't work either. She didn't care, and neither do I."

"I don't have time to unpack your relationship drama. The meter's busted. It rejected my quarter, ignored my card, and didn't respond no matter how much wrist action and enthusiasm I offered up."

"Listen, doll, I don't make the rules. I enforce them. Your kind of vehicle—" he nods toward my car "—tends to attract attention in this neighborhood."

"First off, it's a Lexus. It might not be up to your aesthetic, but it's legally registered, insured, and entitled to park at any *functional* meter."

"Lady, this is Beverly Hills. If you can't maintain our standards, you should consider parking... elsewhere," he says, ripping the ticket from his printer.

The subtext isn't even subtext at this point: *You don't belong here.*

I pull out my phone and start snapping pictures—of him, his badge, the parking meter, my car.

"What's with the paparazzi treatment?"

"Just documenting evidence for my court case," I say sweetly, zooming in on his nametag. "Officer... Cockburn?"

He sighs. "Yes. That's my real name."

"Wow. That explains... honestly, a lot."

"I'd watch that attitude if I were you. We take note of... problematic vehicles in this district."

My stomach boils at the not-so-veiled threat.

He holds out the paper. "Save yourself the legal fees and pay the seventy-five dollars. City policy is so simple, even a kindergartner gets it. Broken meter? Don't park there."

"Listen up, Officer *Cockburn,*" I say, drawing his name out obnoxiously. "You might think you're the king of the sidewalk, but that badge doesn't make you special. I'm fighting this ticket. See you in court."

I snatch the paper from his hand and unlock my car. I can feel his beady eyes as I slide into the driver's seat, slam the door, and toss the ticket onto my messy dashboard. Another financial hit I can't afford. But I'll be damned if I'm going to let Officer Little Dick and his broken meter win.

At least Jim got lunch. I'll count that as a win, even if the scoreboard's on fire.

***

This day needs to die. Full-on Viking funeral—torch it, sink it, and let a shark crap it out.

I scan Sterling Tower's 32nd-floor boardroom—a shrine to capitalism, where twenty suits with perfect hair sit around an obscenely long glass table, flanked by a dozen more faces on a wall of monitors. Floor-to-ceiling windows offer a sweeping view of LA—the city where money talks, and the rest of us clean up after it.

My seat? Dead last—right next to the Wi-Fi hub, the projector, and a tangled mess of power cords. But hey, it's closest to the tray of untouched artisanal muffins. *Untouched* because in Beverly Hills, no one eats carbs without an Ozempic chaser.

SqueeEEEP!

I shift, and my leather chair rips a fart. *Awesome.*

What I really don't need is to become the center of attention in this meeting.

I made it here with twelve seconds to spare, which meant no bathroom stop, no lipstick fix, and zero lunch. I had to park on the street again *(garage was full),* and while the meter actually worked this time *(small miracles)*, it only gave me an hour. I've got a timer set on my phone to run down and feed it in exactly—thirty-seven minutes.

I can't have Officer Cockburn popping out of a shrub like an angry leprechaun with a citation instead of gold.

"We are on the edge of a pivotal moment," Gavin says, commanding the room as if he was born to do it. "In two weeks, we go public. This is not about ringing the bell; it's about opening a new chapter for our company. We need to hit the ground running on day one."

My big brother, Gavin Brinkman. Six feet of sharp suits and sharper ambition. His dark-brown hair is cut and styled with precision, and his hazel-green eyes—the only feature we share besides our smart mouths—scan the room like lasers. The women here are openly salivating. One exec is tongue-bathing her Montblanc pen like it's foreplay. Gavin doesn't care. Sex comes third for my brother—first is business, second is more business.

The Rolex on his wrist catches the light, and my heart does that stupid squeeze. Mom and I busted our asses for that watch—she scrubbed extra toilets while I served burnt pancakes and bottomless coffee at Denny's. Seeing him open that box on his graduation day was the last time I saw him truly smile.

And the fact that he still wears it? Every damn day? Instead of upgrading to some flashy billionaire flex? Yeah. That's an emotional Rubik's cube I'll never solve.

The Brinkman siblings. Two sides of the same fucked-up coin. Gavin took the "work harder than God" route out of poverty—found himself a billionaire best friend, learned to speak fluent Country Club, and never looked back.

Me? I took the scenic route. The "set it on fire and see what happens" path. While Gavin was shaking hands with the elite, I was collecting detention slips like trophies and perfecting the art of making rich girls cry with nothing but words.

He built an empire. I built a rap sheet of minor offenses and major disappointments.

And yet... seeing him now, owning a room full of people who would've ignored him as a kid? It makes me puff up with pride. My brother did this. The same kid who used to share his school lunch with me when Mom couldn't afford to pack two is now a fucking financial god.

I just wish success hadn't made him so... *them.*

"Going public will give us the resources to expand our services and reach more people who deserve a chance to grow their wealth." Gavin pauses. "Petra... next slide."

Oh, shit.

My fingers attack the laptop. Slides go flying on the screen. Growth charts, retention stats, stock photos of unnaturally happy couples.

"The personalized investment tools slide," Gavin says, jaw tightening.

"Yep. Working on it. Uh—one sec."

I overshoot again. Finally, I land on the correct slide.

And then… it happens.

GRRRRROOOWWWLLL.

My empty, CPK-deprived stomach howls like it's about to club something and eat it raw.

He clears his throat. "As I was saying, our proprietary algorithm has shown remarkable—"

GRRRRRRROOOOOOOOWWWWLLLLL.

My stomach is possessed by a hungry demon. Gavin's forehead vein pulses, and the suits around the table shift uncomfortably.

GRRRRRRRRROOOOOOOOOOOOWWWWLLLLLL!

"Petra! Please grab a damn muffin. If your stomach gets any louder, we'll need to give it a seat at the table and offer it voting rights."

Laughter erupts—tight, amused, and at my expense. Even the woman eye-fucking my brother lets out a dainty snort.

I stand up and reach past the crystal pitchers of water for the pile of pastries when—

"Apologies. My jet's Wi-Fi was out over Colorado. Please continue."

That voice.

There's only one voice on this godforsaken planet that can make my thighs quiver, instantly ruining a perfectly good pair of panties.

My head snaps up to the wall of screens, where a new Zoom window has appeared, and there he is.

Bryce. Sterling.

My fingers freeze mid-grab, suspended in pastry purgatory. Every cell in my body goes on high alert.

Even in digital form, the man is unfairly gorgeous. His golden-blond hair is short and sleek, and my fingers itch to run through it. He's wearing a charcoal gray suit, the kind with a subtle pattern that whispers *custom.* Those piercing blue eyes survey the room with quiet authority. His head tilts, eyes shifting ever so slightly.

Is he... Is he looking at me? Oh God, I'm pathetic. But what if he is?

"Petra, the next slide!"

Shit. Slides. Right. I'm the slide girl. Why am I not sliding?

I jolt backwards, landing hard on the leather chair.

PPPBBBBBTHHHHHHHRRRRRT!

It's not a squeak.

It's not a groan.

It is a full-blown *nuclear fart trumpet.*

Every face turns toward me in collective panic. On screen, Bryce's eyebrows shoot up so high they nearly leave his forehead.

"It was the chair!"

I shoot up—trying to clear my name—when my elbow clips the water pitcher.

WHOOSH! SMACK!! SPLASH!!!

A tidal wave sloshes across the table.

My laptop? Baptized. The Wi-Fi hub? Gone. There's a soft hiss, then a *pop*, lots of sparks, and the entire Zoom screen goes black.

Bryce? Vanished like a gentleman ghost.

"OhmyGod—I can fix it!" I lie, napkin-bombing the tech as if tissue paper stands a chance.

"Sorry, everyone," Gavin says to the room, already pulling out his phone. "We'll need to reschedule."

He doesn't raise his voice. Doesn't throw anything. Doesn't even scowl. But *everyone* evacuates as if the floor just caught fire.

When the last person escapes, he turns to me. I freeze mid-pat.

"Before you say anything, I know this looks bad—"

"Bad? This week's been a disaster. If you really want my help paying for college? Earn it. I challenge you to make it through one day without a crisis."

"Bro, I get it, okay. I am a flaming dumpster of incompetence."

"Enough jokes. No more excuses, sis. I already had to cancel two investor calls, and we did not have time to reschedule this meeting."

The disappointment in his voice makes my stomach twist. "I'm trying, okay? I *swear.*"

"I didn't bring you on to be your babysitter, Petra."

"It was an accident."

"I want to see you win. I wouldn't have crafted this plan if I didn't see your potential. But you need to step up, believe in yourself, and take this seriously."

MWARP! MWARP! MWARP!

Shit! My meter alarm. I slap at my phone blindly.

"Is there something more pressing than this discussion?"

"Nope."

"Good. I need you to head to Harry Winston and retrieve the custom cufflinks Fiona commissioned. The gala tonight at Bryce's mother's is very important to her, so I want everything to be flawless."

The name hits me like a slap across the face.

Fiona. As in Fiona Whitfield.

My brother's future wife. My former high school tormentor.

A slideshow of humiliations flashes through my brain like a horror movie marathon:

Fiona, in homeroom, whispering *(at full volume)* that my mom cleans her toilets.

Fiona telling the entire school I was pregnant—twins, apparently—with the janitor's babies.

Fiona organizing "Poor Petra Day" on my sixteenth birthday—a theme where everyone at school showed up in ripped clothes, dirt on their faces, and the team mascot gathered money in a glittery donation jar labeled: HELP THE LESS FORTUNATE (LIKE PETRA).

Sometimes I wonder if she put some kind of rich-girl voodoo spell on my brother, because the Gavin I know wouldn't willingly choose Satan as a life partner.

"You're making that face again," he says.

"What face?"

"That expression you make every time I mention my fiancée. Fiona is not the same person she was in high school. People change."

"True. She's upgraded her nose and has clearly perfected her gaslighting technique."

MWARP! MWARP! MWARP!

I toss Gavin a salute and pivot toward the door.

"No face. No problem. Just very, very concerned about cufflink logistics."

Gavin yells as I run down the hall, "Work on the face. In two months, she'll be family. Make an effort."

The elevator takes forever. My head is spinning with visions of Bryce in a tux at that ritzy gala tonight. The one at his mother's house—a soirée I'd never be invited to, not in this lifetime.

Forget Bryce. Forget Fiona. Focus on the mission. Get the damn cufflinks. Don't get fired.

I scramble out of the building when—

NO! No no no no no.

My car is being towed.

Officer Cockburn—yes, still his real name—is standing beside it, looking like he's climaxing over the sight of my misery.

I bolt toward him, a total crazy person, waving my arms. "WAIT! That's my car! I'm literally right here!"

CRACK!

My fake-ass heel—the one I lovingly Frankensteined with nail polish to pass for Louboutins—snaps.

One minute I'm upright. The next?

SPLAT.

Face-first into the sidewalk.

Hard.

"OW! MOTHERFUCKING COCKSUCKER!"

Today started at rock bottom. And now? We've tunneled into a level of hell so fresh, Lucifer hasn't even unpacked. And I still have to go pick up the cufflinks. Lucky freaking me.

CHAPTER TWO

BRYCE

I MADE IT OUT. Barely. And yet, it feels like I've returned from a war I never stood a chance of winning.

I swing open the grand double doors of my residence. My Italian leather shoes echo against the marble floor, announcing my arrival. The foyer stretches out before me: pristine white walls, soaring ceilings, and modern art. Each piece—a testament to wealth—provides the only color in this otherwise stark mausoleum posing as a home.

It's a glass and steel palace, perched on the edge of the Hollywood Hills as if it owns the horizon. The wall of windows offers an expansive view of Los Angeles: the glinting downtown skyline, the hazy coastline in the distance, and the sun setting in a blaze of orange and pink over the ocean. It's a city I once thought was mine for the taking.

"Amanda?" I call out, my voice swallowed by the vastness.

No answer. Not surprising.

I hadn't planned to come back from New York today, but Mother insisted I attend tonight's charity gala—something about yachts for youth or champagne for chickens or whatever cause is fashionable this quarter. The Sterling name must be represented properly, of course. Heaven forbid we miss a photo opportunity with our checkbooks.

My girlfriend is likely upstairs getting ready. I choose not to call out again, instead savoring the rare gift of silence before the next storm of social obligations.

I drop my briefcase by the circular monstrosity Amanda calls a couch—a ninety-thousand-dollar designer piece that looks stunning but feels like a concrete slab. The entire house is like this. Trophy furnishings selected for appearance rather than function.

Two people do not need nine bedrooms, fourteen bathrooms, and twenty thousand square feet. Unless, of course, those two people want to easily avoid each other. *Guilty as charged.*

The glass doors to the patio slide open with a whisper. I step into the night, warm air brushing against my skin, and lower myself into a teak lounge chair facing the infinity pool and twenty-five-person jacuzzi that I've used exactly twice in the past year.

I loosen my tie and breathe.

Just for a second.

Just long enough to pretend this is the life I chose. That I'm not some obedient legacy soldier.

"Better enjoy the view while I can."

In one week, I'll be calling New York home as the new CEO of Sterling Industries, my family's empire. Trading California sunshine for Manhattan streetlights. Swapping a career I built for one I inherited when I drew my first breath. Another Sterling man taking his predestined place in the corner office with his name already on the door.

The Sterling name is synonymous with wealth. Every major city in the world has at least one building with our name emblazoned across it in gleaming letters. Over a billion people carry Sterling Bank cards in their wallets. And not one of them could tell you who I am.

I learned early that wealth isn't freedom.

Not when it owns you.

Not when it turns your choices into obligations and your name into a leash.

I pull out my phone and scroll through an avalanche of emails that accrued during my week in the Big Apple. Subject lines scream for attention: quarterly projections, board meeting minutes, and Heartvest's looming IPO.

This past week was an exercise in futility. I'd gone to Manhattan with one mission: convince my father to give me more time at Heartvest, the company I built with my best friend Gavin from the ground up. Instead, I got a masterclass in Reginald Sterling's particular brand of negotiation.

"The agreement was thirty, Bryce. You turn thirty next month." His voice was steady, emotionless, as he swirled eighteen-year-old scotch in a crystal tumbler. "A Sterling man honors his commitments."

As if I needed the reminder.

This is the deal I made after Princeton. Five years to stretch my legs. Get my hands dirty in something "real" before being dragged back into the family dynasty. Five years to pretend I had a say in the matter.

I spot an email from Gavin: *Board impressed with projections. IPO on track. See you at the gala.*

Gavin Brinkman. My chosen brother.

The guy who worked three jobs so his mom could keep their two-bedroom rental in Beverly Hills. The guy who tutored rich kids to cover tuition. The guy who looked at me—a symbol of privilege and legacy and everything he didn't have—and chose friendship over resentment.

The guy I'm going to abandon.

Heat floods my chest, a mixture of shame and regret bubbling up like acid. *How the hell am I supposed to tell him?* Over canapés at Mother's charity soirée? "Splendid affair, old friend. Oh, by the way, I'm cutting ties on the eve of our company going public. More champagne, perhaps?"

My throat tightens. After high school together, getting him into Princeton with me was the least I could do. My father called it "misplaced charity." The truth was far more selfish: I couldn't imagine navigating those ivy-covered walls without the one person who made me feel I was more than just another Sterling.

Heartvest was Gavin's vision from the start. We were in our senior year, drunk on mid-tier Merlot, when he pitched it—his eyes alive with an excitement I had never felt, his hands gesturing wildly as he laid it all out.

"Wealth management for the working class," he'd declared. "Your family's bank requires what, a million minimum, to get a meeting? My mom worked her fingers raw cleaning toilets for twenty years and still doesn't understand how to save for retirement. That's fucked up. We're going to fix it."

I'd nodded along, mentally allocating the seed funding he'd need. But it was more than money—for the first time, I saw a path that wasn't preordained by my last name. Something that mattered beyond quarterly returns and shareholder value.

Five years later, Heartvest has sixty million users: everyday people investing spare change, learning financial literacy, building nest eggs.

We're two weeks away from a public offering that analysts are calling "the democratization of wealth building." Our users have collectively saved over half a billion dollars.

And I'm walking away.

My phone vibrates—my mother's aggressive text glows accusingly on the screen.

Mother: *Car arriving in 40 minutes. Wear Armani, not Brioni. Giorgio Armani's niece Roberta will be attending tonight.*

I drop my head into my hands, palms pressed to my eyes, until I see stars. *Tonight. I have to tell Gavin tonight.*

I drag myself toward the master bedroom, each step heavier than the last. I press on the large bedroom door. The room yawns open, revealing a space that could comfortably house a family of four. The bed alone is obscene.

It's not a king-size bed. It's a *king plus a side of king.*

I glance at my reflection in the expansive mirror and groan. "Christ, you're already falling apart—and it's only been one week working alongside him."

My blue eyes are haunted, my usually neat blond hair flops over my forehead, and the five o'clock shadow darkening my jaw would have my mother *tsking*. I can already hear her clipped tone: "Appearance is currency in our world, and you look positively bankrupt."

Still no sign of Amanda. *Strange.*

Collapsing backward onto the bed, I pull up my favorite playlist—classic rock ballads. Songs that are supposed to be ironic but somehow end up punching me in the damn feelings.

Steven Tyler wails through the speakers. "Dream On."

How fitting.

I close my eyes and let the music drown out the world. Let it press back the expectation. The deadlines. The inevitability.

My mind drifts to the boardroom disaster from earlier today.

To Petra Brinkman—Gavin's fiery little sister, whom I nicknamed Pip. It's been two years since I last laid eyes on her. Her jet-black hair, pale skin, and full red lips were unmistakably the same, but still... She seemed different.

A snort of laughter escapes as I recall her horrified expression at today's meeting. The sight of her unleashing a tsunami of water, taking out the entire Zoom session.

Poor Gavin. He's got his hands full trying to harness that tornado. He loves his sister fiercely, always has, but Pip has never been one to color inside the lines. The idea of her conforming to corporate culture is about as plausible as my father showing genuine emotion. Oil and water. Fire and ice. Petra and rules.

Teenage Petra was all attitude and eyeliner. Her smart mouth was always loaded and ready to fire, especially in my direction. "Hey, Moneybags," she'd say. "Decide which country you're buying today?"

The music shifts, one ballad fading into another. The first, yearning notes of Heart's "Alone" fill the room, and every muscle in my body goes rigid.

Dammit.

Not this song.

Not this memory.

But it's too late.

I see it like it's happening again.

The moment I've locked away breaks free, playing as vividly as if it happened yesterday, not seven years ago.

Petra's high school graduation party. The one no one came to.

I remember standing in her bedroom doorframe. A vintage record player sat atop a milk crate playing this song. Rock band posters were plastered over her walls. Her desk was cluttered with sketchbooks and colored pencils.

"Pip? Just wanted to say goodbye."

She looked up at me from where she sat on the bed.

Crying.

Knees pulled to her chest.

Graduation gown crumpled on the ground.

Mascara smudged under wet, furious eyes.

She swiped at her cheeks with the back of her hand. "Guess you jet-setted over here for nothing, Moneybags," she snarked. "Well, at least you got your daily dose of watching the peasants fail."

I'd never seen Petra vulnerable.

Angry? Constantly.

Sarcastic? Her native language.

But sad? Actually wounded? This was uncharted territory, and it made my chest hurt in ways I didn't have words for.

"You deserve better than this," I said simply.

"Wow. Did your butler teach you that line, or did you come up with it all by yourself?"

The mattress dipped as I sat awkwardly at the end of her bed.

She glanced down, avoiding eye contact. "Don't worry. I'm used to disappointment."

"You're tenacious, Pip. Always have been," I said, the words drawn from some concealed part of me. "Intelligent. Unapologetic. You're extraordinary. You don't require anyone's validation."

For one unguarded second, her chin lifted, eyes wide with genuine surprise. Then—and I still have whiplash from how fast it happened—she lunged forward, grabbed my shirt with surprising strength for someone her size, and kissed me.

I froze. Before I could think, before I could remember all the reasons this was a catastrophically bad idea—

Something electric ignited at the base of my spine, sparking through my nervous system like a live wire dropped in water.

My body seized control while my brain was still spinning.

I kissed her back.

Not gently. Not properly. Not with the restraint I'd been taught was appropriate for a Sterling.

My hand slid up to cradle her jaw, tilting her head to deepen the kiss. Her surprised gasp opened against my lips, and I took the invitation without hesitation. Her fingers twisted in my shirt. My free hand found her waist, fingers splaying against the warm strip of skin where her shirt had ridden up.

My world narrowed to nothing but sensation: the softness of her lips, the subtle sound she made deep in her throat as my tongue touched hers, the way her body arched toward mine—unrestrained and more alive than anyone I had ever known.

Until...

A thunderous voice shattered the moment.

"Bryce? You ready?"

Gavin's voice bellowed up the stairwell, and reality came crashing back with nauseating force.

My best friend. Her brother. The man who'd promised bodily harm to anyone who touched his baby sister.

"Oh God. I—Damn." I stumbled backward, nearly tripping over her graduation gown. "I shouldn't have—Pip. I apologize."

Petra rolled her eyes, composure snapping back into place with terrifying speed. "Relax. No biggie." Her voice was cool, dripping with sarcasm, as if it had all been a joke. "It's not like you're into me. I kissed *you*, Moneybags. It's fine."

We've never spoken about it since. Not once in seven years. I assume she didn't tell Gavin—he would've taken a swing at me by now.

After all this time, it is impossible to hear this song without feeling the sensation of her lips on mine.

BRINGG. BRINGG.

The melody cuts off mid-lyric, ripping me straight out of the past.

Caller ID: Amanda Tenley. Her profile photo exudes polished confidence—pearl earrings, glossy blonde waves, and that serene, unbothered expression only girls raised on country club rules can possess.

I swipe to answer. "Hello, I'm almost ready. Just need a few—"

"You didn't even notice, did you?"

"You'll have to be more specific."

"I moved out, Bryce."

I stand up so fast my head spins, and suddenly I'm seeing the room with fresh eyes. Her bedside table is bare. No silk sleep mask. No crystal-studded charger. No glossy stack of *Vogue*.

I bolt to her walk-in closet and throw open the door.

Empty. Completely bare except for a few stray velvet hangers. The rows of designer dresses, the color-coded shoe collection, the Tiffany-blue jewelry boxes—all gone.

"I didn't think you were serious."

"I've been waiting for your call for three days, Bryce." Her voice hardens. "I warned you that at twenty-eight, I'm approaching my expiration date. My mother has suggested cryogenic egg freezing more than once. You are aware of what she calls unmarried thirty-year-old women in our circle, right?"

I wince, already knowing the answer.

"Unfuckable." The crude word sounds wrong in her cultured voice.

"Amanda, I'm sorry."

"Are you? Because if you've changed your mind, I can have my things moved back this evening. We can salvage this... hiccup."

"No," I say, surprising myself with the firmness in my voice. "I'm not interested in marriage. Not right now. Maybe never."

The silence stretches so long, I check to see if we've been disconnected.

"Did you ever love me, Bryce?"

There's a sudden drop in my stomach. I should say yes. It would be kinder. Easier. But my silence speaks volumes.

"That's what I thought."

"I never meant to hurt you," I say, the words sounding hollow in my ears.

"As your father always says, intentions are irrelevant. Results are what matter. I trust you'll wait to announce our separation. Give me time to establish my next steps?"

"Of course."

"Tell people I'm staying at the lake house to care for my mother. She's had another anti-aging teenager blood infusion and neck rejuvenation."

"Whatever you prefer. And, Amanda, I wish you luck."

"I won't need it, having dated a Sterling now. When I find someone more deserving, I'll let you know—might even save you a seat at the wedding. However, if you do come to your senses, you have my number."

The call ends, leaving me staring at my darkened screen.

Amanda was precisely the type of woman I was expected to marry. Beautiful, polished, socially connected. The female equivalent of me—bred for a life of luxury and trained to keep up the façade.

But did I love her? *Hmm.* Since when did that matter?

I can't think of a single couple in my social circle who are actually in love. Before they divorced, my parents treated marriage like a business arrangement with occasional photo opportunities. My father's friends trade in wives as if they're depreciating assets. My mother's circle views husbands as necessary accessories, like statement jewelry but with stock options.

Even Gavin—practical, focused Gavin—is marrying Fiona Whitfield to cement his place in Beverly Hills aristocracy. His new wealth paired with the Whitfield real estate old-money empire creates a power alliance that benefits them both.

Love means risk, and no one I know is willing to roll the dice on that. When it comes to duty or desire, duty always comes first.

And speaking of duty—I have a gala to attend.

***

I NEED SOME AIR.

Less than an hour into this party, and I'm calculating my escape route. How many more politicians' hands must I shake? How many more soul-numbing conversations about market fluctuations and property values will there be? My mother's grand ballroom is suffocating—a sea of designer gowns, custom tuxedos, and practiced smiles.

"And where is that lovely girlfriend of yours?" asks the governor's wife, Mrs. Harrington.

"Amanda's at her family's lake house. Her mother needed her assistance after a... procedure." The lie rolls off my tongue for the thirty-eighth time. Each repetition digs the hole deeper, and I know when the truth finally surfaces—that Amanda left me because I wouldn't propose—the gossip will spread through Beverly Hills faster than wildfire.

Her final revenge: leaving me to face the social firing squad while she licks her wounds in private. *Well played.*

I adjust my bow tie and slip out the back, leaving behind the glint of diamonds, the murmur of polite malice, and the opulent pretense of my mother's charity gala.

The scotch burns my throat as I head past the tennis court. It's quiet here—tucked behind a guesthouse, surrounded by manicured hedges and strategically placed greenery. The only place that ever felt remotely private growing up.

Which is ironic because the estate that glows behind me could have its own zip code. My mother's mini-kingdom is a monstrous testament to excess. Staff living quarters, bowling alley, home theater, spa, gift-wrapping room, an indoor Greek-inspired pool, and a garage that could house a small dealership. All guarded twenty-four hours a day by ex-military men in suits who report to my mother like she's the head of Homeland Security.

I linger in the shadows, downing the last of my scotch. I'm debating whether to commit the social sin of getting a second drink far too early when something catches my eye.

A rustle.

Then a *snap*.

Probably just some raccoon poking around the perimeter. We get coyotes sometimes. Even a peacock once, thanks to Mother's exotic pet phase. But then—

A human leg.

Then a body *plummets* from the foliage.

THUMP!

What the—

I scan for security, but the guards are stationed at the front entrance, where the guests and their million-dollar jewelry collections are clustered. None of the other partygoers have wandered this far into the garden. No one else has witnessed this breach.

"Hey!" I bark, voice sharp and immediate, instinct overtaking etiquette.

The intruder bolts upright and *runs*.

"Stop!" My glass drops and shatters on the stone path, but I'm already sprinting. "Security!"

They're fast. But not faster than me. I gain ground as they dart toward the casita, feet pounding the pavement, dress shoes be damned.

I reach out and grab their arm.

Gotcha.

"Hands off, Rent-a-Cop!" a woman's voice shouts.

A heel stomps on my foot. Hard.

"Jesus Chr—!"

Her elbow slams into my ribs before I can finish the curse. I double over, sucking in air.

Who the hell did I grab? Female John Wick?

I can't see the intruder's face under her hoodie-covered head, but she's racing for the pool house entrance.

"Dammit," I mutter, dragging myself upright and giving chase.

She reaches the door and yanks on the handle. It doesn't budge. Locked. A string of muffled curses fills the night air as she slams a fist against the glass. Moonlight glints off the surface as she rattles the handle again, frantic.

Instinct kicks in. I don't think—just react. Four years on the Princeton Prep wrestling team. Three Ivy League championships. That kind of muscle memory doesn't vanish just because you trade in singlets for suits. If I can get this trespasser pinned until security shows up...

I charge forward with intent to takedown and pin. A drill I've done a thousand times.

My arms hook around the intruder from behind, trapping her in a textbook restraint that would make Coach Stevens grunt with pride. I don't squeeze too tightly because, well, she's a woman. But she's behaving like a cat in a bathtub, kicking and thrashing.

"Let! Me! GO!"

"Surrender before you make it worse," I bark in a low voice.

"Where's the fun in that, Security Ken?"

I firm up my hold, arms forming a human straightjacket. The little maniac braces both feet on the pool house door.

Wait, what is she—

With extreme force, she pushes off the door, launching us both backward. For one suspended moment, we're airborne—a tangle of limbs rocketing toward the ground.

SLAM!

My back hits against the stone path with bone-pulverizing force. All the air in my lungs evacuates in a *WHOOSH*. My vertebrae feel rearranged.

This was definitely not covered in *Princeton's Advanced Takedown Techniques.*

She scrambles free. *Not on my watch.*

Pure reflex takes over. My arm shoots out like a spring-loaded trap, fingers latching around an ankle mid-stride. I feel leather, a boot, and then—

WHAM!

She hits the grass face-first with a satisfying *OOF.*

"Miss, are you okay?" I wheeze, my voice barely recognizable.

"You call that a takedown?"

She wriggles, trying to escape. I yank hard, pulling her across the grass as if I'm reeling in an alligator.

She's fast. I tighten my grip. She kicks back viciously, catching me square in the stomach. I groan, but I don't let go.

No, I *clamp down harder*.

I haul her leg toward me, crawling up her body like a deranged octopus, and manage to lock my own legs around hers in a perfect body scissor hold. Her back is pressed against my chest. I'm a human pretzel with my arms wrapped around her torso.

We're a twisted, breathing, cursing mess in the damp grass.

She's still fighting dirty. Bucking. Twisting. Throwing elbows.

"GET. OFF!"

"SECURITY!" I yell out.

Nothing. *Where the hell is everyone?*

An arm slips free. A small victory for her. A tactical error for me.

"Hey, asshole!" the female voice shouts. "Take your hands off my boobs, perv!"

And then—

CRACK!

Her elbow connects with laser-guided precision to my groin.

Holy mother of—

White-hot agony explodes through my body. I'm not sure if I'm screaming out loud or if it's just inside my head. Either way, the universe tilts sideways, and I see every bad decision that led me to this moment.

This gala? Bad call.

Impromptu wrestling? Bad call.

Chasing some lunatic intruder through my mother's estate? Extremely bad call.

I roll to my side in the fetal position, the cool grass against my cheek providing little comfort for the inferno raging below my belt. Through tear-blurred vision, I see the intruder scramble up, poised to sprint away.

That silhouette. That leather jacket. Those combat boots.

"Pip?"

She freezes like she's been caught sneaking out of detention. Slowly—*very slowly*—she turns and pulls the hoodie off her head.

Wide hazel-green eyes blink down at me, framed by a wild mess of tangled black hair and a smear of dirt across one cheekbone. But what I notice most are those full red lips.

"Oh, shit," she says brightly. "Hey, Moneybags. Fancy seeing you here."

"DON'T MOVE!" a deep voice shouts.

Two security officers lumber onto the scene, tasers drawn, faces set to "imminent threat" mode.

Petra raises her hands, totally unfazed. "Easy there, *Paul Blart Mall Cops*. I lost my invite. Figured the hedge was the VIP entrance."

"You again!" The burlier security guard points accusingly. "We told you at the front gate—no entry!"

"And as I explained, I have a right to be here." Petra crosses her arms. "You didn't listen, so I was forced to trespass. That's on you."

I stagger to my feet, brushing grass off my tux. Trying—and failing—to look as though I wasn't just taken down by a woman half my size. "It's fine, gentlemen. She's with me."

"Are you sure, Mr. Sterling?" The second guard eyes Petra suspiciously. "Her car looks like it was in a drive-by."

"Excuse me?" she fires back, pointing aggressively. "Are you seriously profiling me based on my vehicle? What kind of classist, elitist bullsh—"

Jesus. She's going to end up tased in front of Mother's rose garden.

"Thank you for your diligence," I cut in. "There's been a misunderstanding. Ms. Brinkman works for my company."

The guards exchange skeptical glances.

"I asked her to come tonight because..." I pause. I have absolutely no idea why she's here.

Petra yanks a velvet box from her pocket and waves it around. "Cufflinks! Special CEO delivery for this fancy schmancy snobby event."

I blink at the box. Then at her. "Yes. Cufflinks. Let me show you inside, Ms. Brinkman."

The guards lower their weapons. "Very good, sir," one of them mutters.

I nod as though this is all totally normal and not the single most unhinged moment of my adult life.

As the security team reluctantly retreats, she falls into step beside me like she owns the damn place.

We start walking, and I steer her off the main path to the side servants' entrance.

"Nice save, B. Though I could've taken those lightweights with my eyes closed."

"After what you did to me, I believe that." I wince, each step sending a fresh reminder of her combat effectiveness. "I may never father children."

"Please. I barely tapped you. Besides, consider it payback for the pervy boob grab."

"I assure you, that was not intentional. You were flailing like a marlin on a fishing line."

"So, you admit there *was* boob contact."

"I admit to nothing beyond the immediate need for an ice pack to my nether regions."

She bursts into laughter, and I find myself grinning. Pip's always had that effect on me. She was Gavin's shadow growing up, and so many of my high school memories are filled with her loud, defiant presence. Back then, only Gavin could match her quip for quip, and I miss seeing that side of him.

As we approach the main house, the noise of wealth grows louder. The clear notes of an overpriced string quartet, the gentle clink of champagne flutes, the distinct voices of people who've never worried about their credit scores.

Petra halts suddenly, glancing down at her all-black outfit complete with wrinkled AC/DC shirt. "Whoa there, Richie Rich. I can't go in there looking this way. Your mom will have me black-bagged and vanished faster than you can say 'wealth disparity.'"

She's not wrong. Judith Sterling-Holloway would rather serve boxed wine in plastic cups than allow someone in a leather jacket and combat boots to cross the threshold of her charity gala.

I take in the full spectrum of Petra's dishevelment—from the leaves still tangled in her hair to the grass stains marring her hands. Her jeans, already distressed by design, now sport a large, fresh tear across the thigh, revealing a tantalizing glimpse of pale, creamy skin.

Yet, inexplicably, it's the delicate curve of her collarbone that draws my attention—exposed where her shirt stretched during our impromptu wrestling match. My gaze, defying propriety, drifts lower to the soft rise of her breasts beneath the worn band tee. The cool night air has made certain... *assets*... unmistakably alert, and the thin fabric leaves little to the imagination.

She's not wearing a bra.

Look away. This is Gavin's little sister.

I suppress a shudder as a wave of heat courses through me. "You look..."

"Like I just body-slammed a Wall Street exec into his hedge fund?" She cocks an eyebrow, the quirk of her crimson lips daring me to disagree.

What the hell is wrong with me? These inappropriate thoughts need to stop. Now.

I need to quit thinking about where my hands were—gripping bare skin, skimming places I have no business remembering in this much detail. How she moved, what she let me touch... *Jesus. I'm going to get slapped if she sees how hard I'm getting.*

"I was going to say 'distinctive.'"

"If this is your rich-boy version of flirting, I give it two stars. I'm guessing you're one compliment away from asking if I do yoga."

She rakes her fingers through her wild mane, dislodging more foliage—as if intentionally doubling down on her freshly ravished look.

And now I'm picturing her sprawled across my king-sized bed, that midnight hair fanned out against white Egyptian cotton sheets, those defiant eyes molten with desire as I hover above her, ready to—

Sterling, get your shit together. This is Pip. The same woman who just tried to relocate my testicles to my throat. And the last person on earth I should be fantasizing about.

"Whatever, B. Help me find your bestie so I can hand off this fancy man-jewelry and ninja-vanish Homer Simpson style back through the bushes."

"Vanish? You're as subtle as fireworks at a funeral."

"Well, I'll be damned. Bryce Sterling cracked a joke. I guess all that money finally bought you a sense of humor. What's next? Eating frozen dinners and firing your personal chef?"

I fight back a traitorous smile. This is the problem with Petra—she's insufferable in the most entertaining way possible.

"Through here." I gesture toward the side entrance.

"Ooh, the secret poor-person door," she stage-whispers, leaning in close enough that I catch her scent—an intoxicating blend of jasmine mixed with fresh brewed coffee. "Why do I feel like I'm about to be initiated into some weird cult where you all wear Prada robes and sacrifice tax returns to the god of offshore accounts? Do I need to know a password? Is it 'the peasants don't deserve healthcare'?"

"It's an art auction for charity. The only ritual sacrifice happening is my sanity suffering through small talk. Try not to attack anyone, please."

"No promises, Moneybags. If some lady tries to shank me with a Gucci stiletto, it's go time."

I should be concerned.

I should have security escort her off the property immediately.

Instead, an unexpected flicker of curiosity stirs in my chest. Something tells me I want to witness what Petra Brinkman is going to do next.

CHAPTER THREE

PETRA

Group Chat : CPK Forever
Me: *Soooo I may have neutered Bryce.*
Cam: *WAIT? WHAT!*
Katie: *What did you do??*
Me: *Elbow. Balls. Direct contact. Long story.*
Me: *¡Dios mío! That'll get a guy's attention.*
Katie: *Gavin's gonna disown you. You should start practicing the phrase "Hi, I was once a Brinkman."*
Me: *He can get in line. All I know is RIP future baby Sterlings—they died doing what they loved: absolutely nothing.*

I'M FUCKING MORTIFIED.

Like, cram me in a cannon, aim for the sun, and blast me into another galaxy.

This never-ending day keeps finding new ways to suck!

Behind Bryce's perfectly tailored Armani-clad shoulders, I'm skulking through his mother's mansion like the world's worst cat burglar. We've invaded a kitchen plucked right out of a Nancy Meyers wet dream—gleaming copper pots, marble everything, and wicker baskets bursting with overly photogenic fruit.

The kitchen staff is in wealthy-people-feeding mode, operating as a well-oiled machine. White-gloved hands arrange tiny cucumber squares topped with what I'm guessing is caviar, but let's be real, my reference for fine dining is gas station sushi.

I look behind me to see one chef is using tweezers to place microscopic flowers on a cracker the size of my thumbnail. What is this? Food for ants?

The moment I turn back, I plow into a waiter carrying a tray of fancy desserts.

SMASH! CRASH!

Every single person in the kitchen halts mid-action, eyes now on me. Bryce tosses a glance over his shoulder so disapproving that I almost explode into flames.

"Are you incapable of keeping a low profile?"

"Sorry. I'll try to channel my inner duchess." I lick the frosting off the sleeve of my jacket. "Ah, splendid! The sugar-to-cake ratio is simply divine. Do carry on, my dears. Everything looks marvelous."

That earns me a chuckle from… no one.

Yep, reminder number 435,701 why Bryce "Suave, Sophisticated, and Stuck Up" Sterling would never go for Petra "Forever Fuck-Up" Brinkman.

I pick up my pace as he leads me into the tightest hallway I've ever seen. If I breathe too hard, I'll scrape paint off the walls.

"What is this? A secret mistress tunnel? Do I get to see what goes down at your mom's rich-people ragers? I bet it's a human sacrifice to the Illuminati. No, a piñata full of stock options. Wait... If I'm supposed to be the virgin sacrifice, I have bad news for you..."

Bryce ducks under a low-hanging light fixture. "This is a direct line to the kitchen to make it easier for servers to refill their trays without disturbing guests."

"Are you telling me your house has secret passages? Did you ever sneak in here as a kid? Spy on people? Please tell me little Bryce engaged in at least one act of childhood rebellion."

He stops so abruptly, I smack into his broad back. He spins, glacier-blue eyes locking onto mine—so intense, my lungs forget how oxygen works.

"What do you think?"

"Right. No fun. No snooping. Only WWE takedowns of female party crashers."

I see it.

A glint.

The tiniest, most microscopic twinkle of amusement in those arctic eyes.

I want to dive into that twinkle and live there forever.

Because here's the thing:

I've always known how to get under Bryce Sterling's skin.

I used to think if I poked him enough—teased, flirted, dropped an inappropriate joke or ten—he'd stop seeing me as Gavin's annoying shadow and see me as something more.

He didn't.

Focus on the task, Petra. Hand over these stupid cufflinks, make a semi-graceful exit, and then find the nearest hole to crawl into for... I don't know... ever. Seriously, being around this man makes my brain go berserk in ways that should be studied by scientists.

Bryce stops outside a heavy-looking door that blends into the wall so perfectly I almost walk past it. He holds out his palm expectantly. “I can handle the delivery from here.”

“Nope. I’m already late because my car got arrested. Gavin’s got this whole thing about *personal responsibility.* I need to hand these over or he’ll think I’m flaking again.”

“I could explain—”

“You clearly don’t know the full extent of my fuckup history.”

He sighs. “Stay here. I’ll track him down.”

“Sure thing, Moneybags.”

“I mean it, Pip.” His eyes narrow. “Don’t. Move.”

I cock my hip and smirk. “If you want to handcuff me right here and now, I support that kink.”

For a glorious second... he blushes.

If I were keeping score—and mentally, I am—I’ve bagged a grin, a twinkle, and a blush all in one night. The microsecond when his control slips and the honest version of him emerges from behind the Sterling family crest is highly addictive.

Seriously, what are you doing? Stop flirting with him. You know it’s hopeless.

He clears his throat, adjusts his bow tie, and disappears through the door. Beautiful chamber music filters in from the adjoining room.

God, he looks... *Unfair.*

That tux isn’t just fitted—it’s a freaking exoskeleton, engineered by fashion sorcerers with doctorates in Making Bryce Sterling Look Like a Golden God Among Mortals. And the way he moves—measured, precise, as if every molecule in his body knows exactly what to do.

If confidence had a scent, it would smell like him. Expensive. Sharp. And completely untouchable.

I glance down at myself and immediately wish I hadn't. *Ugh.* The idea of me in his world?

Laughable.

He has me stashed behind a door like the help he forgot to tip. Not even allowed to step inside with the real guests. As though I'm too wild, too messy, too damn... *me* to be seen.

The music crescendos with a violin solo so intense, I swear the instrument is having an extended orgasm. I check my phone. 8:07. *Shit.* I'm late for my bartending gig. Julio is going to have my ass. I fire off a text:

Me: *Stuck in Beverly HELLS. Be there soon.*

I exhale, letting the wall take some of the weight off my feet. My shoulder bumps something.

CLICK!

A small panel slides open, like something straight out of a Scooby-Doo episode.

A peephole.

Well, what do we have here?

I can't speak for others, but when the universe offers me a backstage pass to the glittering freak show of the one percent... I take it. No questions asked.

At first, it's what I expected.

Rows of powerful people in opulent chairs, dripping in jewels and designer clothes. A sea of tuxedos and tulle gowns, champagne flutes balanced on manicured fingers, expressions arranged in polite boredom.

But what they're all staring at... in the center of the room... is weird. Super weird.

In the middle of this grand, high-society gala—

A man.

Wearing nothing but a pair of tighty-whiteys.

Standing in a circle of white canvases.

His face is obscured by thick blue and green paint that drips down his chiseled torso in psychedelic rivers. And around him?

Models.

Lots of models.

Also in their underwear, their petite bodies gleam under spotlights as they dance and flail like interpretive chickens who took jazz in third grade and quit before the recital.

The paint-faced man lifts a bucket high above his head with the dramatic flair of a Vegas magician.

"I AM LIMITATIONS!" he bellows.

Before I can blink, he dumps the red paint over his hair. It sloshes down his toned body, clinging to the bulge in his underwear and pooling at his feet like a crime scene.

The models surge forward like paint-starved zombies. They run their hands over his slippery body, gathering the crimson on their palms before spinning away to smack their hands against the pristine white canvases.

SMACK! SLAP! WHACK!

Each slap sounds like someone getting spanked in a sex dungeon.

The paint man thrusts his pelvis at a canvas, smearing a rainbow streak across it with alarming enthusiasm.

"I AM BROKEN!" Paint Man screams, dropping to his knees.

The models respond by falling dramatically to the floor and writhing like they're being simultaneously electrocuted.

"I AM REBORN!" he shrieks, jumping back to his feet and spreading his arms wide. Paint flies off his body, spattering the front row of Chanel and Armani.

"Cool cool cool..." I whisper to myself. "We've entered the *Eyes Wide Shut* cult portion of the evening."

The door beside me swings open. Bryce enters with my brother in tow. I instantly morph into Innocent Petra Who Definitely Wasn't Spying On The One Percent's Paint Orgy.

"What the hell?" Gavin's voice is tight, controlled.

I thrust the velvet box at him. "Ta-da! Your sparkly wrist decorations, as requested. Before you ask, my car was detained by Officer Cockburn, and yes, that's his real name. You're welcome, by the way."

"For what? Doing your job?" He snatches it. "These are late."

"Oh no. Did the champagne warm by two degrees while you waited?"

He drags a slow, soul-killing gaze over my disheveled appearance. "Hold on. How did you manage to get into this party?"

I freeze. Because the real answer?

Involves bushes.

Security threats.

And a criminal-level tackle on Bryce's ballsack.

"I escorted her in."

I whip my head toward him so quickly, I pull a neck muscle.

Bryce Sterling covered for me. Why?

I don't let my shock show—I've got enough street smarts to not blow up my own lifeline.

The ballroom music dies mid-swell. There's a beat of expectant silence followed by applause.

And then, like a blast from my high school traumatic past, an all-too-familiar voice wafts from the microphone, sending shivers down my spine.

"Thank you to the supremely talented artist Echo for his exclusive performance!" she says. "It was transformative, wasn't it?"

Fucking Fiona Whitfield.

My brother's fiancée.

My never-ending nightmare.

Imagine a life-size Barbie—glossy lips, sweet voice, perfect hair—possessed by a PR-friendly demon. And I'm the only one who sees the spinning head.

"And of course," Fiona continues, "we must thank Mrs. Sterling-Holloway for hosting tonight's spectacular silent auction for one of the most near and dear causes to my heart. Nip, Tuck & Woof—giving our pets the dignity to age gracefully with wrinkle-free doggy brows and lifted jowls!"

Another polite golf clap from the room. The groan that escapes me is so loud, it ricochets down the hallway. Gavin shoots me a warning glare.

"And now I have a huge surprise!" she trills. "Gavin, dearest, come on up. My perfect fiancé. Where are you, my little venture capitalist?"

A titter of laughter from the ballroom.

He points at me sharply. "Stay here."

"Yeah, no. I've had enough of... whatever this is. I gotta get to work."

"Stay," he commands like I'm a disobedient bulldog.

I'm ready to argue, but he returns to the ballroom. The door clicks shut, and suddenly the hallway feels incredibly intimate.

Now it's just me.

And Bryce.

Holy crap, he's close.

So close I can feel his breath on my face. Last time we were this cozy was that night in my bedroom when...

Oh, hell no. Don't even think about dusting off "Petra's Most Mortifying Moments" playlist. He probably doesn't remember. Billionaires like him have a built-in memory eraser for stuff like that—like blocking out a tax audit or the trauma of slumming it on someone else's jet.

Or maybe he does remember. Maybe he's thinking about it. What if he wants me to reach out and... *Snap out of it, brain! In case you've forgotten, he has a girlfriend. A live-in, long-term, joint-bank-account kind of girlfriend. So, keep your fantasies at bay and your hands to yourself.*

I'm about to spiral further when Bryce speaks. "Where do you work?"

"Why do you ask? Jealous I'm giving my loyalty to someone else?"

"Maybe you're selling company secrets," he says dryly.

"Don't sweat it, B. My customers are usually too drunk to find their own shoes, let alone steal IPO insider tips."

One of his eyebrows lifts so subtly, it's almost imperceptible. Which, from Bryce, is basically him flashing his underwear on a parade float.

"So you're a bartender."

"Yup, at the Broken Bottle on Sunset in Hollywood. Come by sometime. First round's on you."

"Isn't that a dangerous part of town?"

"Awww. You worried about me? Don't be. I can take care of myself, Moneybags. I've got a right hook and a taser if customers get too frisky." I angle my head, studying him. "Why aren't you back at the party? You don't have to hide here in the cheap seats with the staff. You're allowed to be with the beautiful people."

"Someone needs to keep tabs on you," he says, his face so serious, I can't tell if he's joking.

"Don't wanna leave the wild child unattended?"

He doesn't deny it. *Sooo, not joking.*

Tap. Tap. Tap.

There it is—that quiet, persistent tapping of his finger against his thigh. It's Bryce's tell, the little sign that he's feeling uncomfortable.

And it's the reality check I need.

Seriously, Petra. You've moved on from this fantasy, remember?

I force myself to turn and gape through the ballroom peephole again.

Fiona, is front and center, owning the stage with those platinum blonde curls that cascade down her back. Her skin's glowing like she's been rolling around in diamond dust and the souls of the damned. And that floor-length dress? Champagne-colored and hugging curves that were definitely purchased with Daddy's credit card.

By her side, Gavin is her shiny accessory—tall, handsome, and imposing.

They look perfect together. It's disgusting.

Fiona grabs Gavin's hand, and even from this distance, I see the flash of her engagement ring.

That diamond?

Ten. Freaking. Carats.

Her ring was the final nail in the coffin, sealing my brother's fate to the dark side. The second I saw that rock, I knew—he was a goner.

"As you all know," Fiona coos into the microphone, "Gavin and I are getting married in a few months. But oh, we have the most fabulous surprise! We've been invited to say 'I do' at the utterly exclusive Casa Cashmere estate in Mexico! So, we're moving the wedding up to next week! We jet off tomorrow!"

The crowd erupts in gasps and excited murmurs. "Casa Cashmere?" several voices exclaim in unison, like Fiona just announced they're getting married on the moon.

But what catches my attention isn't the audience's reaction—it's my brother's face. For a split second, shock takes over his usually controlled expression.

I have no freaking clue what a Casa Cashmere is, but it's obvious he's not happy about it.

***

I'M GETTING FULL-BODY HIVES.

Gavin dragged me into this Sitting Room of Doom after Fiona dropped her surprise wedding timeline bomb. I'm standing in the corner, trying not to breathe on the many things that look like they came from the Vatican. I can't even with this wallpaper—some antique monstrosity featuring... Constipated cherubs? Riding narwhals? Through clouds made of... dollar signs?

Rich people are so weird.

I count exactly seventeen ornate vases in this room. Breaking one would bankrupt me so fast, I'd have to auction off both kidneys, sell my eggs to science, work triple shifts at the bar, and still offer hand jobs on the side to make payments.

I scan my leather jacket for tiny red dots. *Phew—so far, not marked for death by snipers.* Though honestly, I'm not sure what worries me more: getting shot for standing here or staining this fancy rug with my blood.

My plan was simple: Deliver the cufflinks. Avoid Fiona. Get out.

Instead, I'm watching my brother and his fiancée in full soap opera mode, staging their little "discussion" about the sudden wedding acceleration.

"I thought you'd be happy, Gav-Gav," Fiona says with a breathy little pout. "This is my *dream*. I've always wanted to get married at Casa Cashmere."

He exhales, slow and measured. "It's just... sudden."

"I got so excited when they had a cancellation," she says, eyes watering. "It's fine. I already told them yes, but we can keep the original wedding date."

I have to hand it to her—there's a reason she was voted most dramatic in our senior class.

"Daddy will fix it. Cancel the helicopter parade and the underwater drone photographer. Tell the sand sommelier that we won't be needing a curated barefoot walking experience. And I'm sure the bioluminescent jellyfish wrangler can release them back into the ocean."

"I didn't say no, Fi. This is... a big change. We need to talk it out. You know how important the next two weeks are for the company.

We timed the wedding for after Heartvest goes public so I could focus on us."

He pulls her close, and she nuzzles his chest. *Nuzzles.* I might vomit into the nearest vase.

To the outside world, Fiona is the walking definition of flawless.

But I know better. I know the truth behind the sparkle. I know the *REAL* Fiona.

The one who told our entire class I had chlamydia—*CHLAMYDIA*—and then passed out "Petra Protection Packs" with condoms and pamphlets like I was the poster child for abstinence.

Never in a million years did I think I'd have to endure Fiona Whitfield again.

Much less have her join my family.

"Fi, I want to give you everything your heart desires, but this one might not be possible. A wedding in one week is a big lift."

"Don't you think it would be *amazing*?" she purrs. "Eight whole days celebrating us. Our love. With our closest friends." She waggles her eyebrows. "I'm already picturing you in that little blue Speedo."

"Okay, can I leave now?" I ask, raising a hand. "Or do I have to stick around and watch you two *mate*?"

"Petra, come say hello to Fiona."

Oh, this sneaky bastard. That's why he made me stay in this museum of ugly expensive crap. He knows I've been avoiding her since they started dating.

"Petra!" Fiona gasps. Before I can dodge, she's wrapped me in a tight perfume-clouded hug. "Oh my gosh, I forgot you were here! Your brother... He makes me melt. Like *ugh*, how did I get so lucky?"

"Not sure. I'm guessing *hypnosis* or CIA-level *blackmail*."

"It is wonderful to see you!" she gushes, finally letting go. She holds me at arm's length, scanning my outfit. "Look at this... creative ensemble. So brave to wear that to a formal event."

"Thanks," I deadpan. "I was going for 'woman who'd rather be anywhere else.'"

Gavin clears his throat.

"Fiona's been looking forward to catching up," he says.

I snort. "Really? Because you've been engaged for six months, and this is literally our first conversation."

"That's my fault," she says, pressing a hand to her heart like she's pledging allegiance to the flag of bullshit. "I've been *inundated* with wedding planning and my charity work, but that's no excuse." Fiona's voice drips with manufactured concern. "Petra, I know we had our differences in high school, but I've forgiven you—and I hope one day you'll—"

"Disappear?" I smile sweetly. "Same."

Fiona chuckles—a tinkling, practiced sound. "You always made me laugh."

"Aw. That's the nicest way I've ever been called a punchline."

"I can't tell you how thrilled I am to be marrying your brother. He's the love of my life. And that means you're... well, you're part of that too."

I tilt my head. "Right. Like that sprig of rosemary on your dinner plate—technically food, but everyone knows it's pointless and should be ignored."

"I sense you're skeptical, but I've changed. I'm not that girl anymore. More than anything, I'd like us to be friends."

"Friends? You're kidding, right? You switched my senior yearbook quote to 'Live. Laugh. Lube.' You announced over the morning intercom that my hair was 'bravely resisting shampoo.' Don't even get me started when you told the school counselor I—"

"That's enough." Gavin's voice drops an octave, signaling his warning. "Fiona has apologized—more than once. I want you two to get along. You're both my girls."

"Ooh, I have the most wonderful idea! We should do a spa day—getting pampered with gold-leaf manicures, sake baths, stem cell facial treatments, and some deep tissue bonding."

"Great idea," Gavin says, kissing her temple. "You're incredible. Always thinking of others."

Yeah, she's a real patron saint of passive-aggressive revenge.

The moment Fiona is done pitching her *spa day trap*, the sitting room door swings open. In waltzes Judith Sterling-Holloway, Bryce's mother and Beverly Hills' reigning queen of judgment. Her silver hair is swept into a complicated updo. Not a strand dares to misbehave. She's wrapped in a gown the color of midnight, and a constellation of diamonds drips from her ears and neck.

I dive behind an oversized potted palm and nearly take out a porcelain vase. From behind the fronds, I check for sniper dots once more. *Phew. Still clear.*

Through the greenery, I spy Bryce—standing next to his mother, his expression unreadable, his posture impeccable. The Sterling family portrait of perfection, framed by the doorway's gilded molding.

"Fiona, darling," Judith's voice slices through the air—sharp as a paper cut but somehow melodic. "Having your wedding at Casa Cashmere? How *thrilling*!"

"Sadly, Gavin might cancel because of work."

"Nonsense." The ice in her martini tinkles as she waves her hand dismissively. "Gavin, you're the CEO. You make the rules—everyone else falls in line. That's how power works."

I glance at Gavin, whose jaw is clenched so hard, the air pressure in the room has shifted.

Until now, I've never wanted to punch an old lady in the throat before.

"Besides, you do NOT turn down an invitation from Miss Muffy Von Cashmere. That's social suicide. People wait *years* just to apply for the chance to be rejected."

"That's what I told him," Fiona says, nodding.

"Bryce, darling. You remember when we took you there for your eighth birthday?"

"Yes, Mother. The bird-watching observatory was particularly educational."

Judith takes a delicate sip of her martini. "Bryce wanted a silly carnival. Hot dogs, face painting, bumper cars... Can you imagine? But then I got the invitation to Casa Cashmere from Muffy herself, and well. We weren't going to pass up that opportunity."

Tap. Tap. Tap.

That quiet, steady tapping starts again, his finger brushing his thigh like he's trying to ground himself. A blinking light that says something's wrong. Most people miss it, but I've learned how to spot it. I feel it in my chest before I even see it.

I'm picturing eight-year-old Bryce, dreaming of cotton candy and carousel rides and then getting dragged to some snooty billionaire compound.

Did he ever get that carnival?

Did someone at least let him eat a hot dog?

The thought gives me an odd disappointment. Like when you find an old toy still in the box that never got played with.

"Gavin, this invitation cements your status. It's on the top of my list for Bryce and Amanda's wedding. Either there or Buckingham Palace. Though really, that place could use a facelift. So drab."

Wedding? He's engaged?

Why am I surprised? Of course he is.

Fiona vibrates with excitement. "We were lucky because the king of, oh, some tiny country—I forget which one—was supposed to vacation there, but he got food poisoning and almost died. Now he's in a coma and can't use his reservation."

"That is a stroke of luck," Judith says. "Well then, it's settled."

"I think my brother can decide for himself what he is and isn't going to do."

Dead silence falls over the room as all eyes lock on to my plant hideout.

Oh shit. Guess I said that out loud.

"Security!" Judith yelps, clutching her necklace like I might try to steal it.

The door bursts open, and in rush the two goons from my garden wrestling match. They skid to a halt when they spot me, recognition dawning on their faces.

"Hey fellas, miss me?" I step out from behind my botanical shield, wiggling my fingers in a wave.

Bryce steps forward, slipping into diplomat mode with practiced ease. "Mother, it's fine. This is Petra, you remember? Gavin's younger sister. You've met her before."

"I don't see the resemblance," she says, blinking slowly. "Gavin looks... successful."

Ouch. True, but ouch.

Before I can shoot back where I'd like to shove her martini olive, a security guard touches his earpiece.

"Ma'am," he says. "The governor is departing, and your husband is requesting your presence."

Judith sighs dramatically. "Naturally. The man can't locate his own handkerchief without staff assistance." At the threshold, she pauses to address one of the guards. "Keep an eye on… that." She waves vaguely in my direction. "I want her searched when she leaves. This is a charity gala, not a shelter."

I scan my body once again for sniper dots as she leaves. "Well, she didn't have me shot on sight, so that went better than expected."

No one laughs.

Tough room.

Gavin shifts his stance and turns toward Bryce, all business. "Can we make it work? Shift the IPO prep around the ceremony?"

Bryce hesitates for half a beat. "Honestly? It's risky. We're two weeks out from going public. There's always a surprise this close to the finish line."

I catch it. The flicker behind his eyes. Something he wants to say. Something important. But Bryce locks it down tight.

I move toward the door. "All right. I'm gonna peace out before I get cavity-searched in the driveway. Sorry I can't help with all the Miss Muffy stuff and royal coma logistics. Best of luck with the marital jellyfish."

"That's it," Gavin says, snapping his fingers. "Petra's the answer."

"Say what now?"

"You come to Casa Cashmere," he says, stepping closer. "You run point. Manage the wedding week with Fiona. Handle logistics so I can stay focused on the business."

"Yeah, that's gonna be a hard pass," I say, backing toward the exit.

"Gav-Gav, honey, she barely agreed to be a bridesmaid. I don't think wedding coordination is her... strength."

"But, Fi, this is what you've been wanting. You said yourself you want to bond with Petra."

I watch Fiona's face, catching the flare of panic that darts across her features—gone so quickly I might have imagined it. But I didn't. She doesn't want this any more than I do.

Gavin cups her face. "Fi, I trust my sister. There's nothing she won't do for the people she loves. When it counts, she shows up."

Why is he saying that? I've been nothing but a nonstop disappointment since I dropped out of college. And this week at his company, I have not been killing it.

"I want you to have your dream wedding," Gavin tells Fiona, his gaze intense. "And I'll make it happen. That's what I do."

She softens, her expression melting into practiced adoration. "If this is what it takes for you to say yes... then yes."

Gavin adjusts his suit jacket. "New deal, Petra. Eight days. You help me get through this wedding, and when it's over? You're done working for me. I'll pay for college. No more strings attached, Wildcat."

Ugh. Using my childhood nickname means he's serious. The promise dangles in front of me like a carrot on a stick—another hoop to jump through, another test to prove I can be the version of myself Gavin isn't embarrassed of. Behave. Blend in. Don't talk too loud or say too much.

If I follow the rules for a week, maybe I'll finally earn more than a dismissive sigh.

I wish—just once—his love didn't feel like something I had to earn.

"I'm sorry, big bro. The answer's no. I don't do dress-up games and seating charts," I say, standing my ground. "This isn't my world. And frankly? I like it that way."

And I'd rather gouge my eyes out with a spork than pretend to be friends with Fiona Whitfield.

"I'm sticking to our original agreement," I say. "I'll finish out the summer working for your company like I promised. I'll come to the wedding and play the dutiful bridesmaid. I'll even bring Mom—but I'm not going to help decorate the fairy tale."

I turn on my heel and head for the door.

It opens before I touch it.

Because of course the security guards are there waiting for me.

I pat myself down with exaggerated motions. "See? No centerpieces in my bra. No antique silverware taped to my thighs. And no decorative Fabergé eggs hiding in my reproductive system."

They nod. One gestures—*after you.*

I know I should walk away.

But I am weak. I am human. And the Bryce-shaped temptation is too strong.

I start to turn back, a parting zinger locked and loaded. "Later, Moneyba—"

WHAM!

My arm swings wide and connects with a massive vase.

CRASH!

The sound of shattering porcelain is deafening. A standing ovation for my performance of *This Bitch Doesn't Belong.* Starring me, Petra Brinkman.

Suddenly, I'm being escorted—*fine, physically hauled*—toward the exit, and the last thing I see is the disdain on Bryce's face.

"Don't worry," I call out. "I can cover that... My uterus hits the dark web tonight."

CHAPTER FOUR

BRYCE

I shouldn't be here. Full stop.

A grown man in a five-thousand-dollar Armani tux with Sterling blood running through his veins does not loiter outside Hollywood dive bars at one in the morning like he's waiting to make a drug deal.

And yet—here I sit.

I could've called. Texted. Sent a car service. Hell, I could've drafted a strongly worded email. But no. Here I am—camped out in my car across from the Broken Bottle, looking less *CEO* and more two-bad-decisions-away from having my own TMZ headline.

And why?

Because apparently convincing Petra Brinkman to do one decent thing for her brother requires an intervention.

This isn't about *her.*

It's about Gavin.

About cushioning the fallout I know is coming.

I'm here to get Petra on board. Convince her to agree to his Mexico wedding plan. Stabilize the situation before I upend it with my own bombshell—and walk away from the only real friendship

I've ever built. Before I disappear into the empire that's been waiting to chain me to a gold desk since birth.

First, get Petra to Mexico.

Next, tell Gavin the truth.

Then, pray he won't hate me for the rest of his life.

A simple, manageable sequence.

Still... I tap my thumb lightly against the steering wheel of my Aston Martin. *Tap. Tap. Tap.* If I'm being brutally honest—a habit I usually try to avoid—there's a second reason.

Curiosity.

Dangerous, inconvenient curiosity about the woman who turned another boring gala into a full-contact sport—who came and left like a human tornado in a room of marble statues.

I hold up the picture on my phone sent courtesy of my mother's private security detail. It matches the vehicle I see parked on the street. They weren't kidding about her rolling death trap. The driver's door is held on by duct tape. The back left window is covered in plastic wrap. The trunk proudly displays: CHOKE ON IT in spray paint with a giant pink penis.

Jesus, Pip.

Why does she insist on driving something so blatantly... subversive? Pride? Stubbornness? The perverse joy of knowing it makes people like me uncomfortable?

I could buy her a new vehicle. Have it delivered anonymously. One that's sensible. Safe.

But I can already see how that would go. She'd track me down, those hazel-green eyes blazing with fury, and set the car on fire in my driveway to prove she doesn't need handouts.

Heat rushes through my body at the mental image—Petra silhouetted by flames, defiant and wild and so goddamn gorgeous.

"Get a grip, Sterling."

The bar door swings open. A group of guys spill out, laughing and shoving each other. One of them vomits into the gutter. *Lovely.*

Through the grimy windows, I catch occasional glimpses of my best friend's sister behind the counter, slinging drinks with the same take-no-prisoners efficiency she applied to demolishing my family's priceless antiques.

The sound of porcelain shattering echoes in my memory. Five hundred years of ancient Chinese artistry, reduced to dust beneath Petra's combat boots.

And God help me, I'd found myself fighting back a smile.

Should I waltz in? Just march across those sticky floors and drag her out? That would go over well. Nothing says "do your brother a favor" like being dragged away from your workplace by a billionaire on a power trip.

Besides, one photo of me inside that establishment, and the headlines would write themselves.

BILLIONAIRE CEO SLUMMING IT AT HOLLYWOOD HOLE IN THE WALL

HEIR TO STERLING FORTUNE CAUGHT IN SCANDALOUS NIGHT OUT

MONEY MOGUL'S SECRET TRYST WITH TATTOOED VIXEN

Not that Petra would care what they write. Those are the things that keep men with empires to protect awake at night.

Money. Image. Power.

She doesn't give a damn about any of it. Never has.

In a world where I've spent twenty-nine years navigating the intricacies of salad forks and PR crisis classes, Petra Brinkman is a bomb of authenticity. She refuses to put on a show or fake politeness. She enters a room as herself—attitude problem and all—daring anyone to challenge her right to be there.

A feeling dangerously close to envy coils in my chest.

When was the last time I did anything without calculating the optics?

I'm considering texting her—though what I'd say, I have no idea—when the bar door opens again, spilling yellow light onto the dirty sidewalk like a beer puddle.

And there she is.

Petra steps out, a vision in black leather and defiance. She slides in her AirPods, pulls up her hood, and grabs something from her shoulder bag before taking off down the street toward her car. She moves like a girl on a goddamn mission.

I toss my phone onto the passenger seat, open the door, and swiftly exit. My Aston chirps as I click the key fob.

"Hey!" I call after her.

Nothing. Not even a hesitation in her stride. Either those AirPods are blasting death metal at eardrum-rupturing volume, or she's deliberately ignoring me.

Based on our history, I'm betting on the latter.

I pick up the pace, the sidewalk slick under my dress shoes. "Slow down. We need to talk."

Still no response. I'm momentarily captivated by her swaying hips. *Damn.*

"Wait a second—"

I reach out and tap her shoulder.

Mistake.

Huge, catastrophic mistake.

The world explodes into pure, undiluted agony. Pain detonates in my chest, shooting down my arms, locking my knees. My entire nervous system declares mutiny. Every cell in my body launches into a simultaneous riot. My blood is replaced with Pop Rocks and Coca-Cola.

BZZZZZZZZZZZZZZZZZ!!!

My teeth chatter like castanets in a flamenco band. My eyeballs are trying to escape my skull to save themselves.

"GLARB-NURBLE-GNAAAAARGH!"

Is that sound coming from me?

I can't stop shaking.

Why am I shaking?

I think I'm going to piss myself.

Is this death? Am I ascending?

No, you idiot—the microscopic part of my brain not currently being jelly-fied forms the realization:

I'M. BEING. TASED.

Through the static frying my neurons, I hear Petra shriek: "OH FUCK! BRYCE?!"

Yes. Hello.

I'm the human marshmallow you're currently roasting.

I try to answer, but the only thing that comes out is a mangled, "Blarghh—

My legs give out.

I hit the ground hard, the key fob flying from my hand and bouncing into the street. The asphalt is cold and gritty under my palms. I blink up at the sky, my vision swimming with neon halos.

"Shit, shit—okay—don't move," she pants, patting me down as though she's checking for smuggled weapons. "You're fine. You're... fine-ish."

"FNNNNGGG-WIZZLE-GUBB!"

What the hell just came out of my mouth?

She places her hand firmly on my chest, feeling my heart race, and leans in close. From this position, I have a clear view down her shirt.

I've closed million-dollar deals while half-asleep. I've given keynote speeches in front of Fortune 500 CEOs. I've led high-stakes negotiations without breaking a sweat.

But right now? All my brain can manage is:

Boobs.

Boobs.

Holy shit, Petra's braless. Naked. Boobs.

I make an embarrassing whimper noise in the back of my throat.

She frowns, leaning closer. "Stay with me, okay? Focus. How many fingers am I holding up?"

"Plurple-fish boobs," I answer with absolute confidence.

Her eyebrows shoot up into her hairline. "Oh my God, I liquified your brain. Gavin is going to murder me. Moneybags, if you can hear me, tell me your name."

"Blue. Blue hamblurgers."

"I need to take you to a hospital!"

"No stabular. No hob bub. No snorck-slickle."

"Are you trying to say no hospital?"

"YEEP-DE-DOOP!" I confirm solemnly.

I make an effort to lift my arm, wanting to brush her hand. Assure her I'm not brain-dead. Maybe... touch those perky—

"If you don't want the ER, then let's get you home to Amanda. Where's your driver? Wait. Did you drive here?"

"Car Vrooooom-zoom-Vrrrr-SKRRRT!"

"Now we're getting somewhere. Where are your keys?"

"House lake... Amanda? *Poof.* Teenagers. Vampire blood?"

"Annnnd we're back to gibberish. Seriously, what were you thinking? You can't sneak up on a woman after dark! Do you have any idea how the real world works?"

I lift my right hand triumphantly. "Key!"

"There's nothing in your hand, B. You must have dropped them."

I stare at her as she crawls around the sidewalk, voice muffled as she peers under a parked car.

"I'm a menace. I tased a billionaire. Don't need a law degree to know I'm definitely going to jail for this."

Even half-electrocuted, I'm powerless against the pull of those tempting lips. Still painted that defiant red—like the warning signs my brain should have registered before I climbed out of my vehicle to pursue her. Red like the embarrassment that'll eventually replace the numbness in my extremities... if feeling ever returns.

"Aha!" Petra bolts upright, pointing triumphantly toward the center of the road. "Found your fob! Stay here. Don't move a muscle."

I would laugh at the absurdity of her instruction if my facial muscles were cooperating. Instead, I manage what I suspect is a horrifying grimace.

She gets to her feet, brushing dirt off her jeans as—

A giant street sweeper with spinning brushes and industrial-strength vacuum power rounds the corner. Its headlights are blinding.

"No, no, NO!" She breaks into a run, arms windmilling.

Too late.

WHIRRRRRR-SLUUUUURP-CLUNK!

My fifteen-thousand-dollar Aston Martin key fob is slurped up by the city's cleaning behemoth.

"Are you freaking kidding me?!" she shouts at the retreating machine. "These streets are never cleaned. Ever! What, did you sense the billionaire and send out the emergency sparkle team? Trying to make the gutters nice and shiny for Mr. Moneybags here?! UGH. Great job! You missed the used condom!"

Petra stomps back to me, each footfall an exclamation point of rage. I'm still sprawled on the concrete feeling like a gooey puddle.

"Okay, you're clearly disoriented, you don't want a hospital, I don't know where the hell you live, and your keys are somewhere inside the Bermuda Triangle of the L.A. Sanitation Department."

She exhales sharply, like this next part physically hurts her.

"I can't believe I'm saying this... but I'm taking you to *my* place. Come on, B. Push up on three," she instructs, gripping my waist. "One... two... THREE!"

Somehow, through sheer brute strength and an unholy amount of grunting, Petra gets me vertical.

Or vertical-ish.

She half-drags, half-shoves me toward her beat-up vehicle. She kicks open the passenger door, and a cascade of papers and crumpled napkins fall out.

"VIP treatment, Moneybags."

I survey the passenger seat—currently home to what appears to be half of her worldly possessions. Fast food wrappers. Crumpled receipts. A textbook on constitutional law. And at least six empty coffee cups with varying levels of lipstick stains.

She scoops up the debris with one arm, maintaining her death grip on my waist with the other. The contents are unceremoniously dumped into the back seat.

"Bet your fancy car doesn't come with artisanal garbage."

Folding my six-foot-two frame into her compact car is an exercise in human origami. My knees hit the dashboard. My shoulders scrape the doorframe. My head finds every hard surface on the way down.

"Bend! You have to bend!" she shouts, pushing on my shoulders. "Your legs go INSIDE the door!"

"Spaghetti legs are jellyfish," I inform her helpfully.

After an impressive string of creative profanity, she manages to stuff me into the seat.

"Seat belt," she pants, reaching across my lap. Her face is inches from mine, close enough that I notice tiny flecks of gold in her eyes. A loose strand of hair brushes my cheek. My heart rate doubles instantly.

God, she smells good.

Or at least I *think* she smells good.

Could be the electrical burn still cooking my brain.

She slides into the driver's seat and jams the key into the ignition. Nothing happens. Not a single sputter.

"Come on, girl," she coos to the dashboard, patting it lovingly. "Start for Mama. I just fed you the expensive gasoline yesterday."

She tries again. And again. On the ninth attempt, the engine coughs to life like a pack-a-day smoker.

I stick my tongue out to celebrate.

It feels... wrong.

"Hairy tongue. Like kitty cat. Meow." I attempt to demonstrate a cat licking its paw.

"Oh, I'm in so much fucking trouble with my brother," Petra groans. "I've kidnapped a tased billionaire who thinks he's a cat."

I wiggle my tongue again, trying to see it in the rearview mirror.

It looks normal. It does not *feel* normal.

I scratch frantically at my tongue like I can scrape the imaginary fur off it.

Petra watches out of the corner of her eye. "So, your arm works now. Miracle one complete. Time to jumpstart those legs, and you might survive climbing two flights of stairs to my apartment."

Two flights? That feels... ambitious.

I concentrate hard on my lower extremities. Are they tingling? Something is definitely waking up down there. A very specific throbbing begins to register.

"Legs move," I announce proudly.

We come to a stop at a red light. Petra turns to check my progress—and her eyes go comically wide.

"I hate to break it to you, B" she says slowly, gaze fixed firmly below my waist, "but that's your, uh, third leg you're... flexing."

I peer down at my crotch and—oh.

OH.

My penis is at full attention, creating a tent in my dress pants. And it's... twitching. Rhythmically. Like a dog's tail wagging with hyper enthusiasm.

I should be mortified. I should be apologizing profusely and covering myself with the closest object.

Instead, I find myself grinning like an idiot. Why? Because this isn't real. It can't be.

Nothing—absolutely nothing—in my careful, overly planned existence has ever been this unhinged, chaotic, off-the-rails insane.

That's how I know this is a dream. I'm safely at home, in my king-plus-king-sized bed, experiencing the most vivid dream of my life.

Or I'm dead.

***

This is fucking real. Turns out, not a hallucination.

I suck in a breath, the air reeking of smoke, urine, and what I assume is the shattered dreams of everyone who's ever walked down this block.

There's a burning trash can on the corner, flames licking at the night sky, surrounded by a bunch of men passing a bottle in a brown paper bag. Barred windows jut out like warning signs, and graffiti scars every building. Streetlights flicker, casting shadows that prowl like predators. Police sirens scream in the distance—and then not-so-distant.

Petra's neighborhood is so bad, her car actually blends in.

"Almost there, B. Just ten more steps."

My thighs are shaking. My lungs are staging a protest. I lean more heavily on her than I should, but Pip doesn't slow down. She manhandles me up another flight of stairs, until finally—*finally*—she fumbles a key into a dented door and kicks it open.

I stagger inside... *Good God.* Her apartment is a crime scene.

"You've been robbed."

"Well, well. Look who can form full sentences again. Shame. I was enjoying your billionaire babble."

The space assaults all my senses at once. A mattress on the floor drowning in a sea of mismatched blankets and pillows. An orange couch that looks like it was rescued from the curb. The "kitchen" is a mere mini-fridge with a two-burner hot plate. Books are stacked in precarious towers, clothes draped over every available surface. Christmas lights zigzag across one wall, providing the only warmth against the harsh overhead lighting.

I'm frozen at the threshold, afraid the floor might collapse if I step too hard. Or that whatever's living under that pile of laundry on the couch might bite.

I rub my forehead, trying to remind myself why I'm here. *Get Petra to say yes to Mexico.* That's it. Convince her, call my driver, and get the hell out of here before I need a tetanus shot.

"Is this your first time seeing how the other ninety-nine percent lives? Should I prepare a guided tour? 'And to your left, you'll see the exotic sight of someone living paycheck to paycheck.'"

"Do you even have a restroom?" I blurt out, scanning the chaotic open area.

"I'm not *that* poor," Petra snorts. She crosses the limited floor space in three strides and flings open the only interior door with a dramatic flourish. "Ta-da! Indoor plumbing. Ain't I fancy?"

The bathroom is so small it appears to have been an architectural afterthought, as if the contractor remembered humans have biological functions only after finishing the rest of the apartment.

"It's efficient," she says, patting the doorframe. "I can brush my teeth, shower, and pee all at the same time. Real time-saver on busy mornings."

There's no tub, just a shower stall so narrow it makes the lavatory on my private jet look like a Roman bath. "I've seen bigger showers on sailboats," I mutter, immediately regretting the observation.

"Sorry the poverty tour isn't meeting your standards. Next apartment viewing, I'll request the deluxe model with gold-plated bidets and oyster dispensers."

She's living like this. Every day.

And somehow, she still smiles as if she's daring the world to knock her down again.

A knot forms low in my stomach, tight and ugly and complicated as hell.

Petra flops down onto the mattress and kicks off her boots, her bare toes wiggling in triumph. She carelessly tosses her leather jacket onto a nearby pile of clothes. Her shirt rides up, exposing a delicious sliver of smooth, sinful skin and—*is that a tattoo peeking above her waistband?*

"Make yourself at home, Moneybags. But be warned—if you see something skitter across the floor, don't try to fight it. You'll lose."

If my mother saw me like this, she'd have an aneurysm.

"And if you hear my front door open, it's either a robber or a ghost, because I sure as hell don't have a roommate."

"I honestly can't fathom where a roommate would sleep."

"The couch, obviously." She props up on her elbows, those full red lips curving into a smirk. "Or if they're hot enough, they can share my bed."

She pats the mattress, and the image of some random guy under her sheets sends a strange discomfort sliding through me. I'm not sure why I care. It shouldn't matter.

Her *type* is probably muscle-bound bartenders from the low-light liquor lounge where she works. Or tattooed bikers with greasy hands and grimy fingernails.

This is ridiculous. Her dating life is not my concern.

"This was fun, but you should probably call your security detail to come get you. I'd rather not have a SWAT team rappelling through my window at three a.m. I'm already kissing that deposit goodbye—let's not add broken windows to the bill."

I pat down my pockets, coming up empty. "My phone's in the Aston."

"Fantastic. Okay, Billionaire Boy, you can't just stand there looking traumatized by my poverty all night." Petra jumps up from the bed, sweeping a mountain of clothes off her couch with one dramatic arm gesture. "Let me check out the damage I inflicted on you."

"I'm fine."

She presses a single finger against my chest—pain explodes like fireworks beneath my skin. I collapse onto the sofa with an embarrassing groan.

"Dear God," I wheeze. "What did you do?"

"Fifty thousand volts of 'don't creep up on women after dark,'" she says. "Now take off your shirt so I can see how bad it is. But don't get too comfortable, or I'll charge you rent."

I shrug out of my ruined tuxedo jacket and start unbuttoning my dress shirt. When I glance up, Petra has gone uncharacteristically quiet.

Her gaze tracks my fingers as I undo each button. The faintest hint of pink spreads across her cheekbones, and for the first time since I've known her, she looks almost... shy.

"Damn, Moneybags. I'm surprised the taser even penetrated that wall of muscle."

I can't help the small, satisfied smile that escapes. Seeing this girl flustered is both unexpected and oddly gratifying.

"Dude, you should tell your trainer to up your weights. Since I took you down twice in one day."

She leans in to examine the angry red mark blooming on my chest, her fingers—surprisingly gentle—trace the outline of what will no doubt become an impressive bruise. My skin ignites wherever she touches, a completely different kind of electrical current now racing through me.

I should be terrified of her. She literally brought me to my knees tonight. But goddamn I want more of it, more of that delicate press of her fingertips against my bare skin.

Do not focus on her hands. Not her pale, soft skin. Not the fact that she smells like jasmine and fresh morning coffee. Not those red lips that are inches from my chest.

Her touch softens further, featherlight fingers stroking across my pecs with hypnotic rhythm. The pad of her thumb catches on my nipple, and we both gasp. Then—as if burned—she jerks her hand back.

"Oh yeah, that's gonna bruise. Let me get you an ice pack."

She practically sprints to the mini-fridge and yanks the door open so hard the whole thing wobbles.

"So..." Petra says, her head buried in the freezer, "what was that nonsense you were spouting about Amanda? Something about teenage vampire blood and a lake house. Sounded like a weird *Twilight* sequel."

I freeze. The haze of post-taser delirium had me forgetting the Amanda situation and the well-rehearsed story we'd agreed on.

"She's at her family's lake house. Her mother's recovering from a procedure."

For a moment—a single impulsive, reckless breath—I consider telling her the truth.

"Anti-aging treatments," I say instead. "Her mother is very dedicated to them."

"Rich people. Always finding new ways to avoid reality."

Petra places a plastic freezer bag in my hand, filled with small green balls. The weight is substantial, the cold seeping through instantly.

"You'll have to forgive me. I don't have ice cubes in my budget. This should work."

I lift the bag, eyeing it with deep suspicion.

"Are these... narcotics?"

"God, I wish. No. It's cookie dough." She unzips the bag and holds it under my nose. "Take a sniff, Moneybags. I promise they're not edibles, though I would love to see what you're like high."

The scent hits me immediately—sweet, earthy, with a weird green tea aroma.

"That funky smell? Matcha," she says, grabbing a dough ball and tossing it into her mouth like popcorn. "Fancy word for 'dirt that tastes expensive.' Matcha chocolate chip, my specialty."

"You... make cookie dough to freeze?" I ask, trying to imagine this menace in eyeliner whisking away in the kitchen.

"Pro tip for single life survival: Always have emergency cookie dough on standby. My friends and I make giant batches and freeze 'em. Then when life sucks—and spoiler alert, it always sucks—you can reward yourself with warm cookies on demand."

I press the bag to my ribs and hiss as the ice-cold dough sears against my skin. "Christ!"

"Aww. Poor baby. Billion-dollar body, two-cent pain tolerance."

I grunt, repositioning the bag. "Are these 'friends' guys?"

The second the words leave my mouth, I want to bite them back.

Smooth, Sterling. Real subtle.

"Spying for my brother, B?" she teases. "Tsk, tsk. Very uncool." She pops another ball of dough onto her tongue. "Not men. Katie and Camila. My besties from college." She licks a smudge of chocolate from her thumb with deliberate slowness. "But for the record, dudes do *love* my cookies, if you want to include that in your little spy report for Gavin."

I adjust the makeshift ice pack over my heart to hide the heat creeping up my neck. Pain ignites. "Holy mother of—"

"You definitely need drugs. I'm making dinner, and you're eating. I've got painkillers that require food." She heads toward her kitchen area then glances back with a devilish grin. "But if you want a cookie, you better be a good boy and take your medicine."

The words "good boy" in that husky voice of hers does irreparable damage to my insides.

While Petra bangs around in her sorry excuse for a kitchen, I take the opportunity to further examine my surroundings.

Stacks of textbooks are shoved into every available space—Contract Law, Property Law, Civil Procedure. Thick volumes with sticky notes and highlighter explosions leaking out the sides.

Law books?

I push up off the couch with a groan, wandering over to the closest stack. I open my mouth to ask—*Why law books?*—but then something else catches my eye.

A record player.

Not just any record player.

The record player.

The same vintage turntable that was in her teenage bedroom, perched atop a milk crate overflowing with vinyl. The exact setup from that graduation night seven years ago when she kissed me and my world slowed down—for a fleeting moment.

"This is quite a collection you've got here," I say, flipping through the albums.

"Well, there's no Mozart in there, if that's what you're wondering."

I keep flipping. Led Zeppelin. Fleetwood Mac. Nirvana.

And then—

Heart. Their *Bad Animals* album.

My pulse spikes. The primitive art design on the cover reminds me of Petra herself—raw, powerful, untamed. But more importantly, it holds track two, the song that was playing when her lips touched mine.

"Mind if I play something?" I say before my brain can stop me.

"If you think you can resurrect that fried record player, be my guest. It's been dead for months. Which sucks because pawning that thing was my backup plan to make rent this month. My 'Nips for Tips' campaign's been underperforming lately. Guess even the creeps are on a budget in this economy."

I slide the album back into the milk crate as she approaches, juggling two mismatched bowls in her hands.

"Dinner is served, Your Highness. Feast of champions. Zero Michelin stars guaranteed."

"What exactly is... *nips for tips*?"

"Basic bartending economics 101. No undergarments increases revenue." She gestures toward her chest with the bowls. "The girls earn their keep."

Do not stare at her breasts, Sterling. You are not a hormone-addled teenager. You are a grown man. A professional. An heir to billions. Stop. Looking.

I'm definitely still looking.

I cough into my hand, immediately wincing as pain shoots through my taser-fried muscles.

Petra grins, knowing exactly what I was looking at.

"Okay, tough guy. Let's feed you before you pass out and sue me."

We settle onto the couch, and she drops two white pills into my palm, passing me a chipped glass of water.

"What are these exactly?"

"Like Tylenol, but stronger. Trust me, it's fine. Probably."

"You inspire exactly zero confidence."

"Relax. They're not roofies. If I wanted to take advantage of you, I wouldn't need pharmaceutical assistance."

I choke mid-swallow. *Why do I have the impression that's not a brag but simply plain fact?*

She hands me a steaming bowl filled with a vibrant, unnaturally orange... *pasta?*

"Eat up. Those pills need food, or you'll be barfing all over my vintage couch."

I raise my fork, eyeing the bright-orange mound, then take a bite. "Your mom used to make this when I'd stay for dinner!"

"I remember!" she says, laughing. "You thought it was a science experiment. And you're right, it is. Nuclear-orange goo that's pure magic. But it's gotta be Kraft Mac & Cheese. I'd rather eat out of a dumpster than go generic."

"Marcel, my personal chef, would hate how much I'm enjoying this," I mutter, chewing.

"Oh my God. That's the most billionaire thing you've ever said."

We both go quiet, totally absorbed in our bowls. Petra polishes hers off and places it on the coffee table with a *CLINK.*

"All right, B. Why were you lurking outside my bar like a handsome stalker? I'm enjoying this twisted little reunion, but we aren't in each other's lives."

Tell her what's going on. Tell her you're leaving Heartvest. Tell her you feel as though you're breaking something with Gavin you can't fix.

"Your brother wants you in Mexico. I came here to convince you."

"I figured. The answer is still no."

"Think about it logically. In exchange for a paid vacation in a private Mexican paradise, you'll get your college paid for."

"Look around, Moneybags! Am I a person who makes decisions based on good financial plans?"

"You said yourself you need the money."

"And I'll figure it out like I always do," she counters, chin jutting forward defiantly. "Without selling my dignity to be my brother's performing poodle for his bridezilla fiancée."

"It's eight days, Pip. That's it. Why are you being so stubborn?"

"Eight days of pretending to be someone I'm not for people who've never respected me. No amount of infinity pools or free champagne is worth that."

The conviction in her voice floors me. *What the hell can I say to that?*

Then I feel it—the drugs kicking in, my body sinking deeper into the couch, muscles liquefying.

"I'm sorry to inconvenience you further," I mumble, my words slurring, "but I think I need a nap… right here. Just a little."

"Lightweight," she teases, but her expression softens as she grabs a blanket from a nearby heap and lays it over me.

"I'll be over there if you need me," she says, pointing awkwardly toward her bed. "Normally I sleep naked, but I'll keep the goods covered tonight. You're welcome, Moneybags."

My eyes betray me instantly, drifting to where her nipples press against the thin cotton of her T-shirt. I rest my head against the couch, my vision blurring.

After a good night's rest, I'll convince her to say yes.

For Gavin.

That's why I'm here.

That's the only reason.

CHAPTER FIVE

PETRA

Group Chat : CPK Forever

Me: *Quick Poll: On a scale of 1 to felony, how bad is accidentally tasing your brother's business partner, drugging him, then maybe—just maybe—cuddling him a little while he's unconscious?*

Katie: *PETRA! Please tell me you didn't kidnap Bryce Sterling!*

Me: *Kidnap is such an ugly word. I prefer "non-consensual hangout."*

Cam: *Girl, this sounds like the start of a Lifetime movie.*

Me: *He had the AUDACITY to ask me to help with Fiona's wedding.*

Cam: *Oh HELL NO! Tase him again!*

Bryce made his escape while I was sleeping.

No surprise there. Bet he bolted the second his billionaire brain realized he'd been held hostage in this glorified shoebox with plumbing.

Sunlight sneaks through my "blinds"—aka the shower curtain I taped to the window *(because real curtains are expensive).* I stretch my back, and it cracks like a glow stick.

"Guess my hospitality skills didn't impress," I grumble, tossing off the blankets. "What? No mint on your pillow? No champagne brunch? Sorry to burst your bubble, Moneybags."

I groan, dragging myself to my feet and ignoring the fact that every part of me is lowkey vibrating with his memory. Of him sleeping on my couch. Of his distinguished body crammed into my messy living room, looking wildly out of place and somehow... right.

No, it was wrong. Last night was a freak occurrence, an emotional blackout. Like drunk dialing your ex, but instead of a slurred voicemail, I kidnapped him. He's gone back to his life. Reality check complete.

I shuffle into the kitchen.

"Honestly, what kind of love story starts with, 'when I sorta combo-attacked his balls with an elbow and a taser—that's when fate stepped in'?" I snort. "Yeah. That's a fairy tale to tell the grandkids."

Our worlds don't even share the same laws of nature. He wears shoes worth more than everything I own, and I eat cereal with my hands because who has time to wash a spoon?

Plus, he's engaged to Amanda "Probably Pisses Rosewater" Tenley. *If word got out that he was even here, we'd be front-page news*:

Billionaire Ditches Socialite Goddess for One Night with Bartender Gutter Rat!

I give the coffeemaker two smacks—the magic touch to make it cooperate—then pour in the last handful of grounds from the bag. It gurgles like a cat hacking up a hairball, and the brew that comes out is basically brown water. But screw it. I can't afford the double espresso from the corner café today. Belt-tightening mode: activated.

While it wheezes, I grab a mug from the drying rack—the one that says: I Survived my Childhood: Where's my Fucking Medal? Camila gave it to me after I told her about my dad walking out and leaving us penniless.

I yank my Contract Law textbook off the kitchen counter where it's been marinating in a pile of unopened bills and dirty dishes. *Focus, Petra. Your shit's not going to pull itself together.*

Lately, I've been reading everything I can about law. At first, it was just curiosity—could I hack it? Did I have what it takes? I had no intention of wasting time and racking up mountains of debt, only to find out I'm as suited for law school as a penguin in the Sahara.

I've learned this about myself: I thrive on the warrior side of law. I love fighting for people who can't protect themselves, building cases tight enough to survive a black hole, and then verbally throat-punching asshats with arguments so tight they squeak like dollar store chew toys. The rush of a powerful debate is addictive—more potent than caffeine—and it's where I come alive.

But reading lengthy legal texts or conducting extensive research? I'd rather eat broken glass. These headache-inducing paragraphs with their convoluted, deliberately obtuse language are pure torture.

Good thing I've got stubbornness in spades. I'll read the same page fifty times if I have to. Break it down. Wrestle it into submission. Make it my bitch.

I sink onto the couch, curling my feet under me with my book balanced on my knees. As I set my mug on the coffee table, I spot it—Bryce's bowl, sitting next to mine. The same one that held mac and cheese a few hours ago. And there, neatly folded at the end of the sofa, is the blanket I'd tossed over him.

Before I can stop myself, I scoop up the blanket, press it to my face, and inhale. *Fuck—it smells like him.* That distinct Bryce scent that's haunted me since high school. Crisp pears and sandalwood. Expensive and intoxicating.

A memory trickles in—seventeen-year-old me stealing his navy sweater after he left it at our house. I hid it under my pillow for months, obsessed. I cherished the way it smelled like him. But eventually my mom found it, washed it, and ruined my life.

I hurl the blanket across the room, but the damage is done. All I'm thinking about is his chest from last night—broad and muscled and right there under my fingertips. How he looked at me with those intense blue eyes. How his gaze kept dropping to my breasts when he thought I wasn't looking.

When his breath caught after my thumb grazed his nipple... *Oh my God!* Every cell in my body lit up at that tiny point of contact. *I'm getting wet just thinking about it.*

"Study, you thirsty disaster. Study!" I command myself, smacking my forehead with the textbook.

I open the law manual to the chapter I left off on—prenuptial agreements.

"Fuck me with a spatula."

Prenups. The magical legal shield my mom didn't have when my father swapped us out for a newer, shinier family. She was already barely scraping by, so hiring a divorce attorney—let alone a good one—might as well have cost a million dollars. She got steamrolled. And by the time it was over, we were left with nothing.

I bet Bryce will have a prenup the size of the Oxford English Dictionary when he marries Amanda. Pages and pages of legalese making sure the family's priceless art collection stays safely out of his wifey's manicured clutches.

The thought of Bryce getting married sends a sharp pain to my ribs.

"Nope. Hard pass. Let's see what other kind of legal misery we can learn about instead."

Next chapter: post-nuptial agreements.

"What in the rich people fuckery is this?"

I lean closer to the small print, reading out loud in my best courtroom voice: "Similar to prenups, postnuptial agreements are legal contracts created after marriage that determine how property and finances will be handled in the event of divorce or death. To be valid, they must be signed by both spouses, and notarized, blah blah, soul-crushing blah."

Wait. Now *that* has possibilities.

A wicked little grin curls across my mouth as I picture it. Perhaps some light tasing would persuade dear old Dad to sign one? *Surprise, jackass! Half that mansion you bought your new, younger wife? Yeah, Mom's coming for it with blood in her eyes and receipts in her hand.*

I grab the highlighter and start mauling the page. "This is how we launch the revenge tour."

KNOCK KNOCK.

I freeze.

Shit.

There's only one person who knocks around here—and it's not the good kind of knocking.

It's landlord-knocking.

Late-rent-knocking.

I shrink back into my couch as though I'm a possum playing dead. Maybe if I don't move, he'll think I'm a corpse. Or that I joined a doomsday cult. Or that I'm too broke to be worth the hassle.

KNOCK! KNOCK!

"Pip, are you home?"

I fall off the couch. "Bryce?"

"Yeah," he calls through the door. "You mind letting me in? If I loiter out here much longer, I'm confident I'll be mugged."

"Shit, shit, shit," I hiss, frantically running fingers through my black hair, which only makes it worse. Screw it. He's already seen my rock-bottom life. What's a little more humiliation?

"And please note: I am verbally identifying myself. Loudly. So there's no need for elbowing, kicking, tasing or, really, assault of any kind."

"Ha-ha," I deadpan, opening the door.

There he is. My heart sighs.

Holding two coffee cups and a pastry bag, standing in the walkway like some absurd fantasy. He's showered and shaved. His blond hair is neatly styled. The fitted blue suit he's wearing brings out the deep color in his eyes. His pocket kerchief compliments his tie in a way that confirms someone is paid an obscene amount of money to make sure Bryce Sterling's accessories coordinate at all times.

"Look who's back for round two of 'Slumming It with Petra.'"

"Didn't want to wake you. I took a wild guess you're an espresso drinker."

I snatch the cup from his hand and our fingers touch. Literal arm-tingling fireworks shoot up my arm. "God, yes," I moan unashamedly.

Bryce's mouth twitches, fighting a smile.

I'm so busy having an inappropriate relationship with my espresso that I almost miss the gleaming stretched limo parked at the curb behind him.

"Shit, Moneybags, you can't roll up in that! People around here will think I really *do* sell meth."

"After last night, you made it clear you can't be bought. But that doesn't mean you can't be bribed to come to Mexico."

I take another sip of my liquid orgasm, eyeing him over the rim of my cup. "Does the word 'no' mean something different to billionaires? Or maybe the voltage scrambled your brain, because I told you I'm *not* going."

"Hear me out." His eyes dance with mischief—an expression I've rarely seen on his overly serious face. He reaches behind him and pulls out a cardboard box, setting it at my feet.

It's a case of Kraft Mac & Cheese.

"Thirty-five boxes," he says. "Only the good stuff."

"Glad to see you were listening," I say, nudging the box with my toe.

"I haven't finished." There's that spark again, that little flash of the real Bryce peeking through the tailored suit. He extends an arm backward and produces another box. "Bribe number two."

"Let me guess. You got me a yacht?"

Nope. A box of tasers. Actual, honest-to-God tasers.

Cute ones. Small enough to fit in a lipstick tube.

"This special model has the same fifty-thousand volts with a built-in flashlight. Which makes me feel safer about you walking on dark streets alone at night. And I got a dozen so you can have one for your car, in your purse, in your pocket, and multiples here at your apartment."

"I like the idea of multiples," I quip before crossing my arms, trying to ignore the warmth spreading through my chest. *Is he... worried about me?*

No! Stay mad. Stay strong. Do not be wooed by electroshock weaponry.

I give a lazy shrug. "It's not *that* bad around here."

Bryce glances behind him toward the street—and right on cue, some dude is spray-painting a glorious pink penis across the wall of the laundromat.

"Ohhh, so when rich snobs do it, it's *performance art.* But when it's poor people, suddenly it's *graffiti*? That guy's the next Banksy. You should buy that wall before it appreciates."

For a second, I think he might chuckle, but he stays glued to his usual stoic expression.

"This is nice and all, B, but—"

"Hold on. I'm still attempting to bribe you."

He turns and reaches once more, carefully lifting something bulky wrapped in bubble wrap. With reverent hands, he unwraps it to reveal...

My record player.

Not a new one. *My* record player.

I whip my head around to check, and sure enough, the spot where it usually sits is empty.

"I had it repaired. Apparently broken belt drives are common in these models."

"You stole my record player?"

"Borrowed. Can I come in and return it to its rightful place?"

"Be my guest. How did you get it fixed so fast?" I watch him kneel on my stained carpet and set the player carefully back on the milk crate. "That model is ancient. Parts are impossible to find."

He shoots me a look over his shoulder, and God help me, the sight of Bryce Sterling on his knees in my apartment does dangerous things to my self-control.

"Billionaire, remember?"

Is this some misplaced big brother syndrome? Like he's channeling Gavin's overprotective energy because my actual brother is too busy being engaged to the princess of darkness? It's clear that seeing where I live has triggered his white knight complex. Now he feels sorry for poor little Pip.

"Why go to all this trouble? What's in this for you?"

My question catches him off guard. As he stands, his finger starts tapping against his thigh—tap, tap, tap.

What is he not telling me?

"I had another conversation with Gavin this morning. This abrupt change in plans is causing him a great deal of stress."

He pauses, his eyes dropping to the floor for a split second before meeting mine again. "And unfortunately, Amanda is unable to attend. I'd... prefer not to go alone. Engaging in small talk with strangers at these events is something I find quite dreadful."

Something flutters in my chest like a trapped butterfly. Bryce wants me there. Not for Gavin. For him.

"Whoa, whoa. You don't want to go either? New plan: We both ditch the shindig."

A dangerous thought creeps into my head. *What if I did go with him?* Eight days of Bryce all to myself. One last time to be near him. Living the fantasy that he's mine, if only for a while.

Yeah, that's pure crackhead logic, Petra. Let's not veer into "accidental trophy wife" territory.

"Suppose, hypothetically, I said yes. Am I required to participate in all the luxury torture? As in... snail mucus facials with Fiona and 24-karat gold colonics?"

"If I have to, you have to," Bryce says without blinking.

"So we're a package deal of mutual misery?"

"Yes."

"You make it sound so romantic."

Bryce shrugs. "Not trying to."

I sigh. Loudly. "You're not going to give up, are you?"

"No."

Katie and Cam would duct tape me to a chair if they knew I was considering this. But I can't help myself. Not because I believe in fairy tales and all that happily ever after crap. I just wanna bite into that poison apple, savor the taste, and prove it won't take me down again.

"Fine, I'll do it," I snap. "I'll go to Mexico. Mainly because I want to see Fiona break down over lukewarm mimosas and off-brand humidity. That's peak entertainment. But if this goes to hell—and it will—I'm tasing you again."

"Deal." He holds out his hand like we're sealing a blood pact and not the worst idea I've ever had.

I shake it. Then he glances at the mountainous piles of laundry around my apartment.

"Which one of those is the formalwear heap?"

"Eat a brick."

"Pack your essentials. We have a stop to make before the jet."

Then he smiles—a genuine smile—and my heart does a damn triple axel. Seeing that grin light up his face is my new addiction.

This is bad. *I have royally fucked up.*

***

Let's set things straight. There are a million places I'd rather be than parked in front of a fancy-ass store on Rodeo Drive. First things that come to mind:

1. Getting pap smear from a drunken clown.

2. Holding Fiona's hand during her weekly colonic.

3. Hell.

"I'll save you the trouble, B. I'm not getting out. Beverly Hills is the enemy."

Through the tinted limousine windows, I notice this particular store has no flashy signs. No mannequins. Just a solid gold plaque with some fancy script that probably translates to "Broke Folks, Keep Walking."

"Beverly Hills is a zip code, Pip. It doesn't have an agenda."

"I packed clothes. Perfectly acceptable clothes. My trusty black dress. The good jeans without rips in the crotch. And my slutty heels. I'm all set."

"There is an expected attire for Casa Cashmere."

"I won't pretend to be someone I'm not."

"No one's asking you to."

"Oh, yeah? Don't think I don't see the *Pretty Woman* rebrand happening."

He winces, then opens his mouth to speak, but I'm on a roll. "This is how it starts. First you stuff me into a blazer dress, and next thing I know, I'm married to some real estate developer named Doug, saying crap like 'We simply adore summering in Saint-Trop ez.'"

He wants me to look the part. Translation: He's embarrassed by the real me. The *me* with tattoos and opinions.

"Pip, I'm asking for less friction. A few pieces. Things that'll make the week easier. Do it for Gavin."

"You rich boys are all alike. Why you want to marry the same blonde cheerleader is beyond me." The words tumble out before common sense kicks in. "It's okay to go against the grain sometimes, ya know. Try the rebel, not the debutante. The dark side's got cookies and orgasms that don't require access to your bank account."

Bryce's eyebrows shoot up so fast, I'm surprised they don't fly off his forehead.

Shit. The words hang there, sharp and stupid. *Nice one, Petra. Great start to the trip. You lasted a whole twenty minutes before hitting on the hot engaged billionaire.*

I clear my throat, shifting gears. "What about *your* clothes? When's the last time you went on an actual vacation?"

“I travel constantly.”

“Business trips don’t count. I’m talking tequila with your morning coffee, sand stuck between your toes, and swimwear that’s a little too revealing.” I lean forward, narrowing my eyes. “I bet you’ve never even worn flip-flops.”

“I own appropriate footwear for every occasion.”

“Here’s my counteroffer. I’ll go in there, let the fashion critics pick apart my second-hand wardrobe and resting bitch face. I’ll even ooh and ahh, pretending I know which overpriced designer made the clothes. But only if we *both* get vacation wear.”

His expression suggests I just proposed he do a striptease while riding a unicycle on the beach.

“I’m talking sunglasses, butt-ugly Hawaiian shirts, and at least one pair of shorts. If I have to pretend to be someone else for a week, then *you* have to take a vacation from being a buttoned-up CEO.“ I cock an eyebrow. “You said it. If *I* have to, *you* have to.”

“You’re going to make me regret this trip, aren’t you?” he asks, but there’s a strange light in his eyes—*a flicker of anticipation, maybe?*

“Oh, hell yes, Moneybags. Now, let’s go see those pretty ankles.”

The moment we step through the threshold, I’m assaulted by sheer... emptiness. This place isn’t a store; it’s a temple of minimalism. The marble floors are polished to perfection, reflecting all my shortcomings. And those velvet chairs? Art pieces, not meant for actual human asses.

Most disturbing? There are *no clothes.* None. Not a single rack or hanger.

“What the hell is this place?”

As if summoned, a man materializes before us like Dracula’s fashion-forward twin rising from a velvet coffin. Tall, rail-thin, dressed in funeral-black from neck to toe, tiny round glasses perched on his beaked nose. In one hand, he holds an iPad. In the other, a microscopic espresso.

When his eyes lock on me, he physically recoils. *Ah yes. The Beverly Hills Welcome.*

"Absolutely. Not," he says, voice dripping in condescension. "We do not accept foot traffic, walk-ins, and certainly not—" his glare performs a scathing inventory of my entire existence "—whatever *this* is."

"Take a breath, Mugatu," I fire back. "I'm not here voluntarily. I'm being forced to dress like a society-lady robot so I don't embarrass the billionaire elite." I hook a thumb toward Bryce.

The man's entire demeanor transforms. "Mr. Sterling! It's been too long! Too tragic!" He swoops closer, air-kissing in Bryce's general direction.

"Sebastian." Bryce nods with that infuriating rich-person calm. "Good to see you again. We need a complete vacation wardrobe. For my... um... for Miss Brinkman.

"Mistress," I supply helpfully. "He meant mistress."

"Ah. That explains the confidence," Sebastian says.

"Petra." Bryce's voice has that scolding edge that makes me go all gooey.

"What? It's classier than 'hooker,' which is clearly what Fashion Frankenstein thought."

Sebastian doesn't deny it.

"This is Gavin Brinkman's younger sister."

"Impossible!" Sebastian's eyes narrow as he scans me. "That breathtaking specimen of masculine refinement and this street pigeon share DNA? The universe cannot be so cruel!"

"Well, this is off to a super fun start," I mutter.

"Accompany me!" Sebastian commands. "Time is evaporating, and we have mountains to scale!

We're given no choice but to follow him into... *The Room.*

Sweet baby RuPaul, this isn't a dressing room—it's a palace! Crystal chandeliers dangle from the sky-high ceiling with white carpet so plush, my boots sink in with every step. There's a champagne bar sparkling in the corner. Empty clothing racks line the walls, and a circular platform with a tri-fold mirror setup stands in the center, ready to showcase every possible angle of my self-loathing.

"Let us begin the transformation. But first, Mr. Sterling, is she allergic to anything? And by that, I mean fabrics, not quality and taste."

"Just judgment and pretentious assholes," I shoot back. "Oh, and polyester. My nipples aren't a fan."

"How very... specific." Sebastian lifts his iPad and jots something down.

Bryce clears his throat. "She'll need options for daytime excursions, poolside attire, and... sleepwear."

"B, you know my thoughts on sleeping in the nu—" I start.

"And," Bryce cuts me off, "several appropriate dinner options for Casa Cashmere."

Sebastian, who's been scribbling notes with manic intensity, freezes mid-swipe. "Casa Cashmere?" He whispers the name like a sacred incantation.

His head whips between Bryce and me as his eyes bulge with horror, and he clutches his iPad to his chest.

"You bring me THIS—" he gestures at me as if I'm a contagious disease "—for CASA CASHMERE? The SANCTUARY of

STYLE? The EPICENTER of ELEGANCE? Where Muffy Von Cashmere herself holds court, passing judgment on the fashion elite?"

"Well, she sounds like an absolute peach," I say dryly.

"It is beyond impossible! The style chasm is too vast! It would be kinder to send her naked."

"If anyone can make her Casa Cashmere-ready, it's you," Bryce says smoothly. "And I'll increase your commission by ten percent for the challenge."

"It is true. Sebastian Bellini has never encountered a fashion crisis he couldn't reinvent. I embrace this test!"

He snaps his fingers twice. On cue, a dozen women materialize from hidden panels in the walls. Long limbs, glossy hair, cheekbones that could cut a diamond—all in sleek black outfits and stilettos that make no sound when they walk. They don't blink. I'm not sure they even *breathe.*

Sebastian addresses them. "Today we transform this fashion catastrophe from a rebellious trash-dwelling troll... into a resplendent Rivera goddess!"

With a wild gleam in his eye, Sebastian is now a commander pacing before battle.

"I require Chanel—the *good* pieces, not the tourist collection! GUCCI—but only ones without those nightmarish logos! Valentino. Oscar de la Renta. No Prada. No Dior. Too many florals this season, and God knows her personality brings enough unsolicited color to any outfit!"

The model-assistants all nod in unison.

"And I want accessories. Bring me Cartier, Tiffany, something aggressive. Something that warns the other guests. Something that says: *I bite.*"

He snaps again. They vanish.

Thirty excruciating minutes and several unwanted measurements later—including my left ankle, which Sebastian insists is a crime against symmetry—I'm stuffed into a cream Chanel tweed suit that feels like a suffocating straightjacket.

"Well?" I attempt a graceful twirl, but my legs are practically zip-tied together. I wobble on heels thinner than medical needles. "Do I look the part? Like I marry for money and can fake climaxes with enthusiasm?"

"The tragedy is unbearable," he deadpans. "This woman is the CEO of a startup that sells overpriced candles smelling of peppermint and regret." He snaps twice. "Next!"

I'm whisked straight to the dressing room and crammed into something infinitely worse—a pastel pink romper with satin bows that must have been designed by a five-year-old going through her princess phase.

"Whoever designed this genuinely hates women," I announce, yanking at the hem to dislodge the perpetual camel toe. "Why does this scream *costume for a grown man with a doll fetish*?"

Sebastian's jaw drops in horror, and all the color drains from his face so fast, I briefly wonder if he's having a stroke.

"DESTROY that ABERRATION! Burn it and scatter the ashes across different continents so it can never reassemble!"

"We do have a schedule to keep," Bryce reminds him with controlled authority. "The jet is waiting, and there's a welcome dinner to attend."

"This creature descended upon us with the fashion sense of a Walmart parking lot at three a.m., and I am tasked with transforming her into Casa Cashmere-worthy splendor in a few hours!" Sebastian exhales dramatically. "TRUST the PROCESS! I have never failed, and I will not blemish my legacy on this day!"

I take advantage of their back-and-forth to scratch furiously at my inner thigh, where the romper has left an angry red welt.

An assistant tiptoes over with something clutched between two fingers as though she's carrying nuclear waste.

It's... my bra.

"Oh sweet Dior above, what is this monstrosity? My eyes! They're melting."

"It's fine. It does the thankless job of holding up my boobs."

He snaps, ignoring me. "La Perla! One of EVERYTHING! Bras, panties, slips, garters, silk, lace, mesh, divine intervention—GO! Fetch me a goddamn miracle, stat!"

I glance at Bryce, expecting him to be mortified by this intimate garment discussion, but he appears absorbed in his phone, thumb scrolling.

Then, without looking up, he says, "Include red."

The blush that starts at my hairline travels south with alarming speed.

Bryce has *opinions* about my underwear?

"Excellent suggestion, Mr. Sterling. Back into the wardrobe chamber, Miss Brinkman!"

I trudge into the fitting room, where they force a nightmare of a dress over my head. When I see it, my breath catches—for all the wrong reasons. It's loud, yellow, ruffled, and did I mention loud?

One shoulder. Eight million ruffles. So much satin that it actually makes *swish-swish* noises.

"No! CATASTROPHIC! Escape while you can!

"I'm done!" *swish-swish-swish* "Where's my taser?"

"Your rage will not shield you from your poor style choices."

I'm ushered away too soon—robbed of my chance to unleash a decent comeback.

But then I see it. Hanging apart from the rejects is a long, sleek, crimson halter dress that oozes liquid sex. I put it on, adjust the straps, and take a breath.

The neckline is high, elegant, and the cutouts offer an enticing glimpse of side boob. The back is completely open, swooping low and giving a peek of my hip tattoo. I step out, and the entire room goes silent.

"Call VOGUE! Inform the internet that Sebastian Bellini has triumphed *again* with his unparalleled genius!"

My gaze stays locked on Bryce as *his* sweeps up my body, slow and deliberate, sending a shiver down my spine. For a breath, his mask slips, and I catch a flash of something primal woven into his stare before he reins it back in.

"Yes, we'll take that one," he says, his voice a touch deeper than usual. Then, as if nothing happened, he returns to his phone.

But that *tap-tap-tap* of his finger against his thigh tells a different story.

After the red dress breakthrough, everything Sebastian puts me in just *works*—white rompers, ivory power suits, champagne silk tunics with wide-leg trousers that somehow make *comfortable* pass as couture.

We run out of time before I can try on the swimwear, lingerie, and pajamas, but Sebastian insists: "I have cracked the code of your essence! The collection I have picked will be transcendent!"

I'm in front of the mirror wearing a cream-colored sleeveless vest with matching wide-legged pants and leather sandals. I hardly recognize myself.

I look... elevated.

Bryce is across the room, hovering by the jewelry tray and treating it like a charcuterie board. He casually points at a piece.

Then our eyes meet in the mirror, and something electric passes between us—a current so strong, I'm surprised the lights don't flicker. He walks over, holding a simple Tiffany solitaire diamond pendant.

"This goes perfectly with that outfit," he says, "May I put it on?"

My fingers fumble as I gather my hair, lifting it away from my neck. Bryce steps behind me, his knuckles grazing my skin and lingering longer than necessary as he fastens the clasp. My entire body is one giant goosebump.

"There," he murmurs, his breath warm against my ear. "See?"

I let my hair fall back down and stare at our reflection—a snapshot of possibility. Of what could be, if we both lived in this world. If I were someone who belonged in clothes like these. If he were someone who would choose a girl like me.

Sebastian claps his hands. "Our guests depart for Casa Cashmere in seven short minutes!"

I spin around, breaking Bryce's gaze. "Wait! Where are the items I asked for?"

Sebastian's face contorts like he's sucking on a lemon dipped in pickle juice. "They are in *there.*" He points to a black shopping bag tucked discreetly behind a chair. "But they are HIDEOUS! So TERRIBLE! I cannot believe that Versace even makes something so GROTESQUE! Do *not* tell anyone that I styled those... outfits. I will deny it until my dying breath!"

Sebastian does a slow, theatrical scan as though he's admiring his own reflection. "There she IS. My masterpiece! You walked in a snarling little street creature. Now *look* at you. The tattooed butterfly has emerged from her clearance-rack cocoon. You are Casa Cashmere ready!"

"I'll never forget you, Sebastian," I deadpan. "But God knows I'll try."

We're walking to the front doors when Bryce nods toward the black bag dangling in my hand. "What did you get from Sebastian?"

I can't help the wicked grin that spreads across my face. "It's for our agreement. If I have to, so do you."

We step out onto Rodeo Drive, and something strange happens—or rather, doesn't happen. No one gives me side-eye. No security guards monitor my movements. No salespeople size me up.

In my cream linen ensemble with a diamond sparkling at my neck and Bryce Sterling's arm hooked with mine, I've somehow become... immune to judgment.

Don't get used to this. It's temporary.

A costume change. A week-long masquerade.

The second this trip ends, I go back to my life, dealing with my usual crap. Back to the real world, where Bryce doesn't lavish me with attention and gifts.

Don't let yourself be fooled by the fantasy, Petra. You don't belong to him.

CHAPTER SIX

BRYCE

Red? I said red?

Why—*why*—would I make comments on her undergarments? Not just comments. Preferences. I requested red. What the hell is wrong with me?

That is not something a man says to his best friend's little sister. It's wildly inappropriate. But dear God, all I'm thinking about is her bold red lips in matching red lace.

My collar suddenly feels three sizes too tight.

Petra is sitting as if the leather seat might bite—arms folded, ankles crossed, back hovering like the chair's rigged to explode. She's so tense, as if one wrong move will wrinkle her new cream outfit. *Is she... nervous?*

Christ, you idiot. You brought the damn limo. Of course she is.

Even my driver raised an eyebrow when I requested the stretch today—especially after I told him *what* part of Hollywood we were headed to. He didn't say a word, just gave me a look that said: *Bold choice, my guy.*

Petra shivers—a subtle movement, but it catches my attention. Her bare arms prickle with goosebumps.

I lean forward and press the intercom. "Carlos, let's give the A/C a rest."

"Right away, Mr. Sterling. ETA to the airfield is twelve minutes."

I settle back, watching her. "Better?"

"My hero." She smirks. "I lost feeling in one nipple, but don't worry, I can still feel sarcasm."

My gaze flickers—one second, tops—to the deep V of her vest. And I swiftly avert my eyes toward the bar. "Help yourself. Water, juice, whatever you prefer."

She scans the selection. "Five kinds of water? I always thought you wealthy folks only guzzled champagne and the tears of the less fortunate. Surprise me, Moneybags. Show me how billionaires stay moist."

There she goes. That criticism. The flirting. She's doing her damnedest to provoke me, but it's my turn. I grab the tall, sleek glass bottle with the wooden cap. *This will set her off.*

She eyes the label like it insulted her mother. "Svalbardi? Polar iceberg water? Let me guess... From endangered icebergs?"

"Close. Norwegian."

She unscrews the cap, slow and taunting, like it's an overly sensual act, keeping eye contact the whole time. My eyes take in the tattoos on her wrist, and then focus on those red lips as she wraps them around the bottle.

And my brain shorts out.

It's water, Bryce! H2O is not seductive. But she moans like the bottle whispered something filthy. My jaw clenches. My pants tighten. My IQ plummets.

"Mmm. Tastes like tax evasion." She pulls away, lips shiny, then takes another sip.

I fidget with my collar. "There are only twelve bottles left in the world. You're drinking six thousand dollars."

She chokes, sputtering all over my face like a sprinkler. "Fuck, Bryce! Are you kidding?"

I hand her a napkin, trying to look helpful and *not at all* like I'm fighting an erection. "You did say to surprise you."

"I was expecting like... a splash of lime. Maybe cucumbers. Not penguin bath water."

I swipe at the moisture on my face, hoping to erase the utterly inappropriate thoughts that have clouded my judgment.

"In proper society," I say, a little too sharp, "knowing what you want is considered a virtue. This week, you'll be asked a lot of questions about your preferences. I suggest you come prepared with appropriate responses."

"Should I practice my opinions now?" she asks, slipping into an accent suspiciously like my mother's. "I simply cannot tolerate Cristal. It's Dom Pérignon or death."

"That's actually a perfect response."

I unlock my phone, needing the barrier of technology between us because every part of me wants to touch her. Badly. Recklessly.

This isn't me. I don't lose control. I don't fantasize like some blue-balled teenager.

This has to be about Amanda. Post-breakup rebound confusion. My mind latched on to the nearest attractive woman as some sort of coping mechanism. That's logical. Why else would I be consumed by thoughts of—

Red underwear... red lips... that red dress.

Pip is unmistakably a woman now. No longer the teenage girl who used to steal Gavin's car and sneak out to concerts. And those tattoos, especially the ink above the low back of that dress, disappearing beneath crimson fabric. *What is it? How far does it extend? What would it feel like under my fingers?*

Yet another stark contrast between us. I'm defined by corporate suits and boardrooms; she's characterized by tattoos and dive bars. I adhere to rules; she delights in breaking them.

And she's Gavin's sister.

Off-limits with a capital fuck no.

The nuclear option of friendship destruction would be sleeping with his little sister. I'm hoping to save our partnership, not detonate it from the inside.

Would she even desire me like that? The flirtation, the innuendos—is that merely Petra being Petra? Her approach to all men?

Obviously, you moron. She's a bartender. She explained her "nips for tips" strategy. And here you are, another gullible fool falling for it.

Nevertheless, the idea of other men flirting with her makes me feel... tense.

Enough. Her interactions with men are none of my concern. From this moment onward, there will be no further inappropriate thoughts about Pip.

Twelve minutes later, we're boarding my jet.

Petra stops dead at the entrance, her eyes widening as she takes in the interior. "Holy shit."

The cabin is decorated in Sterling corporate colors—navy walls, brown leather seats with brass fixtures, cream carpeting that looks new despite routine use. The forward section holds six reclining chairs arranged in pairs, facing each other across polished walnut tables. Behind them, a curved leather sofa faces an entertainment center.

"You have a couch?" Petra points toward the back. "Wait. Is that a bedroom?"

"For longer flights."

She peeks behind the suite partition. "Oh. My. God. This isn't a jet. It's a private mile high club. Now I get why you were so harsh about my bathroom. You could fit three of them in that shower. Four if you stack 'em like Tetris."

My earlier comment stings, hearing it from her point of view. I hadn't meant to insult her living situation, though that's precisely what I accomplished.

After takeoff, Petra keeps adjusting her seat belt, then her collar, then picking invisible lint from her designer vest. The nervous energy radiating from her is distinctly un-Petra-like.

"Not a fan of flying?" I ask.

"What? No. I love traveling." She forces a laugh. "Just, bracing myself for the inevitable shitshow that's gonna go down at Casa Rich People."

"I think it would be helpful if I were to teach you certain etiquette guidelines, to avoid any awkward situations."

"Charm school with Professor Manners? Let me guess... First lesson is 'How to Not Embarrass the Billionaire at a Fancy Dinner.'"

Our flight attendant Christine appears with her practiced smile. "Mr. Sterling, Miss Brinkman. I have fresh peanut butter cookies from the galley. Still warm."

Petra perks up. "Did you say warm cookies?" She grabs one and takes a bite. "Oh, my sweet buttery lord," she groans. "This is a cookie-gasm. *Almost* as good as my matcha chocolate chip." She wraps three more cookies in a cloth napkin and stuffs them into her pants pocket.

"You realize Casa Cashmere has a full culinary staff?" I point out.

"Who probably makes those teeny portions like at your mom's fancy gala. I've seen heartier meals in a doll house." She pats her pocket. "Trust me, backpacking through Europe teaches you a thing or two. Rule one: Always carry snacks. Rule two: Never, ever trust a jacuzzi at a hostel."

I want to ask her everything.

Why she dropped out of college. What Europe gave her that school didn't. What she was pursuing during those two years. How it felt to go off the grid.

I want to know it all. But my phone buzzes.

The name on the screen makes my stomach clench.

Reginald Sterling.

"Excuse me. I need to take this."

I retreat to the rear bedroom, closing the frosted glass door. The plush executive chair sinks as I settle in at the desk, already steeling myself.

"Father," I answer, knowing pleasantries are futile.

"We're moving up the timeline," he says. "The CEO announcement happens this week. The board wants something concrete for the shareholders meeting."

I grit my teeth. "That's not possible. I haven't finalized things with Heartvest yet."

"You haven't told Gavin you're leaving."

It's not a question. It's an accusation wrapped in disappointment—his signature move.

"There have been complications. But I'm handling it."

"Don't tell me you're handling it, Bryce. Just handle it."

The line goes dead.

I don't know what hits harder—the command, or the fact that it didn't surprise me at all.

Reginald Sterling doesn't waste breath on feelings or emotion.

Through the closed door, I hear Petra laughing at something Christine said. The sound is so genuinely carefree, it causes a pang in my chest. When was the last time I laughed like that?

I step out and find Petra lounging on the leather couch as if she's back in her apartment. Legs crossed, one sandaled foot is bouncing to some internal rhythm only she can hear.

Christ. The difference between her and Amanda is staggering. Amanda would have positioned herself elegantly, spine rigid, a flawless ornament, expecting admiration from a distance.

But Petra? She sprawls without a care, wild and defiant, daring the world to question her.

Her words from the limo circle back: *"Try the rebel, not the debutante."*

"I have to admit, B. This whole private jet thing? Not terrible."

She shifts and stretches full length on the cushions with a sigh that sounds like pure sin. My mind paints her in nothing but attitude—those red lips ghosting down my neck, her thighs open, my fist tangled in that dark hair while she begs for—

"When I flew to Greece, this guy sitting next to me decided to have a spa day." She rolls onto her side. "He whipped out a whole pedicure kit. I'm talking files, clippers, those weird toe separator things. Then—" she mimes an explosion "—toenail shrapnel directly into my pretzels."

And my penis shuts down.

"That's revolting."

"Exactly! And that's why I'm glad I got stuck next to him. This is all fine and dandy, but if everything's always perfect, you miss out on the good stuff. You won't have any wild travel stories if you only fly private. The chaos... That's what makes life interesting."

She shifts on the couch, trying to get comfortable in the sleeveless vest.

"This fancy outfit is *not* made for lounging."

Her arms go behind her head as she wiggles and—

"Petra."

"What?"

"Your, um..." I clear my throat, looking anywhere but directly at her. "You're having a wardrobe malfunction."

"Oh, for fuck's sake. See! This is why Sebastian should have let me wear my bra," she mutters, hastily adjusting the fabric.

It's too late. The sight of her exposed breast is seared into my mind. The delicate dusty rose of her nipple contrasting against her pale skin. The perfect curve. Her bud, hard from the cool cabin air.

My tongue—*God help me*—tingles with the desire to lick her.

That is the final straw. I'm confining myself to the bedroom for the rest of the flight. Nothing good can come from being in such close quarters with Pip.

***

Three hours later, we land at the private airfield in Puerto Vallarta, Mexico. The second the aircraft doors open, the next wave of logistical choreography kicks in. A matte black helicopter waits on the tarmac, rotors already slicing through the air. Behind it, two cargo trucks idle—ready to haul our luggage to the estate.

I confirm the transfer protocol with the ground crew chief—a former Marine who runs travel like a military operation. One pilot. Two drivers. Three handlers. ETA: forty-two minutes post-arrival.

Things are in order, just as I like it.

"Ever consider carrying your own underwear?" Petra's eyebrow arches. "Might give you a cheap thrill."

"You're mocking me."

"Only a little, Moneybags."

"At Casa Cashmere, self-service is considered a system failure. They have staff whose entire job is anticipating needs you're unaware of."

"They should get hazard pay for dealing with especially difficult guests... Ya know, like Fiona."

"She's not that bad."

"Fiona Whitfield is a high-maintenance red flag disguised as a person."

"That must be why your brother needs your assistance. You speak fluent chaos."

She smiles as I place my hand on the small of her back, steering her to the helicopter. Petra doesn't flinch. She walks toward it like she's heading into a rock concert, not a flying metal blender. No death-grip on the door handle. No hesitation. Just hops in like it's an Uber.

Amanda treated helicopter rides like dental surgery—necessary but traumatic. She once cried the entire flight to Napa because it ruined her blowout.

Petra? She's buzzing as she settles onto the passenger bench, fastening her seat belt.

As soon as we're airborne, wind whips through the cabin. Her dark hair transforms into a wild storm cloud, strands attacking her face.

"This is amazing!" she shouts over the engine noise, holding her hair back.

I catch a rogue strand between my fingers and tuck it behind her ear. My thumb lingers against her cheek, tracing the firm bone beneath her soft skin. Her pupils dilate, transforming her hazel-green eyes into pools of molten gold.

"Headphones!" I shout, jerking away to grab the aviation headsets. "Here."

She slides them over her ears while I adjust my own, willing my pulse to stop sprinting.

"Can you hear me?"

"Loud, commanding, and vibrating in all the right places. Keep going."

"Petra." My voice hardens *(in solidarity with my cock).*

"What? I'm talking about the helicopter ride. Obviously."

I point to the sweeping landscape. "That's the Puerto Vallarta coastline."

"Looks like L.A.'s prettier cousin. Mountains, beaches, but the water isn't sewage gray—it's actually blue. And the mountains are green. What kind of high-society witchcraft is this?"

"The picturesque views come free of charge, Pip. You can thank Mother Nature. See up there, beyond the resorts? We're heading into that jungle. The estate sits on a hill right in the thick of it."

"Hold up. *In* the actual jungle? With the snakes and spiders and things that want to eat my face? If something bites me without my consent, I'm suing."

"I would be fascinated to see that lawsuit. What grounds would you have?"

"Endangerment. Emotional distress. Forcing a civilian into wilderness conditions wearing couture, and hot billionaire negligence."

"Excuse me?"

"You're the one who lured me here and won't let me wear my combat boots to defend myself. If I die from a spider crawling into my panties, you better avenge me."

"Rest assured, I will instruct my assistant to attend to that."

"Outsourcing the job? Damn, B. I thought I meant more to you."

Petra shoots me a wink before glancing back at the coastline. "So what's the deal with this place we're headed to? Why does everyone gasp like they spotted Taylor Swift shopping at Target?"

"Casa Cashmere is invitation-only. A gathering place for the ultra-elite."

"How elite? Like, private-island elite, or we-secretly-run-the-world elite?"

"Both. It's a playground with absolute privacy. When I visited as a boy, they had an ice rink, movie theater, bowling alley, spa, cigar room, Olympic-sized indoor pool, bird-watching observatory—"

"Wait. A room just to stare at birds? What, regular windows weren't boujee enough? God forbid you spot a macaw without climate control."

Her eyes sparkle with a challenge, daring me to justify the ways of the affluent.

"The estate was built by a British aristocrat as a winter retreat from England. Somewhere to entertain guests without—"

The words die in my throat when I see it.

Casa Cashmere.

"Holy fuck, B! That's not a house. That's a... I mean... look at the size of that thing. That's some serious supervillain lair shit."

It rises out of the wilderness like it doesn't belong to this era—or planet. White limestone and Spanish tile and sunlit archways, perched arrogantly on a jungle-covered hilltop that rolls all the way down to the ocean. The main house alone could swallow a city block. Twin bell towers anchor the corners while endless balconies and terraces cascade down the façade.

At least twenty additional buildings share formal gardens that stretch in engineered elegance. Their manicured hedges and marble fountains form an absurd contrast to the wild jungle pressing in on all sides.

From this angle, you can see the plank extending down to a private dock—where a superyacht waits, lazy and hulking, as if it owns the sea. Surrounded by 150 acres of untamed jungle and coastline, the nearest hint of civilization is miles away from this paradise cove.

"It's just as majestic as I remember."

"Wow! There's only one kind of money that builds a hidden jungle palace with a yacht docked in the front yard. Oil."

I nod. "The Von Cashmeres made their fortune in oil. At their peak in the late 1800s, they controlled twenty percent of global reserves."

She whistles. "Not bad. But don't be jealous, Moneybags. The prestige of your family name wins. You've got buildings named after you in every major city, and your family personally sends me a 'Hey girl, your credit card is maxed out' letter every month. I feel special. Like getting scolded by a rich king of finance."

My spine stiffens.

"I guess someday you'll be the king sending me those 'you've been a bad girl' letters, huh?"

The observation hits like ice water as we descend toward the landing pad—a concrete circle surrounded by grass so green it seems spray-painted. The helicopter touches down, and before the rotors even slow, a small army materializes. Staff in crisp white uniforms swarm as we exit in a well-choreographed ballet.

"Refreshment, Mr. Sterling?" a server asks with a silver tray balanced on his palm, crystal glasses catching sunlight like prisms. Pink liquid swirls inside, dotted with fresh strawberries and mint sprigs. Another attendant offers warm, lavender-scented hand towels, while a third snaps open a white umbrella above our heads, shielding us from the Mexican sun.

I accept a towel, demonstrating the ritual for Petra's benefit—wipe hands, fold neatly, return to tray. Then I take the drink, nodding my thanks.

"Are you kidding me?" Petra stage-whispers, mimicking my actions with dramatic flair. "There's etiquette for washing your hands? Where's the guidebook for blinking correctly?"

She finishes with a mock curtsy, and I notice one of the male attendants letting his gaze linger on her cleavage, enhanced by her tailored vest. Something hot and territorial flares inside me.

Keep your focus, Bryce. You succeeded in getting her here, but the real task is helping her to fit in.

Petra may be dressed the part in her designer clothes, but she's still Petra—unfiltered, unimpressed by wealth, unafraid to ask questions that make people squirm.

"Mr. Sterling." The man's voice carries generations of British refinement. "Allow me to officially welcome you to Casa Cashmere."

The gentleman before us could've stepped out of a PBS historical drama. Silver hair parted like it was combed with a ruler, steel-blue eyes that miss nothing, dressed in a crisp, charcoal morning coat with tails. His pocket square forms precise triangular points, and his black shoes gleam like they've never met a speck of dust. He looks so frozen in time, he could moonlight as a haunted portrait.

"I am Nigel Featherwick, estate manager and personal butler to Miss Muffy Von Cashmere II." He executes a flawless bow. "Should you require anything—anything at all—please do not hesitate to contact myself or my assistant, Miss Thistlewood, who has been briefed on your caviar pairings, preferred conflict de-escalation phrases, and the angle at which your morning toast must lean upon the plate."

"No wonder the *butler* has a butler," Petra whispers.

"Indeed, Miss Brinkman." His tone remains neutral. "Miss Whitfield alerted us to your... impromptu inclusion. Lodgings have been secured, albeit in the East Wing, regrettably separated from our principal guests."

The East Wing. Code for social quarantine.

"Miss Brinkman will stay in the suite adjacent to mine. She's my... companion."

Wonderful. Now I've actually implied she is my mistress.

"Of course, Mr. Sterling." Nigel bows again. "I shall alert the Pillow Attendant, Bathroom Amenities Coordinator, and Room Fragrance Technician of this alteration immediately."

We follow Nigel across the stone path that snakes through the grounds. Impeccably trimmed garden hedges line the walkway, fountains trickle nearby, and birds chirp in the canopy above as though they're whispering gossip.

I clear my throat. "The room assignment. I meant—so you're not wandering this palace alone. I asked you to spare me from small talk, remember?"

"Thank you," she says with startling sincerity.

A beat passes before I add, "You'll be more comfortable... That is, it might help if you follow my lead a little."

"Or I could do my thing and see how ruffled Lord Britchybottom gets when I wear pajamas to dinner. Think he'd have a stroke if I asked for ketchup?"

"His name is Nigel Featherwick."

"I stand by my version."

As we cross the grounds, the estate's true scale is revealed. Staff members appear and vanish like well-trained ghosts—gardeners pruning already-perfect shrubs, maids carrying fresh linens, security personnel in dark suits murmuring into earpieces. The whole operation runs with the precision of Buckingham Palace.

"Is this place a house, or did we barge headfirst into a small sovereign nation?" Petra whispers. "Do I need my passport to use the bathroom?"

A rustling draws my attention. Petra is fishing for something in her pocket—the crumpled napkin from the jet emerges, and—*dear*

God—she's unwrapping contraband peanut butter cookies like we're in a prison yard.

"Are you seriously eating?"

"What? You want one? They're only slightly pocket-warmed and I'm guessing sixty percent cookie and forty percent lint."

My internal panic meter shifts from yellow to flashing red. The path beneath my Italian loafers suddenly feels as though I'm walking on quicksand.

I've made a catastrophic miscalculation.

I've brought Petra "Chaos" Brinkman into the most etiquette-obsessed environment on the planet without providing a single word of preparation. No crash course in silverware hierarchy. No primer on acceptable conversation topics. Not even basic instructions like "don't eat cookies while walking through a billionaire's estate like it's a mall food court."

It's as if I handed a tornado a crate full of scissors and aimed it at a paper factory.

Before Nigel's eagle eyes can spot this breach of decorum, I snatch the cookie bundle and hastily rewrap them. "Put these away," I hiss.

"Jeez, don't have an aneurysm." She tucks the bundle back into her pocket with a dramatic eye roll. "I forgot rich people only *pretend* to eat. Lucky for you, poverty's made me excellent at intermittent fasting."

My pulse hammers in my ears. Gavin will never forgive me if I allow his sister to become social cannon fodder. My mother will disown me. Every Sterling in history is probably rolling in their monogrammed mausoleums at my recklessness.

In approximately thirty seconds, we'll walk into a room filled with people who consider jaywalking a capital offense—and I've brought someone who teases customers with her nipples for tips.

"Take my arm," I command rather than offer, extending my elbow. "Do not make a move again without consulting me first. I'd prefer not to have any more surprises."

As soon as the words escape my lips, I know I've made mistake number two. Telling Petra not to do something is like telling a storm not to rage. She doesn't just double down—she triples down, adds fireworks, and invites spectators.

Her lips—those full, dangerous, perpetually sassy red lips—curve into a smirk that makes my blood run simultaneously hot and cold.

"But surprises are the best part, Moneybags." She slides her arm through mine, her body heat seeping into my side. "And if it really bothers you, then why do your pupils dilate whenever I'm being naughty?"

I cough lightly into my fist—the most professional move I can manage while my brain fights my body's suggestion to kiss her hard against the nearest statue.

"I think," I say carefully, "it would serve us both if you tried—just this once—to be ladylike."

She leans in, whispering in my ear, "Fine, I'll play your little arm-candy charade. But, so we're clear"—her voice drops to that dangerous purr—"there's not a single ladylike thing about me. Especially between the sheets."

There's the proper reaction to that line. And then there's the one I'm having… in my pants.

She flashes a smile that says, *busted.* Hard.

Get it together, Sterling. You're about to face Gavin, and explaining why you're mentally undressing his sister is not going to help your CEO exit strategy.

"Your party has assembled in the drawing room," Nigel announces, ushering us forward.

I nod, then immediately turn to Petra. "No touching the art, no asking people their net worth, and please—for the love of God—don't challenge anyone to a drinking contest."

"So basically, you want me sedated." She bats her eyelashes innocently. "What about breathing? Is that allowed?"

"Breathing is permitted. Minimally."

The doors swing open to reveal a room that makes the Palace of Versailles look like a fixer-upper. The ceilings soar two stories high. Chandeliers twinkle with the soft glow of aged crystal. Everything is baroque or Victorian. The air smells of beeswax, old books, and that indefinable scent of extreme privilege.

Clusters of people are spread out across the room, but Petra's focus goes directly to the huge oil painting above the fireplace.

The nameplate reads: MISS MUFFY VON CASHMERE.

The elderly woman in the portrait stares down with the kind of aristocratic disdain that only comes from generations of people bowing upon your entrance. Her silver hair is sculpted into an architectural masterpiece. Her face is a map of refined wrinkles—the kind that come from pursing your lips at inadequate table settings.

But the true masterpiece is the dog in her lap—a pristine white Maltese with fur so perfectly groomed, it makes the woman's hair appear unkempt. The pet wears matching pearls and a custom Chanel suit identical to its owner's, down to the black piping and gold buttons. Somehow, the dog's expression is even more judgmental than the woman's.

"Seriously? The old broad who plays dress-up with her dog is the one looking down on everybody?"

"I should tell you, Miss Mu—"

"Gav-Gav! Look who's arrived," Fiona says from the other side of the ballroom. Petra's body tenses by my side.

"Bryce is here with Amand—" The sentence stalls on her tongue as we turn from the oversized canvas to the group.

"Petra?! Oh my God, is that really you?" Fiona's eyes perform a head-to-toe scan of Petra's outfit, her expression cycling through shock, confusion, and unmistakable jealousy. "I hardly recognized you."

Gavin swoops in with a surprise bear hug that pries Petra's arm from mine. Her warmth vanishes, and disturbingly, I'm already calculating how many seconds I need to wait before reclaiming her arm without seeming like a caveman.

"Thanks for coming, sis."

"That vest," Fiona says. "Is that Valentino's new collection? I've been waitlisted for months."

"Beats me." Petra shrugs. "You'd have to ask Sebastian."

"Sebastian Bellini styled you?!"

"Yeah. Weird, right? Though you gotta be careful with wardrobe malfunctions in this thing. One wrong move, and it's hello, nipple city." She throws me a wicked grin.

I extend my arm toward her. "Well, since we've just arrived, we should freshen up in our room—" Horror dawns as I hear my own words. "*Rooms!* Our separate rooms. That are near each other."

"Nonsense!" Fiona interjects, slicing through my humiliation. "You must wait. Nigel told us Miss Muffy has awoken from her nap and is coming to greet us personally."

I lower my arm, resigned to prolonging this torture. My eyes meet Petra's, silently pleading for her to behave just a little longer.

And that's when I hear it.

CLICK-CLICK-CLICK-CLICK.

Tiny footsteps. Clicking across the marble.

The entire space falls silent, attention shifting toward the entryway. She appears.

The small white Maltese from that regal portrait, dressed in pearls and a custom designer outfit, trots into view with absolute purpose.

The dog pauses dramatically, surveying the guests with beady black eyes.

She sniffs the air.

And then charges—barking loudly—straight for Petra.

"Oh hey! You're the doggie from the painting! Hi, cutie," she coos, scratching behind its ears. "You smell my cookies, don't you?"

My brain fires frantic signals: *Intercept! Create a distraction! Release the emergency sprinklers! Do SOMETHING!*

Before I can stop her, she scoops the fancy Maltese into her arms.

And all hell breaks loose.

Security emerges from nowhere like ninjas. Earpieces. Suits. One of them actually grabs the gun at his hip.

Petra stiffens, eyes going wide as she clutches the squirming furball. "Uh... what's happening? I haven't even fed her the cookie yet. Technically, she assaulted me."

"Madam." Nigel's voice is polite enough to butter toast, but there's no mistaking the command in it. "I must insist you release Miss Muffy IMMEDIATELY."

Her eyes ping to the guards. To the shocked guests. Back to me.

"Pip..." My voice is controlled. I take another step closer, ignoring the security team tracking my every move. "You're holding the heir to the Von Cashmere oil dynasty," I explain slowly. "And our hostess for the week. Miss Muffy Von Cashmere... the Second."

Petra glances at the furball in her arms and then at the portrait on the wall, comprehension dawning with horrifying slowness. Her mouth drops open.

"Are you fucking kidding me? THIS DOG is a BILLIONAIRE?!"

And that's the moment I realize my gravest error in preparing Petra.

The primary rule of surviving Casa Cashmere: Never touch the dog who owns her own mansion, staff, and twelve-figure trust fund yet occasionally still drinks from a toilet.

CHAPTER SEVEN

PETRA

Group Chat : CPK Forever

Me: *Quick Cam question: Do you speak enough Spanish to explain to a judge why I'm not ACTUALLY a menace to society?*

Cam: *We might need my Abuela for that.*

Katie: *PETRA! Are you really in jail?*

Me: *Not yet, but the day is young and I'm feeling ambitious.*

Katie: *Please don't become an international fugitive.*

Petra: *At this point, prison might be the safer option.*

I fondled a billionaire Maltese in front of half the Forbes list. How is that a thing? What kind of upside-down elite world have I stepped into? Pocket cookies are a crime, but some crazy old broad can leave her entire fortune to a dog?

Right now, I'm hunched over a tufted bench in the bathroom, grunting as I try to hook sixty-two microscopic demon-clasps along the spine of this dress. My fingers are useless—like I'm defusing a bomb in oven mitts. Every time I fasten one, another pops open. *Shit!*

This dress is a catastrophe. Dusty rose ruffles, gauzy layers—like someone turned a wedding cake into a gown. Strapless. Puffy. A-line. And the leg slit? It goes up to places my gynecologist explores annually. The corset top is so tight, I'll be coughing up a lung before the shrimp cocktail hits the table.

"Fucking pink. Sebastian, you vindictive fashion tyrant."

These hooks aren't having it. I drop my arms, gasping as though I've lost a wrestling match.

"Hair down it is." I yank the curls out of their clip and let them tumble over my shoulders, covering the back of the dress.

I collapse onto the mattress and take a moment to acknowledge the room I've been stomping around in for the last half hour.

It's obscene.

The suite is a clash of cultures so absurd, it somehow works—European grandeur meets Mexican coastal chic. Soaring ceilings with exposed dark-wood beams and whitewashed walls, and big-ass arched windows framing panoramic views of lush jungle and sparkling ocean.

French doors lead to a private balcony. The bathroom is a marble shrine where rich people worship their own naked reflections—complete with an exhibitionist tub facing a wide, uncurtained window.

"Because nothing says 'I'm wealthy' like flashing your fun bits to passing toucans."

Inside the walk-in closet, my new wardrobe has been *Marie Kondo'd* into submission. Each outfit hangs on its own velvet hanger with a laminated cue card featuring instructions.

I snatch the note from tonight's selection, reading aloud in my best snooty Sebastian accent:

To Miss Brinkman, My Most Challenging Project:

It has become PAINFULLY clear that, left to your own devices, you would pair Versace with gym socks and strut like it's revolutionary. This. CANNOT. Happen. Not on my watch. Karl Lagerfeld would claw his way out of hell and slap us both in the face. I have therefore taken the liberty of providing toddler-level instructions. Follow them PRECISELY. These notes are your style defibrillator—use them or die in pleats. Your wardrobe rehabilitation is my cross to bear.

—Sebastian Bellini. Fashion Savior. Miracle Worker. Long-suffering saint.

"Understood. A subway rat in a designer gown is still a subway rat."

My mind recalls the scolding from Butler Lord Britchybottom and how Bryce's voice was tight with embarrassment as he apologized.

"Miss Brinkman's not accustomed to Casa Cashmere's protocols," he'd said. "This is her first exposure to... this level of society."

What the fuck am I doing?

I've been throwing myself at Bryce—an engaged man—who clearly sees me as nothing more than an embarrassing obligation.

Every eyebrow raise?

Polite discomfort.

Every moment I felt special?

Damage control.

He's Bryce freaking Sterling. And I'm Gavin's little sister—aka the problem to be managed.

God, I've been acting stupid. Whatever this twisted thing is, it ends now. No more fantasy. No more flirting. I'm not here for him. I'm here for Gavin.

I'm going to help my brother survive his wedding to Miss Satan in stilettos. To prove, for once, that I can show up and shut up. That I'm able to hold my own in a world that never wanted me in the first place.

That I deserve a future that doesn't come with a tip jar.

"They want proper? Fine, I'll be a proper fucking lady in this stupid princess costume."

I flip Sebastian's instruction card over.

WELCOME DINNER ENSEMBLE (Dusty Rose Oscar de la Renta)

Mr. Sterling personally selected this Tiffany ten-carat Mozambique ruby ring as the focal accessory. I've sized it up considerably to accommodate your working-class knuckles. Try not to get it caught in your hair or use it to open beer cans.

I grab the Tiffany box and march to the balcony. *I need air.* I should fake an illness and escape this whole bullshit dinner. When I push through the French doors, the warm evening breeze ruffles my dress. I slump onto a curved iron chair, watching the sun dip below the horizon.

The jewelry box feels unusually heavy in my palm. I lift it to reveal—

"Holy shit."

The ruby is enormous, a deep, bloodred stone that seems to pulse with its own heartbeat. A halo of diamonds surround it, catching the fading sunlight and scattering tiny rainbows across my skin.

I slide it onto my finger—my left ring finger, because apparently my newfound resolve hasn't caught up to my brain yet. It twirls loosely, at least two sizes too big, spinning around and resembling a tiny, sparkly hula hoop.

"Thank you, Sebastian, for your vote of confidence in my sausage fingers."

I hold my hand up, watching the light play through the deep red stone. The exact shade of my favorite lipstick. My lips I've caught Bryce staring at more than once.

He chose this. Specifically this color. For me.

For one dangerous, indulgent moment, I let myself slide down the slippery slope of what-ifs.

What if he picked this ring because he has feelings for me?

What if he wasn't engaged to Perfect Amanda and this was actually my ring?

What if Bryce wanted to marry... me?

God, you're embarrassing! No more thoughts of him. No more daydreams.

"You want dignity, Petra? Start acting like you've got some..." I push up from the chair, determined to go back inside and channel my inner duchess or debutante or whoever the hell manages to look elegant while secretly spiraling—

—and promptly trip over the massive poufy ballgown wrapped around my legs.

"Motherfu—"

THUD!

I faceplant.

The floor is stone. The pain is instant. The sound… is worse.

Tink-tink-tink-tink.

The ring. The *stupid ring* popped off my finger and—"No-no-no-NO!"

I scramble to my knees and lunge toward the balcony edge in time to see it disappear over the side.

Gone.

Straight into the jungle landscaping, swallowed by thick ferns.

"Fuuuuuuuck."

I leap to my feet, grabbing my heels, phone, and designer clutch, and barrel out the door. Panic floods my system, erasing any thoughts of ladylike behavior.

If I'm lucky, I'll find it before I have to explain to Bryce I was playing fake fiancée like a lunatic.

I burst into the garden, my bare feet slapping the stone pathway as I skid around the corner of the building. The silky tulle of my dress catches on a sculpted bush, and I yank it free with zero regard for Sebastian's masterpiece.

"If I were a ruby the size of a grape, where would I hide?"

I press my cheek against the cool grass, peering under a massive shrub with orange flowers, then push my way deeper into the foliage. A sharp thorn rakes across my forearm, leaving a long red scratch. "Son of a—"

I bite back the expletive as I hear voices from above. A familiar blonde head appears two balconies over.

Fiona.

I scramble behind an enormous hedge and peer through the leaves.

Standing next to her is a man I do *not* recognize. A man who is definitely *not* my brother.

He's tall, lanky, with long wavy dark hair cascading to his shoulders. He's rocking extra-tight leather pants, a paisley vest with nothing underneath, and more scarves than a magician's sleeve. Rings decorate every finger. A feather earring dangles from one ear. His vibe? Black-eyeliner rock star meets Renaissance Fair enthusiast meets thrift store on an absinthe bender.

Their eyes are locked on each other, bodies way too close to be considered *just* friends.

"What the shit?" I mutter.

I strain to hear their conversation, the breeze carrying fragments down to my hiding spot.

"...everything we've planned..."

"...Gavin has no idea what's coming..."

I open my camera app.

"Say cheese, Home Wrecker Barbie," I whisper, extending my arm to get an angle of them together.

They disappear into the room. *Dammit.*

I stretch farther, lengthening my reach, when a hand clamps down on my shoulder.

Instinctively, I whirl around—my phone gripped like a weapon—and go straight for the throat.

THWACK!

"HRRNNGGK!"

Bryce makes a sound like a goose being strangled, stumbling backward with his hand flying to his neck. His face contorts—first surprise, then pain—as his eyes bulge and he struggles to breathe.

"Oh my God, B! I'm so sorry. Seriously, though. Do you have a death wish?"

He makes another concerning noise, more wheeze than words, and tugs at his bow tie as if it's suddenly become a noose.

"Are you dying? Please don't die." I step closer, genuinely concerned now. "I can't afford the legal fees for manslaughter, and orange is a worse color on me than pink."

"What—" his voice is raspy "— are you doing out here?"

"Communing with nature," I say flatly, brushing a leaf off my gown. "You know how us broke people love hobbies that are free. Tree-hugging, dirt whispering, ring scavenging..."

Do not acknowledge that he is handsome AF in that tux.

That little crease appears between his eyebrows. "Pip, about earlier—"

"Let me guess—you're mad I didn't curtsy before causing a scene in front of your country-club cult and their four-legged dictator. Don't worry. I got the message loud and clear."

Something flashes in his eyes. Regret? Frustration? *Who cares.*

"That's not what I—"

"Save it." I brush past him without slowing. "You've made it clear I'm an embarrassment."

"Let me escort you to dinner."

"As charming as that sounds, hard pass on your escort service." I'm already walking away. Fast. Determined.

"Petra, wait—"

I don't look back.

Bryce Sterling isn't my concern. Gavin is. And he deserves to know what I just witnessed.

***

I STORM DOWN THE main hallway, a woman on a mission. The waiting area outside the formal dining room is next-level luxurious—marble floors polished to an ice-rink sheen, chandeliers dripping like diamond waterfalls, and the distinct scent of money, which I guess is the smell of fresh flowers and furniture polish.

Somewhere in the distance, a harp is playing.

Because of course it is.

All I want tonight is to stay ten football fields away from Bryce and figure out what the hell Gavin's shady, fake-ass fiancée was doing with that wannabe pirate.

I scan the crowd of guests—each one glammed up and chatting in designer evening wear. I spot my brother's coiffed dark-brown hair near a massive floral arrangement. He looks every inch the financial titan in his tailored Tom Ford tuxedo.

"Hey bro. Where's Fiona?" I ask, tugging at my bodice as I sidle up to him.

Gavin turns, champagne flute in hand. "Had something to attend to. She'll be down soon." His eyebrows lift, amused. "That's... quite a gown, Wildcat."

"I look like a marshmallow had a baby with a lampshade."

I straighten my spine, ready to drop my bombshell. My mind races through possible openers:

Option 1: Blunt-force truth bomb. "Hey, Gav, your bride-to-be is cheating. Not a hunch. Not a maybe. I saw her with my own eyes. Surprise! I was right."

Option 2: Casually unhinged. "Okay, quick question, and I swear I'm not trying to start a wedding fire—but is Fiona, by chance, supposed to be seducing dudes in flower gardens like some Real Horny Housewife?"

Option 3: The slow burn. "Remember when I told you Fiona was evil? Well, Satan called, and he wants his handmaiden back."

Before I can decide between sarcasm or scorched-earth honesty, Gavin cuts in.

"The dog incident was unfortunate, but let's move past it."

"I didn't know it was their furry overlord. There wasn't exactly a sign saying 'Do not touch: canine billionaire.'"

"Petra." There's that tone—half exasperation, half grudging affection. "You need to—"

"Gavin, I must apologize." Bryce's smooth voice interrupts from behind me. "I failed to properly brief her on the protocols here. I'll make sure she understands what's expected moving forward."

As Bryce stands beside me, his arm brushes mine—a hot whisper of contact that lights me up. I'm turned on, off-balance, and pissed about it. My body goes into fight-or-flirt mode, and I choose fight.

"That won't be necessary, Moneybags. I'm a big girl. I can navigate rich-people nonsense on my own."

Gavin sighs, giving me the *you're-being-difficult-again* face. "This isn't your world, sis. Let Bryce help you."

"I don't need a warden. I'm not little Pip anymore."

"Could you, for once, not fight me on everything?" Gavin steps closer, lowering his voice. "One week. That's all I'm asking. Be nice to Fiona. Let Bryce guide you. Can you do that for me?"

I start to bristle, but then he places a hand on my arm. The weight is firm, grounding. And there it is—that damn Rolex. The one Mom and I bought him. For all his hard-ass tendencies, Gavin's always been my rock. He stood up when Dad left. He worked his way through college while sending money home. He's given me more second chances than I deserve.

A single week of playing nice is more than reasonable. Besides, I shouldn't bring up Mystery Man until I have real proof. My suspicions won't cut it—only solid evidence will survive Gavin's scrutiny.

"Fine, I'll let Moneybags be my fairy godmother."

Bryce's mouth twitches at the corner.

Gavin switches instantly to CEO mode. "Great. You're my point person for wedding logistics. I'm depending on you to stay on top of things."

My phone's out of my clutch, and I'm opening my notes app as he launches into his list.

"Confirm the fire dancers have a safety perimeter set up for the reception, and Fiona wants an ice luge for the tequila tasting at the bachelorette party. Make sure it's the one carved like a Mayan jaguar, not a walrus penis."

I glance up from my screen. "Ice sculptures? In Mexico? Why not set fire to your money instead? It's more efficient."

"Miss Muffy has very specific aesthetic preferences," Gavin says, ignoring me. "The gift bags for tomorrow's excursion will require her final sign-off before distribution. Then, confirm the satellite hookup for the virtual guests. Mom wants to make sure Uncle

Charlie can see from his hospital bed in Palm Springs. He's doing great, by the way, recovering from hip surgery."

"Lucky Uncle Charlie. He doesn't have to be here."

"Petra, focus up. It's expected that you ask Miss Muffy for all approvals—or consult with Nigel, who acts on her behalf."

"I'm sorry... The *dog*? I need *the dog's* permission?"

The silence hits hard. For a moment, I think I've stepped in it. Thankfully, every head swivels toward the entrance.

Fiona floats across the ballroom toward us, oozing old Hollywood glamour. Her gown is a masterpiece of silver beading and crystal work, creating the illusion she's glittering on ice. Her blonde hair is twisted into an elaborate updo.

"Fi, you're a vision," my brother says, kissing her cheek.

"Thank you, Gav-Gav," she purrs, her hand landing on his chest with practiced delicacy. "Sorry I'm late. Had a last-minute detail to handle."

Oh, I bet you did. In a candlelit room. With Mystery Man's scarf tied around your hands.

I search for evidence on her wrist, but if it's there, it's hidden beneath a massive diamond bracelet.

"Petra! Playing princess tonight?" she says, eyeing me. "That dress is... surprising. So edgy-meets-elegant. Like a tattooed Cinderella."

The insult is wrapped so beautifully in compliment paper that if you're not fluent in Fiona's backstabbing, you'd totally miss it.

"Wow thanks," I reply with artificial sweetness. "Your outfit is stunning too. I especially love how it matches your personality—cold, sharp, and *shine* over substance."

Gavin's eyes narrow to deadly slits, sending me a clear warning shot across the bow.

"What I mean is," I say through gritted teeth, "you're gorgeous. Like an angel who fell from heaven..."

Fiona beams, smug as ever.

Gavin claps a hand on Bryce's shoulder. "We need to talk Heartvest. I received a call earlier about some wording Legal flagged in the press packet. Might be smart to pivot to an early media hit—"

Fiona clears her throat. "I thought we agreed on no business talk at wedding events."

"You're right, Fi. I'm here. All in."

He kisses her cheek again, and I glance at Bryce.

Tap. Tap. Tap.

He's a statue everywhere else—jaw tight, shoulders square—but that finger? It's sending a distress signal in Morse code.

What's got him wound so tight? The business? Fiona? Or maybe... me?

BWONNNNGGGGGGG!

The sound vibrates through my bones like a church bell, making me jump so violently, I nearly lose a shoe.

"Holy shitballs!"

"Language, Pip," Bryce grumbles under his breath.

I spin to see Nigel standing beside an enormous bronze gong, his white-gloved hand still gripping the mallet. He's now wearing an even more formal tuxedo with tails that makes the previous one look casual. His silver hair shellacked in place, expression as frozen as a wax figure.

"Esteemed guests," he announces in his crisp British accent, "dinner is served."

Two men also dressed in black tuxedos part the towering double doors.

Bryce catches my elbow as Gavin and Fiona sweep into the dining room like they're on a red carpet. I try to follow, but his grip gently holds me back.

"A moment, please," he says quietly.

"Can we not? Whatever lecture you're dying to give me, shove it in a Tiffany bag and deliver it later."

"That's not my intention. The back of your dress is undone."

I twist, fumbling behind me like a feral raccoon pawing at a snack bag, and yeah. My spine is... out. Exposed. Back door open. Peekaboo hour at Casa Cashmere.

"Turn around," he says firmly.

My brain does a full somersault.

Because *oh hell no.* Those two words shouldn't be that hot. But they are. They are panty-melting, command-me-Daddy levels of hot.

I should punch him. But instead, I obey and turn.

Big mistake. Huge.

Because I'm weak. Because I hate the way I want him to see my back. My ink. My skin. All the pieces of me that say *I'm not who you think I am*—but also, *I wish I was good enough to be who you want.*

I stare at a sconce on the wall as though it's the only thing anchoring me to this dimension.

Behind me, Bryce moves—measured, deliberate.

My breath catches as he finesses the tiny hook-and-eye, knuckles brushing the bare skin between my shoulder blades. His hands are infuriatingly warm, annoyingly gentle, and way too restrained. My skin prickles. My stomach flips. Every nerve sings, like maybe he wants to rip this dress off, not fix it.

This is not foreplay, Petra. He's simply being helpful. A gentleman.

"You're trembling."

"I'm allergic to you," I snap.

"Your tattoo here. Are these wildflowers?" he says, his finger tracing the floral design along my shoulder blade, leaving a trail of fire in his wake.

"Look at you, Moneybags, knowing your roadside weeds."

He leans in and whispers against my ink. "I like them."

Three words is all it takes, and I fall into the fantasy I promised myself I wouldn't entertain again.

Him. Me. This room.

I imagine that tux sliding off those broad shoulders. My hands on him. This ridiculous dress sliding down my hips as he kisses every inch of my body. The weight of his hard cock pressing against my stomach while his mouth devours whatever sounds he can draw from me.

My spine arching off the velvet chaise, body yearning beneath his. Those big hands pinning mine above my head—rough. Commanding.

I bet he whispers when he fucks.

Those perfect, proper lips, turning filthy in my ear. His control cracking as he thrusts—composure slipping—losing himself inside me.

I bet he's a contradiction. Touches me like I'm breakable but fucks like he's breaking apart. Like a man who's been quiet for too long and he needs a place to be loud.

I hate that I want to be that place.

I'm unraveling under his touch. And he's not even trying.

"What does this tattoo mean?" he asks, brushing behind my ear with a curious touch.

"That I'm a fool who makes bad decisions with cheap tequila."

The real story is more pathetic. *It's the broken heart you never knew you gave me.*

His hands fall away, but the echo of him pulses through me like a held breath.

"Okay, B, dress disaster averted. I'll try not to collapse face-first into the soup course."

He doesn't move. Just stands there.

"You look beautiful, Pip."

"Must be the soul-crushing corset. Nothing says glamor like strategically redistributed organs."

"Not the dress. You."

My stomach drops straight into my stilettos.

Stop blushing, slut-brain.

Don't fall for his "rich boy manners" routine. Give him two minutes, and he'll be telling our dog hostess she's the belle of the fucking ball.

He doesn't mean it the way you're hoping.

I can't go back to being fifteen and naive. My law books don't have room for *Mrs. Bryce Sterling* doodles. I've got to be careful, or I'll waste another decade on this infatuation.

He holds out his arm for me. "We need to discuss dinner protocols."

Nope. No more touching. I need serious distance. Like, force-field-level. Or one of those grabby claw things they give to senior citizens so they can reach high shelves.

Stick to the plan. No more reckless thoughts about this unattainable man.

Abort this lust.

Abort the whole damn man.

"No thanks, B." I take a deliberate step back. "I've managed to avoid stabbing myself with a fork since preschool. My eating skills are pretty much the same—just with fewer crayons. Usually."

I spin toward the banquet hall before my traitorous body can stage a full-blown mutiny against my better judgment.

I'm not a girl who will be turned into a puddle by one well-timed compliment. I am woman. Hear me roar. Or at least hear the rustling of my dress as I flee.

Swish-swish-swish.

The dining chamber is a shrine to over-the-top wealth and questionable taste. It looks like Marie Antionette and Liberace had a decorating showdown and both won.

A single, ridiculously long table dominates the room, encircled by thirty chairs, each intricately carved with gold leaf and adorned with pale-blue velvet cushions. The place settings are terrifying—layered with six plates, three napkins folded into origami swans, and silverware arranged in a way that suggests measuring devices were involved.

And at the head of the table? Not a chair. A throne. For a dog.

A dog with more money than I'll earn in fifty-thousand lifetimes.

I scan the monogrammed place cards.

There I am. Petra Brinkman.

And right beside me? Bryce Sterling.

Fuck.

I pick up his name tag, scanning the seating area for somewhere—anywhere—else to put him. Maybe inside the flower arrangement. Or under the dog's butt. Or I could just eat it.

"Trying to move me toward the exit?" Bryce appears, reclaiming the slip and putting it back.

"I'm trying to create some healthy social distance. For *your* protection."

"I'll take my chances."

His gaze locks on to mine, and holy hell—something has shifted. Gone is the polite restraint. Something heated is lurking behind those cool blue eyes. Something hungry... and suddenly my thighs have opinions. Dangerous ones.

The air between us thickens, charged with an energy that makes it hard to breathe. The background noise of polite murmurs fades, leaving nothing but the sound of my own heartbeat thundering in my ears.

"Our conversation from earlier isn't finished," he says sternly.

"In my world, when someone walks away, that's the universal signal for 'conversation over.'"

"Good thing we're in *my* world. Different rules apply." His gaze drops to my mouth for a fraction of a second.

The smallest, most insufferable flicker of a smirk crosses his sculpted lips. It transforms him from handsome to devastating, and something molten spreads through my belly.

Who is this man, and what has he done with the buttoned-up Bryce Sterling?

The warmth of him seeps through my dress's thin material, flushing my skin like a physical caress. He's standing so close that if I shifted forward ever so slightly, my chest would brush against the solid wall of his arm. The temptation is maddening.

"Fight it all you want, Pip, but you're not getting rid of me," he bites out. "This is Gavin's week. His wedding. I'm the best man, and he asked me to keep an eye on you."

"Lucky me. My own personal billionaire babysitter." I flutter my eyelashes. "Will you be checking under my bed for poverty monsters?"

"Whatever helps you accept it. But you're stuck with me until this wedding is over."

The cocky way he says *"stuck with me"* drips with heat, not obligation. My internal temperature skyrockets.

"If you think I take orders that easily, you have another thing coming, Moneybags." I step into his space, daring him to push back. "I don't wear collars for spoiled rich boys, and I sure as hell don't fetch, stay, or roll over."

His gaze doesn't waver. It deepens—hungrier, dominant, electric.

"You've never had the right handler." His voice drops. "If I clipped a collar on you? You wouldn't be fighting. You'd be purring."

And then he smirks. Not a subtle grin—a full-on smolder.

Did Bryce Sterling—Mr. Fortune 500, King of Composure, Goldenboy by-the-book Billionaire—just imply he wants to... dominate me? In the biblical sense?

My brain is a toaster short-circuiting in a bathtub.

What the hell do I say to that?

CHAPTER EIGHT

PETRA

***Oh fuck.* I'm toast.** Burnt to a crisp.

Mr. Suit-and-Tie is a hair's breadth away from me, smirking—deliciously dangerous. The air between us crackles with so much tension, I could slice it with one of these dainty forks. That voice of his? Straight out of the world's dirtiest audiobook, and my brain is begging me to misbehave.

"If I clipped a collar on you... you'd be purring."

My core ignites at the image—me in nothing but that ruby ring and a collar, on my knees, eyes yearning for only him.

My skin flushes hot, then cold—a rollercoaster of arousal crashing into suspicion.

What. The. Actual. Hell.

This isn't the Bryce I know. Moneybags maintains a ten-foot radius of professionalism at all times. He says things like "portfolio diversification" and "appropriate decorum."

Is this some twisted new tactic to control me? Flirt with the chaotic little sister to keep her in line for his best friend's wedding? Seduce the problem child into submission? Because if so, that's... that's...

Genius. And infuriating. And embarrassingly effective.

Except... *The joke's on you, B. I figured out your petty game. Think you can tame me with a few dirty words? That because you've released your inner Christian Grey, you can put me on a leash?*

HMPFH! Think again!

If Mr. Billionaire wants to be the etiquette police and my personal Dom-for-dinner, bring it on.

You've met your match, B.

I yank my chair to sit, but his grip stops me. This time, on my forearm.

"Wait," he says. "No one's seated yet."

"Hands to yourself. Unless you're prepared to use them properly."

"Be careful what you wish for," he says, like it's a promise.

"I didn't take you for the kinky type, Moneybags. Always assumed you'd be missionary-with-the-lights-off boring. The kind who says 'pardon me' when you come."

His pupils dilate. *Victory!*

Bryce's palm moves to my wrist, the pad of his thumb finding my pulse point and circling slowly. "Do you want to test that theory, Pip?"

For a heart-stopping moment, he looks prepared to pull me against him, consequences be damned. His attention lingers on my red lips, hungry and intent.

Words hover on my tongue—*I dare you to take what you want—*

"OHMYGODHI!"

Before I can register what's happening, I'm engulfed in a hug of exotic perfume and designer silk and being treated like I'm someone's long-lost bestie.

"I'm Hana! Hana Choi! Maid of honor." She pulls back, grinning at me with the blinding intensity of a sunbeam who's never had a bad day in her life.

If Disney created a modern-day Korean princess, she would 100 percent resemble Hana Choi. Her face is heart-shaped perfection—high cheekbones, flawless porcelain skin, and almond eyes that sparkle with perpetual excitement. Her black hair falls in a glossy waterfall past her shoulders, each strand moving with choreographed grace as she bounces on her toes in a lavender silk gown.

Diamonds adorn her throat, wrists, and ears. Her teeth are aggressively white. And her voice? Somewhere between a Miss America contestant and a talking cupcake.

"You're Gavin's sister! Fiona has told me all about you!"

"Well, that's terrifying."

Hana giggles. "She said you were super spicy and unpredictable. Like a jalapeño in a mimosa!"

I force a smile. Am I supposed to believe *this* seat just happened to be open for Fiona's BFF? Sure.

It's surveillance, plain and simple. Hana's here to monitor my every move, gather information against me, and report back to her queen B-word.

She clutches my arm, her bracelets digging into my skin. "This week is a full-blown fairy tale. The yacht party, the spa day, the sunset ceremony—it's like living in a bridal magazine! Aren't you totally over-the-moon excited?"

I would respond, but Hana's already yapping away.

"Oh, silly me! Of course you're excited! Gavin is your brother, and now you are getting the best sister-in-law on the planet. You and Fiona are going to be like, *real* sisters!"

My face freezes in what I hope passes for a friendly smile. *Real sisters?* It's more of a Cinderella-stuck-with-evil-stepsister situation.

BOOOOOOONG!

Everyone in the room goes still—mannequin-level, no-body-blink, first-date-fart-slip kind of still.

"Distinguished guests," Nigel announces, "it is my most profound honor to present the hostess of this night—her grace, her legacy, her unparalleled taste—Miss Muffy Von Cashmere the Second. Heiress to the Von Cashmere Fortune, Empress of the Jungle Estate, Patroness of the Arts, and Beloved Mistress of Casa Cashmere."

And in she trots.

Miss Muffy Von Cashmere the Second.

The dog.

She's a spectacle. Her snowy fur is blown out within an inch of its life, her tiny frame swaddled in a green velvet couture evening gown with a gold satin sash cinched at the waist. Topping it off? A tiara.

The Maltese saunters down the center of the table on a raised platform designed specifically for her grand entrance, her little paws clicking against the polished surface. She reaches the end of her royal runway and ascends a set of carpeted stairs to her throne, turning once to survey her subjects before delicately sitting down.

Chairs scrape as the entire room sits. Synchronized. Like this is a very *normal* thing we're doing.

Before I can inhale, a tuxedoed server appears, lifts the napkin with quiet precision, and arranges it neatly in my lap.

Good God, these rich people don't know how to do anything for themselves. What's next? Personal fork lifters and mouth openers? Professional chewers to masticate our food before swallowing?

"Miss Muffy," Nigel continues, "wishes to extend a warm welcome to you this evening, with special recognition to our honored bride and groom, Mr. Gavin Brinkman and Miss Fiona Whitfield."

On cue, the dog lets out a single, sharp yap. Everyone breaks into polite applause.

"Thank you, Miss Muffy, for this extraordinary reception," Fiona coos. "We're overwhelmed by your legendary hospitality."

Another bark. More applause.

"Isn't she inspiring?" Hana says. "She's so elegant. I keep thinking she's like... a duchess instead of, you know... a dog."

A fleet of servers glides into the room in formation, each carrying a covered silver dish. With seamless coordination, they set the first course in front of the guests. I watch my lid lift with a whisper of steam and something... gooey.

What's in my bowl stops me cold: a milky white broth with clear, jelly-like blobs floating in it, garnished with unidentifiable brown bits.

"What *is* this?"

Hana squeals. "Ooh! Bird's nest soup! What a treat!"

"Is it?"

"Oh yes. It's made with real bird saliva, along with pieces of the actual swiftlet's nest. Each one is *hand-selected* for quality. Think about how many birdies had to work overtime with their little mouths to create thirty servings!"

"Bird drool? A delicacy?" I mutter. "Any chance there's an alt soup of the day, like chicken noodle?"

I reach for what I assume is the soup spoon *(thimble-sized, because rich people prefer microscopic portions).* Bryce leans over, his lips not quite touching my ear, and the heat of his breath sends an electric zap straight to my nipples.

"Wrong utensil, Pip," he murmurs. "Keep breaking the rules, and I'll have to discipline you."

"Does it involve restraints and safe words?"

"Only if you're very, very good for me."

A sharp inhale betrays me. "Are you this forward with all the women you babysit?"

"Only disobedient ones who need a firm hand."

Well. That's... disturbingly hot.

No. He's not steering this horny Titanic into an iceberg of bad decisions. I am.

I fake an exaggerated yawn, as though I'm unaffected by his boring advances. "Promises, promises. You high-society pretty boys are all bark, no bite."

"Trust me, Pip... I bite."

The spoon slips from my grasp, clattering against the china. Every head at the table swivels our way. I snatch it off the plate, gripping it with the proper technique.

His eyes drop to my bare fingers, then back to my face with a hint of disapproval.

"Where's the ring you're supposed to wear with this gown?"

The question throws me. Several snarky responses flash through my mind:

Option 1: Blasé Indifference. "That hideous thing? It clashed with my middle finger."

Option 2: Playful Misdirection. "I loaned it to Miss Muffy. It complimented her crown. Who am I to deny our high priestess?"

Option 3: Theatrical Distress. "Holy shit, you're right! Someone must have stolen it! Alert security! Unless... Wait, do you think the butler did it? He seems shifty."

I settle on: "Would you believe I dropped it off the balcony while fantasizing about your romantic proposal?"

He smirks. "Very amusing. I chose that particular ruby to compliment your... dress."

"Well, I rebelled. Call it my protest against being packaged as some kind of sexy party favor."

"It's fine. You don't need the ring," he says, his gaze dragging over me like a fingertip. "You're still temptation itself."

Time out! Shut it down. I gotta collect myself before I lose it.

I break the connection between us and notice Nigel approaching Miss Muffy's throne with the reverence of a monk at an altar. He bends slightly, careful not to crease his uniform, and takes a delicate sip from the dog's bowl.

"It is, as always, perfection, madam."

Only *then* does Muffy lower her snout to begin eating.

Spoons clink. Conversation resumes. The orchestral harp picks back up like it's scoring a BBC miniseries about snobbery and mild incest.

I reluctantly dip into the gelatinous goop. The smell hits me. Is that *sulfur*? It's warm and... slightly salty? I part my lips and let the tiniest blob land on my tongue.

My taste buds stage an immediate revolt.

It's as if someone liquefied a fart and garnished it with fish food. I not-so-discreetly spit the unholy concoction out, then wipe at my tongue frantically with my napkin, trying to erase the trauma of fermented parrot drool.

I glance at Bryce, who's sipping the fancy bird barf soup as if it's delicious. His eyes dare me to say otherwise.

Nuh-uh. I need a distraction from this bowl of sinus gravy and the temporarily insane billionaire beside me. *Hana!* Maybe I can extract some useful Fiona intel from her bubbly sidekick. Keep your friends close and your enemy's oversharing bestie closer.

"So, Hana, tell me about you."

"Oh! Me?" She seems genuinely surprised. "Nobody ever asks. My family owns ChoCorp—the Korean tech giant inside everyone's phone—but they won't let me work there. They said my talents were better used elsewhere."

She says this with the same breezy tone a person might use to mention they prefer chocolate over vanilla.

"They won't let you work at your family's company?"

"Of course not, silly! I'm engaged to marry my daddy's business competitor!" She flashes her left hand, where a diamond the size of a walnut sits. "It's a strategic alliance thing. Daddy says women are better at mergers through marriages than with board meetings."

I'm stunned silent by this casually delivered bombshell.

"Fiona is just *so lucky* to marry someone handsome and under fifty! My fiancé is seventy-five and has this weird breathing thing when he sleeps, but my mother says that's a plus because I'll inherit sooner! What about you? Has your family chosen your husband yet?"

"I don't have to get married. I've made my own fortune, selling meth."

Hana's eyes go wide before bursting into tinkling laughter. "You are *too funny!* Fiona said you had the most amazing sense of humor!"

Beside me, Bryce clears his throat pointedly, but I stubbornly keep my attention on Hana.

"Aww, look at them," Hana sighs dreamily. "Gavin actually gives eye contact to Fiona when she talks! That's like, *relationship goals!* My fiancé's assistant gave me an entire document about which topics I'm not allowed to bring up at dinner. Apparently, his first three wives did not understand the importance of proper conversation filtering!"

"Yeah, I've never had much luck with filters. I'm more of a say-what-I-think-and-let-the-jaws-drop kind of girl."

She giggles. Again. "Oh my God, I love that about you! I can tell we're going to become best friends this week."

"Who knows?" I say through gritted teeth.

I glance sideways and catch Fiona... *talking* to Muffy as though she's hosting a podcast with a Maltese.

BWONNNNGGGGGGG.

Hana gasps and turns toward the sound, attention temporarily hijacked.

Perfect.

With the precision of a spy and the nonchalance of a street magician, I tilt my bowl ever-so-slightly and *pour* my untouched congealed bird phlegm soup into hers.

"You're such a naughty, naughty girl," Bryce murmurs. "What am I going to do with you?"

"No idea what you mean," I say, the picture of innocence as I set down my empty bowl. "I made sure to lick up every drop. It was delicious."

"Such a waste," he says, his knee brushing mine under the table. "I could've shown you how to properly... swallow."

My thighs clench. My ovaries squeal. My entire pelvic floor stages a rave.

He's waiting for a response. Somewhere in the control room of my body, my lungs smack the panic button and scream at my brain: *HELLO? Suck in some oxygen, bitch! Then speak!*

"Sorry," I say sweetly. "I can't hear you over the sound of your ego inflating."

"Strange. You heard me perfectly fine when I said you needed a firm hand."

"I have selective hearing. It filters out boring stuff and only tunes in when the conversation gets... stimulating."

His smile is slow and dangerous. "Then I'll be sure to keep you... stimulated."

Body, we need to have a chat. No, not you, lungs—you're trying.

You, vagina.

Me: *We had an agreement. You were supposed to be on team self-respect, remember?*

Vagina: *But he said "swallow," Petra. With that voice.*

Me: *No.*

Vagina: *But—*

Me: *Shut it. We're in public. There's a tiara-wearing dog five feet away.*

I discreetly pinch my own thigh under the table, and ouch!

Nope. Not dreaming.

This is real. Bryce Sterling—*my brother's best friend, my teenage crush*—is saying every filthy thing I've ever fantasized about... and somehow he knows *exactly* what buttons to press.

Which is *unacceptable*, because there are only two people aware of the full extent of my unholy Bryce Sterling fantasies: Me. And my vibrator.

He's playing a game. That's what this is. A twisted high-society chess match where seducing the chaos gremlin earns him good boy points with the well-mannered butler.

He's distracting me. Manipulating me.

Well, not today, billionaire. But you can bet my little lady and I will be discussing your tactics later.

"Excuse me. Hana and I are having a very *important* girl talk. We're analyzing the serious epidemic of billionaires with super teeny tiny... tax write-offs."

I shoot him a sweet, innocent smile. "*What* did you think I was gonna say?"

His nostrils flare. That's right, Moneybags. Choke on it.

The servers swoop in with the next round of edible punishment. In one overly theatrical move, they lift the domes to reveal tiny bowls of lumpy beige sludge. *This is what cottage cheese might look like if it spent six hours rotting on hot concrete.*

"Ooooh!" Hana claps her hands together like an excited toddler. "Escamole! I heard Miss Muffy serves the most spectacular authentic Mexican delicacies."

"Esca-what-the-hell?"

"Escamole! It's the caviar of Mexico. This delicacy is the larvae and pupae of large black ants! Isn't that the *neatest* thing?"

My stomach answers the question for me, and my esophagus tightens in self-defense.

"Too bad I'm full from the last course to dig into this bug buffet."

"Stop!" Hana slaps my arm playfully. "You are cracking me up!"

Once again, Nigel approaches Miss Muffy's dish like it's baby Jesus... and he's trying to get an invite to the Last Supper. He takes a modest spoonful of the insect nursery, tastes it, then nods his approval. "Exquisite texture and seasoned as you like it, Miss Muffy."

Only after the Maltese takes her first dainty lick does the room lift their spoons. I watch in horror as thirty absurdly rich humans cheerfully shovel insect offspring into their mouths like it's Cocoa Puffs.

I put a small amount onto my spoon, examining... *itty-bitty alien eggs? Rice that's gone horribly wrong?* The individual grains have a slightly translucent quality that reminds me of maggots. I see tiny black specks inside that I'm pretty sure are innocent little baby ant eyes staring back.

"Mmmmmmmm." Hana's moan is so explicit, it would get flagged on YouTube. "So divine! It's... nutty and buttery and gooey—but, like... chunky."

My stomach heaves.

That's it. I'm going to vomit into this bowl.

And honestly? Nobody will notice. It'll blend right in. They'd probably think it's a garnish.

I set my spoon down in quiet surrender. "So what's with the butler eating the dog's food?" I ask because my mind needs the diversion.

"That's billionaire safety protocol. He's Muffy's official taster. You know, in case someone tries to poison her. Only last week, there was this king—I forget which country, but somewhere with mountains—who almost died from an appetizer."

"So the dog has bodyguards and a personal food tester. How relatable."

"I know, right! That's how Fiona was able to secure this place for the wedding. The king had to cancel, so Casa Cashmere had an unexpected opening!" she sighs. "Fiona is always so fortunate with things like that!"

"Yep. His near-death experience is our gain. Total stroke of luck that we're all here feasting on bugs and bird snot."

"Fiona told me that Gavin lets her eat carbs. He's so progressive! My prenup requires one weekly weigh-in with the family nutritionist and includes a whole appendix of acceptable food groups."

She shovels another spoonful of ant larvae into her mouth with genuine enthusiasm, and I have no idea how to respond. It just might be the most fucked-up thing I've ever heard. Should I be planning her escape? Slipping her the number for a women's shelter? Is there a hotline for women trapped in dystopian marriages?

"What's wrong, Pip?" Bryce asks, "I thought you were fearless."

He nudges the bowl of ant baby tapioca looming on the table. It jiggles.

"I've done many questionable things in the name of proving a point, but voluntarily eating insect fetuses at a billion-dollar dinner party is where I draw the line."

"I assumed you got off on dares." His eyes twinkle with pure trouble. "I dare you to eat one bite."

"Why would I torture myself?"

"Because if you don't gag, I'll stop correcting your etiquette for the rest of dinner."

His relaxed expression infuriates me.

"And what do I get if I *do* gag?"

His gulp is audible. "Then we'll have to spend the night exploring what else you enjoy choking on."

Okay, who the hell spiked the water with horny juice?

You know what? *I'm calling his bluff.*

I steal the spoon from his hand without a word. The metal is warm from his touch, and God help me, I feel it everywhere.

I scoop up a wriggling pile, forcing myself to look. The larvae glisten and shimmy under the chandelier light. *Nightmare fuel.* But if this is the price for a night tangled in Bryce Sterling's lap? Pass the damn salt. I'll lick the plate clean.

Because the way he's looking at me? I really hope he'll make good on it.

I shove the entire spoonful into my mouth. It's warm. Slimy. And it pops. SOMETHING POPS!

My whole body jerks. My shoulders stiffen. My throat convulses.

Chew, Petra. CHEW.

I can't.

There is no way in seven hells I'm swallowing this abomination.

With zero regard for propriety or manners, I lunge for the napkin in Bryce's lap. My other hand lands on his muscular thigh for balance. I spit into the napkin as if survival depends on it.

I'm about to grab his water when I realize my grip is on his very firm—

Wait.

That is *not* his wallet. Not a phone in his pocket. Not a bonus breadstick tucked under his pants for later.

Our eyes lock, and in that split-second, I get it.

Me: *Holy shit. He's as turned on as I am.*

Vagina: *Told you so.*

Me: *Not. Now.*

This isn't a power play. Not some *distract Petra* game. He's very aroused by whatever the hell this is between us.

And the proof under my palm is wood big enough to build a canoe with.

"Bryce, darling!" Fiona's voice slices through our tension. "When can we expect Amanda to join us this week? I enjoy her company so much."

I snatch my hand away from Bryce's lap so fast I nearly dislocate my shoulder.

Amanda. The woman he's going to marry.

Bryce goes rigid, his warmth turning to stone. That nervous tic starts up—tap-tap-tap against his thigh where my fingers were moments ago.

"Sadly, Amanda is unable to make it," he says with practiced politeness. "Her mother continues to need her assistance with recovery. But she sends her warm wishes."

"It's probably for the best," she agrees with a dismissive wave. "When you get engaged, we wouldn't want her to be jealous that your wedding can't be at Casa Cashmere."

When they get engaged?

I thought they already were. At the gala, his mother definitely implied it.

My mind pinballs between confusion and clarity. The flirting. The innuendo. The gifts. He's been doing all this while he has a girlfriend back home. A girlfriend he's on the verge of proposing to.

And then—like a brick to the face—I remember the joke I made earlier to Sebastian at my fitting. The one about being Bryce's mistress.

Did he take that seriously? Is that what this is?

Oh God.

That's why he arranged our rooms to be next to each other. Not because of proximity or convenience. No. It was logistics. Privacy. Strategy.

A fucking affair.

I glance around the opulent dining room, taking in the sea of polished, powerful guests. This is how their world works—wealthy, restless people locked in loveless marriages made for money, image, and legacy.

They play the part in public, then scratch the itch in private. With someone reckless. Someone forbidden. Someone forgettable.

Someone like me.

Is that what Fiona's doing too?

My gaze darts around the dining area, searching for the lanky man in tight leather pants. He's conveniently not present *(same as Bryce's conscience)*.

The one percent understands how to cover their tracks. How to lie with a smile and a napkin on their lap. How to raise a toast with one hand and stab you in the back with the other.

The thought makes me ill.

I flirt. I tease. I joke. But this? *This* is not a game I signed up for.

He's got a girlfriend. I've got a line. And I don't cross it.

And I *sure as hell* will not be a pleasure toy for a bored billionaire.

"Still, it's sad," Fiona chatters on. "Amanda will be missed. She always makes things more fun when it's the four of us. But it's nice making new friends too, right Petra?"

I'm so done with the lies. My brother and I both deserve better. He's a good man, and I won't sit by and watch Fiona cheat her way down the aisle.

I lean forward, elbows planted firmly on the table *(screw it)*, and the dam breaks.

"Ya know, speaking of new friends. Somebody is missing from this dinner party," I say accusingly. "Fiona, where's that guy I saw you with earlier?"

Her smile doesn't just falter—it *malfunctions*. "I don't know what you're talking about."

"Really? That wasn't you with the artistic, Jack Sparrow–looking dude? I was sure it was you, but hey, maybe there's another platinum blonde heiress wandering this castle."

"How funny you are, Petra!" she exclaims, her voice soaring like a helium-filled balloon ready to pop.

"She's the *absolute funniest!*" Hana chimes in, her head bobbing so frantically I can hear her diamond earrings clacking against her jawline.

"It's not a joke. It's what I saw."

Gavin sets his fork down—hard. "Fi, what is she talking about?"

I part my lips, ready to deliver the killing blow—to describe in vivid detail how his bride-to-be was practically glued to another man—when I feel it.

Heat. Pressure. Skin against skin.

Bryce's caress curled around my bare thigh, his palm scorching through the high slit of my dress. His eyes lock with mine—a clear warning. *Stop talking. Don't make a scene.*

Fat chance, buddy.

But then—God—his fingers sweep upward, tracing delicate patterns on my inner thigh, inching higher with devastating precision. My entire body liquefies on the spot, muscles turning to warm honey. The dining room dims at the edges as all my blood rushes south to follow his tapered touch.

What was I saying? Those things with... letters? How do they work again?

My legs part slightly of their own volition.

Wait. What the actual hell am I doing?

I slam my thighs shut with the force of a Venus flytrap, nearly crushing his fingers in the process. My knee knocks against the table hard enough to rattle the crystal. Miss Muffy lets out an indignant yap from her throne.

I toss Bryce a look that could freeze tequila: *Touch me again, and you'll be eating escamole larvae through a straw.*

"Petra, how could you?" Fiona gasps. Tears—actual, glistening tears—well in her eyes. "You've ruined the surprise!"

I'm sorry, the what now?

My brain screeches to a halt like a cartoon character leaving skid marks.

Fiona presses her napkin delicately to the corner of one eye. "Miss Muffy, would it be acceptable to present my surprise ahead of schedule? It seems the secret is out."

The Maltese gives a crisp, pointed bark.

Nigel translates. "Miss Muffy graciously permits Miss Whitfield to begin her presentation ahead of the planned schedule. Send in the special guest!"

The ballroom doors fly open, and through a cloud of literal smoke, in saunters... Mystery Man himself.

"Ladies and gentlemen," Nigel announces, "the renowned performance artist and painter... Echo."

He struts forward, straight to Miss Muffy, and lowers himself in front of her throne in a deep, sweeping bow. Then, he lifts her paw and kisses it.

"Your grace," he says solemnly. "It's an honor."

Hana squeals quietly. "Oh my gosh—it's ECHO! He's the hottest up-and-coming artist in the world! Billionaires literally fight over him! The Rockefellers offered him their summer château just to attend their anniversary, and the Sultan of Brunei sent his private jet filled with rare ghost orchids, hoping to have him perform at his granddaughter's sweet sixteen!"

Oh fuck.

This is the nutjob from the art show at Bryce's mother's house. The guy who stripped down to his skivvies and had rainbow paint poured over him like a human sundae.

Echo's gaze sweeps across the banquet area, making intense eye contact with each guest. "Lovers of beauty with elevated taste, I am humbled to reveal my purpose at this most exquisite gathering!"

He lifts his bejeweled hands toward the ceiling, and light dances off his rings matching the sparkle in his smile. His grin is wide and full of creative glee as he commands the room like a maestro.

"For the next glorious week, I shall be creating a SPECIAL COLLECTION inspired by the transcendent union of Fiona and Gavin! A collection that captures the very essence of their love story—LIGHT and DARKNESS! LOVE and CHAOS! The duality of souls merging into one magnificent entity!"

The room bursts into wildly unearned applause. *Fucking rich people.*

Fiona stands. "We're also thrilled to announce that following our ceremony, there will be a special art charity auction featuring Echo's new collection! All proceeds will benefit homeless seagulls in Venice Beach, ensuring they receive fresh caviar daily!"

She turns to my brother. "Darling, do you like my surprise?"

"It's incredible. You never cease to amaze me." he says, pulling her into a kiss.

"Isn't that just *so* Fiona?" Hana whispers. "Always thinking of those less fortunate. Especially the ones with feathers. Did you know that Fiona basically discovered Echo? She has an eye for talent."

Ugh. I was wrong. God, even saying that makes my soul itch.

But something still feels off. This guy gives me major slimeball vibes. If I were bartending and he walked in, I'd peg him as the douchebag who orders complicated cocktails, hits on everything that moves, and leaves his number instead of a tip.

"SILENCE!" Echo suddenly cries out. "The muse strikes—I must listen!"

He sways as if he's channeling a ghost from the Renaissance.

"There's an energy here," he whispers. "Raw and ripe with contradiction. Someone in this room and I were *passionate* lovers in a past life. I *sense* it."

"This is exciting!" Hana squeezes my arm. "His last muse was a Monegasque princess! The paintings he created of her are now worth millions!"

Echo prowls around the table, extending fingers as if feeling invisible currents in the air. "She burns like a fever!" he declares. "She defies gravity with her spirit! She carries divinity and decay in equal measure!"

He takes hold of my chair.

Please, fuck no.

"Her."

He drops to one knee and kisses my hand—he *clings* to it. Lips pressed, lingering as if he's trying to draw inspiration through osmosis.

"You are my muse. Fire and frenzy. Sex and envy. Hunger and absolution!"

The room gasps before applauding again. Hana is hyperventilating with excitement.

I look to Bryce, hoping for a lifeline. But all I get is buttoned-up rage.

His eyes—those impossibly blue eyes that had teased and tormented me all evening—turn to arctic ice. His jaw flexes hard, the muscle in his cheek ticking with restrained fury. Tension radiates off him in waves—dark, coiled, and aimed solely at me.

He's mad... at *me*?

Why? I didn't ask to be Echo's muse.

And *Bryce* is the cheating asshole who's practically engaged. What the hell gives him the right to be angry?

I thought I understood Bryce Sterling—beneath all that wealth and family legacy. I thought he was better than this world of smoke and mirrors. But this man, whom I've measured against all others, is nothing but a beautiful lie.

CHAPTER NINE

BRYCE

I won't jerk off to my best friend's little sister... again.

Hot water pelts the back of my neck like liquid bullets, steam curling up around the marble shower, heavy with judgment. I brace both hands against the slick tile and stare down at my traitorous cock, fully alert, completely unbothered by the moral implications of its current state.

Droplets bounce off my sensitive tip, sinful, provocative taunts running down my length. My hand hovers—hesitating. Threatening. A tremor of restraint coils through my gut.

This is absurd.

I am a grown man. A man with responsibilities and self-discipline. I will not enter into negotiations with my own rock-hard dick about Petra Brinkman.

Technically, this is the third time I've given myself this lecture.

The first instance was last night, after that trainwreck of a dinner. After the... audible foreplay? I stripped out of my tux, still smelling her on my hands—jasmine and sin. The lingering presence of her thigh under my palm. Her fingers—*God, her fingers*—landing on my erection. The challenge in her eyes as she whispered, *"And what do I get if I do gag?"*

I came in record time, biting my fist like a goddamn teenager.

And then at 3:12 a.m., I jolted awake from a dream so vivid, I could almost feel the ghost of her weight on top of me. Hear her throaty voice in my ear. My hand was already gripping my cock, stroking. Urgent. Instinctive.

This isn't me. I've spent twenty-nine years building a life defined by discipline and restraint.

And yet here I am, starting my morning as if I'm some unhinged pervert in a luxury rain shower, contemplating round three like it's medically necessary to keep me from losing my shit.

This would make it an unholy trinity in under twelve hours. A personal record I'm not proud of.

I don't indulge. I don't fixate. I don't *obsess*.

Except… it's Petra.

My brain's been rewired. Every thought loops back to her. The way she leaned into my touch as I fastened her dress. The way her body trembled when my knuckles skimmed her spine. Ink painted over her curves, begging to be explored.

God, her tattoos.

I can't stop thinking about the wildflowers etched across her shoulder blade. When my fingers traced their outline, she shivered. And that broken heart behind her ear—so small it was nearly missed—until my thumb brushed it and she went rigid.

There's history inked on that skin. A warning label—and an invitation.

Who broke Pip's heart badly enough that she needed to immortalize it? The thought stirs something possessive and primal in me.

I'd love to peel that pink dress off her body, exposing each hidden tattoo one by one. I'd start at her neck, pressing my lips to her pulse point, feeling it race beneath my mouth as I worked my way down. Would she be soft or sharp with me? Would those clever retorts dissolve into sighs if I used my teeth on the sensitive skin below her ear?

My hand wraps around my cock before I even realize it.

"Fuck."

I stroke once, slow. Then again. My hips twitch forward, my eyes slam shut, and a guttural sound escapes my throat. Shame flickers. Followed immediately by a vivid mental reel of Petra straddling my lap, lips parted, pupils blown wide as she dares me to ruin her.

I've never acted this way. Not with any woman. Certainly not Amanda. In five years, I never once felt this consuming, desperate hunger. Sex with her was *routine*. A scheduled appointment. An emotional *ceasefire*. Always efficient. Always polite.

This—this obsession with Petra—is something else. It's ravenous and unhinged and frightens me even as I chase it.

What is it about Pip that dismantles me? Is it because she's forbidden fruit? Because she's Gavin's little sister? Is it her rebellion? Or is it simpler than that?

She's real in a way no one in my world has ever been.

Or perhaps it's because she called me *missionary* and *boring*, making me want to pin her to a wall and *prove* her wrong?

My hand moves faster now, my breathing ragged.

I told her: *"We'll have to spend the night exploring what else you enjoy choking on."*

Christ.

Who the fuck was that man? Not Bryce Sterling, heir to a financial empire.

I've never uttered words like that to any woman.

Amanda would have fainted dead if I had suggested such a thing. Our bedroom talk consisted primarily of "Is this satisfactory?" and "Be sure to let me know when you're approaching completion."

But with Petra? Some dormant beast clawed its way to the surface the moment she challenged me, awakening desires I wasn't aware I had. Urges that involve holding those small wrists above her head while I make her beg.

With her, it doesn't feel dangerous to be known. Like peeling back my layers wouldn't scare her off.

My cock strains against my palm, the head swollen and sensitive, pre-cum mixing with water as I stroke from base to tip with increasing need.

The fantasy takes hold again, darker this time. My strokes turn rougher, faster. My hips jerk forward. I'm chasing it now—chasing her.

Would she want it this way?

Fast. Dirty. Rough.

Would she taunt me? Push me to go harder?

Beg me not to stop?

"Petra..." Her name escapes on a ragged exhale.

What would she say if she saw me like this? The great Bryce Sterling, reduced to jacking off in the shower? Would those red lips curl in her knowing smirk? Would she let out her smoky laugh that makes my cock twitch?

Or would she press that spectacular body against mine, rise up on her toes, and whisper, "Need some help with that, Moneybags?"

I'd have an aneurysm and die smiling. But last night, the mood snapped like a rubber band. I still don't understand what happened.

Did I go too far?

Was it the ring?

Echo?

The moment he declared her his "muse," her expression shifted. One second she was teasing me, pushing me, daring me to cross the line, and the next, she was ice.

No smile. No jokes. No comebacks.

She didn't say another word to me the rest of the night.

I wanted to go to her room. Ask. Demand. Hell, *plead* for an explanation.

But I didn't.

"Goddamn it," I growl.

I lean my face against my forearm on the shower wall, my jaw locked with the sort of guilt that never washes off.

I chose a million-dollar ruby to match the shade of her lips. Of course she refused to wear the damn ring.

What the hell was I thinking? Petra hates flashy wealth. I should've known she'd see it as an attempt to dress her up like some Sterling-approved showpiece. Or worse—she was afraid of the responsibility, worried she'd lose something so valuable.

Regardless, I backed her into a corner with my expectations. And once again, she defied them.

Her name pulses through me with each punishing stroke. *Petra. Petra. Petra.*

I can almost feel her in here with me—pressed between my overheated body and the cool marble wall, water plastering that wild black hair to her skin, red lips parted on gasps bouncing off the tiles.

One of my hands would be in her strands, angling her head back to expose the pale column of her throat. The other gripping her hip as my fingers dug in hard enough to leave marks. I'd say her name with every thrust then demand she say mine in return.

"Say it, Pip. Say my name."

"Make me, Moneybags," she'd say, gasping and fighting her growing arousal.

My muscles coil tight as I near release. I imagine those plump, red, dick-sucking lips. God, I crave that mouth—around me, on me, *owning* me. I want to be fucking her mouth with the kind of hedonistic pleasure I've spent my entire life denying. And when her rebellious hazel eyes stare up at me through dark lashes, it's game over.

My orgasm slams through me—no warning this time. Just *detonation.*

Rope after rope of come sprays against imported marble before being washed away by the water, evidence of my weakness disappearing down the drain.

"Jesus fucking Christ," I gasp, chest heaving like I've run a marathon, my cock still pulsing in my grip.

I have no idea how many more releases I'll need today. Five? Ten? Before I finish drying off?

Because this?

It's the only choice I have.

I *have* to keep my distance.

***

I haven't seen Petra all day. Not that I've been looking for her.

Okay, fine. I have.

The tearoom. The gardens. The waiting area outside the massage cabana. I engineered three unnecessary trips past her suite, lingered in hallways with no purpose, and subjected myself to a fifteen-minute conversation with Hana Choi about the "transformative power of jade face rollers"—all in hopes she'd seen Petra earlier.

Still no sign of her.

Now I'm seated with Gavin for our lunch meeting at Casa Cashmere's poolside outdoor pavilion, barely tasting the exquisite meal in front of me because I'm busy monitoring the perimeter like a Secret Service agent watching for threats. Or in this case, a 5'9" woman with a smart mouth and black eyeliner.

The pavilion exudes tropical luxury. A thatched palapa roof soars overhead, supported by bamboo columns wrapped in fairy lights. The teak floor shines. White curtains flutter, showcasing twin infinity pools that disappear into the Pacific. The jungle provides a lush, private setting.

Despite the midday Mexican heat, we're both in suits. I was raised that Sterling men don't "dress down," even when the humidity makes it feel like we're wearing portable saunas. My navy Tom Ford clings to my back, while Gavin's charcoal Armani stays impeccable. The man could walk through a hurricane and be runway ready.

Hidden fans and a top-notch cooling system keep the air pleasant and scented with plumeria. Three motionless servers in matching white uniforms blend into the décor so well, they're barely visible. One materializes to refill my water glass the instant I glance at it, then swiftly disappears.

"What do you think about the stockholders' first quarter projections?" Gavin asks.

"What?"

"I asked what you think." His tone's tight. Buttoned. "Which you would know if you'd listened to a single word I've said since we sat down."

"I apologize," I say, straightening my already straight tie. "I've been… distracted."

"No shit." Gavin's eyes narrow with laser precision, his expression shifting into what his competitors call the "Brinkman Bullshit Detector." "You've been off since we got to Mexico. What's going on? And don't tell me it's nothing, because I'm not leaving this table until I drag it out of you."

This is Gavin's superpower: weaponized silence. He simply sits there, sharp hazel-green eyes locked on you—until your nerves snap and the truth spills out. Same eyes as Petra. Same ruthless tenacity.

Tell him the truth. In a matter of days, I'm leaving the company.

"Amanda moved out," I say instead.

Gavin's eyebrows shoot up. "As in, you're over?"

I nod.

"When did this happen?"

"While I was in New York. I came home to an empty closet and a note."

"And you're just now telling me this?"

"It's not exactly cocktail party conversation," I explain, keeping my voice level. "She wanted a ring. I wasn't prepared to give her one."

"Let me get this straight. The woman who sat through sixteen hours of your mother's Christmas gala planning, who learned golf just to join your father's corporate tournaments, who basically ran your entire life for you... asked for a commitment—and you balked?"

When he puts it that way, I sound like a heartless cad. But he doesn't understand how empty the relationship was, how it was built on mutual benefit rather than any genuine connection.

"That's essentially correct."

"Fucking hell, Bryce." Gavin shakes his head. "No wonder you've been walking around like you swallowed a lemon. Does Sterling Senior know yet?"

"Not yet, no."

"Well, that'll be a fun conversation. 'Sorry, Father, I've failed to fulfill item six on the Sterling heir checklist: acquire suitable breeding partner.'" His imitation of my voice is eerily accurate.

The mention of my dad sends a wave of discomfort through me. This is my chance. Time to rip off the Band-Aid. *Tell him about Sterling Industries now, you coward. Just get it over with.*

"Listen, I'm here for you." he says, softening his voice. "I mean it. If you need anything, consider it done."

I nod, throat tight. "Appreciate it. But you've got your hands full with the wedding. And I have Pip to keep me company."

Gavin exhales, running a hand over his jaw. "I'm starting to worry that all this luxury and seeing the wealth gap firsthand is backfiring. The last thing I need is for her to rebel again, skip out on college, and decide slinging drinks in a dive bar is the life she actually wants."

Something protective flares inside me. "She is making an effort to support you. I wouldn't write her off quite yet."

"Since when are you on *Team Petra?*" Gavin asks. "Yesterday, you looked ready to strangle her for picking up Miss Muffy."

"I'm not siding with Petra. I'm simply stating that being here can't be easy for her."

"I love my sister, but she's got to finish that art degree, no matter how ridiculous it is. After that, I'll make sure she gets an MBA and a real job. We can't have her ending up like that pretentious artist, Echo. What kind of name is Echo, anyway?"

"An absurd one," I agree, grateful for the subject change. "That entire spectacle last night was preposterous."

"Total bullshit. And if being his *muse* means laying a finger on my sister, there's gonna be a problem," he says. "But Fiona thinks it's highbrow, so... she wants a Jackson Pollock burlesque show, she gets it. That's the deal with marriage, right? Compromise."

"That's what I've heard," I reply dryly. "I wouldn't worry about Petra. That girl's a fighter. She'll finish school and make you proud."

"Let's hope she doesn't throw any real punches this week. Fiona's been on edge about having her here. She's convinced she'll sabotage the wedding on purpose."

"Petra would never. You know that." The defense comes out more forcefully than I intended.

Gavin studies me for a moment. "Yeah, you're right. She'd walk through fire for family. Even if she's the one who lit the match."

BUZZ! BUZZ!

Gavin's phone lights up on the table.

"It's Fiona. She's set us up for a *Vogue* feature interview." He sighs. "Maybe one day my headline won't be 'Poor kid from Beverly Hills makes it big.' It'll be about the work I do. The company. The damn vision instead of the 'rags-to-riches' angle they're all so fucking obsessed with."

As he stands to leave, his expression falters, certainty slipping to reveal a glimpse of something I rarely see: vulnerability.

"I'm not the superstitious type. You know that."

"Of course."

"But I've got this feeling. A bad one."

Does he suspect the truth? Did my father already tell him?

"About the IPO," he continues. "I don't know. Something doesn't feel right. Maybe we're rushing it? Maybe there's a blind spot? The market's unstable or the valuation's bloated? You've told me horror stories—your dad spending more time calming shareholders than running the business."

That lands hard.

Gavin has forever been the visionary, the one with unwavering faith in our mission. To see him in doubt now, when I'm about to pull the rug out from under him, makes me feel like the worst kind of traitor.

"There's always a cost when a company goes public," I say carefully, "but any failure won't be due to our lack of preparedness." I force a smile. "Besides, you're aiming for equal footing, right? Once we go public, I won't be the only billionaire."

"It's hard to believe," he admits. "I... I don't want this change to take away from our customers. The second we prioritize shareholders over users, we're another soulless finance app."

Pride swells in my chest, quickly followed by crushing guilt. This isn't only about me abandoning our company—I'm leaving behind the best part of myself. The version of me that believed in something beyond money for money's sake.

Gavin is more than a friend. He's my conscience. My moral compass. He reminds me daily that wealth means nothing if it isn't used to help others. Sterling Industries may have my name etched into its marble entrance, but my family's company will never have Gavin's passion, his fire, his absolute conviction that financial security should be a right, not a privilege.

BUZZ! BUZZ! BUZZ!

"Duty calls." He steps away, then pauses. "And hey—thanks again for staying glued to Petra. I understand she's... a handful. But there's nobody I trust more."

I nod, unable to speak past the knot of self-loathing lodged in my throat.

He walks off, totally unaware he just split me open.

Which betrayal is worse? The cowardice that keeps me from telling my best friend I'm disowning everything we built together?

Or my burning desire to cross a line with his sister?

***

My balls are sweating. And I don't mean metaphorically. This is full-on, ball soup sweltering.

Moisture trickles down my spine, collecting in the waistband of my boxers. My white dress shirt has gone transparent, plastered against my chest like shrink wrap. Every step releases another droplet down my temple.

"Good God. I'm being slow-roasted in Italian wool," I mutter, yanking at my tie.

I should go back to my room. Shower, change, and lie to myself about having self-control before, once again, finding relief with my hand and visions of Petra.

Instead, I keep walking.

Because after the conversation I had with Gavin—where he told me he trusted me *like family*—I need space. Room to breathe. Somewhere quiet to pull myself together and pretend I'm not mentally undressing his sister every five goddamn minutes.

I venture deeper into the jungle, following the dirt path that's shaded by a canopy of tangled vines and swaying palms. Every few steps, I pass a leaf the size of a Prius. The rainforest is humming—a cacophony of unseen creatures, rustling leaves, and distant water. The scent of damp earth hangs thick in the air.

Mosquitos buzz in a halo above my head as though I'm some kind of overpriced blood smoothie. My Italian loafers crunch over gravel and roots, and then I spot it—a wooden sign half-strangled by creeping vines and dense foliage: "Bird Watching Observatory."

Relief washes over me. I remember this place from my childhood. Glass-walled, blissfully cold, and most importantly... vacant. The rich don't come to Mexico to look at birds unless those birds are made of gold or willing to carry a tray of cocktails.

I round the corner ascending the small incline to the observatory—and stop.

She's here.

Behind the pristine wraparound glass, Petra sits.

Perched cross-legged on a sleek bench, dressed like she's heading into a corporate takeover, not a jungle trek. A pastel-blue Chanel skirt rides high on her thighs, paired with a boxy tweed jacket. Those damn sleeves hide the tattoos my tongue can't stop fantasizing about.

I'm halfway to the door when I notice her holding binoculars—not aimed at the tropical birds fluttering through the canopy, but down at the trail below.

Curiosity flares. I follow her line of sight.

Oh, for fuck's sake.

Echo.

Today's outfit is a paisley fever dream. His pants are so wide and flowy, I genuinely can't tell if he's wearing two colorful hammocks tied at the waist. A mesh tank top clings to his wiry frame like cobwebs revealing nipple piercings that nobody asked to see. Beaded necklaces jangle as he moves, and topping it off? A goddamn beanie.

And sweet mother of—*is he licking a tree?*

Not a symbolic lick. No. This man is giving bark a full-on, open-mouthed, tongue-on-the-grain lick.

And now he's... ugh.

He's *grinding* on it.

Sweet hell, he's giving the tree a lap dance.

"My artistic loins ignite with your ancient vibrations!" he proclaims.

What does Petra see in this cliché performance art disaster? The thought sends an uncomfortable jolt through my system. *Is this her type?* Theatrical, boundaryless, and clinically delusional?

He throws his head back and releases a howl that resembles a wounded coyote mating with a kazoo.

What a tool.

That's the thing about the one percent. They don't *want* to be told what's good. They prefer to hear about what's expensive. What's *scarce*. What's *coveted*. So they can scramble after it, bid on it, then flaunt that they got it first.

Echo. What a name. Who dreams up a pompous jackass name like that anyway? I bet his driver's license says "Brandon" or "Kyle."

I dab my forehead with my pocket square, which is pulling double duty as a sponge.

He suddenly springs away, sketchbook in hand. "I hear you! I must follow her siren song into nature's throbbing core!"

Petra doesn't waste a second. She slips out the opposite door of the observatory, her Chanel-clad figure disappearing into the emerald maze with surprising speed for someone wearing four-inch heels.

Decision time.

I push through the entrance, and—holy merciful air conditioning. The climate-controlled sanctuary envelops me in its refrigerated embrace. Goosebumps erupt across my overheated skin as the sweat cools on my body.

But Petra is getting away.

With physical pain, I burst through the far door, plunging back into nature's sauna. The humidity hits like a wet mattress to the face.

The path slopes downward, narrowing between towering ferns and hanging vines. I catch glimpses of Petra's blue outfit ahead.

"Unleash your root chakra! Let the trees enter your spirit hole!"

I have no idea what that means, and I'm sure I'll be angrier once I figure it out.

I shift my weight, trying to find footing on the uneven slope, when I step on a branch shaped like a damn baguette.

CRACK!

The sound echoes (*FYI, that's how you properly use the word, you self-absorbed hack)* as if I fired a weapon. Birds scatter.

Petra stops. Whips around.

Shit.

I raise my hands in surrender. "I can explain."

She stomps right up to me, poking me in the chest. "Are you stalking me? This is harassment! I know my rights!"

Echo moans somewhere up ahead. "Nature is *wet* with revelation! She offers herself to us, moist and pulsating with ancient longing!"

Her mouth opens, closes, then opens again. "Whatever. I don't have time for this."

She spins on her heel and plunges off the path deeper into the wild. Without hesitation, I pursue her into the green chaos. I dodge one branch, then another. My blazer sleeve snags on a thorny, overachieving plant. There's sweat pooling in my shoes… *Inside them.* I trudge onward as my designer loafers squish with every step.

"So… this is your type? Guys who hump tree trunks and yell about chlorophyll?"

"You just can't leave me alone, can you?" she teases. "No need for jealousy, Moneybags. I do not find Echo and his woodland orgy charming. My gut is telling me he and Fiona have a secret. I'm guessing *affair*."

"I know you aren't exactly a Fiona fan—"

"Understatement of the decade."

"Do you really think she'd do something to hurt Gavin?"

Petra stops so abruptly, I nearly crash into her. She turns, eyes blazing. "Abso-fucking-lutely."

She drops into a crouch behind a massive fern and yanks me down with surprising strength. A cloud of tiny insects scatter into the air as my knees connect with the jungle floor. I groan as I slam my arm down to avoid faceplanting into the mud.

"Shh," she hisses, raising the binoculars. "If you're going to spy with me, Moneybags, be quiet."

I don't respond because my brain is melting—*literally melting*—inside my skull. If Satan opened a sauna in the ninth circle of hell, it would be ten degrees cooler than this Mexican jungle.

Why does Petra have two heads?

I blink hard, trying to clear my vision, but that simply redirects rivers of sweat directly into my eyeballs.

Through the salty sting, I see Echo—or what I'm increasingly convinced is a heat-induced hallucination—standing in a clearing ahead.

"I must release my artistic spirit from these fabric prisons!" he bellows.

Then he growls and rips open his mesh shirt. He quickly shimmies out of his pants and is now fully nude—twirling in the mud like a twerking caterpillar.

He flops to the ground. Rolls. Stretches his arms wide.

"The earth accepts me as its lover," he moans, thrusting his hips against the ground. "I become blank canvas. I become vessel. I become—"

"AHHH! MOTHERFUCKER! MY BALLS!" He leaps to his feet, slapping wildly at his groin. "FUCKING ANTS! THEY'RE BITING MY DICK!"

I slap a hand to my mouth to keep from snorting.

Echo takes off sprinting down the path toward the house, bare buttocks clenched in terror, abandoning his clothes and sketchpad.

"Jackpot," Petra says, eyes lighting up. "If there's anything shady between him and Fiona, it's going to be in that notebook."

She scrambles down to the path where Echo's belongings lay scattered. I make an effort to follow, but my whole body is moving in slow motion. My vision fractures into a kaleidoscope—one Petra becomes three, then six, before merging back into a single figure as she snatches up the abandoned sketchbook.

"Got it!" she announces, waving it triumphantly. "Let's peek inside the twisted mind of a tree-humper."

The ground feels unstable. Wobbly. Like it's breathing.

And then the jungle starts to blur at the edges.

My knees buckle.

Everything.

Goes.

BLACK...

...

...

... somewhere above me, a voice.

There's wind. Blessed wind. Where's it coming from? Heaven?

Am I dead?

Is this what the afterlife feels like? Sweaty, confusing, and vaguely arousing?

My eyes flicker open, but things are fuzzy.

Light. Leaves. Boobs.

There's a face. Hovering. Lips. Red, shiny, moving. Loud. *Definitely loud.*

Petra.

On top of me.

Breathless. Frantic. Shouting.

Oh.

OHHHH.

Is this sex? Are we having jungle sex?

It has to be. I'm flat on my back. She's straddling my thighs—yelling my name. She's sweating. I'm sweating. And there's jiggling.

"Bryce?! Bryce—oh God, oh God, stay with me!"

Yup. Definitely sex.

Focus, Sterling. Jungle sex requires active participation.

I attempt to form words. What emerges is: "Flubbity gubwah sexyboobs?"

Nailed it.

"FUCK. Fuck fuck FUCK!" she shouts, red-faced and desperate.

Yup. She's into it.

I want to taste her.

No—I *need* to taste her.

Now. Take control. Show her Bryce Sterling understands how to please a woman.

I lift my arm—barely functional—grip her waist, and pull.

"What the—!"

She pitches forward, and the moment her chest hits mine...

I kiss her.

Hard. Messy. Greedy.

I kiss her like it's a command, a question, and an apology all at once. Her mouth opens. She makes a noise—something in the back of her throat that's half gasp, half *don't stop.*

Then her lips move. She kisses me back. Her fingers grab my shirt. Her body sways.

Ohhh yes.

My hands slide down, over her curves, guiding her to where I need her most. My hips thrust upward, grinding against her core.

She moans into my mouth.

I do it again.

If this is my last act on earth, I will die doing whatever it takes to make Petra Brinkman come in the jungle.

The kiss goes molten. Then—

SLAP.

Pain detonates across my cheek.

"What the fuck, Bryce?!" she yells, scrambling off me.

I blink. "Did you orgasm?"

She looks like she might slap me again. And enjoy it.

I think I might enjoy it too.

My brain struggles to catch up. Not sex? Not sex. *But she was... and I was... and we were...*

"You were straddling me," I explain, as if this clarifies everything.

"To SAVE you, not SEDUCE you!"

"But you were shouting my name."

"Because you. Were. Unconscious! I can't believe you kissed me!"

Oh.

Well.

This is awkward.

"Listen up, overdressed billionaire. Either drink this or die dramatically. Your call."

I weakly raise a finger. "Water, please."

She huffs, leans down, and unscrews her travel bottle, shoving it at me like hydration is a personal insult. I drink it down in three gulps.

"In my defense, your mouth was making very sexy emergency noises."

Her eyes narrow. "Don't move. I'm going for help. And don't kiss anything while I'm gone."

Easy for her to say. She gets to strut off, while I'm left whispering sweet nothings to my overly enthusiastic erection and still convinced she moaned into my mouth on purpose.

That kiss lit a fuse I can't put out. But unless I want to blow up everything with Gavin... I need to find a damn fire extinguisher.

CHAPTER TEN

PETRA

Group Chat: CPK Forever

Me: *Quick poll: Does it still count as cheating if the guy kissing you was hallucinating from heatstroke?*

Cam: *Let me guess. Mr. tall, blond, and financially irresponsible with his mouth?*

Katie: *WHAT?! Bryce kissed you?*

Cam: *Did his girlfriend fall into a convenient coma or…?*

Me: *I SAVED HIS LIFE, and this is how he repays me—by making me an accessory to infidelity.*

Katie: *Was it hot?*

Me: *Fucking incredible.*

Cam: *Hmm. Maybe what happens in the jungle stays in the jungle?*

Yacht Day Ensemble *(Dolce & Gabbana Maritime Collection)*

To Miss Brinkman, my reluctant protege,

Today, you embark on a nautical journey. The black plunging one-piece features dramatic white bow—DO NOT untie it unless you fancy yourself as the ship's entertainment. The midnight sheer cover-up and wide-leg trousers will flutter elegantly in the ocean breeze, assuming you don't get tangled and fall overboard. Your accessories include 1) a sun hat large enough to eclipse the moon and 2) sunglasses that would make Jackie Kennedy's ghost jealous. Don't remove the hat. It is doing most of the work to distract from your personality.

—With dwindling faith, Sebastian Bellini, Fashion Emergency Responder

"Yacht day," I mutter, staring at my reflection. "I look like a widow who poisoned her husband with a martini and then cried at the funeral to throw people off the scent."

I adjust the bow again. It somehow grew twenty percent in the last sixty seconds.

Is it too much to ask for an easy breezy afternoon of margaritas on the beach? No yachts. No billionaires. No tiny swan-shaped sandwiches.

I sigh and reach for my phone, scrolling through old photos until I find it—the pic of Katie, Cam, and me, sunburned and grinning beneath a plastic Corona umbrella.

It was spring break, sophomore year. We scraped together enough cash for a cheap motel in Cabo. Katie spent the week finding *(and scheduling)* free excursions, while Cam filmed literally everything, determined to document our "epic poor girl" adventure.

On our last night, we spotted a massive yacht anchored offshore. Young, drunk, and spectacularly stupid, we decided to crash the party. We didn't get far—security stopped us before we even touched the gangplank. So, we ended up on the beach passing around a bottle of cheap tequila and declaring it the best vacation of our lives. And honestly? *It was.*

I'd give anything to have them here—Katie and Cam, laughing beside me *(*and probably *at* me in this getup*)*. But no, they're off on their own summer adventures, and I'm stewing in my latest judgment fail.

The kiss.

It wasn't a maybe-kiss. Not an oops-our-faces-brushed moment.

Our mouths moved as if they understood the choreography by heart. His lips were strong but gentle—ravenous and eager, like he'd been imagining how I would taste. And when he rocked up into me, his thick erection pressing against my clit, well... my body responded without permission.

For those few seconds, I forgot everything. We were all that existed. Only the sensation of him. The feel of his hands on my skin. The way he was moving against me. *God, it was hot.* But then my brain kicked in and reminded me that I'm nobody's side piece.

I give myself another look, the bow now slumped at an angle like a disapproving head tilt.

How could I have been so stupid? Bryce is with Amanda—his almost-fiancée.

I've spent years telling myself he was different. That under all that money and privilege, he was a good man. Not the type of guy who screws around in secret, then marries the pretty princess with the family seal of approval.

What a fucking joke.

How many times did I tell myself? Rich men don't fall in love with my type. They use us.

Flirt. Fuck. Discard.

We're a cheap thrill, something fun to play with. They get bored and move on. The same way dear old dad left my mother.

Bryce crossed a line by kissing me. I should be devastated. But honestly, he deserves a thank-you card. It'll be so much easier to get over him now that I know he's a fraud.

Time for a distraction. I grab Echo's sketchpad from my bag. Might as well review the contents of that lunatic's mind before I climb onto a ship filled with people who think dogs deserve inheritances. Maybe there's something in here that proves my suspicions about him conspiring with Fiona. I need a mystery to solve that doesn't involve my talent for falling for unavailable, out-of-my-league men.

I flip it open. The first few pages? Food. Sketches of tiny sandwiches. So many sandwiches. Cracker stacks. Crostini. An entire page of what seems to be a club sandwich dissected and labeled as if it were an anatomy diagram.

"So Mr. Tree-Humper has opinions about fancy snacks. Disturbing—but nowhere near scandal material."

Then it gets weirder.

MARVIN.

Scribbled.

Everywhere.

Manic handwriting, resembling a ransom note made by someone who's been left on read too long—big letters, small letters, cursive, print.

"What in the true crime podcast is this?"

More pages. Same name. Over and over. MARVIN MARVIN MARVIN—scribbled like a spell, a plea, a breakdown in ink. Scrawled across every inch of white space until the paper is practically bleeding.

Then portraits of an older gentleman.

Balding. Slouching. Always drawn from weird angles. Close-ups of liver spots. Nose hair. Ear hair. Wrinkles.

And scattered around each sketch, two words are drawn in angry capital letters: GROSS and MAN.

I study the images, trying to decode this bizarre obsession.

Gross. Man. Marvin.

Who the hell is Marvin?

No idea.

Maybe he's a vision Echo had after licking too many trees? Or perhaps he's part of a love triangle with Fiona and some GILF sugar daddy? Could be a metaphor for how repulsed he is by the aging process?

None of it adds up, but then again, welcome to my week.

KNOCK KNOCK!

So much for my subpar detective skills. I open the door to find three Casa Cashmere staffers standing outside.

"Apologies, Miss Brinkman," a worker says. "We didn't realize you were occupying the room. We try to go unnoticed during guest transitions."

"You're good," I say, letting them inside. "And heads up—I'm not one of the trust fund babies. I'm team paycheck-to-paycheck, like you."

I wave Sebastian's instruction card as if it's a white flag. "Need evidence? They literally write step-by-step directions for how I should dress myself. Like they're afraid I might accidentally wear my underwear as a hat."

The youngest guy—probably my age—fights down a grin.

I haul my ancient suitcase from behind a decorative chair. "This duct-taped Frankenbag is the real me. Can you get it to the floating mansion?"

"Of course, miss."

"But don't let that beauty out of your sight. If this whole thing goes sideways, I'm gonna need it to paddle my broke ass home to reality," I add with a wink.

The young guy smirks. "We'll be sure it is accessible for any escape plans."

Ten minutes and one half-assed sunscreen application later, I'm being chauffeured in a luxury golf cart down the long wooden dock.

And then—there it is.

The superyacht.

That word feels criminally inadequate.

This isn't a boat. It's a floating skyscraper that chose to take a swim. The gleaming white hull rises from the water and stretches longer than a city block. Multiple decks stack up toward the sky, crowned with a helipad at the stern.

I head up the gangplank, and the front deck opens into a stunning view of whitewashed wood, striped cushions, and umbrella-shaded seating that's begging me to spill tequila on it. Staff members discreetly slip across the decks in matching white and navy uniforms with nautical gold accents.

And waiting there is Hana—all sparkle and bubbles, like a pitcher of sangria in heels.

"Petra! Oh wow! You look like Audrey Hepburn, but if she traded her tiara for tattoos. Who knew elegance could be so edgy? I love it."

I scan her ensemble, wanting to return the compliment. She's wearing a ruffled rose-colored bikini top with a matching high-waisted skirt. "Pink is definitely your color! Very Barbie heiress on spring break."

"Oh stop, you're making me blush! That is *exactly* what I was going for!"

Hana loops her arm through mine. I let her. Mostly because she smells like vanilla bean and joy.

"Yacht excursions are the best! Well, except for charity luncheons and private shopping appointments, but it's totally in my top three! What's your favorite part of yacht trips?"

"This is my first one."

She gasps. Her hand covers her heart. "That is the saddest sentence I've ever heard. And I follow Fiona's foundation newsletters. Last month, they featured this pet psychic who helps animals relive their past lives. You won't believe it, but Judith Sterling-Holloway's parrot was Shakespeare. That's why he was always squawking sonnets at three a.m. but needed a translator. I had my fiancé donate half a million dollars."

I grab a fruit-flavored water from a server and choose not to acknowledge that bat-shit crazy nonsense.

Why do Fiona's charities all sound like rejected TLC reality shows?

I try to choke down the usual bitterness about the one percent throwing money at vanity projects instead of causes that actually ease human suffering. It's hard, because people like my friend Jim, a veteran sleeping on the street, don't fit Fiona's aesthetic.

"Her most recent cause offers higher education for socialites' canines," Hana continues. "Pets can enroll in courses like Barkonomics, Paw-litical Science, and Canine Culinary Arts—all inspired by Miss Muffy Von Cashmere the Second. Isn't that neat?"

Because the universe needs more dogs with degrees and fewer hands-on solutions to real-world problems.

Other guests trickle onto the deck, and my eyes do an automatic sweep. I'm scanning for Bryce without meaning to. It's muscle memory—like checking your mirrors while driving or looking both ways before jaywalking.

Gavin appears with Fiona welded to his arm, and they're giving off "You Too Can Be Effortlessly Wealthy" seminar vibes. My brother's rocking a crisp, ivory linen suit. He's handsome, charming, and confident as hell.

Fiona beams beside him, her cream-colored crochet bikini top complemented by a matching jacket and a form-fitting maxi skirt. Her accessories are minimal but flawless—thin gold chains and delicate hoop earrings that glint beautifully in the sunlight.

Still no sign of Bryce. I'm imagining him overheating on the dock in his wool suit, having absorbed zero lessons from yesterday's jungle heatstroke disaster.

"Hana! Darling!" Fiona glides with the grace of a swan.

"Oh my gosh! You're a real-life sea goddess!" Hana squeals. "And such a trendsetter dressed in vintage. That gorgeous piece is from last season, isn't it? You look so effortlessly fabulous!"

"How sweet of you to say," Fiona purrs. "I thought re-wearing something understated would be appropriate for our little nautical adventure. I didn't want to outshine the ocean."

"And Gavin," Hana coos. "Your outfit is so distinguished, but also casual, but then daring at the same time! On my fiancé's yacht, he wears this old captain's hat, and with his white beard, he looks like a Civil War fisherman. But Mother says I can't leave him in the sun too long, or he'll shed his skin from head to toe—like a molting snake!"

There's a mental image.

Hana may toss compliments like confetti, but they seem genuine. Is she a little clueless? Sure. Brainwashed by her controlling parents? Maybe. But she's growing on me, and she's my best bet to getting dirt on Fiona.

So today, Petra Brinkman plays... the heiress bestie.

"Hana's totally right," I say. "You two are like a yacht magazine cover story."

"Makes sense," Gavin replies. "We had our first date on a yacht."

Hana squeals. "My fiancé and I had our first date on his yacht too! We started our prenup paperwork right there over dinner! Well, it was split pea soup. My fiancée purees most of his meals. His doctor says anything chunkier might 'overwhelm his aging jaw muscles.'"

I hide my laugh *(this poor girl)*. "That's... sweet. What about you, Fiona? Any cute prenup signing stories? Did you and Gavin celebrate with champagne after dotting all the i's of who will get the private island?"

Fiona's eyes narrow and her lips flatten, as if I just dropped a threat. *What the fuck?*

Hana giggles. "Oh my gosh, yes! Marriage starts and ends with paperwork. We were just talking about that, weren't we, Fiona? My prenup includes a 'no discussing his ex-wives' clause. If he mentions wife number one, I get a girls' trip. I love traveling, so let him complain about her taking half his first billion. It's a win-win!"

The look of horror on Fiona's face is a dead giveaway that I'm on to something.

I slap on my best pageant smile and press further. "So spill! Tell us your prenup situation. You guys have it all worked out? Any fun clauses, like if my bro works on Christmas, you get to spank him with a monogrammed paddle?"

"Well, sis, prenups are complicated, but if you must know, we're still—"

"Gav-Gav. We agreed that's our personal husband and wife affairs."

"You're right, Fi. That's Mr. and Mrs. talk." He kisses her cheek. "Petra, have a minute? I need updates on the wedding logistics plus a few other business details."

Fiona sighs. "Okay. But after this, no more work. You promised."

He gives her a nod, then leads me away from the others while Hana and Fiona initiate a selfie marathon. If he thinks I'm letting the whole conversation die, he has another thing coming. My Fiona radar is a car alarm going off in a bad neighborhood *(I should know!)*.

"Have you seen Bryce?" he asks, scanning the deck. "He's not usually late."

"He's a big boy with a family bank account that solves everything. If he's running behind, he'll just helicopter in like the dramatic billionaire he is."

"Petra." Gavin's voice takes on that *dad* edge I hate. "I know busting Bryce's balls is your go-to hobby, picking on the rich guy or whatever, but do me a favor. Cut him some slack."

"Why would I do that?"

Gavin steps closer and whispers, "Listen, this has to stay between us, okay? Bryce and Amanda split up right before this trip."

Everything tilts sideways. The ocean starts spinning.

He's single?!

Bryce Sterling is fucking SINGLE!

Which means yesterday in the jungle when he kissed me like I was oxygen—he wasn't cheating. He wasn't some bored billionaire treating me like his dirty little secret while his girlfriend was off manifesting their wedding.

That was him. Kissing me. For real?

Holy shit holy shit HOLY SHIT!

"Wildcat? You okay? You look as if you're going to pass out."

Act normal, Petra. Do not start squealing like a teenage girl. Play it cool—no one needs to know your ovaries just high-fived because your dream guy is officially up for grabs.

I blink rapidly, trying to reboot my brain. "Yeah. Fine. Um... surprised is all. They seemed pretty serious."

"He's dealing with the fallout. So I'm telling you—go easy on him. Bryce is family, and *family* sticks together, especially when personal shit hits the fan."

"All right, I won't give him a hard time," I manage to croak out.

But in my head?

It's chaos.

Screaming chaos.

He's single.

He's single.

HE'S SINGLE!!!

Breathe, you maniac. You're spiraling harder than a washing machine with a brick in it. He kissed you because of heatstroke. Not because he like, WANTS you, wants you.

Vagina: *But what if he's secretly harboring feelings?*

Me: *Shh. You just liked his glorious cock tap dancing against your clit.*

Vagina: *It was sensational. Let's do it again!*

Me: *Shut your horny hole! I need to think.*

This isn't real. This is heatstroke and hormones. My vagina's writing fan fiction about a guy I've wanted for a decade. *Facts, not fantasies—that's what matters here.*

And then Bryce appears on deck.

Oh. My. Fuck. He's actually wearing it.

Our deal from the limo. If I had to dress like a proper socialite, he had to dress like a normal person on vacation. I never thought he'd really do it. I figured he'd find some loophole or show up in a ten-thousand-dollar "casual" linen suit.

But there he is, sporting the fashion hate crime I forced Sebastian into styling.

Imagine a piña colada threw up on a Bass Pro Shop then got lost on its way to a Jimmy Buffett restaurant.

Banana-yellow board shorts covered in tiny hot-pink flamingos doing yoga poses and a salmon Hawaiian shirt loud enough to guide ships to shore. He's also wearing a wide-brimmed straw hat with a tropical print band. And, I can't believe it... neon orange Crocs.

Gavin chokes on his cucumber water. "Jesus Christ. Told you he's having a breakdown."

Yeah. So am I.

"Hello, Gavin... Petra," he says.

I squeak. Actually squeak. "Hey, Moneybags. Nice... outfit."

"Glad you're amused." His lips curve into a subtle smirk.

Oh fuck nuggets. He smirked. At me. Shit. Why am I suddenly fifteen again and worried my crush knows I like him? What do I do? What do I say?

Brain cells, report for duty! I need at least one of you functioning.

Actually, scratch that. Don't say anything. No talkie, no explode-y. Because you will fuck this up—that's your superpower. You turn perfectly good moments into flaming garbage fires.

Fiona materializes. "Oh dear LORD, Bryce! What are you wearing? I honestly thought you were some homeless beach bum who stumbled onto the ship."

Bryce shrugs. "I don't claim to understand fashion. But Sebastian styled it specifically for yacht day. I believe it's Versace... with Pip's added inspiration."

"Well, you know what they say about guys who wear Crocs," I snort. "Big feet, huge di—dimensions."

Did I just make a dick joke? To Bryce Sterling? While standing next to my brother?

Yes. Yes, I did.

Bryce's eyes flash with barely hidden amusement, and I tumble deeper into my personal anxiety tornado.

Breaking news: My ovaries are barking like deranged seals.

Stop reading into it, Petra. He's humoring you. This is Croc fashion banter, not a declaration of love.

Vagina: *Sweetie, he wants to explore us like we're the Mariana Trench—only wetter and more dangerous.*

Me: *I said no talking.*

Fiona chirps, "Oh, if Sebastian approved it, then it's groundbreaking. He's never wrong."

I catch Gavin's detective eyes ping-ponging between Bryce and me as if he's tracking evidence at a crime scene. My panic meter swells.

"Yeah, well, Sebastian's track record isn't exactly flawless," I babble. "He warned me not to untie this bow contraption, or it's gonna be *boobs ahoy.*"

Bryce's eyes drop to the giant white bow covering my chest, and his pupils dilate.

This is either the most *mortifying* or the most *arousing* moment of my life.

DING DING DING!

The ship's bell clangs. *Thank God!*

Nigel—Lord Britchybottom—Featherwick glides across the deck in his damn tuxedo, resembling a butler who's been cryogenically frozen for centuries. *How is he not melting? Maybe he's an old-timey ghost? That would explain the wardrobe.*

He raises one pristine gloved hand. "Before our imminent departure, Miss Muffy Von Cashmere the Second wishes to extend a personal maritime welcome aboard her floating estate, *The Pawseidon.*"

Miss Muffy emerges—the queen of the seven seas—holding her head high, the very picture of four-legged regality. White sunglasses are perched on her furry little snout.

Except. *Oh my God.*

She's wearing *my* outfit.

A black swimsuit with the EXACT same white bow. She's me. I'm her. We're twins *(minus the opposable thumbs).*

"You have got to be shitting me!" I shout.

Miss Muffy stops in front of me, giving me a short, icy bark. I'm guessing it translates to "Bitch, how dare you copy *my* look on *my* ship. Who do you think you are?"

"Oh, Miss Muffy!" Fiona gasps. "I am absolutely mortified for you!"

The dog yips rapid-fire, her tiny body quivering with aristocratic outrage.

"What's she saying now?" Hana asks.

Nigel clears his throat. "This is an unprecedented breach of vessel etiquette. Miss Muffy finds it deeply inappropriate that someone would wear her signature ensemble."

"We are so sorry, honey!" Fiona coos to the dog, then places her gaze on me. "Petra! Go change this instant."

I stare at the assembled group, waiting for someone to crack a smile or admit this is an elaborate prank.

Nobody does.

"You're serious," I say slowly. "You want *me* to put on a different outfit because I'm accidentally twinning with a dog."

Every single person on deck—including my supposed brother—stares at me like *I'm* the one being unreasonable.

Miss Muffy delivers a final, authoritative bark as though to say: "Don't forget who runs this ship. Begone, peasant!"

"Fine." I throw my hands up in defeat. "I'll go. Wouldn't want to offend Her Highness."

Honestly? I'm relieved to escape this circus. I need to wrap my head around the fact that Bryce is available now, decode his smoldering stares, and maybe—*just maybe*—not sabotage the only shot I have at happiness.

***

"**Fucking dog fashion police,**" I hiss, stomping down the hallway as the yacht sways beneath my feet. "This whole billionaire week can kiss my ass. I'm done pretending this is normal."

But then my brain—that traitorous bitch—circles right back to the image that's been torturing me since I stepped onto this floating palace.

Bryce. His eyes drinking me in—

No! I stomp the mental brakes so hard, my thoughts screech. The second I let myself think about the way his pupils dilated when I mentioned untying this bow, my thighs start quivering like they do when I'm about to make spectacularly bad decisions. And my core? Already throbbing with its own goddamn heartbeat.

I scan the empty corridor, hearing the distant sounds of conversation and clinking glasses from above. The guests are probably playing boat bingo, or pin-the-tail on the servants, or whatever wild games the elite dream up for fun.

Which means this is prime snooping time.

I need to get my hands on Gavin's prenup. The way Fiona's face went all twitchy when I mentioned it? That wasn't bride jitters. That was full-blown panic mode. Something's rotten in the state of Gavin's love life, and I'm going to figure it out.

A crew member appears around the corner and immediately tries to blend into the mahogany paneling like a chameleon.

"Excuse me," I call out, switching to my most harmless *I'm-not-about-to-ask-you-to-break-the-rules* voice. "I'm in a bit of a bind here. My brother—Gavin Brinkman—asked me to send some emails from the laptop in his suite, but I'm a total idiot who forgot to grab his key, and now—"

"Not a problem, Miss Brinkman," he says, unlocking a door halfway down the hall and stepping aside. "Will you need anything else?"

Seriously? That worked? I've seen tighter security at a Motel 6.

"All good, thanks," I say, slipping inside and sealing the door behind me.

Without hesitation, I plop my enormous sun hat onto the table and flip open his laptop.

Password screen. Dammit.

I glare at it, hoping my sheer determination can will it to unlock. What would Gavin's password even be? Some pretentious Warren Buffett phrase about compound interest? His favorite tax loophole spelled backwards?

The door swings open behind me. *Shit.*

I'm about to dive into the coat closet and pretend to be a very unconvincing jacket when... Bryce steps in.

"Thank you for helping me locate her."

My heart starts doing that fluttery dance. I slow my breathing, trying to rein it in.

"You're sneaking into your brother's room. Do I want to know?" he asks, shutting the door.

I lift my chin, defiant. "Technically, so are you."

"I caught the intruder. That makes me the hero of this story."

His mouth quirks up, that almost-smile. *Stop. Staring. At. His. Lips.*

"Well, don't get too excited about pressing charges. Turns out I'm a shitty spy. I can't even guess his damn password."

"Is this some good-natured sisterly snooping, or should I be prepping for a court subpoena?"

"Shh. Don't ruin the surprise. You and my brother have never been to prison before, right?"

Bryce steps up to the laptop, and his fingers fly across the keyboard. The screen unlocks immediately.

"You know his password?"

"You do too." He glances at me with impossibly blue eyes. "It's your birthday."

The words are a punch to the sternum. *My birthday?* The workaholic, perfectionist older brother uses my birthday as his computer password.

"Well, shit. Way to pour on the guilt, Moneybags."

"Just pointing out that he loves you."

"Yeah, *conditional* love. The 'be a good girl and jump through the flaming money hoops' kind of love."

"Care to explain what you're hunting for? We both know Gavin wouldn't want you poking around."

"Look at you, all suspicious and detective-y."

Bryce levels me with an intense stare. "Pip."

I roll my eyes, refusing to let him rattle me. "That stern billionaire glare loses some of its intimidating factor when you're dressed like a retired surfer."

"I'll have you know this ensemble is quite liberating."

I'm about to deliver a scathing comeback when I catch a detail on the screen—an email from Gavin's lawyer.

The subject line reads: WHITFIELD-BRINKMAN PRENUPTIAL AGREEMENT - PENDING ITEMS.

"Their prenup?" Bryce reads over my shoulder. "First you suspect Fiona is having an affair, and now—"

Suddenly, we hear Gavin's voice echoing through the corridor, growing louder. He's on a call, and even through the closed door, his words are loud and commanding.

"Shit!" I slam the laptop shut right as footsteps settle by the door.

Without thinking, I grab Bryce's arm and yank him toward the small coat closet. I shove him inside as the electronic beep indicates the door is unlocking.

I spot my sun hat sitting on the table like a giant "Petra was here" beacon.

"Fuck!" I whisper-yell, darting across the room.

I snatch it right as the door handle turns, throwing myself into the closet and closing the door.

The space inside is ridiculously small—barely big enough for one person, let alone two. We're pressed together, chest to thigh. A sliver of light slips through the door frame. Bryce's eyes sparkle in the dark, locked on to mine. His unsteady breathing matches mine.

I fumble for my phone, my hands shaking. I switch it to silent. The screen illuminates our faces in the tiny space. Bryce nods, pulling out his phone and doing the same.

Through the thin closet door, Gavin's tone switches into pitching mode. "That's exactly right, Marcus. Heartvest was built on the principle that financial literacy shouldn't be a luxury reserved for the wealthy..."

I type a message to Bryce.

Me: *He won't be long. Promised Fiona no more work today.*

Bryce nods, eyes fixed on me as if he's trying to solve a puzzle. The butterflies in my stomach are having a flutter orgy as I write.

Me: *Why did you wear that outfit?*

He pauses.

Moneybags: *Because I promised you I would. And... also figured I owed you after what happened yesterday.*

Me: *Owed me for what? An apology for the kiss, or for mistaking me for your girlfriend while you were sun-drunk?*

His response comes lightning fast.

Moneybags: *For taking something I had no right to take.*

Me: *What if I wanted you to, but I thought you were still with Amanda?*

He starts to speak then catches himself.

Moneybags: *Gavin told you.*

Me: *Yeah. Bright side, now I know you're not a cheating dickhole.*

Moneybags: *Christ, Pip. That must have looked... I'm sorry. I never meant to put you in that position. The idea that you thought I could be that kind of man... I would never be unfaithful. Never.*

Gavin's muffled voice shifts gears. "Listen, Marcus, I better finish up. It's my wedding week, and my fiancée is blowing up my phone. You know how it is—got to keep the future Mrs. Brinkman happy, or her old man will stick me with the catering bill!" His laughter fills the room.

My pulse hammers against my throat as I type out the question that could change everything.

Me: *So yesterday in the jungle... was that a heat-induced hallucination, or did you actually want me?*

He stares at his screen. I detect the telltale vibration of his anxious finger drumming against his leg. The nervous habit makes me bolder.

Me: *Because... I want you.*

I watch as the tiny dots on my phone appear and disappear—a dance of indecision. He writes, then deletes. Starts typing... and deletes again. Then, without warning, he powers off his phone like the conversation is over—and shoves it deep into his pocket.

Fuck. I pushed too hard. *Way to go, Petra.* I turn off my phone too, the little glow winking out as I shove it into the waistband of my stupid swimsuit.

The silence in the tiny closet is suffocating. I'm grateful for the darkness hiding the mortification burning my cheeks, the sting behind my eyes that I refuse to acknowledge.

And then, his hands capture my jaw and he seals his mouth over mine.

He's kissing me.

The impact detonates my system like a nuclear bomb, sending shockwaves of heat and electricity racing through every nerve ending. When I inhale sharply against his lips, he takes ruthless advantage, his tongue sweeping inside with the kind of controlled aggression that makes my spine melt.

His grip shifts to my lower back, hauling me flush until we're sealed together everywhere that matters. I sense the rapid thrum of his heartbeat, the tension coiled in his muscles through that ridiculous Hawaiian shirt.

My arms lock around his neck, fingers tangling in his hair, and that's when I feel the rigid length of his arousal branding my hip bone.

A quiet whimper escapes my throat before I can stop it.

He retreats immediately, his breath hot against my ear as he whispers, "Easy, Pip. You have to stay quiet for me."

The endearment in that gravelly whisper unravels me. Then his teeth graze my earlobe, and my knees buckle. His lips blaze a trail down my throat, each kiss a promise that has me trembling. I'm drowning in sensation, in his sandalwood scent, in the heat that's radiating from his body.

Oh fuck. I'm going to come. His hands are finally on me, and I swear to God I'm going to come. The sheer intensity obliterates every midnight fantasy I've tortured myself with, every desperate moment when I'd close my eyes and pretend.

His hands slide over my body—rough, greedy. Like he can't decide if he wants to memorize every inch or devour me whole. But he's not tearing at the swimsuit like he's aching to get inside me. He's savoring. Licking, sucking, breathing me in as if he's waited years for this moment like me.

Every place he touches comes to life, my skin pebbling, tremors racing through my body like aftershocks. My nipples are straining against the fabric of my swimsuit. I arch greedily into him, pressing my chest against his so he knows exactly what I need.

He lets out a rough, needy breath that sends my core clenching.

I reach between us with shaking fingers and grab his wrist, guiding his hand to the giant white bow on my chest.

He understands immediately. His fingers work the fabric loose, and the bow falls open like a present being unwrapped. He gently pushes the material aside, and cool air hits my exposed skin.

I'm half-naked in a coat closet with Bryce Sterling, having my seven minutes in heaven. I could die of happiness.

His finger starts its descent from my throat, drawing lazy patterns between my naked breasts before tracing the curve underneath one. His palm cups the weight of me, and then his thumb is stroking across the hardened peak in devastating slow motion—

WHOOSH!

The door to our secret hideaway swings open.

Light explodes in. I yank the swimsuit fabric across my chest.

"My deepest apologies, Mr. Sterling. Miss Brinkman." The staff member is mortified. "I was fetching Mr. Brinkman's dance shoes. I'll return later."

"No need," Bryce replies smoothly. He steps out and pulls a blazer from a hangar. "Petra, put this on."

Now in proper lighting, our intimate encounter is written all over him. Bryce's hair is wildly disheveled, sticking up at impossible angles. His lips are swollen and painted fire-engine red from my Wet n' Wild lipstick. Scarlet smudges decorate his neck where I marked my territory.

And somehow, those god-awful tourist clothes make the whole picture even more mouth-watering.

The worker snatches the shoes and flees as if the room's on fire.

Bryce finger-combs his makeout hair. "I believe we're supposed to be at some sort of dance instruction."

"Oh. Right. Dancing." I glance down at his very prominent erection protruding in his ridiculous shorts. "You planning to tango like that?"

"I require a few minutes to... address the situation." He stops at the door, shoulders rigid. "Petra, this... We need to put a pause on this. Be logical. For your brother's sake."

Then he's gone, leaving me standing in a borrowed jacket, half-naked, and completely wrecked. My brain is a tornado of lust and confusion, but one thing is crystal fucking clear through all the noise:

Fuck that noise.

That man just gave me a preview of the main event and thinks he can call intermission? Wrong. Dead wrong. I've waited ten long years to feel Bryce Sterling lose control.

There is only one way this ends. With him buried deep inside me, consequences be damned.

CHAPTER ELEVEN

BRYCE

I despise dancing.

The Pawseidon dance studio leaves me nowhere to hide. Its mirrored walls, polished bamboo floors, and judgmental lighting make it the perfect stage for my impending humiliation. One wrong step, and I'll shatter my tailbone *and* my dignity—not necessarily in that order.

For the next hour, this room is my personal torture chamber.

I put myself in the corner like I'm being punished. I'm a sulking statue—pressed khakis, every shirt button clamped shut, a collar so tight you'd think it had a choking kink. But I need the discipline. I don't trust myself around a certain brunette in red.

Thirty minutes ago, I was in my cabin having what I'd describe as the fastest, most pathetic orgasm of my life. Three pumps and I was done, courtesy of replaying Petra's moan when I grazed her nipple.

Now she's ten feet away, wrapped in a crimson dress that clings like guilt. Strategic cutouts reveal flashes of inked skin, deliberate and taunting. She's scrubbed away every trace of our encounter—hair flawless and wearing a fresh coat of red lipstick.

Fiona spins by in a blinding pink disco ball gown. Hana twirls in a fringe tornado.

But Petra... She hijacks every molecule of my attention.

Christ. I kissed her again. I have zero self-control when it comes to her.

I'm the biggest piece of shit alive. Gavin trusts me, calls me family. And here I am, one heartbeat away from ripping off that sin-red fabric and finishing what we started in the goddamn closet.

Our eyes lock, and she shoots me a wicked grin, as if she's heard my thoughts and is daring me to act on them. My dick twitches at the invitation.

Out of the question. I'm leaving this class right now. One more seductive glance and I'm a dead man.

"¡Buenas tardes, mis amores!"

A petite Mexican woman with silver hair and a flower in her bun bounces into the room, her jewelry chiming with each step.

"I am Rosita Salinas, and today we discover the language of passion through movement!" She shimmies dramatically. "Salsa maintains the fire between two hearts long after the vows are spoken. My Enrique and I have been dancing for thirty years, and—*¡madre mía!*—we still burn for each other."

Hana releases an appreciative sigh.

"Sadly, *mi corazón* cannot join our lesson today. He's teaching at the weeklong summer festival in Puerto Vallarta with drinking, dancing, and"—she winks—"passionate encounters beneath the stars."

My mind conjures images of Petra moving against me under cover of darkness, and I shift uncomfortably.

"But first," Rosita announces, "you must witness true dedication! Allow me to present my most accomplished students!"

The studio door swings open, and I'm fully unprepared for what emerges.

Miss Muffy Von Cashmere II struts in wearing a rainbow-sequined dress possibly stolen from a Vegas showgirl.

And then comes Nigel.

Gone is the butler suit. In its place: a matching colorful shirt unbuttoned to reveal glittery chest hair and pants so tight they look sprayed on.

"What fresh hell is this?" I whisper.

Latin music floods the room.

What happens next will haunt me forever.

Miss Muffy rises on her hind legs, places her paw in Nigel's hand... and they dance.

Like, *actual salsa*.

Miss Muffy's tiny legs work in perfect time with the beat as Nigel guides her through choreographed turns and spins.

"This cannot be real," Gavin mutters.

The music builds, and Nigel drops into a split—a full split—while Miss Muffy leaps over him. Nigel springs up as if he's got coils in his shoes, and they kick into side-by-side footwork that would shame professional humans.

My stunned brain forgets how time works—because suddenly, it's the finale.

Nigel lifts her overhead, a spinning glittery cyclone, and throws her skyward. She rotates midair.

A double backflip!

He catches her in a dramatic dip. For her ending pose, she kicks out one leg, her tiny paw poised in perfect prima ballerina precision.

The room explodes with applause.

Fiona and Hana are on their feet, shrieking with delight. Even the normally reserved guests are clapping.

"¡Magnífico!" Rosita beams.

My brain's still buffering from the dog ballet when *WHAM!* Rosita pounds her cane on the floor with fury.

"Now, find your partners and prepare for romance!"

I'm halfway to Hana when Echo slithers toward Petra like a shirtless snake.

"My radiant muse," he purrs. "You've invaded my subconscious. I spent all evening clothed only in moonlight, attempting to translate your beauty onto canvas. I must have you tonight for a private modeling session. Naked, of course. For art."

I'm across the room and claiming her before I know it. "She doesn't dance with anyone but me."

That dangerous spark ignites in Petra's eyes. "Did I agree to that? My memory's fuzzy. Hmm. This is a pickle, isn't it? Who should I dance with?"

"The guy who bought your dress," I say firmly, closing my fingers around her wrist and steering her away.

"I'm enjoying this dominant side of you, Moneybags," she murmurs breathily.

Fuuuuccccck. This is not good. But it's too late—the class has started.

Rosita paces like a general in stilettos, her cane tapping out the rhythm.

"¡Uno, dos, tres, cuatro!"

At first, we practice the steps on our own. *WTF?* Petra failed to mention she had a previous life as a professional backup dancer. *Where did she learn this?*

Me? I'm a sweating pile of panic in khakis, moving as though I've got concrete shoes and a spreadsheet for a soul.

"*Señor* Sterling! You are too buttoned up! We must liberate you!"

Before I can object, she's rolling my sleeves and popping buttons like it's an F1 pit stop. Cool air hits my skin, and suddenly I'm the reluctant star of a *Magic Mike* sequel.

With a firm push, she shoves us together—tight. My palm lands on the curve of Petra's waist, our fingers lock. We're pressed so close that my dick is already third wheeling us in the salsa.

"*¡Excelente!* Now feel your partner's body moving against yours."

Petra presses in, nipples grazing my chest. And—

Ooof! I trip over her ankle.

"Awesome! I'm stuck with two left feet over here," Pip announces.

"Petra, go easy," Gavin says, half laughing.

"Oh, I'll go easy—once he stops dancing like he's dodging bullets." Her hand slides up my neck, fingers slipping into my hair.

Stop getting hard. Think about quarterly earnings reports.

"Feel the music, Moneybags," she says playfully, then leans in. "Would it help you to remember how I tasted? Or how I'd taste if you licked me... other places."

I clear my throat. "Gavin asked me to look after you. Not... this."

"I don't need a babysitter, B." Her tongue darts out to wet her lips. "A facesitter, maybe..."

Focus on the steps. Left foot. Right foot. Don't think about licking that sweet cu—

"There ya go, Sterling, now you're getting it," Gavin shouts.

Against my best efforts, the lesson transforms into a fever dream of vertical foreplay scored to Latin music.

"Whoopsie," she says, fake falling. Her hand shoots out to "catch herself" and lands directly on my straining erection. She gives me a gentle squeeze that makes my vision blur.

"My, my. Now that's what I call a dance partner."

I close my eyes, swallow down a groan, and try to find my sanity somewhere in the pounding music. My best friend's watching. My entire body is on red alert. My Sterling sword is doing a dance routine of his own, and Petra's loving every second.

"Everything okay over there?" Gavin calls out.

"Just peachy!" Petra chirps, still cupping me before pulling back slowly. "Trying to help your bestie find his rhythm. He's incredibly... *hard* to work with."

"Pip," I rasp.

"What?" she asks innocently. "You look so damn hot, I can't help myself. And that monster in your pants has me gushing." She edges closer, breath scorching my neck. "Knowing how much you want me... is making me so fucking wet."

Her purring slides down my ear like a shot of whiskey—smooth, hot, and meant to burn. The sensation rockets through my spine, landing low in my stomach like a lit match. My grip tightens as I spin her away—too hard, too fast—and she crashes straight into Gavin and Fiona.

"Sorry!" I yelp.

"¡Cuidado!" Rosita chuckles, helping Petra to her feet. "This is salsa, not bumper cars."

Petra laughs, eyes glittering as though she's committed a felony and gotten away with it. She presses back into me, hips swaying slow and lethal.

"What's the matter, Moneybags? Worried I'll break you in front of everyone?"

Think about interest rates. Tax codes. Anything except how good she feels grinding against my dick.

"*¡Muy bien,* Senior Sterling!" Rosita shouts over the chaos in my head. "I see the chemistry building! Allow your bodies to communicate!"

My voice comes out hoarse. "Thank you. Very... educational."

Rosita claps. "Now try the dramatic finish! This is where passion explodes!"

Poor choice of words.

"Yeah, B. This is supposed to be sensual," Petra says loudly. "Not like you're afraid I have cooties."

As she's calling me out, her fingers glide across my chest, lighting me up. She spins, her leg sliding up my thigh, and then wraps my arm around her. I catch her in a low dip, my hand skimming the edge of her dress's daring neckline.

I pull her up with agonizing slowness.

She leans in, lips brushing my neck. "I'm dying to know," she purrs. "Do you fuck like you kiss?"

Her hips roll against my erection with dirty intentions. My control is shaking like an overstretched rubber band.

"Because Bryce, you don't have to be gentle with me."

Snap.

I lose my footing and fall backward, knocking into the sound equipment, creating a domino effect of destruction.

The room goes silent.

"Minor technical difficulties!" I announce from the floor, scrambling to cover my arousal. "Nothing to worry about!"

Everything to worry about. Your hard-on can be seen from space.

"Shit, man, you okay?" Gavin approaches with genuine concern written across his face.

"Leg cramp," I lie, untucking my shirt. "Need to… ice it. Pulled something. Cold shower. Emergency ice situation!"

I flee like a teen boy trying to hide his erection from his grandma's Bible study.

That smug little menace. A few filthy words, and I'm one grind away from combusting in my pants.

New plan: Build a fortress. Moats. Guards. Maybe a steel cage for my dick.

Because if she touches me again, I won't just lose control—I'll lose everything. Including my best friend.

***

"Behold! The sun spreads her golden thighs above the horizon, offering herself to the ocean's thrusting waves!" Echo thrashes his paintbrush, splattering orange across the canvas. "Witness the sky's erotic climax!"

I massage my temples and contemplate jumping overboard. We're all held captive as Echo *performs* on the front deck. The yacht's elite guests nod in agreement, calculating the millions his latest masterpiece will fetch at auction.

Since the salsa class catastrophe, I've executed a much-needed avoidance strategy. Four hours barricaded in my suite, drowning myself in quarterly projections, payroll documents, and IPO updates—whatever it took to scrub the memory of Petra's body grinding against mine.

At dinner, I used Hana Choi as a human shield, positioning myself between her and Gavin.

Genius move, actually.

Hana proved to be the ideal distraction—a rambling, giggling chatterbox of low-effort conversation. For ninety minutes, she regaled me with riveting tales of her seventy-five-year-old fiancé's nightly skincare routine, his collection of vintage handkerchiefs, and his adorable sleep apnea.

The woman described his snoring patterns with the enthusiasm of a biologist discovering a new species.

Pure conversational white noise. Exactly what I needed.

Petra kept her distance—physically, anyway. But not with her eyes. The looks she shot me from the other side of the table? Volatile. A flash of challenge and promise in the curve of her lips. I kept my head down, playing the disinterested observer.

If I can maintain this tactical approach for the remaining wedding festivities—strategic seating, human buffers, mundane small talk—I'll survive with no further lapses in judgment.

It's a foolproof plan.

Except, I see Petra slipping away from the crowd like a master thief mid-museum heist. One second she's lingering by the Miss Muffy-shaped ice sculpture. The next she's rounding the corner—gone.

No one else has noticed Pip's escape.

Stay put, my rational mind commands. *Do not follow her. You've maintained boundaries all day.*

But what if she trips in that gown? What if she leans too far over the railing? Someone should ensure she's safe. It's the responsible thing to do.

Everyone else is hypnotized by Echo's creative breakdown. When he launches into a soliloquy about penetrating "the virgin canvas with my artistic seed," I slip away.

I find her at the stern, leaning over the polished railing, her gaze fixed on the distant shoreline where carnival lights pulse like a neon heartbeat. Music echoes over the waves—mariachi trumpets and laughing voices from Puerto Vallarta's summer festival.

The sight of her in that dress stops my heart mid-beat.

Nude silk that looks like liquid champagne poured over every damn curve, overlaid with intricate black lace. The off-shoulder cut shows off her collarbones, and the plunge flashes enough skin to ruin me.

When did Gavin's rebellious little sister transform into such a temptress? As a teenager, she was all sharp edges and defiant energy—beautiful in an untamed, dangerous way. But this woman before me...

She's a celestial storm sent to test every ounce of willpower I possess.

"Well, looky here. If it isn't the man who spent dinner learning about geriatric respiratory disorders just to avoid eye contact."

Caught red-handed.

"I was being polite to a fellow guest."

"Mmm-hmm," she says with those probing hazel-green eyes. "It had nothing to do with me turning you into a malfunctioning robot during class."

"You're overestimating your influence, Pip. I simply lack coordination when it comes to Latin dance."

She rubs her arms. On instinct, I shrug out of my tux jacket and drape it over her shoulders.

"Thanks, Moneybags. Though I should warn you, accepting gifts from billionaires goes against my principles."

"It's a jacket."

"That's how it starts. First clothes, then jewelry, and before you know it, I'm getting weekly Botox and referring to my housekeeper as 'the domestic staff.'"

A snort escapes. "Impossible. You'd never be open to that type of corruption. You're too... *you*."

The words hang between us, more honest than I intended.

We fall into comfortable silence, facing the shore where the distant carnival pulses with life. I study the way the lights twinkle and blur across the water.

"You know what's ironic, B? Those people are probably blowing their grocery money on overpriced rides and street tacos, but they're having more fun than anyone on this boat."

"You think money makes experiences less... authentic?"

"I think when you can buy anything, nothing feels special." She shifts, my jacket slipping off one shoulder. "Seriously, when's the last time you wanted something and had to question whether you could afford it?"

"You assume because I'm wealthy that I have unlimited choices."

"That watch you're wearing is worth more than most people's houses."

I glance down at the custom Patek Philippe—my grandfather's watch. Four generations of Sterling expectations tick with every second.

"This watch comes with a price tag you can't see. When you're born with someone else's ambitions, wanting things for yourself is a luxury that gets revoked."

"Jesus. That's the most beautiful description of a prison I've ever heard."

"I never said it was a prison."

"You didn't have to. It's written all over your pretty face."

"What about you? You're quick to dissect everyone else's motivations. What drives Petra Brinkman?"

"Easy. Justice, fresh coffee, and to never have to wear a bra again."

I find myself fighting a smile. "That simple?"

"The best things usually are, Moneybags," she says, something earnest flickering in her eyes. "I give you a lot of shit, but I'll say this. You're one of the good ones, Bryce."

My stomach goes tight. She doesn't know... *I'm about to abandon her brother. Leave him to run our massive business alone. He's not ready for that, and if she knew, she'd despise me.*

For a beat, we're just here. No distance, no flirting. I don't know how she does it—those piercing eyes see through the crafted Sterling image and straight to the man underneath who doesn't know what the hell he wants.

Except, I *do* know. I want to grab her midnight hair and suck the smart remarks off her tongue, savoring every syllable. I want to own that mouth.

I *want* to press her against this railing and show her how far she's pushed me—how little of my self-control she's left intact.

I'm burning for her. The intensity scares the hell out of me.

Her words from dance class rattle in my brain: *"Do you fuck the way you kiss?"*

The blunt honesty, the sexual challenge, the complete lack of coy games—women like her don't exist in my world. She doesn't want to acquire me—she wants to tear me apart.

I slide my hands into my pockets to resist her pull. "But seriously, what do you really want? Out of life, I mean."

Her expression transforms, igniting with an awakened fierceness.

"I want to fight for people steamrolled by systems rigged against them. People who can't afford good lawyers and deserve better. The little guy who gets buried in red tape and legal jargon while corporations float away on golden parachutes. I want to be the voice for everyone who's been told to sit down and shut up because they don't have the right connections, the right bank account, or the right anything."

She lets out a breath, shaking her head with a wry little laugh. "Wow. Okay. TED Talk over. This conversation has gone way too deep for a yacht at sunset. We should be talking about vacation-y things, like, I don't know... how rich people act super weird on vacation. Don't you guys ever get shitfaced and just stare at tropical fish through a snorkel mask?"

"I don't believe I've ever observed marine life while under the influence of alcohol."

"See?" She throws her hands up. "That's tragic! You billionaires have no clue how to have normal human fun. It's all privately curated tours and seven-course meals with unpronounceable names.

Where's the adventure? The spontaneity? The regrettable sunburn you bitch about for weeks afterward?"

Something reckless stirs in my chest. "You want adventure? Follow me."

Five minutes later, we emerge from the glass elevator onto the bottom deck of the boat.

Spotting the camouflaged wall panel, I place my hand on the smooth, cool surface. With a silent whoosh, a section slides back, revealing a narrow spiral staircase that fades into darkness.

"Troublemakers first."

She doesn't hesitate.

The staircase curves downward, our footsteps echoing softly against metal treads. At the bottom, we step into a small circular room that resembles a high-end meditation pod. A single couch wraps around the entire space, one continuous curve of white cushions.

"Oh wow. A circle couch," she deadpans.

"You still think I can't impress you, huh? I find that oddly motivating. You wanted a fish adventure? How about one only billionaires get?"

Before she can fire off another smart-ass retort, I flip the master switch. The lights cut out, plunging us into inky blackness. Petra's breath catches. Then—*CLICK*—the darkness outside is swallowed up by spotlights, flicking on, one by one.

The walls... aren't walls at all.

They're windows.

The entire circular room is encased in glass, a pod submerged beneath the ocean's surface that offers panoramic views of the illuminated sea floor.

"Oh shit! Are we underwater?"

"It's essentially a submarine merged with a glass-bottom boat," I explain, watching her face cycle through shock, wonder, and pure delight. "Billionaires prefer to observe nature's beauty without risking a wedgie from a wetsuit."

"Did Bryce Sterling just crack a joke?"

She scrambles onto the curved seating, pressing both palms against the window, nose touching the glass. Her enthusiasm is infectious.

"I can see the ocean floor. And holy shit! Is that a dolphin over there?! Fuck me! That's a shark! That's an actual shark!"

A massive hammerhead glides past our window. She squeals.

"I am *not* being sarcastic right now, B. This is genuinely fucking incredible. Sit down. Stop standing there like you're chaperoning a middle school field trip."

"I don't think that's a good idea."

"Why not?"

"Because... I can't resist you," I admit, only realizing I've spoken it aloud when her eyes darken.

"Good. I don't want you to control yourself. Show me the real you, Bryce."

"Pip, we can't. Gavin is my best friend."

"Always with the mood-killing brother talk."

My finger is a machine gun, drumming against my thigh—tap-tap-tap-tap-TAP!

"I should return to the group. If you need anything, press that button. Staff will respond immediately."

I pivot toward the spiral staircase, away from temptation.

"Bryce, wait."

Her quiet voice stops me cold. My hand grips the metal railing—hard.

She sighs. "I... I don't know what's happening between us. I'm just... Well, you have my permission."

Keep moving! Escape. Before you do something irreversibly stupid. You don't have Gavin's permission for whatever this is.

"What I'm trying to say is... however you want me, wherever you want me—I'm completely and utterly yours. No strings, no games, no bullshit. Just yours."

Christ, how could a man resist that invitation? I sure as hell can't. I'm only human.

I turn, cross the space between us in two strides, and crash my mouth to hers. Our lips collide with the force of a small explosion. Desperate. Hungry. Completely unhinged. Her hands seize my hair as we move in a frantic rhythm, stealing each other's breath. I kiss her like I'll die if I stop.

My blood is on fire—my heart pounding so loud I can barely hear over it. My tongue sweeps against hers, claiming her, devouring her, and the only thought in my head is: *more, more, more.*

My mind goes primal, messy—everything in me is screaming: *Bury yourself in her.*

I force it back—*that can't happen.*

Petra whimpers against my lips, and the sound heats up my cock like a lightning bolt.

A growl rips from my chest, raw and animal. *What the fuck? Where did that sound come from?*

Between kisses, I rasp against her lips, "I'm not... fucking you, Pip. I'm just... tasting you."

Petra peels off my jacket she's wearing and hurls it away, her voice husky and seductive. "Whatever you need to tell yourself, Money-bags."

Hands attack my shirt, ripping buttons open in a frenzied rush, sending them flying across the room like shrapnel.

My mouth charts a burning path down her throat, tasting her skin. I drag the neckline of her dress down, exposing the swell of her breasts. I groan, deep and ragged, as I suck her into my mouth, rolling my tongue over her perky nipple. Her other breast fits perfectly in my hand, my thumb circling and teasing.

"Oh God, B. Yes!"

Her nipple grows firm in my mouth. Every pull of my lips makes her arch against me. I switch sides, desperate to feel the other swell against my tongue. I graze my teeth over the taut bud, rough enough to make her cry out.

"More," she gasps. "Please, more."

Something savage unfurls in my gut—a version of myself that's been caged behind boardroom manners and inherited expectations.

My hand slides lower, tracing down the curve of her waist, over the swell of her hips. My fingers hook under the hem of her dress and yank it up, bunching the delicate fabric around her waist. Her breath catches. I glide my hand up her thigh, closer and closer to where I want her most. The instant I make contact with soaked lace, Petra unleashes a sound that nearly stops my heart—pleasure vibrates through the entire room.

Nothing in my groomed existence has prepared me for this rush of dominance. Her body trembles from my touch, and a savageness ignites in me. I was made for a single purpose: to ruin her for anyone else.

My cock is a steel rod of need—so hard, it hurts—trapped behind my zipper like punishment for wanting her this badly. But my orgasm can wait. What I need is to hear every fucking sound she makes. To know if she's all throaty growls or breathy gasps when she comes.

"Fuck me, Bryce. I want you inside me."

I pull back, meeting her eyes. The blue light of the water beyond the glass flickers across her bare skin, her breasts heaving, her nipples swollen and wet from my mouth.

"No," I growl. "I said no fucking, Pip."

She opens her mouth to protest, but the look on my face has her swallowing her words.

"No more talking. The only noise I want to hear from you is my name when you come on my tongue."

Before she can respond, I fist her panties and tear them clean off—not a careful removal, but complete annihilation of expensive lace that goes flying.

She gasps, and I drop to my knees. I'm a man approaching his religion. My mouth waters as my hands grip her thighs, dragging her to the cushion's edge and spreading her wide for my hungry gaze.

I dive in like a man possessed. The moment I taste her, everything else ceases to exist. Sweet and salty and so goddamn addictive. I can't stop. I lap at her, drinking her in, the wet sounds of her arousal filling the small space. Every moan she lets slip—every breathy gasp—floods heat straight to my cock.

I flatten my tongue and press against her clit, feeling her jolt under me. She whimpers, her fingers scrabbling for purchase in my hair. I suck in, and she cries out. Her juicy sounds are music made just for me.

"I can't! It's too much—" she starts, but I cut her off with a look.

"What did I say about talking?" I command.

I grab her legs and hook them around my neck, angling her ass off the couch. She gasps, her stilettos digging into my skin as I hold her there, suspended and trembling.

And then I dive back in.

My tongue parts her, slow and savoring at first, tasting her from the inside out. The way she moves under me, her hips canting forward, those heels digging in while her legs press tighter around my head—it's enough to undo me.

I push deeper, my tongue pressing inside until she's panting. Every vulnerable, breathy noise she makes tells me exactly where to go. My hands rake her thighs, holding her steady as I lick and chase the pulse of her pleasure.

Her breathy pants turn into velvety, languid moans. They slip out like she's trying to hold them in.

I growl against her, the vibration sending her head flying back, her whole body going tight. I know I've found her sweet spot. Her noises climb higher and higher like a song that's about to break. The way her legs are quivering, how she uses those delicious internal muscles like a vise around my tongue—it's everything.

Her soft little pants turning into sighs and moans that melt together. It's a fucking symphony, and I'm the conductor with every greedy thrust of my tongue.

She's close. I feel her thighs squeeze harder, her hips roll faster. I still my body, keeping my mouth right where she needs it, my tongue pumping with steady, firm pressure. She's fucking shaking in my hands.

I'm wild. Unbridled. A man of one purpose.

Then she says it. My name—my name in a voice that's half moan, half sigh, a sound so delicate and sweet, it carves a hollow right through my chest. She collapses back, whimpering, her body going limp and boneless, and I feel her melting on my tongue.

Her satiated sighs continue to play like a melody. A song that's all mine—to memorize and replay in every quiet moment for the rest of my miserable existence.

The underwater lights of the ocean dance across her skin and turn her into something unreal—an ocean-born siren pulled from a sailor's tale. Her lashes brush flushed cheeks, and that devastating mouth curves into the softest smile I've ever witnessed on her.

I did that. Me.

Turned a walking rebellion into a satisfied puddle of a woman. Must say, I'm feeling pretty goddamn pleased with myself.

For once in her life, she's not insulting my lineage, threatening my anatomy, or plotting creative ways to destroy my personal property. She's peaceful. Beautiful. Content.

It's unsettling, because this version of her is even more dangerous. I want more of it. I want all of it.

But I can't let her know that. The moment she sees me as vulnerable, she'll rip me to shreds with her sass, and we'll be right back to her having all the power.

Something tells me she's used to men groveling at her feet. But I'm not most guys. I want her needing me—badly. Petra doesn't respect weakness—she annihilates it. If I want to keep her attention, I need to be the one thing she can't demand.

My hands smooth her rumpled dress back into place, making sure she's covered before gathering the shredded remains of her panties and placing them beside her. A gentleman's courtesy, even in the aftermath of complete debauchery.

I slap my best smug expression across my face and start casually backing toward the staircase. "Sleep tight, Pip. Try not to dream about me too much."

I hear her inhale to fire off a quip—probably something that'll bruise my ego and make me hard at the same time—but I don't stick around for it.

She thinks she's the one in control? Let her think it.

Tomorrow, she'll be the one squirming and begging me to touch her again.

CHAPTER TWELVE

PETRA

He dined and dashed. With a smug grin that said, *You're welcome.*

Next time, I'm either going to slap that smirk off his face or sit on it. *Decisions, decisions.*

I press my eye against my cabin door peephole, fully embracing my inner nosy neighbor.

Across the hall: The Door of Doom, aka Bryce's room.

"Come on out, Billionaire Boy," I mutter. "Face me like a man."

I groan and thunk my forehead on the doorframe with a dramatic thump. I didn't sleep last night—*not even a little.* I kept blaming it on boat stuff: the gentle rocking, the low engine hum, the water lapping at the hull.

Total lies.

The truth is, I spent the entire evening replaying every breathless second in that glass pod on the ocean floor.

His confession. His hands. His tongue—

Nope. Down, girl. It's barely eight a.m., and you've already blacked out three times thinking about it.

I've spent years analyzing Bryce Sterling's micro-expressions. He drums his fingers on his thigh every time he's uncomfortable. His left eyebrow twitches if he's annoyed but trying to be polite. His jaw muscle jumps when he's fighting a smile.

But swagger? Giving me a mind-melting orgasm and walking away with a wink and a one-liner?

I don't know this man at all.

Thank God for Gavin's wedding emergency emails: vendor meltdowns, seating chart crises, and absurd guest gift bags gave my brain something else to spiral over. Who needs bride and groom bubbles when you're gifting exotic vacations and literal diamonds? These aren't party favors—they're dowries.

At three a.m., Katie saved my ass with a FaceTime call—ten in the morning for her in Italy. Despite strolling through an Italian piazza looking chic and stunning, she used her supreme event planner skills to help me. For over an hour, we emailed vendors, fixed monogram font spacing, and translated Fiona's boujee aesthetics.

Apparently, there's a critical difference between cream and ivory, and calling it *white-ish* gets you side-eyed by the bridal mafia.

I did *NOT* mention the mind-blowing underwater oral session.

My besties picked up the pieces of my heart the last time Bryce unknowingly wrecked it. Trying to pass off his skilled tongue as the reason I caved? Yeah, that's not gonna cut it. I swore to them I would never fall for him again.

But my brain? She's a slut for delusion.

Deep down I already know how this ends. This isn't a storybook romance where the rich guy chooses the messy girl with no filter. This is more... hot billionaire has some fun with the troublemaker until real wife material shows up. Someone more blonde. Less sarcastic.

Still, I've been fantasizing about that moment last night since I was fifteen fucking years old. And it was *better*, so much better, than all my teenage dreams combined.

That mortifying slip-up: *"I'm completely and utterly yours."*

Are you trying to fuck this up, Petra?

Bryce cannot discover I've carried this torch since high school. He has to think this attraction is new. Like I just discovered he has a penis and suddenly found it fascinating.

Back to the peephole—no movement. I march to the mirror for a final look at today's unzip-me ensemble.

This olive-green jumpsuit I'm wearing matches perfectly with my trusty black combat boots. It's cinched at the waist, clinging in all the right spots, and says "I'm outdoorsy—let's make out." I ease the center zipper halfway to danger, revealing my crimson bikini underneath.

Secret weapon time.

Digging into one of the many pockets, I pull out my faithful drugstore lipstick and slick on another layer of "come hither" red.

Footsteps in the hallway send me scrambling to my spy position.

Not Bryce. Hana. She's skipping past my room in a tennis outfit so white and bouncy-bright, she looks like she's headed to Wimbledon instead of an off-roading expedition.

We're riding ATVs through the jungle, not sipping cucumber water at the country club.

Suddenly, his doorknob turns and my pulse skyrockets. *Operation Make Bryce Sterling Regret His Smug Exit is officially a go.*

Sarcasm: loaded. Attitude: armed. Fucks to give: zero. He wants to act the elusive, cocky billionaire. Fine. Two can play that game.

Three authoritative knocks echo off the door.

I yank the zipper down to my thighs in an impromptu burlesque move, letting the jumpsuit gape open to showcase my bikini-wrapped assets. Then, I fling the door wide.

Bryce takes one look and clears his throat loudly. "My apologies. I thought you'd be dressed."

"I am."

His gaze trails down my torso like I'm a buffet and he's ranking appetizers to devour first.

I peek down at myself, feigning surprise. "Again? This stupid thing keeps slipping down. You better keep an eye on it, or I might trip and fall directly out of my clothes."

I zip up—*slowly*—watching his finger *tap-tap-tap.*

"Come on, babysitter. We've got a sweaty playdate in the jungle."

I brush past him, my breasts grazing his chest—totally on purpose. His sharp inhale behind me? Music to my chaotic little ears.

Let the games begin, Moneybags.

***

BACK AT CASA CASHMERE, we're greeted by automotive paradise. Talk about sex on wheels—this garage has it all. Ferraris, Lamborghinis, motorcycles, and endless rows of off-road vehicles. Whatever a billionaire fancies, Casa Cashmere has it—detailed, dazzling, and ready to roll out.

Staff in matching blue polos swarm around the wedding party as they prepare for our 4x4 adventure. Helmets snap into place, headsets tangle in manicured fingers, and the row of ATVs rumble in formation.

Bryce and I gear up side by side. I drink in his transformation from corporate clone to rugged outdoorsman. Holy hell, Sebastian deserves a serious bonus.

Dark khakis sculpt his legs while that cream henley hugs his torso exactly where it counts. But it's the half-buttoned olive gray shirt layered on top that causes my thighs to clench, bringing back the memory of his shirt flying open before he sank to his knees.

I want to strip him down, layer by layer, until there's nothing between us but bad decisions.

Nope. Stick to the plan. Make him beg. This richie rich must be mind-fucked.

I snap my helmet into place and tap the microphone. "Testing, testing... So what's the seating arrangement here? Do I get to steer this beast, or will you be maneuvering me like you did last night?"

A chuckle crackles through the receiver. "You're riding behind me, Pip. Get a good grip—I don't go slow."

I cock my head with a teasing grin. "Should I be concerned about your stamina? I mean, you tapped out pretty early yesterday with that 'no sex' excuse."

Before Bryce can serve up a smug one-liner, we overhear Fiona whining.

"But babe. I was picturing a more sensual activity. Like you, shirtless, getting a massage while I feed you grapes. Not ruining my romper on a glorified lawnmower."

She and Hana are both dressed for a garden party and not a joyride through a swamp pit.

"Fi, we had a deal," Gavin says. "One thing. Just one damn thing I wanted to do this week. And this is it!"

"But Gav-Gav, this is so... *barbaric.* I assumed you'd pick something more civilized."

"We have eleven spa appointments on the schedule," Gavin sighs. "I agreed to your group chakra healing, the seaweed wraps, and even the couple's full-moon sound bath. This is the *one* thing I asked for. C'mon. You can survive two hours on an ATV."

Ooh, trouble in paradise. This is the first time I've seen cracks in their pre-wedding love bubble, and I am here for it. Popcorn in hand. Zoomed *all* the way in.

Hana makes a beeline for us, fleeing the tension. Bryce glues himself to his phone, avoiding the chatterbox like a pro.

"Oh my goodness, this is going to be such an adventure! I never get to do things this exciting! My fiancé and I take walks together, but anything past the driveway and he needs his walker. But honestly, it's super convenient because there's a cup holder attachment for my water bottle and extra storage for his heart medication!"

Seriously, what the fuck do I say to this girl's stories?

Hana continues her ramble. "I'm not even strapped in yet, and I already feel like a rebel! Can you keep a secret?"

"Depends." I say. "Will I be legally required to testify?"

"I didn't get permission to do this," she whispers. "I signed the waiver without calling my mom or my fiancé's assistant. I didn't even read it!"

"Hana Choi. You dirty little thrill-seeker. I am so fucking proud."

She starts hyperventilating. "Oh geez. What if they find out? I'm not bold like you, Petra. My heart is racing. Maybe I shouldn't."

I put my hand on her shoulder. "Take a breath. They don't have to like it. You're not a collectible doll, Hana. You're a grown-ass woman."

"You're totally right. I'm doing it. I'm being a bad girl. OH GOSH—I GOTTA PEE AGAIN."

I feel oddly proud as I watch Hana bounce toward the restrooms.

"So... corrupting *all* the rich people now?" Bryce asks. "I thought *I* was your special project."

There's that cocky smirk. *He's so fucking gorgeous.*

"Aw, look at you. Already needy, and we haven't even hit second gear yet."

All these different sides of him—the controlled businessman, the dominant tease, the snarky smartass—it's sensory overload.

"Distinguished guests!" Nigel's crisp accent cuts through the garage chatter. "Your attention, if you please, for our safety orientation."

After yesterday's sequined salsa spectacle, I thought nothing Nigel Featherwick could wear would shock me. Wrong. The man, usually straight out of a period drama, is now in full military camouflage, complete with combat pants and a tactical shirt. His ATV helmet and aviation goggles make him look ready for a fighter jet mission.

"Due to recent rainfall, terrain conditions are especially challenging," Nigel continues. "Please exercise appropriate caution and reduce speed when necessary."

Two Casa Cashmere security guards—clearly ex-military—step forward. One nods. The other salutes. Then... the strapping begins.

They start buckling black padded straps around Nigel's torso with the intensity of someone preparing an astronaut for launch. Crisscrossing chest harnesses. Reinforced shoulder clips. The whole contraption looks like bondage gear meets mountain climbing equipment.

From the side garage door, a third security guy appears. He moves slowly like he's transporting live explosives. Cradled in his arms?

Miss. Freaking. Muffy.

I nearly swallow my tongue.

She's combat-ready: camo jacket, leather shoulder pads, pilot goggles, and a rhinestone-studded helmet. The man straps Miss Muffy *into* the harness on Nigel's chest.

OH.

MY.

LORD.

IT'S A BABYBJÖRN.

For a dog.

I can't even.

Nigel harumphs like none of this is batshit bananas. "Miss Muffy is secured. Mount your vehicles. Remain within visual range. And remember—dignity above all."

I whisper to Bryce, "Are rich people really this bored with reality?"

"Unfortunately, this barely cracks the eccentricity scale."

"Didn't know you had such harsh opinions about your own species."

"There's a lot you don't know about me, Pip." He winks, sliding on sporty sunglasses that reflect my face as he straddles the ATV. "Hop on."

"Oh, honey. You'll need more than two words to get me to *straddle it.*"

I slink toward him and twist up my Wet n' Wild lipstick. "Eyes on me, Moneybags."

Using his lenses as a mirror, I drag the red across my lips in a smooth, sensual swipe, watching my reflection take shape. I press my lips together with a soft pop, and his grip on the handlebars tightens.

"There. Now I'm ready to wrap my lips around something stiff."

His jaw ticks.

Point: Brinkman.

I slip on my sunglasses and mount up behind him, arms wrapped around his chest, and give him a little squeeze, just to test his reaction. I hear it—the breath he didn't mean to let go.

"Think you can give me a ride worth remembering, B? In my experience, rich boys tend to overpromise and underdeliver."

He doesn't respond. Instead, he slips his phone into the handlebar mount and connects it to the ATV's built-in personal sound system—because why wouldn't billionaire off-road vehicles come with surround sound?

He presses play. The distinctive gallop guitar riff is instantly recognizable.

It's *Barracuda.*

Full blast.

No way. Bryce "Buttoned-Up" Sterling listens to hard rock?

But there's no time to dwell on this new development because he revs the engine. "Hold on tight, Pip!"

Then he punches the gas.

The ATV rockets forward like we've been shot from a cannon and my whole body slams backward. My arms squeeze around him for dear life *(his evil plan, no doubt)* and my cheek presses between his shoulder blades.

The other 4x4s explode into motion around us. Nigel takes the lead, Miss Muffy bouncing against his chest. Gavin and Fiona peel out to our left, Fiona's helmet slightly askew as she yells something about her hair. But the real show is Hana on her own ATV, hair whipping behind her like she's competing in the X Games, shrieking with joy.

The jungle rushes by in a blur of sun-dappled green, vines dangling like nature's party streamers. Each breath is thick with wet earth, gasoline, and the sharp bite of adventure. I'm screaming with joy as we dodge mud bombs, and the ATV's power vibrates through my spine while wailing guitar riffs pulse in my ears.

It's like I've been dropped straight into an action movie trailer.

For one dangerous heartbeat, I let myself slip into dreamland. This is our honeymoon. We're madly in love. Tearing through paradise, drunk on adrenaline and each other. The version of us I've always wanted.

But then, the lyrics hit, simple and clear, through my helmet.

Did he pick this song for me?

Am I the wild thing he's trying to tame?

If that's his game plan, he's gonna learn real quick that this barracuda... bites back. And I have more teeth than he's ready for.

I've got my own mission for this ride: reduce the smug billionaire to a puddle of lust. Time to turn up the heat.

I adjust my grip on his torso, sliding my hands seductively down to his waist.

Bryce clears his throat into the headset. "Everything... all right back there? You keep squirming."

"Just getting comfortable," I say innocently.

"Strange. You seemed plenty comfortable last night. That was you, right? Begging me not to stop?"

"I wasn't begging. I was providing feedback."

"You melted like chocolate in my hands."

"Ha! *Melted* is a strong word. I prefer 'temporarily satisfied.'"

The ATV rattles over a rocky patch, giving me the perfect excuse to press even closer. My thighs tighten, and he lets a soft groan slip out.

"You know what I think, Pip?"

"Oh please, dazzle me with your insights."

"I think you haven't stopped replaying every second of our time together."

My core clenches traitorously at the memory, but I keep my voice steady. "Doesn't mean I'm planning an encore performance."

"You sure? Because every time I bring it up, you press those thighs a little tighter around me."

Shit. Busted.

Time to knock Mr. Ego down a few pegs. My years of bartending have taught me that in the art of flirting, you want to lead.

"You're sounding a little breathless there, hotshot. Is that from dodging tree branches or because you can feel my hardened nipples on your back?"

The sound he makes should require a prescription, it's that addictive.

I move my hips. "These bumps keep jostling me around, and I'd hate for anything to accidentally rub your... equipment."

"If you keep running that sassy mouth of yours, I'm going to find us a nice, quiet spot in the woods where I can teach you some manners."

"Big talk from someone who'd have to grow a pair and admit he wants me first."

I feel his laugh rumble through his chest. "Pip, you're going to be the one begging me to pull over before this ride's finished."

He kicks the ATV into high gear and shoots forward.

"Try not to grab my ass when we hit that bump," Bryce says into the headset.

The next thing I know—*we're airborne.*

My body flails like I'm in zero gravity.

Then—*WHAM!*

"What the hell, Bryce?" I shout. "You always drive like this, or are you trying to make me hump you like a jungle koala?"

His laugh is feral. "If the koala moans like you do, I'm all in."

We zip around Nigel's ATV like we're in some billionaire-themed Mario Kart taking first position. Miss Muffy's ears flap in the wind, her tiny pink tongue hanging out in pure bliss.

I need a photo of this madness, or I'll spend the rest of my life trying to convince people I didn't hallucinate the whole thing.

But right now, I've got more pressing matters. If I want to crack Mr. Perfect Control and get him to confess he's secretly craving round two, it's time to deploy the nuclear option.

I dig my fingers into his abs and let out a soft, breathy, "Mmmm," right into the mic.

His shoulders go tight.

I moan again, longer, dirtier. Add a soft sigh. A little inhale. Like I'm being touched in all the right places.

The ATV bounces over a root the size of a telephone pole, and I strike like a cobra.

"Oh! Yes! Right there. That's the spot."

Every muscle in Bryce's body locks up like he's been flash-frozen. "Pip, what are you doing?"

"I'm giving you feedback on your driving technique. This seat really knows how to work a girl's pressure points."

I start panting. Little gasps between the moans. Each one a little louder. A little more… persuasive.

"Oh… oh my… yes, just like that…"

"Petra, stop."

"Stop what? Having a good time?" I moan loudly. "I thought you liked hearing me enjoy myself?"

The ATV suddenly veers left, crashing through a giant wall of tropical leaves before he jerks us back onto the path.

"Son of a—!"

Music to my ears. Mission Scramble Bryce's Brain Eggs is succeeding.

"Bryce! Can't you go any faster? These vibrations are getting me off!" I purr with manufactured lust.

I create a symphony of breathy gasps—louder, needier, filthier.

"Cut it out."

"It's building… Almost…" I dig my nails into his sides. "Oh fuck, yes—"

"That's it. I'm pulling over."

"No!" I gasp dramatically. "Don't stop! I'm so close. Faster, Bryce! Harder!"

His laugh cuts through my performance like a rock through glass. "Nice try, Pip. You forget—I know what you really sound like when you're about to come. I've got your soundtrack memorized."

"So you're some kind of orgasm expert now?"

"When it comes to yours? Absolutely. That fake whimpering is insulting to both of us."

Time to flip the script.

"What about you, Moneybags? Did my performance get you all worked up?"

My palm presses against the front of his pants and—oh. *Hello, monster truck rally.*

"Holy shit, you're hard as a rock. All this from only my voice? I wonder what would happen if I..." I start stroking him over the fabric, feeling him twitch beneath my palm.

"Don't do that while I'm driving."

"Why? Afraid you'll lose control and come in your pants like a good little billionaire?"

He doesn't answer, so I keep rubbing. "Admit it... You're thinking about my creamy pussy."

He jerks the handlebars. "I'm trying to steer."

"Your cock says otherwise. It's begging for attention. Just say you want me, and I'll stop... or say you want me, and I'll keep going."

He lets out a low groan, and I rub harder, feeling him pulse beneath my fingers. "Admit you want to be inside me right now."

"Petra."

"That's not an admission."

I look back over my shoulder. We're in the lead. The other four-wheelers are tiny specs in the distance. So I unzip his pants and reach inside, wrapping my fingers around his hot, hard length and giving him a firm squeeze.

"Christ!" He swerves, barely missing a gigantic tree trunk trying to take us out.

"Great reflexes, B." I start stroking faster, feeling him pulse in my grip.

"Not here! Your brother is catching up to us."

I glance over my shoulder, and sure enough, Gavin and Fiona are gaining ground. "Yup, he is."

"This is crazy."

"You can end this now," I whisper, my hand working him with steady pressure. "I'll tell you exactly how wet I am if you tell me how much you want me. I can feel you throbbing. You're dying to say it. Come on. Just three little words."

I kiss the back of his neck and close my eyes, breathing him in. Sweat, leather, jungle heat, and man. The way his cock twitches in my palm, my whole body is pulsing, aching... *Oh shit.*

I'm climbing for real... Fast.

Whatever's humming down there is obscene. I mean—*truly obscene*. Like, there should be a warning label slapped on this ATV: CAUTION: MAY CAUSE UNINTENTIONAL ORGASMS.

"Bryce, I'm not fucking around—I'm close... Oh... oh God," I moan.

"Jesus, Pip—do you want us to die?"

"Tell me I'm right. Tell me you're aching to be between my legs."

"Christ. Your hand..."

"My hand, my mouth, my pussy..." I purr into his neck. "Admit it, and they're all yours."

WHAM! The ATV hits a colossal bump, and the sensation rockets through my core like lightning. The buzz of the engine, combined with the way I'm pressed against him, sends shockwaves straight to my clit.

The moan that escapes is high-pitched and breathy.

"Shit, that's real," he rasps.

"Told ya." My voice comes out husky as I work him frantically. "Last chance, B. I'm about to come... and you're about to explode in my hand. Say it. Say I'm the one you want, or we both finish right here, right now."

"You're bluffing..."

Another bone-jarring bump sends pleasure ricocheting through my system like a pinball machine made of nerve endings. "Bryce!" My hips buck against the seat involuntarily, seeking more friction, more pressure. "Faster! Gavin's right behind us..."

"AAHHHH-FUCK!" he shouts, making a hard left without warning.

The ATV tears through a thicket, branches slapping at our sides, engine roaring as we veer off the path into the jungle like fugitives.

Then—*SLAM.*

Brakes lock. Dust explodes around us.

"What the fuck?" I pant. "I said *NOT* to stop. I was *so close!*"

He says nothing.

Just climbs off the ATV, rips off his helmet, and throws it to the ground.

"Seriously, did you not understand what I—"

But my voice cuts off as he unbuckles *my* helmet, chucks it next to his, and hauls me off the ATV like I weigh nothing. He slings me over his shoulder, caveman-style.

"Is this you admitting that you're losing your mind over me?"

"I didn't say that. You're the one who needs to get off. I'm just being a gentleman and offering assistance."

He sets me down in a break of trees, shaded and humid, our bodies panting and wild. For the first time since this started, I get a full look at his face. The polished gentleman is gone. His blue eyes are practically black, blown wide with lust. His chest is rising and falling, and when his gaze drops to my zipper...

He's a man possessed.

The front of my jumpsuit unzips with a harsh, dragging sound, exposing the red bikini beneath.

"Fuck," he breathes.

Before I can respond, we're crashing in a hungry, relentless kiss. His mouth is claiming mine—desperate and hungry—like I'm his, like he owns me. My eyes roll back, and I'm so ready to be fucked when—

He breaks away. We're both gasping.

Then, without warning, he spins me around and pulls my back to his chest. His heart pounds through me as his muscular arms snake around, hands groping my breasts. He backs us into a massive tree trunk—anchoring us.

"Put your arms around my neck," he growls.

I can't obey fast enough.

My hands dig into his hair as he gathers my wild mane to one side, exposing the curve of my neck. Then his lips find me, hot and demanding as they slide along my throat.

What have I done? He's out of control.

His hands find my hips, fingers digging in hard on both sides. He presses his hard length to my backside. We both groan at the contact.

I follow his lead, grinding my ass over his hard cock. His sounds tell me exactly how good I'm making him feel. My hips are rocking him into oblivion. I can't hold back a smile.

Bryce murmurs, "Feel that? That's what you do to me. Now, let's see how you like being teased."

The first touch of his fingers dipping into my bikini bottoms and through my slick heat makes me whimper. His fingers drag slowly through my folds, exploring every sensitive inch. When he feels just how wet I am, he moans.

"Oh Pip, is that all for me?"

I shake my head frantically, even as my hips betray me by pressing against his touch. "No. That's for my new ATV boyfriend."

In response, he plunges two fingers deep inside me, and I lose my damn mind.

I throw my head back so hard I nearly concuss myself on his shoulder, a scream tearing from my throat—but his other hand clamps over my mouth, muffling the sound.

"Shh. We're not alone out here. I love hearing the real sounds you make when you come, but this time you have to be quiet for me."

He pumps his fingers in a rhythm made to ruin me—slow, deep, then faster. And then slow again. The thundering ATV already had me on edge. Now every inch of me is strung tight and his to play with.

He crooks his fingers and hits my magic spot. I must give something away—a quiver, a shudder—because he stays right there, repeating that delicious motion over and over.

Twist. Glide. Stroke.

"You still think a machine can do this better? Admit you want me."

I shake my head against his palm, even though we both know it's a lie. I'm seconds from seeing stars, which is when I remember: *Wait. No.*

He can't win. I may be three strokes away from climax, but I have one move left. I reach around behind me—hand sliding inside his boxers—and wrap my fingers around him.

"Petra, no," he growls, but his hips buck forward into my grip.

I feel his precum dripping from his tip. I stroke him slow. Then fast. Matching his rhythm. Mirroring his intent. Reclaiming the power one handsy stroke at a time.

"You like making my dick ache for a release, huh? Is that your game?"

We're both teetering on the edge of complete meltdown when I hear it—the low, rising growl of an engine charging toward us. My heart lurches.

I'm terrified he'll stop, pull away, leave me hanging—but he doesn't.

Instead, his pace becomes punishing, his hips snapping forward with enough force that I stumble, catching myself against the tree roots before finding my footing again.

"You like it hard and messy?"

Yes. God, yes. I want him inside me so fucking bad.

I keep stroking him, gripping tight, matching every pump of his hips. He's close. His breath stutters in time with mine.

The engine noise grows deafening, like whoever it is might burst through the trees at any second.

In his next breath, Bryce sinks his teeth into the side of my neck and *growls.* His body spasms. Warmth spills across my hand in thick pulses. His release coats my skin just as my muscles clamp down around his fingers and my own orgasm slams into me.

I gasp against his palm, my eyes squeezing shut. I sink into him, my body no longer mine to command as he continues slow, devastating strokes, milking every last tremor from my climax.

As my breathing finally steadies, he delicately pulls his hand away. I catch a glimpse out of the corner of my eye—his fingers, glistening and slick. And then, with a wicked grin, he licks them clean.

"The taste of you is so fucking addictive."

I want to say something witty, keep up the pretense that this was just physical, but my brain is fried. Then—

"Bryce! Petra!" Gavin shouts like a bulldozer plowing through our private paradise. He sounds way too close for comfort.

With military efficiency, Bryce strips off his button-down and uses it to clean my hand before gently positioning me against the tree for support. Once he's sure I won't collapse, he uses the sleeve to wipe away the red lipstick stains from his other hand.

One look at my face makes him wince. "Well, shit."

His thumb swipes across my swollen lips, cleaning away the carnage my lipstick has become. "Don't worry, beautiful. Next time I'm kissing every bit of it off."

The promise of *next time* makes my knees wobble.

"I wouldn't count on it," I rasp out.

He smirks. That damn smirk.

"Where the hell are you guys?" Gavin shouts.

Bryce transforms back into a composed gentleman so fast it gives me whiplash.

"We're over here!" he calls out, his hands moving to zip up my jumpsuit while maintaining eye contact. "Be right there! Your sister had to pee and was afraid of getting bitten by something!"

I whisper-hiss at him, "Really? You're throwing me under the bus?"

"I'll take the blame... if you admit I'm what you need."

"Admit my ATV orgasm was making you jealous."

He just grins wider then reaches up to straighten my hair, plucking out a rogue leaf. The casual intimacy of it makes my heart swell.

Get it together, Petra. You're not some billionaire's plaything. You're supposed to be calling the shots.

I straighten up with renewed determination. "Here's the thing, B. Yesterday, you showed your cards. Guys don't eat pussy like that unless they're desperate to get inside of it. Which tells me you want to fuck me... bad."

His eyes twinkle with pure evil. "Interesting theory. But I think you'll be the one knocking on my door tonight begging for more."

I shove past him. "Ha! Dream on, Moneybags. Now, if you'll excuse me, I'm driving this time so you don't cockblock my fun mid-climax."

CHAPTER THIRTEEN

BRYCE

I LOST CONTROL. ***AGAIN.***

I should feel guilty about how quickly I broke—embarrassed, even. But shame doesn't register when I'm still reveling in the *feel* of her pussy's angelic chokehold on my fingers.

My guest suite feels like a prison cell, even with the ocean stretching wide beyond the giant windows. I'm too wound up to appreciate the view. I sit on the edge of the bed in nothing but silk boxers, hair still dripping from the blistering shower I took to erase the jungle heat. And her touch. And her taste.

It didn't work.

I'm supposed to be settling into my evening routine—analyzing market trends and reviewing IPO documents. Instead, I'm rock hard over the phantom sensation of her wicked grip around my cock.

I scrub my palms down my face, rough stubble biting back. She obliterated my willpower in seconds. *What the hell is wrong with me?*

Who does that? Who fingers his best friend's sister against a tree while she jerks him off like it's some team-building exercise for deviants?

Me, apparently.

Sterling men don't lose their composure. We don't make guttural sounds when we come. We don't bite women's necks like predators.

But that's exactly what I did.

The memory sends a wicked pulse of heat down my spine—and lower.

I reach for the scotch, my fingers trembling slightly as I bring the glass to my lips. The amber liquid burns as it goes down. And Christ, tucked away in my suitcase is that damn shirt, stained with her lipstick. I should have thrown it away, but there it is, folded carefully like some kind of twisted souvenir.

The digital clock on the nightstand glows 11:52 p.m.

"You'll be the one knocking on my door tonight."

The arrogant prediction echoes in my head. I had delivered that line with such insufferable confidence, so sure I'd left her dripping for more. Convinced I held all the cards.

And now, it's pushing midnight.

I stalk toward the balcony, anxious for some air. The night breeze carries the whisper of distant waves and the rustle of palm fronds, but underneath it all... silence.

Deafening, mocking silence.

Was the whole thing an elaborate game? Get the billionaire to blow his load in the jungle and walk away laughing? *Was I a conquest?* Her one-time power play to bring the rich boy to his knees?

I bet Petra's in her room right now, texting her friends, rating my orgasm noises on a scale of one to pathetic.

"Guess what, girls? I jerked off Bryce Sterling. He came so fast, I thought he was sneezing. And then he whinnied like a dehydrated pony."

I bury my head in my hands. *Jesus.*

Or maybe—*fuck*—maybe I was too aggressive. Too rough. Maybe when I pulled her back against my chest and covered her mouth to muffle her cries, she felt trapped.

Shit. What if I crossed a line? What if she didn't come knocking because she's afraid to be alone with me?

I fall onto the bed, a man defeated, the Egyptian cotton sheets cool against my overheated skin. The phone on my nightstand is a glowing beacon of bad decisions. I snatch it up, thumb hovering over the screen as my mind cycles through increasingly desperate options.

Maybe I should text Gavin. Not about the sex stuff, obviously. Just... ask if Petra mentioned me. Casual. Brotherly concern. *Hey, how's your sister? She seemed exhausted after the ATV ride.*

"What in God's sweaty name are you thinking?" I mutter to the empty room, tossing the device. "You can't text him. He'll figure it out in five seconds, drag you back to the jungle for a 'bonding hike,' and push you off a cliff."

I pick up my phone again. I could message her. *And say what? Thanks for putting 110% into that handjob. How about we finish what we started?*

No. Out of the question. That's pathetic.

But what if she's lost? It is a huge house. What if she can't find her way to me through this labyrinth of hallways?

"Sterling, you're grasping at straws. She's fine. Her room is literally across the hall from yours. She's probably sleeping and hasn't thought about you once."

My brain isn't listening. It simply plays back a reel of her sweet sounds, smells, sighs, and sensations.

Listen, brain. Petra is trying to one up me. She thinks if she holds out longer, she wins. If I cave, if I go to her first, she will never respect me. This is Classic Pip—rattle the unshakable gentleman.

How did I not see this coming?

I grab the scotch, take a swig, and immediately regret it. The ice has turned to water, transforming aged perfection into lukewarm disappointment—kind of like my entire evening.

Fuck, I want her.

12:03... Blaring proof I'm a failure.

I should let it go. Stay here. Be rational.

Instead, I catapult off the mattress and head for the closet. *If she wants a reaction, very well. She shall have one.* No more games. Just two adults who clearly need to address unfinished business.

I stare at the silk robe just hanging there. Getting fully dressed *is* admitting defeat—as if I'm preparing for a meeting instead of whatever sexual standoff is about to unfold.

The robe wins.

I slip into the midnight blue silk, not bothering to tie it completely—loose enough to appear casual, but still dignified. Not vulnerable. Just appropriately annoyed at being kept waiting.

I storm to my door, hand on the handle, and exhale dramatically. Time to march across that hallway and remind Petra Brinkman who she's dealing with.

I pull it open—

And my brain sputters.

There she is, smirking at the threshold. All my filthiest fantasies in the flesh.

THUD! I shut the door so fast, it shakes the frame.

"Fucking hell."

My hand hovers over the lock mechanism. I flip the deadbolt. Flip it back. Then flip it again.

Open it, you coward. Pretend you have some semblance of game left.

Or you could test your luck, jump off the balcony, and go hide in the jungle.

Stop being pathetic. You're a Sterling. Sterlings don't retreat.

Swinging the door wide, I allow my robe to slip open, revealing my bare chest. I lean against the frame, aiming for nonchalant, hoping it appears effortless.

"Good evening," I say, dragging my gaze up her body. "I thought you'd lost your nerve."

Her grin could power half of Mexico. "You're the one who seems to have lost your shirt somewhere between opening and slamming the door."

Her eyes drop—lingering on purpose.

I cross my arms. "I do not slam doors."

"I'd call that a slam. Unless it was the sound of your composure hitting the floor."

"I was... ensuring proper door functionality."

"For an eternity and then some. What were you doing in there—fluffing the merchandise?"

"It's a complex locking mechanism."

She laughs—this rich, throaty sound that goes straight to my dick. "Right. Well, I'm here to collect on your little wager. You said I'd come knocking *today.*" She taps an imaginary watch. "But it's 12:14 a.m., Moneybags. Welcome to tomorrow."

"So you're winning on a technicality?"

"I'm just showing you who's edging who."

My eyes narrow. "Why are you dressed up? Is there an occasion I'm unaware of?"

"I dress for the mood I want to inspire. Tonight's vibe? Make the billionaire beg."

She executes a ravenous spin. So torturous, my neural pathways scramble.

Jesus fucking Christ, that dress.

It's the crimson halter from when we went shopping at Sebastian's boutique—molten silk that hugs every dangerous curve like a map to temptation. The back dips scandalously low, revealing that tattoo I can't stop thinking about *(and she knows it).*

She peers over her shoulder with calculated innocence. "See anything that needs closer inspection?"

"Wait..." I force my thoughts to align. "You only showed up to gloat about timing?"

"Not exactly." Her eyes rake down my torso, then lower to my hips. "I came to see if your boxer situation had resolved itself. There he is. Mr. Happy, waving his silk flag of surrender."

I instinctively adjust my robe, which is failing spectacularly at concealing his interest.

"You're absolutely maddening."

"Your body disagrees. You're at full mast, and I haven't even touched you yet."

"Do you ever stop?"

"Only when someone shuts me up properly."

My brain glitches. *I can do that.*

She steps closer. "Ready to admit I outplayed you?"

I shake my head, despite every instinct screaming surrender. "Not happening. Sweet dreams, Pip. Try not to lose sleep over what could have been."

I start closing the door with exaggerated slowness—calling her bluff.

She doesn't budge.

Until there's just a sliver to look through.

"Wait." She exhales. "All right, fine. I'll say it... I want you, Bryce."

The confession pours over me like warm honey and wildfire. Everything I've tried not to feel floods into me at once.

I open the door wide. "Thank Christ, because I've been out of my mind wanting you."

One pull, and she's flush against me. My mouth crashes into hers, like she's oxygen and I've been suffocating for years. Her lips part on a breathy noise I *sense* more than hear—and then, it's heat and tongue and her taste flooding my senses.

THUD! Somehow, one of us manages to close the door.

Her mouth is wild and confident. Like she owns my lips and is only here to remind me. I match her intensity, opening her up and sinking in. She fights back, because that's who she is. Who she's always been.

This is exactly what kissing her felt like years ago—like grabbing hold of a live wire and choosing electrocution. Every safe, predictable part of my life is going up in flames, and I'm too far gone to worry about the ashes.

My hands slide down to cup the globes of her ass, squeezing through the crimson fabric. She gasps against my mouth, the noise shooting straight to my groin. Then her fingers twist into my hair at the nape of my neck and yank—hard. There's a sting of pain, and it excites me.

A lot.

I'm outside myself now. Not the Bryce who gives press quotes and signs billion-dollar deals. No longer calculating risks and playing the long game. I am the man who let her jack him off in the jungle like a goddamn animal. I moan into her mouth—savage and greedy. She swallows the sounds, giving it back to me twice as dirty.

Fuck. That alone almost does me in.

The friction of the silk, her warmth pressing into me, triggers a full-body jolt. My eyes roll, and I tighten my grip on her juicy backside. My body drives the rhythm, pulling her hips harder into mine until we're both panting.

Petra kisses like she's corrupting my soul. As if she knows I've spent twenty-nine years being polite, restrained, appropriate—and she's dragging me out of that hell, kicking and screaming.

Then my brain—my perpetually overanalyzing brain—hijacks the moment.

Why would she choose this? Me? When this girl has spent her whole life tearing down everything I represent? Does she think she owes me? Is this some kind of thank-you?

I tear my mouth away, both of us breathing hard. She looks thoroughly kissed—lips swollen, cheeks flushed, eyes dark with lust.

"Before we..." I clear my throat, searching for the words cautiously. "If this isn't what you're here for, say it now."

"What?" She stares at me as if I've sprouted a second head.

"If you don't want to continue—"

"Oh, for the love of—stop being such a fucking gentleman." She pulls back, stepping out of my reach. "I want *you*," she continues. "The guy who grabbed my ass like he owned it thirty seconds ago. The beast you keep caged... The one who forgets to be proper... who takes what he wants. Let me hear those filthy sounds you make when you stop behaving."

Her fingers trace her breasts up to the straps of her dress. Every muscle in my body coils tight.

"I'm not here for the trust fund version of Bryce Sterling. I want the guy who finger-fucked me in the wild."

The crimson fabric slides off her shoulders like water, pooling at her feet. And underneath—

Mother of God.

She's in nothing but red lace and fuck-me stilettos, and damn if she isn't a combination of every filthy thought I've had since puberty. Her black hair spills over one shoulder, and her tattoos peek out from the lace like secret promises. I want her clutching the sheets, screaming my name in pleasure and begging for more.

"You're..." I swallow, my voice thick. "You are the most gorgeous woman I've ever seen."

She doesn't roll her eyes. Doesn't deflect. She stands there. She *owns* it.

Which turns me on more.

I close the space between us, fingertips ghosting along her collarbone then down to the delicate script tattooed along her ribs. I watch her breath catch as her skin pebbles beneath my touch.

Yet again, my brain tries to bulldoze the moment. "I feel compelled to mention. I can't offer anything beyond tonight. My life is... complicated."

What the actual fuck is wrong with me? I should be worshipping this woman.

Her face goes blank for a heartbeat. Then, her wicked smile returns.

"I get it. In your world, girls like me are supposedly looking for a baby daddy and a mansion. But to be clear, I'm not applying to be Mrs. Sterling. I'm just curious to see if your dick lives up to my *very* low expectations."

Her challenge makes me want to test her limits.

"There you go again. Thinking I won't impress you."

"Oh, Moneybags. I'm not one of your *nice girls* trained to lie there and clap politely after two minutes of mediocre effort. If you want praise, you're going to have to earn it."

My cock throbs with purpose, but for one terrifying moment, doubt cuts through the heat.

What if she does walk away unimpressed?

She holds her ground, confident and smug, as if my hesitation proves her point.

Instead, it lights a fire in my gut. *I want to ruin her.*

To prove *her* wrong. To step into this version of me—the one she pulled to the surface—and show her he's not only real...

He's dangerous.

I lean in, my lips teasing the shell of her ear. "What if I can't choose just one way to fuck you?" My fingertips skate across the intricate lace covering her breast. "What if I want to explore them all until I find the position that makes you forget your own name?"

Her breath stutters. "Stop overthinking and show me. I trust you."

Trust? From Petra? That's not just rare—it's sacred.

Every civilized instinct I possess evaporates.

I claim her mouth with bruising intensity as my hands span her waist and lift her up. She's ignited—legs locking around my hips, heels digging into my spine with force, nails carving promises into my skin. The rough lace of her bra collides with my chest, creating delicious friction.

I walk us to the bed, our mouths locked in battle, and drop her—rougher than I intended. She bounces, laughs, and spreads her arms, a delicious offering. She surveys me with predatory satisfaction and a grin that could topple governments.

"What's your personal record?" I ask, prowling closer. "Most orgasms in a single night?"

"Excuse me?"

I glide my palms slowly up her thighs, relishing how they twitch under my touch. "It's a simple question. Give me a number."

She shifts against the sheets, suddenly seeming less sure of herself. "Uh... two, maybe? Hard to keep track when you're swimming in tequila and hoping the dude has a clue where your clit is."

"Then consider this your warning. I will be doubling it. Walking tomorrow is going to be... ambitious."

She reaches for my waistband with grabby hands. "Enough with the threats. I need you inside me right fucking now."

I clutch her wrists to restrain her. "That's not how this works. I set the pace."

The issue is: I'm drowning in options and can't pick a starting point.

Every fantasy I've ever pushed aside about her floods in at once—her riding my face, bending her over the bed, the dresser... trying advanced positions in the Kama Sutra. The sheer number of possibilities has me frozen.

This woman is giving me complete access. But what sends her over the edge? Where should I start? This kind of sexual freedom? It's uncharted territory.

"Bryce." She cups my jaw, anchoring my attention. "Stop using your head and think with your dick. Or swear to God, I'll flip you onto your back and ninja fuck you until that fancy headboard snaps in half."

My cock twitches hard. "Good luck managing that when you don't have the use of your hands."

I pull the silk belt free from my robe and bind it around her wrists—anticipation sparking in her eyes. I cinch the fabric tight. The spindle headboard creaks as I knot her to it, her arms extended overhead, body arched and waiting.

"Well, this escalated quickly," she says, giving the restraint an experimental tug.

She's splayed out before me like a work of art—her bound arms highlighting the sleek line of her torso, red lace mapping out a trail of temptation. Her dark hair is a glorious mess against the white sheets.

Growing bolder, I slide my hand inside my boxers, swiping pre-cum from the tip before bringing my thumb to her mouth. Her eager tongue darts out before I issue my command.

"Now, now. Good things come to bad girls who wait." I pause for a heartbeat. "Taste."

She draws the digit into the wet heat of her mouth without hesitation, her tongue working magic while she hollows her cheeks to create suction. My body shivers. I yank my hand away before she can finish destroying my self-control.

"Nice try, but I'm in charge."

I lean over her bound form and trace my tongue—from the hollow of her throat down to her navel—savoring the way her muscles jump and flutter under my attention. When I venture lower, dipping just beneath the lace waistband, she arches against me with a sharp inhale.

"Aww," I murmur into the damp fabric. "Don't worry, lovely. I'm coming back for you. But not yet."

"Did you just flirt with my vagina?"

"Yes." I press a kiss to her hip.

Every minute with Petra sheds another layer of the man I've been pretending to be. This protective, controlled image I present to the world. With her, I am... free.

I shift over her body, my silk boxers dragging against her lace panties as I brace my forearms beside her shoulders. My mouth hovers just above hers. I speak low, letting every syllable drag.

"I already know how incredible it feels to mouth-fuck your perfect little pussy. So now I need to know how it feels when it tightens around my cock and milks me dry. But first..." I drag my teeth along the curve of her jaw, teasing. "First, I want to hear you sing for me."

My hips drop, pressing the full length of my erection over her panty-covered clit.

Silk meets lace. I roll my hips into her. *Fuck yes!*

A sharp breath hisses between her teeth. Her back arches. I grind harder against the slick center of her panties. My cock throbs at the feel of her wetness, and I haven't even slid inside her yet.

"Still think I'm boring, Pip?"

Petra doesn't answer. She can't. She's making this keening, strangled sound that turns my spine to liquid and makes my balls pull tight. She tilts her hips higher, rubbing greedily against my cock.

I kiss her like a man trying to chew through his own restraint, my hand slipping inside her bra to palm her breast. My rough caress teases her nipple until she's writhing beneath me.

It's too fucking much.

My hips buck forward, and *Christ*, one more stroke like that, and I'm done—and that's unacceptable.

I curse under my breath and slip a hand between us, down the front of her panties, fingers sliding through her inviting slickness.

"Oh, this filthy little thing. She's a bad girl, huh? Not coming when she's supposed to."

"Give her your dick, and she'll sing opera."

"Not yet, beautiful."

I quickly untie the satin belt from the headboard, pulling her arms, still bound, around my neck and securing them like a collar. She blinks in surprise as I hoist her off the sheets effortlessly. Her legs clamp around my waist, and I carry her to the wall, pinning her there with the full weight of my body.

"You need your first orgasm," I murmur.

I rock against her, my hips thrusting with a relentless, bruising force. Her moans shatter into gasps, sounds that imprint into my memory like a melody I'll never unhear.

"Fuck, Bryce—more. Please."

That last word—*please*—makes something inside me snap.

Petra doesn't beg for anything. But she begs for me.

I tighten my grip on her thighs, my hips grinding harder, over and over, crashing my core into hers. Her moans grow louder, more desperate, until...

She holds her breath.

That's how I know.

One second. Two. Then—

She releases this high, helpless whimper—like a whistling teakettle trying to shatter glass. It's her most intense climaxing sound yet.

Damn... I'm officially wrecked.

Her breathing is erratic. Shallow puffs of air brush over my skin as she melts against me.

But I am not done.

Not even close.

"Rest time's over, Pip. I've got a quota to meet."

"Bryce... please. Just fuck me."

The needy moan that tears from her isn't polite—it's carnal. And *fuck me* if I don't get harder.

I release a hand from her waist and slip my fingers under her panties. As I slide along her folds, a groan rumbles through me. "You're dripping with gratitude... I think I better lick you clean first."

She shudders, and I have to pretend I don't feel it everywhere. My body's on fire as I haul her across the room.

The wingback chair waits like a throne, ready for its queen. I lower her, and she sinks into the cushions as though her bones have given out. Her head falls back, arms still tied with the robe sash. When I'm finished with her, this upholstery is going to need a professional cleaning.

I give the belt a firm tug, pulling her limbs above her head. "Unless... you'd rather call it a night? Return to your room and pretend this didn't happen?"

No response. She's conserving energy.

I tug once on the belt. "Stop or go, Pip?"

Her tongue swipes over her bottom lip. "Still waiting to see if your bark has any bite, Moneybags."

There she is.

I secure the belt to the wall sconce next to the chair. Watch her arms pull taut and her spine curve. Her breasts rise beautifully against the lace, nipples stiff and waiting.

I hook my thumbs into her panties and yank. The sound of the fabric tearing is almost as satisfying as her gasp.

"These are mine now," I tell her, shoving the torn lace into my robe pocket.

"Well, you *did* pay for them."

The corner of my mouth twitches. "You're dangerously close to getting gagged."

"Fine," she says, eyes dropping pointedly. "As long as I get to choose what I choke on."

God help me.

I drop to my knees. One swipe of my tongue, and her hips launch upward with such force, she knocks me flat on my ass.

"What the fuck—" I laugh as I catch myself on the floor. "Are you trying to break my nose?"

"How many times do I have to say it? Don't sneak up on a girl like that. Give her some warning, will ya?"

"Spread," I say. No room for negotiation.

She stares me down like a warrior while her knees fall open, eager and seductive, baring all of her to me.

My pulse pounds behind my eyes.

I grab her ass and drag her to the edge of the seat. She's drenched and defiant, trying to take the lead. But she's going to lose. And I'm going to make sure she savors every moment of her defeat. Because I want to ruin her for every other man, make her hear my voice when she touches herself. I want to be the reason no other man can ever satisfy her.

I need to be the one.

I drag my mouth along the inside of her thigh, slow enough to make her curse under her breath. She angles her greedy little thing toward me, a silent plea.

I dive in, my tongue claiming every slick inch like I'll never get another chance.

Her core writhes like she's trying to escape, but I'm not letting her go. I want every last drop she has to give me.

Her moans turn breathless. "Fuck! I can't—I can't—oh my God..."

"You only say one name in this room. Mine. Say it."

She chokes out a ragged, "Bryce."

She's pure music. Every moan, every hitch in her breath, she's a goddamn symphony I'm memorizing note by note.

She tenses, and I can feel her second release coming.

The strangled sound she makes is something between a sob and a scream. "Don't stop. I'm right there. Please—just—"

With a growl, I suck hard while gliding two fingers inside her, curling them until she gasps. I keep pumping until her body tightens, and the sighs she makes are so erotic I want to bottle them.

She shatters.

Her release floods over my tongue, her whole body convulsing, clenching around my fingers as she tries to pull me deeper.

My cock pulses painfully against my stomach. I *NEED* to be inside her.

I untie her wrists, and they fall slack, limp with pleasure. She doesn't speak. Just lies there, glowing and undone.

She's even more beautiful like this.

I can't wait another fucking second.

I scoop her into my arms. She nuzzles into my chest as I cross the room, heart racing, skin tight with anticipation. I yank open the dresser drawer to grab a condom.

I lean her over the glossy wood. Her palms flatten, her spine arches, and her cunt tilts toward me in invitation.

And then I see it.

The tattoo on her hip, hidden until now. A lotus flower cradled in a crescent moon. I trace it with a fingertip, and her curves mold into my touch.

"I want you rough," I murmur as I roll the condom on.

"Same," she gasps.

"Hold on."

She barely grabs the dresser before I bury myself inside her.

And holy. Fucking. Shit.

Heat. Pressure. The slick, tight slide punches the air out of me—it's sheer, overwhelming, sensational friction.

"Jesus, Pip. You're strangling my dick."

She lets out a breathless laugh that melts into a moan. I pull back and slam into her.

Hard.

Her feet lift off the floor.

The dresser jolts forward.

I growl, my hips snapping. "This... This is what you do to me, Pip."

She whines—actually *whines*—and it destroys whatever filter I had left.

"If you're giving me those sounds, they better be real."

"They're—fuck—Bryce."

I pull one hand free and bring it down on her ass with a sharp *crack.*

She yelps. "Oh God!"

"What did I say about names?" I give another slap. Her skin blooms red beneath my palm.

"Bryce!" she screams.

I lose my mind.

I pound into her with abandon, every movement fueled by what I've been holding back—years of restraint, months of denial of what I really want, countless hours spent pretending I don't crave her, all of it snapping under the weight of how badly I need her.

The dresser bangs against the wall. She's set my whole world on fire. The only person who knows what I look like without the armor—and doesn't run from it. She *wants* the beast I hide. She *prefers* him.

A primal sound tears from my throat—a deep growl full of need and possession. Every thrust rips another noise from me, louder now, filthy with want. I can't silence it—don't want to. I want her to hear what she's doing to me.

Our frenzied sounds build and build into a fury of need. Her cries get louder, messier. Her body bows, her moans spilling out and desperate.

Then she clenches. Hard. So tight, it's a goddamn velvet vise sealing around me.

She's coming.

I feel it—rippling, pulsing, a wave crashing over both of us.

My vision whites out.

Everything inside me locks up. I'm right there with her, gritting her name between my teeth as I explode. The orgasm comes with brutal force. My muscles seize, every nerve lights up. I spill into the condom so hard I'm flooding it.

But I don't stop moving. Not until I've wrung out every ounce of pleasure. Until finally, my body gives out and I collapse over hers, panting, soaked in sweat.

"That all you've got, Moneybags? I was promised four."

I huff a laugh. My cock twitches, as if he wants to speak up.

I push her hair aside and kiss the base of her neck. "Oh, Pip. This night's far from over."

And then it hits me.

I thought I'd ruin her.

But she wrecked me.

No other woman will ever make me feel like this.

CHAPTER FOURTEEN

PETRA

Group Chat : CPK Forever

Me: *Quick poll: How wrong is it to ride your ex-crush like a thirst pony?*

Katie: *Petra Monroe Brinkman. You did NOT!*

Me: *Don't lecture me, but yes, Bryce Sterling re-arranged my organs last night.*

Cam: *¡DIOS MÍO! PETRA! After so many "I'm over him" speeches?*

Me: *I am not catching feelings. It's casual. My vagina is very grateful.*

Katie: *Sweetie, you got a tattoo for this man. That's not casual.*

Cam: *Rating needed. Scale of "meh" to "soul left my body?" Spill!*

Me: *There were unicorns leaping over rainbows,*

splashing through candy fountains with glitter raining down like confetti. Just like my teen journal predicted.
Katie: *Happy for you. We just don't want to see you hurt again.*
Me: *My body is satisfied. My heart is locked away. Call it character growth.*
Cam: *Whatever happens, we'll be here with CPK and hugs.*

I WOKE UP IN my own bed this morning with no clue how I got there. Like, *zero.*

If not for the delicious ache between my thighs and suspicious red marks circling my wrists—*are rope burns my new favorite accessory?*—I'd swear last night was another ridiculously hot Sterling sex dream.

But it wasn't.

The orgasm count was real—I lost track after five. The emotional mess I made of myself? Also very real. I told him I wanted him—like a hormonal idiot—with words and everything.

Now I'm sweating my ass off in Casa Cashmere's pretentious art salon, my houndstooth Valentino mini dress trapping heat like it's mad at me. Still, I'm doing my best to resemble a functioning adult.

Unlike Echo—the Human Psychedelic Trip—who is channeling his inner cult leader for a crowd of bored billionaires. His man bun glistens, and his linen pants are soaked in either passion or humidity—I don't want to know which. He's a true showman, grunting loudly and flailing his paintbrush with passion.

His latest creation: *the wedding portrait.*

Bryce isn't here.

No text. No "last night was fun" follow-up. Not even a tragic little emoji. Just... poof. Gone. He might as well have left a hundred-dollar bill on my nightstand.

Ugh. I need to think about something else.

The morning sun cuts through the stained-glass skylight overhead, filling the room in a dazzling array of colors. On a raised platform built for ego and aesthetics, Gavin and Fiona pose with confidence.

My brother is the picture of masculine elegance in his charcoal suit. Beside him, Fiona predictably drips in diamonds, her emerald couture gown a cascading waterfall of silk and sparkle. There's no mistaking it—she's glowing from all the attention.

They look annoyingly perfect. And they *assume* that is the pose Echo is painting.

He is not.

From my strategic corner position, I've got front-row seats to Echo's *interpretation* of wedded bliss.

Holy. Fucking. Hell. This isn't distinguished artwork. This is what happens when Michelangelo gets horny and traumatizes future generations.

Canvas-Fiona is nude. Not *sorta* nude. Not *strategically draped.* No. She is full-on, Renaissance-reclining-on-a-cloud nude. One arm lifted like she's summoning the spirits of lust, the other cradling a breast to an audience of peeping Tom cherubs.

And my brother?

Homeboy has wings.

Massive, iridescent, Victoria's-Secret-model-type wings, spread behind him like he's leading the armies of heaven into war. Instead of a sword, he's clutching Fiona as if she's the last virgin in the apocalypse. A whisper of fabric hovers over his junk—the only thing standing between this painting and an NC-17 rating.

Gavin has no idea.

The poor man thinks he's getting a legacy portrait. Something classy. Something his future children will stand under in monogrammed pajamas while sipping hot cocoa at Christmas.

I'm struggling so hard not to laugh that I might swallow my own tongue.

"Each brushstroke celebrates the mystic union of spirit and flesh!" Echo proclaims, sweeping his brush dramatically over Gavin's painted nipples. "The divine consummation of soulmates reborn in celestial bliss!"

My brother adjusts his pose slightly, appearing pleased as punch. "We wanted something that captures our enduring love."

Oh, it's capturing something all right.

I should tell him that he's the unwilling star of Biblical erotica.

I absolutely will not.

This is my reward for waking up in a post-orgasm shame spiral while my sex partner-turned-ghost haunts me with his absence.

Reluctantly, I return to my laptop. *Petra Brinkman: Wedding Assistant.* That's my role here. Not *Spiraling Girl Who Had Scream-Your-Throat-Out Sex with the Groom's Best Friend.*

I force a reset. Time to get my head in the game. Finish this job for Gavin, secure the college funds, and then go save the world as a kickass pro bono lawyer. I repeat it, a silent promise, even as my brain's rebelling and returning to Bryce. *Damn it.*

To: Casa Cashmere Events Team

Subject: Updated Seating Chart - Please Don't Make Me Do This Again

Hi there! Here's the new arrangement. If anyone asks to switch tables again, I'm setting myself on fire.

Delete.

Hi. I changed everything one more time because apparently I'm a wedding goblin and I hate myself. Chart attached.

Delete.

Dear Team. Seating chart attached. This is version... I don't know, infinity? Let's consider this one locked down or else. Cheers, Petra

Send.

I inhale, and boom—my brain's once again spinning on that what-if carousel, flipping through worse-case scenarios like it's training for the Anxiety Olympics.

What if he's having second thoughts about defiling his best friend's sister?

What if he's calculating the many friendship rules he's violated with his dick?

What if he carried my unconscious body over to my room like he was disposing evidence and wants to pretend it never happened?

What if he's practicing his "lapse in judgment" speech in real time?

I need this humiliating disaster of a trip to end ASAP so I can crawl back to my shitty apartment and never see him again.

"Wildcat, how's it looking over there? We haven't gotten a peek yet."

Gavin jerks me from my daydream *(daymare?)* right as Bryce enters the room.

He claims the empty chair beside me with calm assurance. Not a single word. No hint of a smile. Not a damn thing to show he remembers that less than eight hours ago, I was his willing prisoner, tied to his bed, moaning for him to *please not quit.*

The man's gone full statue. Silent. Expensive. Gorgeous.

From the corner of my eye, I catch the full effect. A navy suit that emphasizes his powerful shoulders, the very ones that pinned me against walls, doors, and his bed. His hair is smugly styled, those dark-blond strands slicked back. His jaw is clean-shaven now, but last night, when that sexy stubble scraped against my inner thigh... *Yes, please.* Dear Lord, I made some indecent sounds last night.

He just sits there as if I'm invisible.

Oh, he's feeling regret. Is that it? Message received. Loud and dickless.

I bet he's already processed his hot, sweaty miscalculation. He took me for a test drive but has swerved back into his emotionally unavailable lane.

Perfect. Absolutely fucking perfect.

He wants to pretend last night didn't happen? Fine. I'm on the brink of not giving a single fuck. And you, Bryce Sterling, can choke on every second of it.

I cross my legs, slap on a serene smile, and stare at Echo as he immortalizes my brother's *(ahem)* angel-winged penis.

"Bryce?" Gavin shifts in his pose. "You've got the best view from there. Initial thoughts?"

"Bold," he responds.

Oh sure, Gavin gets a whole word from Mr. Manners.

"He's giving you more than you asked for," I add. "Really capturing your brand."

"Bryce, can you take over my ten a.m.?" Gavin asks, clearly getting restless. "This portrait session is running long."

"Gav-Gav, sweetheart, this is our artistic legacy," Fiona purrs. "Someday our children will inherit this beautiful representation of our love."

"Yeah," I mutter, "don't think they'll be fighting over this one."

"What's the agenda?" Bryce replies.

"It's the auditing team," Gavin says while maintaining his statuesque pose. "Someone leaked rumors about executive restructuring at Heartvest. They want clarification that there is no shake-up before we finalize the public offering."

The transformation in Bryce is immediate *(and alarming)*. His entire frame goes rigid. That telltale finger starts its nervous percussion against his thigh—tap-tap-tap—and his breathing suggests internal panic.

Whatever this restructuring rumor involves, it's hit a nerve the size of the Grand Canyon.

"SILENCE! The moment is climaxing!" Echo booms across the salon as if he's summoning lightning. "And Gavin, *for the love of Aphrodite's ankles,* stop shifting. Your aura is wrinkling."

"I'll take care of it," Bryce announces, vaulting from his chair like the seat has caught fire.

He's out the door before I can blink. My phone buzzes.

Moneybags: *We need to talk.*

Oh, hell no. Nothing good ever follows those four words. I'm already picturing his cover-your-ass speech about maintaining appropriate boundaries and preserving his sacred friendship with Gavin.

Me: *No need. I had fun. You had fun. One night. That was the point, right?*

The little typing bubbles appear. Then disappear. Then reappear. Then vanish again like they're emotionally conflicted Morse code.

Finally:

Moneybags: *If that's what you want.*

And there it is. The polite agreement to pretend our night of passion never happened. No fight. No protest. Just... acceptance.

My throat splinters like I've swallowed broken glass.

I'm seconds from throwing myself a one-woman sob parade, when Hana plops into Bryce's empty seat with a dreamy sigh.

"This painting is a total fairy tale. I hope my wedding portrait is that magical. Though maybe with a bit more fabric? You know, for my fiancé. He's not one to go shirtless, even at the beach or when he's all sweaty from... um, marital activities. At least that's what his assistant told me."

I'm relieved when she doesn't pause for air, just barrels forward.

"Today is going to be exquisite! Cultural activities followed by spa pampering? I simply cannot imagine anything more perfect."

"I'm less thrilled about the part where a stranger waxes my lady bits in the name of relaxation."

"Oh my gosh, Petra, you're so funny and naturally gorgeous. You have that effortless beauty that takes the rest of us hours and a whole team of professionals to achieve. Your bone structure... is goals."

I pause, mentally bracing for the fine print: "for someone with your vibe," or "if you're into quirky looks"—the usual sparkle-coated stab that girls like her deliver with a smile and a blowout.

But it doesn't come.

Hana keeps grinning at me as if I'm the Mona Lisa with better lipstick. Pure sincerity.

Well, shit. I'm so used to dealing with mean girls and backhanded compliments, I forgot honesty was still a thing.

"Maybe you can teach me how to enjoy all this spa nonsense," I say, surprising myself.

Hana claps her hands and squeals. "YES! I'll be your spa spirit guide! Trust me, I won't steer you wrong!"

"Just so we're clear, though—if you try to get me to wax my butthole, I'm out."

She laughs so hard she snorts. "No butt stuff. Got it!"

And like that, the pressure in my chest releases a little.

Until—

"What on earth is this?" Gavin yells from across the room.

I turn to see him standing next to Echo, hands on his hips, glaring at the painting.

"Fi, there is *no way in hell* this is getting hung in our house."

I raise my hand. "I'll take it! For my bathroom. It'll really class up the whole dropping-a-deuce experience."

Gavin turns and levels me with a glare so sharp it could carve a ham.

I shrug. "Kidding. Mostly."

Something inside me shifts as I soak in the glorious absurdity of this moment—my mortified brother, Hana's contagious joy, Echo's insane artistic passion, and even Fiona's fake-ass pout.

I'm in literal paradise, surrounded by wealth so obscene it feels ripped from a cartoon, and the people in it are somehow more outlandish. Bryce can take his emotional walls and his careful distance and shove them up his obscenely tight ass.

I've got three more days in this overpriced wonderland. Three more days of ridiculous luxury and watching rich people lose their collective minds.

And I'm going to enjoy every fucking minute of it. Starting now.

***

Memo to future me: A Brazilian wax after a night of earth-shattering orgasms is a death wish.

There should be a flashing neon sign outside the spa that reads: *Warning: If you've had a billionaire bang-a-thon and are sore in places on, around, over, under, and in your downstairs, then skip the waxing today, honey.*

My aesthetician is about to apply another steaming eucalyptus devil cloth on my lady bits. Sure, the pain is a welcome distraction from Mr. Emotionally Stunted, but at this rate, I'll be rolling out of here in a wheelchair.

The spa at Casa Cashmere is not your average spa day destination—it's a freaking compound of luxury pampering. Tucked away from the main estate, this place is a quick, serene walk through impeccable gardens with bamboo groves and koi ponds. Inside are arched doorways, the soothing melody of waterfalls, and staff in all white floating to and fro like Botoxed angels.

Every surface shines as if it's been blessed by the patron saint of OCD *(Saint Lysol, perhaps?).* I wouldn't be surprised if my next treatment involved soaking in a tub of hundred-dollar bills while receiving a foot scrub with actual diamonds.

Inside our private suite, the temperature is cranked up to somewhere between a hot yoga class and Death Valley. I'm sprawled out, covered from head to toe in what feels like congealed coffee grounds—otherwise known as volcanic mud—wrapped up tighter than a Chipotle burrito.

I'm slow cooking in my own juices, when one of those ridiculous cucumber slices makes a break for it, sliding off my left nipple and making a slow, dramatic descent down my boob.

Hana lies on the table next to mine. She's a mud-slicked cocoon lounging on a cloud, smiling and humming—*humming!—a*s if she's already achieved Zen-master-level enlightenment.

"Oh my gosh, I can literally sense the stress melting out of my cellular structure," she sighs.

"Really? All I feel is clogged hair follicles and a mild case of claustrophobia."

Hana lets out a string of soft giggles. "Oh, Petra, please stop! You're making me crack my mud wrap."

"Girl, I'm one exhale away from splitting open like a dollar-store piñata."

She snorts. "You're hilarious."

"No. I'm suffering."

"Can you believe this place exists? I've wanted to come here since I was twelve. It's so heavenly, exactly how I imagined it would be!"

"If having your lady parts brutalized by a woman who looks like she could arm wrestle a bear, then yeah, heavenly. Pass the painkillers."

She gasps, laughing. "Do you think Oksana *enjoyed* it? I mean—she made direct eye contact while ripping. That's... intimate."

"She kept giving a thumbs-up before each pull, saying, 'Vis vill hurt!'" I say, slipping into a terrible Russian accent.

"Petra!"

"Seriously, if Oksana can do that to my landing strip, imagine if the CIA recruited her—we'd all be doomed. She'd wax the nuclear codes right out of people."

We both explode into giggles, the kind that makes my stomach ache in the best way. For a split second, I'm hit with that familiar rush, the one I only get when I'm with Katie and Camila. That sweet spot of a friendship where I can let my freak flag fly, say the wildest damn thing, and never worry about being judged. I wonder about Hana. I really hope Fiona is the type of bestie who lets her be her true self.

"Okay, real talk time," I say, angling my head to her. "What's your actual dream? And don't say radiant skin or world peace."

She sighs. "I've always dreamed of experiencing love like you see in K-dramas. Where two people are so connected they can feel each other's heartbreak across oceans. Rain-soaked confessions, a dramatic slow-motion forehead kiss before the train pulls away, that moment when he cups your face and says you're his entire universe... I'm a sucker for that stuff. It's stupid."

Her words trigger a weird discomfort—my emotional shield goes up. *I'm too cynical for this gushy crap, aren't I?* I'm locked and loaded with a dozen sarcastic remarks, but honestly... I want that too. I want Bryce to look at me like I'm his whole damn world. I'd love for him to take in every chaotic, unhinged part of me—and not just tolerate it, but *want* it. To choose me.

No, this is about Hana. I focus back on her, if nothing else but to avoid confessing my pathetic unrequited love story.

"So... how did you go from 'epic soulmates crying in the rain' to signing a marriage contract with someone who witnessed electricity getting invented?"

For the first time since we've met, Hana falters—her sunshiney face dims. She avoids my gaze, staring up at the ornate ceiling instead.

"It's what's expected," she says quietly. "And that movie kind of love isn't real. It's fun to dream, but it's silly. And my family always tells me to get my head out of the clouds."

"Screw that," I say, because somebody needs to. "Love is real. And this is your life we're talking about."

"My parents had an arranged marriage," Hana continues. "Only a thirteen-year age difference, unlike my fifty. And they've built this calm, respectful partnership. Mom insists that's far superior to passionate, emotional relationships because it endures. And Daddy says this marriage is a brilliant strategic move. My family's portfolio will grow thirty percent after the merger, so that's good for everyone."

The silence stretches between us, filled by the rhythmic whisper of waves and gentle trickle of water over smooth stones beyond the windows.

"Ah yes, love—brought to you by spreadsheets and generational wealth."

"Joke all you want, but..." Hana's voice catches slightly. "I cannot disappoint my family. My fiancé? He's... decent. Older, sure, but very kind. And I need to be happy because that's more than most people get."

I study her expression through the steam. This woman has built her whole identity around pleasing others. Trading her happily ever after for a portfolio marriage. And the way she talks about her family's expectations? As if the words "duty" and "desire" are interchangeable.

Holy shit! Bryce is trapped in the same duty-bound prison. Born into tradition. Raised for duty. Groomed to lead.

Unlike Hana, he's expected to not just marry, but also be the future head of his entire family legacy. A goddamn financial dynasty that influences markets globally. The pressure Hana feels from her parents? I bet Bryce feels that multiplied by a trillion.

Of course he could only offer one night.

That's all I ever *could* be to him.

His life isn't about what he actually wants—it's about what he's *allowed* to want. And a working-class bartender with a smart mouth? Not a chance I'm on the pre-approved list.

I have to live with the fact that for a single magical evening, I got to see the man under the polished blueprint. The version of Bryce who let his hair get messy and his hands get reckless. The part of him that isn't the composed heir apparent everyone expects.

He looked at me like I was the only thing he's ever wanted.

Stop torturing yourself, Petra. That hint of something, that flash of connection—it's meaningless. His life is mapped out, a path he's locked on to, and there's no *me* in it.

I was his brief rebellion against a predetermined future. Nothing more.

***

Two hose-downs, three spin cycles, and one extremely targeted jet steam later... and apparently, I'm not done. I'm still at this damn spa. Next up on the itinerary? Gemstone massage.

Turns out my joke about being massaged by diamonds? Not a joke. Rich people *really* do that shit.

I'm gliding down a marble hallway in the fluffiest white robe I've ever worn, spa slippers squishing softly underfoot like tiny clouds hired to love me. The floor is heated—*heated*—because billionaire's feet should never be subjected to chilly floors. But you know what? In my current blissed out state, I get it. I fully, shamefully get it.

Crystals on my ass? Bring 'em on.

Holy shit, my skin. I keep touching my arms like I'm molesting myself in public. Massive PDA. They're so smooth and silky. *What the hell was in that mud?*

Against all odds, I feel surprisingly... zen. Like maybe I could keep it together for more than six consecutive minutes.

Except for one minor issue. My vagina is holding a grudge. Not angry anymore, just... buzzing. She's a well-tuned engine rumbling at a red light. The throbbing is definitely a spa rush. NOT for the person we refuse to think about.

That's my story. I'm sticking to it.

My mind wanders as I walk toward the Crystal Healing Wing.

I wonder why the ultra-rich have gemstones rubbed all over their bodies. Are they trying to absorb wealth through their pores? I'll have to ask Hana.

That thought triggers a memory—me on the balcony, Bryce's ruby ring on my finger. The same band that flew off mid-imagined proposal while I stood there daydreaming like a lovesick teenager. *Why did I ever think him picking that ring meant something?*

Oh shit, I still need to find that.

For a hot second, I consider leaving it. Some groundskeeper will stumble across it and be able to retire to a nice cottage in Tuscany. But then reality puts me in a headlock—it's probably on loan, because that's what high society does. They *borrow* from designers, then return everything like it's a damn library.

I'm assuming after this trip, all the jewelry and clothes will be returned to Sebastian in some kind of highbrow fairy godmother situation. Midnight will strike, and then Cinderella will be back in her rags.

If that's the case, Mr. Bellini can expect a few strategic crumbs in the designer pockets. Or better yet, I'll hide a sardine sandwich in that ridiculous beaded clutch. Let him explain that aroma to his next privileged princess.

I snort out loud picturing his mortified expression.

"This is simply unacceptable!" Fiona's voice is a chainsaw slicing through the peaceful aura of the spa.

I spot a service door ajar, and my eye catches a blur of platinum blonde. My fluffy slippers don't make a sound as I tiptoe closer. From this angle, I'm able to see through the gap.

Jackpot.

Fiona's inside, wearing a spa robe and waving her arms so wildly she might actually achieve lift-off. Across from her—praise be to the spa gods—Nigel is back in his tux, not a glittery chest hair in sight.

"Why am I just hearing about this now? You said everything was approved," she hisses.

Nigel straightens his tie. "Miss Whitfield, I understand your frustration, but the payment authorization has been declined. The account seems to be... temporarily inaccessible."

"Declined? That's impossible! My father owns half of California! There must be some kind of error. Run it again, or call someone... or, I don't know, do whatever it is you people do to fix these things."

Oh, wow. *You people*. Okay, Miss Beverly Hills 9021-No-Manners.

"I have personally attempted to process your outstanding charges on three separate occasions. Each attempt has been rejected due to what appears to be an account freeze at the financial institution. We have dialed the emergency billing contact you provided, but regrettably..." He pauses. "The line redirects to an automated voicemail system. This is extraordinarily unprecedented at Casa Cashmere."

"Well, obviously your payment processing is broken," Fiona snaps.

Nigel's diplomatic smile is a work of art. "Our financial infrastructure, madam, has executed flawless transactions for five decades. I can state with certainty that this is not a processing error. The sudden vacancy you filled, due to the King of Liechtenstein's unexpected and regrettable illness, is an agreeable arrangement for both of us."

Translation: She swooped in like a vulture when some actual royalty's dream vacation was cancelled due to medical drama. How very *Fiona* of her.

Nigel continues dryly, "As long as your expedited reservation is promptly paid in full, it won't tarnish your father's distinguished reputation here."

"Ugh," she huffs. "I'll call Daddy right now and fix this ridiculous misunderstanding. But you cannot breathe a word of this to anyone. The last thing I need is some terrible rumor ruining my magical week."

"Certainly. Casa Cashmere's sterling reputation relies upon discretion. However, I must clarify our position with transparency—we provide extraordinary experiences. We do not bankroll them. Especially one hundred-million-dollar matrimonial celebrations."

"*I'm aware,*" Fiona says through clenched teeth.

My detective brain starts firing on all cylinders: Wedding mysteriously fast-tracked by eight weeks? Yep.

Sketchy chemistry with Echo the Walking Art Project? Double yep.

Prenup weirdness that's got my brother snippier than usual? Triple yep.

And suddenly Princess Perfect's trust fund has apparently evaporated into thin air?

This whole clusterfuck smells fishier than a seafood restaurant dumpster in August.

"If direct contact with your father proves unsuccessful, perhaps Mr. Brinkman could provide alternative financial arrangements—"

"NO! Gavin cannot find out about any of this! He's..." She stiffens. "He's already overwhelmed with his company affairs. I'll sort this out myself. Give me twenty-four hours."

Hold up. Gavin's clueless? Did Fiona just crawl out of a cave, or does she really believe my brother—Mr. "I Can Fix Anything With a Spreadsheet and a Stern Glare"—is okay being sidelined when there's a crisis? Nothing gives him a bigger hard-on than swooping in with his cape and solving a problem.

If she's not going to tell him, I sure as fuck am.

"Very well, but should this financial irregularity persist beyond tomorrow's deadline, Casa Cashmere will need to terminate your wedding ceremony."

"I will sell my dead grandmother's entire vintage perfume collection before that happens," Fiona whispers, her voice cracking as she swipes at tears streaming down her contoured cheeks. "You'll have your money. This wedding is not getting cancelled."

Holy crap. I've never heard Fiona sound anything but smugly superior. She doesn't crack under pressure. She doesn't *do* desperate.

"If you'll pardon me, it is time for Miss Muffy to be retrieved from her hot stone massage. She requires her blow-dry appointment before this evening's dinner service."

Shitshitshitshitshit! Nigel's walking straight toward the door—toward me.

Glancing down the long marble hallway, I know I'm screwed. I'll never make it around the corner without being spotted. I throw myself into a nearby door, praying to whatever gods protect nosy bitches that it's just a boring linen closet.

Please be towels. Please be towels. Don't be a room full of naked oil barons getting their balls shaved.

The door closes with a click, and I find myself in a large dimly lit treatment room that is... blissfully empty. *Thank you, universe.*

My mind spins with unanswered questions. Why did Fiona bump up the wedding timeline? What's the rush? And if she's hiding a bomb this big from Gavin—money stuff, wedding stuff, whatever-the-hell-this-is stuff—what other skeletons is she cramming into her already overflowing Prada closet?

"Excuse me, is someone there?"

My wretched soul leaves my body... I know that voice.

In the dim corner of the room, barely visible in the soft lighting, a figure lies face-down on a massage table.

Oh, for fuck's sake. Bryce.

"I've been waiting for my appointment," he says, shifting like he's about to look up.

Panic hijacks my nervous system.

"Ah! Nyet! No moving, dah?" I bark in a disguised accent. I sprint to the table, shoving his head down into the face cradle. "Ees very, very bad for ze spine vhen you move during preparation of muscles!"

What accent is this? German? Transylvanian?

Nope. It's Oksana. The Russian wax technician who ripped the soul from my bikini line earlier. Her voice must've burned itself into my subconscious, along with the smell of hot sugar and the phrase, "You vill not cry!"

He hesitates. "You're my masseuse?"

"Yes," I say, still doing *The Accent.* "She—I am late. I come here. You relax."

I must be doing a pretty good Oksana impression, because Bryce moans out an "okay" and settles in.

This is catastrophically stupid. Like entering a flamethrower contest while doused in gasoline.

"Could you focus on my glutes?" Bryce requests casually. "They're incredibly tight from last night's... exertions. I think I may have overextended myself."

Oh, did you now?

I peel the towel down just enough to reveal the glorious, unfairly sculpted ass I know intimately well. "Da, glutes is important muscle group. I vill make loose for you, no problem."

My hands hover over his skin. This is where I should run—where any sane person would flee.

But apparently, *sane* is not what I am anymore.

My palms sink into him, and—yep. There go my girly bits. I bite my lip so hard, I nearly give myself a piercing.

Bryce lets out a low, satisfied groan, and my thighs tighten instinctively, every dirty memory from last night plays in high-def across my eyeballs.

No, focus! I must channel my inner Oksana—aim for torture instead of pleasure, keep this professional, and get the hell out of here before he realizes the woman massaging his naked ass is the same one he's ignored all day.

This plan is foolproof.

CHAPTER FIFTEEN

BRYCE

"YOU'VE GOT STRONG HANDS... I like that in a woman."

"Vell, vell," she replies in a truly offensive Russian accent, her thumbs digging deeper into my glutes. "Zis is vhat all ze men tell me before zey cry like leetle babies asking for mercy."

My ass clenches.

That accent should be flagged by Interpol and sent to rot in a Siberian gulag. But those hands... Those warm, smooth, dangerously familiar hands? My body clocks them immediately. They're the same ones that clawed at my back last night. That gripped my shoulders. That clung to me—trembling—when I made her fall apart.

Again. And again. And again.

Six times.

Not that I'm counting *(Okay, I totally am).*

I have no clue why Petra is pretending to be a masseuse, and honestly? I don't care. After a self-inflicted day of icy distance, I'll play along. Let her knead my spine and talk in her ridiculous drawl. If it means I get to be close to her—I'll take it. Being in her presence lifts the weight from my chest.

"You ver' stiff here," she says.

"Yes, I've been carrying some particularly… stubborn tension."

"Must fix."

Her response is immediate and merciless. She drives her elbow into a pressure point just above my hip bone as though she's trying to rupture an organ.

"Christ!" I hiss, fingers curling around the edges of the padded table. "That's… effective."

"Is healing," she chirps. "In my village of… Russi-vania… you want feel good, you first suffer."

Without warning, she pinches my ass. Hard.

I jolt. "Jesus!"

"Much stiffness in ze gluteus butticus."

She has no idea how stiff she's making me, her palms kneading my ass. Lying face down on this table is getting increasingly uncomfortable by the minute.

She pinches harder. "You seem like ze type of man who cannot handle vings vhen zey get difficult. Zis is too intense, dah?"

"It's fine," I grit out.

I deserve every damn ounce of pain she's giving me.

Last night, she entrusted me with parts of herself that I know she fiercely protects. The way she lay against me afterward, all that fierce energy finally at peace, trusting me enough to let her guard down completely. And how did I repay her? By treating her like a mistake, as if she were something to hide, a regrettable lapse in judgment.

I thought having her would set me free—physical release, mutual satisfaction, clean boundaries. Instead, I woke up this morning feeling as if I'd left part of myself in her bed. *What the hell kind of reaction is that?*

I keep trying to classify what happened between us. To place it neatly into a box. But she doesn't fit into any framework I'm aware of. She's not like the women in my world. She wants neither my name nor my money... so what *does* she want?

Her elbows dig into my waist with such force, I almost launch off the table. I mask my pain with a grunt.

There's a very real chance I'll leave this room with a slipped disc and a lifelong limp. This massage was supposed to be my opportunity to strategize—damage control, press statements, my impending CEO coronation. Instead? I'm lying here, surrendering to her torture like a masochist, simply because she's touching me.

This is sheer lunacy. I should end this charade right now. Drop the act, stare her down, have an actual conversation as two adults who've seen each other naked.

I have three days until I leave for New York permanently. Before this fantasy week is over and we return to our separate realities. I'm aware this doesn't come with a future. I get that I can't keep her. So how do I explain I need these next few days with her like I need air?

She's everything my world isn't—uncontrolled, unpredictable, real.

She startles me, delivering a vicious chop to my shoulder blade that resembles being hit with a meat tenderizer.

"Da rich men love vis torture."

"I see. Well, maybe you could shift into something a bit less... medieval," I suggest. "Something with more fluidity. More sensual and graceful."

"I give you superior treatment."

She pauses. Long enough to make me hopeful.

WHAP! Her palm connects with my ass.

"SON OF A—" I bite off the rest of the curse.

She slaps my backside again—and *yanks a leg hair* clean out of my thigh.

"What the hell was that?"

"Siberian bear slap. My babushka always say: 'Man who squeaks during massage don't expect a roar in bed.'"

I could stop this. Turn over, apologize like a grown-ass man, and face whatever fallout's coming. But no. I go full idiot and poke the bear.

"Out of curiosity, what is the official stance of Casa Cashmere on, shall we say, 'happy endings'? Hypothetically speaking... for a friend."

"Tell friend to go home and finish job himself."

I grin against the face cradle. "You see, that's the issue. My... friend had a rather zealous partner last night. Quite vigorous, really went for it. But occasionally, a man requires... a sense of completion."

"Maybe is you—your friend," she stammers in her faux Russian accent, "who has difficulty with... how you say... finishing."

"You're accusing me—*him*—of performance issues?"

"Is common, yes? Vealthy men have big bank, small bang."

Petra's palms press into my back with renewed vengeance—my spine is about to go straight through this massage table.

"Absolutely. Right there," I say, teasing her despite the pain. "So much more effective than last night's encounter. I'm beginning to suspect you might be the woman who can actually... finish the job properly."

The room goes dead silent except for the distant trickle of water over stones and my own thundering heartbeat.

She pulls the towel off my body. A whip of air. Then—

CRACK!

White-hot shock detonates across my left butt cheek.

"Fuck!" I shoot off the massage table from the painful towel snap. One hand clutching the surface, the other protecting my balls.

She's already halfway to the door, her spa slippers slapping against polished stone as she unleashes a stream of pure Petra fury.

"Rich pervert! Dickweasel! Pig!"

"Pip—stop. Please!" I secure the towel around my waist.

She goes statue-still, then pivots slowly, her hazel-green eyes igniting with the force of a controlled explosion.

"You knew?"

"Yes. From the moment you said 'wery important glutes. No real Russian says 'wery.'"

For the first time since she started this ridiculous performance, I can see her face. And damn, it hits me. I've always been drawn to her bad-girl aesthetic—that bold red lipstick, sharp eyeliner, and clothes that say *don't mess with me*. But this unguarded, natural version? It's a new kind of allure.

Her lips are bare and pink. Her cheeks are flushed. Her lashes accentuate eyes that are more vulnerable without the war paint. No act. No armor. Just her.

Two sides of the same remarkable woman, and this one is even more captivating.

I don't stand a chance.

"You are... astonishingly gorgeous," I manage to say.

Something flickers across her features—surprise, possibly pleasure—before she catches herself and lifts a hand to her face, suddenly aware of her natural state. The vulnerability vanishes, replaced by rage.

"You don't get to play with me like some fuck toy then ghost me," she snaps.

"You're absolutely right."

"Great. Glad we agree. Have a nice life, Moneybags."

She spins toward the door, and every trained instinct screams at me to let her go. She is chaos; I am the epitome of order. She acts on impulse; I act on careful consideration.

We do not make sense.

"I can't comprehend what's happening to me," I say, feeling as though I'm stepping off a ledge. "I've never... I'm not usually... *Christ!*" I drag a hand through my hair. "You've completely unsettled me, turned me into someone I hardly recognize, and I'm terrified."

I edge closer. She's facing away, but she's listening.

"I tried to treat last night as though it meant nothing. I convinced myself that I could neatly file it away and move on. But it's impossible. You're in my mind, Pip. Under my skin. And I am unsure what to do about that."

I reach out, gently guiding her to meet my gaze. The anguish in her eyes is my undoing—my silence and cowardice are to blame.

"Tell me how to fix this," I murmur. "Whatever it takes. Just don't leave."

"No fixing needed." She shrugs coolly. "We had one incredible night. Now it's finished. That's how flings work."

"Give me these next three days," I say. "I want to wake up with you and pretend that our lives fit together. I want to be selfish and reckless until reality separates us."

I touch the sleeve of her robe, fingers trailing down to brush hers. She sucks in a sharp breath and holds it.

"I know it's wrong, Petra. And I know it complicates things. But whether it's days or months, it makes no difference. I'll still crave you when this ends. Please, let me drown in you while I can."

Her eyes flash—sharp, assessing, as though she's weighing her options against her better judgment.

Finally, she tilts her chin, defiant. "Then quit talking and fuck me."

I grab her waist and pull her in. Our mouths collide—hot, hungry, and no restraint. I kiss her like I've got something to prove. Our lips push and pull in a perfect storm of contradictions—fierce yet tender, like we're both wanting to savor and devour.

Her hands slide into my hair, deepening the kiss. Her moan vibrates through my chest, a sensual melody that lights me up inside.

I clutch her hips, pressing her right into my growing cock. The towel offers little to cover up my readiness for her.

"God, you drive me insane," I whisper into her skin.

With a hungry urgency, I push the robe down her shoulders, uncovering the silky landscape of her skin. The sight of her, so bare and captivating, sends a tidal wave of desire crashing through me.

Her nimble fingers undo the knot at my waist, the fabric dropping, and she's already wrapping her hands around me.

"I'm thinking you need it rough and quick. Because, holy hell, this—" she gives my throbbing dick a tight squeeze "—is about to burst. And I want you back in action ASAP so we can go another round. Got it, Moneybags?"

"A well-thought-out plan, Pip."

She kicks off the spa slippers, and I lift her effortlessly, her thighs gripping my body as I pin her to the wall. The cool stone on her back makes her arch into me.

"This position suits you perfectly," I say, strengthening my hold on her ass. "You, shamelessly at my command."

My cock glides across her slick heat, and she whimpers, her nails digging into my shoulders. We grind against each other, getting lost in the rhythm—her folds drenching my shaft while my arms guide her up and down.

"Fuck, B. I've never gotten so wet so fast in my life."

I position myself at her entrance, both of us groaning at the contact. "I need you so badly, it's physically painful."

"Then take what you need," she whispers.

We're seconds away from crossing that line when my brain catches up.

"Dammit. I don't have any protection."

I ease her down reluctantly as we catch our breath. My forearms bracket her head against the wall while I try to think past the desire fogging my judgment.

"I've never done it bare, but I'm clean," she says breathlessly. "And I got the shot last week. Good for three months of worry-free debauchery."

Every lesson about responsibility and consequences my father ever drilled into me battles with the primal urge coursing through my veins. "This is precisely the kind of reckless decision I've been conditioned to avoid."

"Am I giving off psycho baby-mama energy?" she asks with typical Petra bluntness. "Trust me, the last thing I want is to explain to my kid why Daddy lives in a different tax bracket."

I drag the head of my cock through her slickness and nearly see stars. "I don't want to stop. I don't want to leave this room. Not for anything."

She presses her lips to mine, gentle this time. "Then don't."

I growl, scanning the space with mounting frustration—massage table, essential oils, decorative water features. Zero contraceptive solutions.

"I thought this place had mind-reading staff?" she deadpans. "Shouldn't there already be a concierge playing sensual jazz and bringing us an antique crystal bowl of condoms?"

I throw open the only other door here: the Ice Room.

The air punches me in the chest like a glacier uppercut. My skin immediately regrets this decision.

Petra leans around me and whistles. "Well, this'll make your nipples angry."

"It's supposed to. You sweat it out in the sauna, then come in here to the Ice Room to stimulate circulation, reduce inflammation, and tighten your pores."

"Do you rich people believe everything you're told?"

The frozen igloo's walls shimmer with translucent blue ice, and a gentle glow lights up the space from beneath. Mist swirls around the floor, giving it this magical, otherworldly vibe. And right in the center of the room, there's a single bench lined in faux fur.

It's as if we've stumbled upon some secret Eskimo love nest.

No condoms.

"This penis-freezing chamber is one way to cool things down," she says as she blows out a breath, watching it crystallize into vapor.

I bark out a laugh. She's not wrong. My balls have sprung up into my ribs.

She doesn't hesitate when I pull her into me. Doesn't flinch when I kiss the column of her neck, then her jaw, then dip to her already-stiff nipples. The contrast between her freezing peaks and my fevered mouth is electric.

"Why here?" she pants, her voice husky. "Are you trying to freeze me solid so I'll be even tighter when you finally get inside me?"

The thought makes me groan. I run my fingers between her thighs, finding her slick and warm despite the cold. "You're getting chilled. I'll have to use friction to heat you from the inside out."

"That's the cheesiest line I've ever heard," she breathes.

"Then why are you trembling?"

"Because I'm literally freezing to death, genius." She shivers against me. "Please tell me this isn't some weird rich-boy kink."

I begin stroking her clit gently, and she pushes into my touch, letting out that musical sigh I can't get enough of.

"You want to hear my fantasy?" I murmur, "It involves those sinful red lips wrapped around my di—"

"Sterling? You in there?"

We both freeze *(pun intended),* our eyes flying wide open in mutual terror.

"He cannot discover us like this," I whisper.

"No shit, Sherlock. Pretty sure I've met my overprotective brother."

Gavin will literally bury my body in the Mexican jungle if he finds his sister naked in my arms.

My eyes scan the ice chamber. One entrance, and Gavin is standing mere feet outside of it. I start backing toward the door.

"If you leave me naked in this freezer, I will castrate you with an icicle," she threatens in a furious whisper.

"I'll handle him," I promise quietly. "Stay put."

Petra shields her breasts with her arms and flips me off with impressive venom. I slip through the door, sealing her inside the arctic chamber.

I cup my hands strategically over my very obvious arousal and pivot to address Gavin, who's standing in the room's entryway, looking every inch the sharp-dressed CEO.

"Gavin," I say with remarkable composure, considering my heart is trying to escape through my throat. I smoothly collect my towel, wrapping it around my waist with practiced nonchalance. My poker face is flawless—minus the slight tic in my left eye.

He lifts Petra's discarded robe from the marble floor with two fingers, like it's contaminated. "You're not banging the staff, are you?"

Gavin's gaze intensifies. *Shit.* I always break under his stare. Everyone does. His interrogation skills are legendary.

Stay strong. Don't crumble. Don't let him discover that his sister is only a few feet away—naked, freezing, and furious.

He glances at the closed door behind me.

My lungs seize.

I snatch the robe from his hand. "I am simply experimenting with some temperature therapy."

Gavin's eyes flick down to the fluffy spa slippers strewn across the floor, then snap back to me. "Look, I get it—the Amanda thing is still raw. But if you're that desperate, I'm sure we can find a bridesmaid to... comfort you."

Part of me wants to inform him that I already have, and it happens to be the most incredible sex of my life.

"Was there something specific you needed?" I ask, hoping to redirect the conversation.

"Emergency board meeting. They want a full debrief on the auditor situation before we involve legal counsel. Can you walk them through it?"

"I'll be there in ten minutes."

Gavin moves toward the exit, his hand turning the door handle—then stops. "If you are involved with the staff... keep it discreet, all right? We can't afford any more issues."

"I don't make a habit of inviting trouble," I reply.

He's halfway out when he adds over his shoulder, "At least make sure she signs an NDA before you explore her pressure points."

And then he's gone.

I wait a beat—long enough for the sound of his footsteps to fade—then launch into motion. Robe in hand, I rush to the ice chamber, fling the door open... and find Petra freezing her gorgeous tits off.

"P-P-Prince FFFF-Freezerburn returns-s-s."

"I'm so sorry," I say, rushing to her, wrapping the robe around her shoulders, and guiding her safely out. "You know how long-winded your brother is."

I slam the igloo door and reel her into my arms, feeling the violent shivers wracking her body. I rub my palms along the fabric to generate warmth.

"This wasn't the friction I had planned," I say, dipping my head to blow warm air along her neck.

"Yeah, me neither."

Thankfully, her warmth returns after a few minutes, and she melts into my embrace. Every curve and contour of her body aligns with mine, and I've never felt so content.

I gently cup her face in my palms. "I have to go—Gavin needs me. But after dinner..." I lean in, lightly kissing her lips, "come to my suite. We're going to finish what we started."

Her wicked smile emerges. "You are officially on thin ice, Moneybags. Literally and figuratively. So be concerned. I intend to make you suffer."

"I'm anticipating every moment of it."

If revenge means her hands and mouth all over me while that wicked fire burns in her eyes as I beg... *then yes, please, punish me.*

Hell, I'll provide the ice myself.

***

Every fiber of my being aches to be inside Petra again.

Since the Ice Room, I've been counting down the hours. Three meetings where I pretended to care about profit margins while my mind replayed her breathy moans. A dinner where her wandering fingers found me throbbing under the table. Her innocent smile was a mask for the torture she was inflicting. I excused myself twice to splash cold water on my face and to will my erection into submission.

Now I'm pacing in my suite, wearing my silk boxers, chest bare to the humid Mexican air. The terrace doors are thrown wide, letting in the sound of rolling waves and night birds. My skin is hot, my jaw tight, and my cock's been hard since the soup course. Every tick of the clock grates on my nerves.

8:12 p.m.

She's testing my patience and she knows it.

I glance at the door as though it owes me an apology. Then I rake my fingers through my hair, already regretting how much of my sanity I've given this woman in a week. Yet, here I am, begging for more.

My mind wanders into dangerous territory—*how would it be if this wasn't temporary?* If I could come home every night to find Petra sprawled across my bed in nothing but that smart mouth and a dare-me expression? Would this fire ever dim? Or would it always burn this intensely between us?

Coming home to Amanda was like entering a museum: sterile and lifeless. I'd find her organizing flowers or consulting with the chef about menus, every conversation centered on our social schedule or her newest charity committee. I never felt a spark of anticipation with Amanda. From the beginning, she was something I selected, like a mutual fund.

Petra is something I *crave.*

It's more than infatuation, I'm gone for her. This woman who argues with billionaires and tasers men in tuxedos. I'm addicted to her chaos.

When this ends, I'll spend the rest of my life comparing every kiss, every touch, every connection to what I had with her. Nothing else will come close. *How the hell can I go back to my life after this?*

Keep her.

The words slip into my brain.

Petra Brinkman isn't the type of woman who gets *kept*. She's not going to host charity luncheons or smile demurely at board dinners while I discuss mergers and acquisitions. She'd tear down the foundation of my world just to watch the rich people panic.

And I'd let her.

Jesus Christ, I am in trouble.

BZZZZ. BZZZZ.

My phone vibrates on the nightstand, and I actually snarl when I see the name glowing on the screen.

Reginald Sterling.

"Perfect timing," I mutter.

Now he calls me back. The second I start envisioning a future with Petra in my life, my home, my bed.

I answer, and my voice slips into the polished tone that's been programmed into me since childhood.

"Father."

"Explain this nonsense about you and Amanda being over?"

No preamble. No pleasantries. Straight to the inquisition, as always.

"I'd expect you to have the foresight to inform me before you burn your most crucial personal alliance to the ground. But clearly, I overestimated."

"That's not why I called you earlier."

"You phoned to confirm I leaked those boardroom whispers," he says with that familiar edge of cruelty. "You know the answer. Consider the rumors a warning shot. I don't fuck around, son."

"Understood, sir." I force steadiness into my voice and will my nerves to behave. "I believed we had an understanding that Heartvest is navigating crucial territory right now. The IPO timing—"

"Heartvest ceased being your responsibility the moment you signed the Sterling succession papers. Accept that truth, or I'll force your hand with a public announcement at dawn."

Heat floods my face while my hands turn numb. My throat constricts, as though someone's tightening a noose, and suddenly the tropical Mexican air feels suffocating. Sweat breaks out across my forehead, and my vision starts to tunnel the way it did when I was twelve and he'd corner me in his office after some perceived failure.

My index finger begins its involuntary staccato against my leg.

Tap. Tap. Tap.

"Amanda's waiting for your reconciliation call. Since both our families have kept your little breakup fiasco under wraps, we won't have to contain any fallout."

The words stick in my throat. "No. We ended our relationship. It was mutual—"

"Mutual?" His laugh is sharp. "That's a generous interpretation. From what I heard, it was classic Bryce Sterling—unable to honor his commitments. Predictable and disappointing."

The blow lands exactly where he intended. He knows my weak spots better than a surgeon understands anatomy, and he never misses.

A Sterling always honors his commitments.

The family mantra sounds noble. But it really means: *no way out.*

"Your mother is livid," he continues. "Amanda is the ideal starter wife and future mother of your children. She checks every box—elegant, obedient, and built to bear heirs. She's been vetted and approved for the Sterling bloodline. You don't discard an asset like that."

My finger drums faster on my leg, beyond my control.

"Amanda will accompany you to New York," he declares with the finality of a judge's gavel. "Your personal preferences are irrelevant.

This is about Sterling legacy, about our empire that employs thousands and influences global markets."

Tap-tap-tap-tap-tap.

"Enough with this dream life you picked up playing entrepreneur in Los Angeles. Real life doesn't accommodate fairy tales, son. This family name transcends our personal desires and will outlive us both. A Sterling leads Sterling Industries—that's always been your destiny."

I swallow hard, tasting copper. "What if... there was another woman? Someone who—"

"You have a woman in mind who can match Amanda's pedigree, social positioning, and readiness to produce offspring immediately? Because you're behind on that requirement too, son."

An image of Petra flashes through my mind—those rebellious eyes that never surrender, that mouth that tells the world exactly where it can go. She's not just the opposite of Amanda. She's the opposite of everything I was bred for.

And that's the problem.

She'd laugh in my face if I asked her to play house and raise heirs. She's made her stance on kids clear: not for her. Especially not with a man like me. And she'd never, not in a million years, wear the Sterling name as a collar.

But damn it... I wish she would.

"Quit wasting my time and get your ass to New York," he snaps. "I don't give a damn about your pet project. If I wanted to destroy it, I could. Don't test me, or I will bury your little startup so deep, nobody will remember it existed."

My blood turns to slush in my veins. When my father employs that razor-edged tone, it means the execution plan's already drafted. He doesn't bluff—he strategizes, then annihilates.

"That Brinkman boy keeps creating headaches for me," he continues. "I should have put my foot down when you wanted to drag that charity case along for your Ivy League experience. Stop showing weakness. Be the man I raised you to be."

My chest caves inward. There's no escape route from this conversation, no clever maneuvering—only surrender. But I can salvage what Gavin and I built together. I can protect the sixty million people who trusted us with their financial futures, the families learning to invest for the first time.

Petra flickers in my mind, but it's hopeless. She was never mine to have.

"I'll do what you ask, on one condition. You delay announcing my CEO transition until Heartvest's IPO completes successfully."

"I'll expect a wedding ceremony within thirty days and confirmation of your first pregnancy by Christmas," he counters without hesitation. "No more delays. You secure what you want, and I collect what I'm owed."

"Yes, Father. I understand. We're in agreement."

"Smart choice, son."

The line goes dead.

My phone drops, hitting marble with a sickening crack. I collapse onto the bed's edge, pressing both palms against my skull, hard enough to make it all disappear for half a second.

But it never does.

I push up. Start pacing. Five steps to the minibar. Back again. The air feels too thick, as though I'm walking through water and every breath is a fight.

I go to the drink cart. Grab the decanter of scotch. No ice. Just a hard pour and a harder swallow. It scalds all the way down, exactly the punishment I deserve.

One more pour. This time, I don't drink it. Instead, I march to the balcony, the crystal tumbler clutched tightly in my hand. And I throw it.

CRASH!

The sound of the glass hitting the tile below shatters the peaceful silence.

My fingers claw through my hair, tugging with enough force to sting. Then I scream. Loud and broken. A sound I didn't know I was capable of making. Years of buried rage breaking loose.

Wetness flows down my cheeks. I haven't shed tears since I was old enough to understand they were weakness. But tonight, my body rebels, against a lifetime of emotional imprisonment. Against the crushing weight of a destiny I never wanted.

Why did I let myself believe for one second that I could choose a different path? *How could I be so delusional?*

KNOCK! KNOCK!

Fuck. Petra's here.

I scrub at my face, eyes swollen and raw. I run a hand through the mess on my head, trying to tame it. I cross the room and square my shoulders. *I'll tell her I'm sick. I'll send her away. I can't let her see me like this.*

The door swings open to reveal Petra clutching a silver ice bucket, her robe cinched tight around her waist, mischief in her smile.

"You ready for your torture, Money—" Her smile drops. "What's wrong?"

"Stomach issues."

"Bullshit." Her eyes narrow, studying my expression. "I know you. Something's wrong."

She *knows* me?

No one knows me—not the real me. I've built walls smooth enough to reflect, tall enough to defend—yet she walked right through them like they weren't even there.

How?

Without waiting for permission, she pushes past me into the suite, setting down the ice. The door clicks shut as she reaches for my hand.

It's shaking.

She doesn't flinch. She just laces our fingers together and pulls me toward the bed.

"Sit, B," she says with gentle authority. "Tell me what's wrong. How I can help?"

Everything in me wants to confess—my future's been sold, my company's being used as leverage, and I agreed to marry someone else tonight in order to protect my best friend.

But admitting the truth means revealing how powerless I am.

"Let me get lost in you," I whisper, hating myself for the selfish plea. "Please."

Her answer comes without hesitation—a single nod that destroys me.

Silently, she surrenders, parting her robe to reveal delicate black lace that steals my breath. I squeeze her hips and pull her close as we sink back onto the mattress. My mouth and hands explore her, and the suite fills with the symphony of her soft moans.

I drown in her. In her taste. Her sounds. Her body.

In everything I want and can never have.

CHAPTER SIXTEEN

PETRA

I'M IN HIS BED.

Wrapped in his arms. Living the fantasy I swore I gave up on.

His breathing is steady beneath my cheek—peaceful, tender—a sharp contrast to the emotional wreckage he showed me last night. Bryce Sterling, always so dignified and distant, let me in. And what I saw, no one else ever has. He fell apart, and then he kissed me like I was the only thing that could save him.

And now?

He's holding me like I'm *still* that thing.

His palm is splayed against the small of my back. The other curls around my shoulder, fingers woven into my hair as though he's claiming every strand. All night he's done this—reached for me in his sleep, pulling me close whenever I drifted. Like even in his dreams, he couldn't bear the thought of letting me go.

"Let me get lost in you."

God, B.

How was I supposed to say no to that?

I stay perfectly still, breathing in the smell of his skin—crisp pears, sandalwood, and the unmistakable aroma of sex. The early morning sun is bleeding through the curtains' slats. I want to tilt my head and admire his sleeping face, but I don't dare move.

I *need* to move. I *should* move. But I won't.

Because the second I wake him, the spell will be broken. He'll remember he's Bryce Sterling, future king of capitalism. I'll remember I'm Petra Brinkman, the poor girl who has more tattoos than money.

Tomorrow, this fairy tale ends—and I'm the one who turns back into a pumpkin.

I've loved him since I was old enough to recognize heartbreak. From when he first walked into our sad little home with my brother, all polished confidence and expensive-looking... everything. Our secondhand furniture had never felt more embarrassing. He didn't belong in my world—but I wanted him anyway.

Even at fifteen, I knew boys like Bryce didn't fall for girls like me. We were from different species—him all sun-kissed privilege and inherited wealth, me all sharp edges and thrift store rebellion.

Hell, I've built an entire personality around being an outsider who never gave a shit.

I've weaponized my mouth into a finely tuned defense system—sarcasm as armor, dirty jokes as deflection. I make things sound casual, like my heart isn't on the line whenever he looks at me. That I'm just here for a week-long ride on the billionaire.

But I'm lying to both of us.

And honestly? It's easier this way.

Because what the hell can you do when the boy you always loved becomes the man you've always wanted—and still can't have? Every fantasy I've ever had is playing out in real time, dragging my heart along for the ride, but I know damn well he's not mine to keep.

I won't ask for more. It's impossible. He'll leave, and I'll pretend I'm fine.

But, before that happens, I'm gonna give him everything I've got.

I'll be unforgettable.

If this is our ending, I want it to be the kind you never recover from. Passion that ruins you for anyone after. I want to leave claw marks on his soul—the way he's been tattooed onto mine.

I can't be his forever girl. But I can be the woman he dreams about. The wildfire in his memories—the one that never quite burns out.

When he's busy playing the role of ideal husband, I want him to look at his trophy wife and wonder why she doesn't light him up the way I did.

I'll be the only woman who showed him how it felt to be wanted for *who he is*, not *what he's worth*. By the time I'm done, he'll spend the rest of his life wondering what the hell happened to him in Mexico.

"You're here," he rasps, his voice laced with sleep.

I smile and feign a groggy wake-up stretch *(complete with exaggerated yawn)*. "Am I supposed to be somewhere else?"

"No, Pip. You're exactly where I want you."

He dips his head, brushing his lips against mine in a kiss so gentle, it makes my heart ache. When he pulls back, I can see the evidence of last night painted across his skin—my lipstick staining his throat, the faint trails of my nails down his shoulder. I see him marked as *mine*, and a swell of emotions threatens to take over.

Don't cry. Plenty of time for that later.

"What are you thinking?" His thumb traces the curve of my bottom lip, those ice-blue eyes studying my expression like I'm a puzzle.

I force a smile. "Just plotting your demise, Moneybags. You're not escaping the torture I still owe you."

He exhales a quiet laugh. "Are you going to be gentle?"

"Not a chance."

He shifts on top of me, pinning me while he attacks my neck with stubble-rough kisses. I howl with laughter.

"You're adding to your punishment," I warn between giggles, trying to squirm.

"Bring it on." His grin is pure sin as he captures my wrists above my head. "I can handle whatever you've got."

"Oh, B. If only you knew."

Twenty minutes later, Bryce is tied up and spread eagle—the world's hottest hostage. Arms and legs flung wide, the smug bastard is full naked starfish. His own silk ties are doing the Lord's work, securing those pricey limbs to the bed. And because I'm merciful *(and trying not to pounce early)*, I've strategically placed a fluffy white pillow over his penis.

I give one of the wrist ties a little tug, testing my handiwork. Solid.

"Comfortable?" I ask sweetly.

He gives a devious grin and lifts a brow. "As excited as I am about this... interrogation, I do have a conference call with Tokyo in ninety minutes."

I trail a finger down his chest. "Don't worry, Moneybags. You won't be late."

I pause. "Though I can't promise you'll be able to concentrate after I'm done with you."

His dark, hungry gaze meets mine. "That's a hell of a threat."

"It's a promise."

With my eyes locked on his, I hook my thumbs into my black lace panties and slowly slide them off. His breathing halts entirely as I ball them up and toss them… on his face.

"Souvenir," I say with a wink.

"Petra—"

"Shh." I climb onto the bed, crawling up his body until I'm straddling his chest, and then I slide up even higher.

Over his collarbone.

His throat.

And then…

I settle my center over his lips like I'm his favorite reckless investment.

I lift my panties off his pouty expression. "Now be a good boy and *lick*."

He doesn't need to be told twice.

He makes a sound—somewhere between a groan and a growl—before his mouth makes contact.

Holy hell.

This man's tongue is a conductor's baton, guiding me with masterful movements. He begins with broad, sweeping strokes against my clit, sending jolts of pleasure through me that make my eyes roll back. Then he shifts to precise, targeted flicks, and I'm clutching the headboard.

He reacts to every sound I make, a man on a mission to drive me wild. His focused intensity leaves my legs trembling and my breath ragged.

I meant to tease him. Work *him* up. But I'm the one unraveling.

Damn him and his silver tongue.

My body moves on instinct, grinding against his jaw, chasing the high he's bringing. His scruff is delicious torture, sharp little bites that send shivers ricocheting down my spine.

He groans into me, and I swear the vibration hits a new nerve. My fingers dig into the headboard. My head tips back.

I'm close. Too close.

When I try to pull away, to regain some semblance of control, his mouth sticks to me like a shadow, never letting up.

"Bryce—Wait—I need—" The protest dies as he adds suction that makes my vision white out.

The orgasm builds and breaks over me in devastating waves, leaving me shuddering and gasping above him. I'm completely undone.

As I slide down his body, boneless and breathless, he wears a grin that says *I won.* His face glistens with evidence of what he's done to me, and he looks utterly triumphant despite being tied up.

"That backfired... spectacularly," I say in between pants.

"From where I'm lying, it went exactly according to plan. When do we start round two?"

"Oh, you cocky billionaire. Payback's just getting started."

He grins. "Great. I enjoy being disciplined by you."

I snatch my panties and use them to wipe him clean, savoring the stunned expression behind his lashes.

"Last chance to pick a safe word, B."

"I have no interest in playing it safe."

He has the *audacity* to wink before I stuff the lace into his mouth.

KNOCK! KNOCK!

His eyes go wide as dinner plates. Mine do too—but for different reasons.

Oh, this is going to be fun.

I throw on my robe and give the strategic penis pillow a little pat. "Showtime, boys! Next time think twice before turning me into a human popsicle."

He tries to talk. "Mmfph. Mmmffphhh."

I dash to his walk-in closet, positioning myself behind the door where I can peek through the gap. From here, I've got a perfect view of Bryce—mid silent panic attack. Unfortunate for him. Hilarious for me.

In my lowest, most serious *Bryce-with-a-stick-up-his-ass* voice, I call out, "Enter!"

Through the crack in the door, I watch as Nigel Featherwick glides into the room in his standard black tuxedo, carrying an elaborate crystal bowl. When he spots Bryce on the bed, he doesn't even pause—just closes the door with the efficiency of a man who's clearly handled stranger requests.

"Apologies for the delay, Mr. Sterling," he says in that stoic, *I-scold-you-so* British accent. "I was informed you wished for me to personally deliver this."

I bite my lip to contain my giggles. This is playing out better than I imagined when I made the call twenty minutes ago, requesting an antique crystal bowl...

Full. Of. Condoms.

"I do hope the presentation meets your exact standards," Nigel continues, holding the bowl at a precise angle for inspection. "The crystal is Waterford, circa 1897."

Bryce responds with an eloquent, unintelligible mumble.

"Shall I temporarily remove the gag, sir?"

Bryce nods solemnly.

Nigel steps forward and delicately pinches the lace with two gloved fingers, like it's a napkin in Casa Cashmere's fancy dining room. He pulls it out and sets it on the nightstand.

"Excellent service as always, Nigel. Please place those on the side table. And might I trouble you to arrange a hearty breakfast from the kitchen? I anticipate an energetic morning ahead."

That's it. I explode—snorting loud enough to shake the door.

Nigel's nose twitches. Barely. He doesn't look toward the closet. But he knows. *Oh, he knows.*

"Of course. Shall I reinstate this oral barrier, sir?" he asks as he delicately raises my underwear.

"No, thank you," Bryce replies smoothly. "But I appreciate your discretion."

"As always, Mr. Sterling."

He bows, sets the panties beside the bowl, and exits the room without so much as a backward glance.

The moment the door clicks shut, I burst from the closet, laughing so hard I collapse to my knees.

"A hearty breakfast!" I wheeze. "The oral barrier! Oh my God, you two were so polite, I thought you might start discussing the weather!" I wipe a tear, still gasping. "See? I told you this snobby place had a concierge with a fancy bowl of condoms. Five-star service strikes again!"

"I'm glad my humiliation brought you joy."

"Indeed it did, good sir," I say in my best Butler Lord Britchybottom impression. "Would you care for the *Wall Street Journal* and a vibrating cock ring to kickstart your morning?"

"Okay, you've had your fun. Untie me now."

"Oh, Bryce," I sigh, sashaying toward the bed with a hand on my hip. "That was your punishment. We haven't gotten to the *fun* yet."

His gaze darkens. "If it involves using those hundreds of condoms, I'm enthusiastically on board."

"Nope. Not the plan. You don't get to touch. You don't even get to *thrust*. You get to *watch*."

I let my robe fall open and position myself between his legs, my fingers tracing up the inside of his thigh. The way he reacts to my touch, fighting the silk restraints, sends me a rush of power.

From my robe pocket, I pull out my tube of Wet n' Wild red. I pop the cap and twist it up with deliberate slowness. Bryce freezes, his jaw tightening, his gaze glued to my mouth as I glide the red across my lips and press them together.

"I was going to make you suffer a little longer, but you've been such a good little hostage."

I toss the pillow aside and wrap my fingers around his length, marveling at how ready he is for me.

"Mmm. I'm in for a delicious challenge. I hope it fits."

His knuckles are white where he's gripping the restraints.

"Keep those beautiful eyes on me, Moneybags. I want you to witness your fantasy."

"Petra, you don't have to—"

His words? Gone. Wrecked by the sight of me bending over and tracing his cock with my tongue. In one long, torturous stroke, I lap him up, base to tip.

Then, I seal my crimson lips around him and take him deep, never breaking eye contact.

"Christ! Fuck! Petra!" The words tear from his throat—a string of broken curses—that have me smiling around his thick shaft.

That's right, B. Burn this image into your brain.

Because I'm making damn sure I live rent-free in your head for the rest of your straight-laced, buttoned-up life.

***

I'M BRACING FOR BREAKFAST.

As I walk through the opulent hallway to the dining area, I have no damn clue what I'm walking into. A quiet meal, or the flaming wreckage of a called-off wedding? It was only yesterday Nigel lit the Fiona Financial Fuse, and I'm guessing the exact amount due was a shit ton.

Fiona was sweating in her stilettos about the bill not being paid for this extravagant shindig. And Nigel made it clear Casa Cashmere will not accept IOUs or emotional excuses. It's cold hard cash only.

Did Daddy come through for her? Or maybe she came clean to my brother? I step into the palatial dining room, prepared for carnage.

Except, everyone looks normal.

Whatever the hell "normal" means in billionaire land.

Nigel gestures toward an empty chair. "Miss Brinkman."

"Lord Britchybottom," I reply with a curtsey.

He nods, unamused.

An hour ago, this man was politely discussing my underwear as an "oral barrier" while Bryce lay naked and bound to his bed. Now he's back to stuffy Butler Mode.

I slide into the seat next to Bryce, fighting the urge to lean over and bite his earlobe just to watch him squirm.

"Good morning, Pip."

"Morning yourself, Moneybags. Trust you got your beauty sleep?"

"Adequate rest, yes. Thank you for asking."

"Hmm." I trace the red marks on his wrist with my finger. "Those aren't the kind of imprints you get from cufflinks. Testing out some new accessories?"

There it is—a tiny twitch at the corner of his mouth. Barely there, but I catch it. Why? Because I've spent a decade memorizing this man's micro-reactions like flashcards for the SATs.

And I love that I'm the only one who knows him that well.

Everybody else sees the golden boy. I see the man who only recently discovered he has a kink for being tied up and bossed around.

Fuck, I want to drag him back to bed and corrupt him some more.

I should stage a kidnapping. Find some remote island where we can live out our lives in a sex bubble of perpetual happiness. Once he got over the initial shock, I bet he'd be into it. I can always tase him if he doesn't come willingly.

Nigel clears his throat. "Miss Muffy will not be in attendance this morning. She requires additional time with her styling team following a most vigorous walk on the beach."

PING! PING! PING!

He rings a little silver bell. "Breakfast is served."

Synchronized staff descends on the table, placing tailored plates before us.

I glance down at the masterpiece before me and nearly moan out loud. A full English breakfast—eggs, bacon, sausages, baked beans, mushrooms, tomatoes, black pudding, and toast. And I've already devoured half of it in three bites.

The espresso alone is a religious experience. The best fucking coffee I've had in my life, and that's not just post-orgasm hunger talking *(I don't think).*

If I do kidnap Bryce, this espresso comes with us.

Across the table, Fiona is sipping celery juice. "Smells delicious, but I'm fasting for my dress fitting later," she says sweetly. "Hana's joining me in solidarity."

"Only juice 'til noon," Hana chirps. "Petra, that bacon looks scrumptious. Is it crispy? I bet it is. I adore bacon. I wish I had your metabolism."

I grin. "That's why God invented Spanx."

Gavin narrows his eyes at me over the rim of his coffee. "Since when do you eat breakfast, Wildcat?"

"I woke up with an appetite."

Bryce's hand pauses mid-toast buttering. Then his hand slides under the table and squeezes my thigh with affection.

Tink! Tink! Tink!

Fiona taps her spoon against her glass. "Attention, please. We've decided to cancel the joint bachelor and bachelorette parties for tonight. Instead, Gavin and I are going to have a romantic evening on the beach, privately."

"Since we're forgoing a honeymoon with all my work responsibilities," Gavin says, "Fi figured we should have one night free from wedding chaos and company stress."

"Nigel," Fiona says, "our fabulous sunset beach picnic will be ready by tonight, correct?"

"Indeed, madam," he replies smoothly. "And the matter from our conversation yesterday has been handled in full."

Fiona nods. "As expected."

Nigel continues, "Arrangements are underway for the additional wedding guests arriving tomorrow. Some shall be lodged at hotels in town, while others will reside here on the estate."

My detective-brain does the translation:

The money came in. Everything is paid for. Problem solved. Nothing to see here.

Gavin thanks Nigel for the excellent service, then lifts Fiona's hand and presses a kiss to her knuckles. She glows with what could actually be... true happiness.

For a split second *(and I can't believe I'm thinking this)*, the smitten look she's giving my brother seems genuine.

C'mon, brain... That's crazy talk. I need my besties.

I reach for my phone and shoot off a text.

Group Chat : CPK Forever

Me: *Quick poll: Do people ever change? Really?*

Cam: *Define "change." Like start recycling? Or like, thinking my influencer bosshole will change from being a prick to a tolerable human being?*

Me: *What if this Fiona grudge isn't about her anymore—and I'm just clinging to it?*

Katie: *I don't know. Your bullshit detector is usually spot-on.*

"Oh my gosh, Fiona!" Hana squeals, bouncing in her chair. "Your newsletter yesterday about that sweet bulldog needing eyelid surgery to blink again? I didn't even finish reading—I hit donate on the spot!"

Fiona preens. "What's the point of living our dream if it doesn't ripple out and help others?"

I almost roll my eyes—*almost.*

Maybe she means it.

Perhaps I am dumping my own issues onto Fiona because I can't let go of the past. Maybe she's actually doing some good in this crazy world of the one percent. Maybe my bitterness has been blinding me.

"You know what? I'm gonna sign up for that newsletter," I say, mouth half full. "Hana tells me it's life-changing."

Fiona pauses, caught off guard. "Oh. Well... In that case, you simply *must* check out my new auction site—PawsitivelyPosh.com! It features Echo's latest work. All proceeds benefit Furry First-Class—we provide spa treatments for shelter animals with abandonment issues."

Spa therapy for anxious rescue pets? That's... actually kind of sweet.

"Let me see," I say, opening the site on my phone.

The homepage loads... *and wow!*

Painting one: Echo, in all his shirtless glory, is a centaur using his feet to play a trumpet. Naturally.

Scroll.

Painting two: Echo, fully nude, curled around a banana tree, surrounded by flamingos in togas mid-jungle orgy. *Yikes.*

Scroll.

Painting three: Echo, buck naked again, breastfeeding a sloth. Tender. Unsettling.

And seared into my memory banks forever.

I can't stop scrolling. Most of these paintings have already been sold. For millions of freaking dollars.

I pause on a portrait still up for sale. This one is... surprisingly ordinary. An elderly man with sharp eyes, a strong jaw, and silver hair. There's a familiar quality to his face, but I can't quite place where I've seen him.

"Time to make the magic happen," Gavin says, standing and pressing a kiss to Fiona's temple. "Looking forward to our beach evening, babe."

"It's going to be so fabulous, Gav-Gav," Fiona purrs.

Bryce squeezes my leg once more before rising, a promise that sends my pulse into overdrive.

He politely nods. "Ladies, if you'll excuse us."

The second they're gone, my fingers fly across my screen.

Me: *Change of plans. I've got a surprise for you tonight.*

Moneybags: *Should I alert my lawyer or my doctor?*

Me: *Depends—how do you feel about putting something long and hot in your mouth?*

Moneybags: *Jesus, Pip. Are you trying to kill me?*

Me: *Not kill. Just full-body surrender.*

Moneybags: *I'll bring my silk ties.*

Me: *Meet me at the garage after your last meeting. And B? Come hungry.*

***

"Would you hurry the hell up back there?" I call out, drumming my fingers on the steering wheel. "We're burning daylight, and I didn't go through all this trouble just to watch the sunset from a parking garage."

Lord Britchybottom made me sign my life away to borrow this vehicle. One scratch and I'm his indentured servant for life.

The SUV rocks slightly as Bryce changes in the back seat. I sneak peeks at his bare ass in the rearview mirror, and yep, it's doing things to me.

"*You* insisted I change back here," he mutters, followed by the sounds of rustling fabric, whispered cursing, and one very stubborn zipper.

"Want me to hop back there and lend a hand? I'm excellent at taking your clothes off, so the reverse can't be too hard."

The door opens and Bryce steps out. My ovaries slow clap.

"Well, shit," I breathe, climbing out to get the full visual.

He's wearing distressed Ralph Lauren jeans and a crisp white tee that hugs his chest in the yummiest way. He completes the look with a light gray bomber jacket, giving off that effortless cool-guy aura. His tousled blond hair says *I'm a gentleman—until the door locks.*

"You are absolutely fucking edible. I should be arrested for the thoughts I'm having."

"Noted. Pip has a thing for denim."

"Zip it and give me a spin, Ken doll. I want the full 360 on the billionaire booty."

"Where exactly did you acquire this wardrobe?" he asks, running a hand over the smooth cotton shirt. "And how did you know my measurements?"

"I have my ways."

He raises a brow.

"Fine. I blackmailed Sebastian. He had a local stylist rush the whole thing."

"You blackmailed a celebrity stylist?"

"Threatened, really. There's a difference." I pull out the note that came with the clothes, clearing my throat dramatically. "Sebastian's exact words: 'Miss Brinkman, I find your threat to hide sardine sandwiches in vintage Chanel both disturbing and effective. Consider this my final act of charity in your hopeless pursuit of… whatever. I don't care.'"

"Sardine sandwiches?"

"Specifically in the clothes you'll be returning to him. Figured the smell would make a nasty impression on his next client."

Bryce laughs—*actually laughs*—and it makes my whole body tingle. "You're diabolical."

"Speaking of which, time for the main event."

I hold up a silk blindfold.

"Not happening in public."

"Where we're going, nobody gives a shit about your net worth or your family name. That's exactly why I got you the disguise—so you can blend in with us normies."

His gaze sweeps over me, taking in my standard outfit of dark jeans, vintage band tee, leather jacket, and combat boots. "Before we go anywhere, I need to tell you something."

"What?"

He moves closer, backing me against the car. "You in that leather jacket and those boots? It's been destroying my concentration since you tackled me at my mother's house."

His mouth is on mine before I know what's happening. He kisses me like it's been killing him not to. It's… longing. Possession. Appreciation. Promise.

When we break apart, I'm dizzy. "Damn, B. We should get matching tattoos to remember that mind-blowing kiss."

"Is that the surprise?"

"Nope. No surprise unless I'm running the show." I wiggle the blindfold at him. "You can be a good boy, or I can use one of those tasers you got me. Your choice."

His gaze smolders. "Why don't we stay here and see where the back seat takes us?"

To prove his point, he kisses me so hard my toes curl in my boots.

I force myself to break away. "Tempting offer, but we've got a sunset to catch. I did not arrange all this so we could make out in a parking garage. Tonight's about you being a regular dude. With incredibly tight jeans."

"Fine." He fake-sighs but lets me tie the blindfold on, muttering, "I swear, if I wake up duct-taped to a piñata—"

"Can you see me flashing my boobs right now?"

I wave my hand in front of him.

He lifts up the blindfold.

"Aaand that was a test. You failed," I say, smacking his wrist and yanking the blindfold back down. "No peeking. This whole thing only works if you commit, Moneybags."

"I'm blindfolded in public wearing denim. I'd say I'm all in Pip."

I loop my arm through his and start guiding him across the garage. "Trust the process."

We fall into step, me leading him down the sidewalk, my fingers laced with his. The sunset's already throwing orange and pink across the pavement.

The man who calculates each move like it's a stock trade let me cover his eyes, in broad daylight, for a surprise.

God, what does that even mean?

As we get closer to our destination, the world around us explodes with sound and smell—kids laughing and squealing, music thumping from speakers against the backdrop of crashing waves, the thick scent of sugar and fried batter in the air. It's sensory overload, and Bryce is tensing up beside me.

I spot what I'm looking for—a street vendor with a cart that has the scent of heaven wrapped in grease—and make a beeline for it, pulling one bewildered billionaire along with me.

"*Dos, por favor*," I say to the guy, butchering my high school Spanish. I hand him some cash. "*Muchas gracias, señor.* Keep the change."

"Are we there yet?" Bryce asks, his head tilting toward the sounds of sizzling meat frying. "I'm famished. Whatever that is, it smells incredible."

"Poor sheltered rich boy, never had to practice patience," I tease, accepting two foil-wrapped bundles that are almost too hot to hold.

"Guilty as charged," he admits with no hint of shame. "Though, I did wait seven years to taste you again."

I stumble slightly, nearly dropping our food.

Seven years?

Oh my God.

Our kiss. That night. That awkward, desperate, perfect collision between two people who weren't supposed to collide.

Has he been carrying it, too? Holding it the way I have, all this time?

I want to ask him. Want to spin around and grab his face and demand answers. *Was it more than a kiss for you? Was it the moment that ruined every person after?*

But fear chokes me.

I don't say a word and keep walking. I bury the questions deep—into that hidden place where I stash things I'm too scared to want.

"Almost time for the big reveal."

I line him up like he's about to be let in on a surprise party. Because he is. Tonight is for him.

I strike a pose with my arms raised high and a cheesy grin across my face. "All right, B, take off the mask!"

He pulls away the blindfold, blinks against the sudden light, and his entire body goes stiff.

Behind me, the beach is a golden halo of lights. A full-blown carnival by the freaking ocean. Spinning rides, game booths with stuffed animal prizes, the sweet scent of cotton candy mixing with fried food and ocean salt. Families wander between attractions, kids shrieking with delight as they race from ride to ride.

Bryce isn't smiling.

He cycles through emotions I cannot read.

Oh fuck. This was a horrible idea.

"Shit, Bryce, I'm sorry. This was stupid," I babble, words tumbling out. "I should've thought this through. I—I heard what your mom said about your eighth birthday. That you wanted a carnival with hot dogs. And she said, '*We* don't do tacky carnival birthdays.' So then you got shipped off to Casa Cashmere for some boujee, rich-kid snoozefest."

He's still frozen.

"GAWD, I'm sorry… I must seem like some kind of emotional terrorist. We can leave. We can go anywhere else. I can get you a steak, or an emergency scotch. We can go make out in the back seat if you—"

He reaches out, cradling my cheeks, and kisses me. The breath whooshes from my lungs.

When he finally draws away, his eyes are glassy. "This is the most thoughtful gesture anybody has ever done for me. Thank you. I cannot believe you remembered something so insignificant."

The truth slips out before my filter can catch it. "If it's important to you, it's important to me."

The confession hangs there, sticky and exposed. I quickly shove the hot dog at him.

"Anyway! Let's inhale this street meat, and then we're hitting every ride until one of us pukes or passes out. That's the authentic carnival experience."

CHAPTER SEVENTEEN

BRYCE

"It's meat... ish, Moneybags. Be brave."

The suspiciously shiny hot dog wiggles in my hand. Heat seeps through the wrapper, the bun is damp from steam, and some viscous goo glistens on the surface—ketchup, allegedly. I have no clue what the protocol is here. Do I unwrap the entire thing? Peel it like a banana? There should be instructions.

I tilt it.

Rotate it.

Sniff it.

It is—without a doubt—the most unappetizing food I've ever considered eating. And I once sampled casu marzu, the world's most dangerous cheese... intentionally infested with live maggots.

"Earth to Bryce," she sing-songs. "Food goes in mouth."

"I have never... I don't—" I glance down again. "It's wet."

"Watch and learn, B." She parts her lips and wraps them slowly around the end of the bun, taking a deliberately slow bite. Her tongue darts out to catch a drip of relish.

"I'm experiencing... a different kind of hunger now."

She waggles her eyebrows. "Fun first, naughty times later. Eat the damn hot dog."

I take a breath. Tilt it... And bite.

It's unholy. Greasy, salty, spicy. My tongue is confused and delighted. My eyes close with pleasure.

"Oh my God," I moan loudly.

"Okay, easy there, Fifty Shades," Petra says through a laugh. "There are children here."

I finish it in four rapid bites. "Another!"

"Slow down. We've got a whole night of artery-clogging deliciousness ahead. Fried Oreos, fried funnel cakes, fried corn dogs. Sensing a theme here?"

"Explain *corn dog*."

"Oh, you delicate rich boy." She pats my cheek condescendingly. "I'm about to ruin your taste buds forever."

That wicked smile. I'd follow her into hell.

I take her hand in mine. "All right, show me how to misbehave."

"Careful what you wish for, B. Now, how's your stomach handle being flipped like a pancake?"

Ten minutes later, we're at the base of a towering beast of twisted steel and flashing lights. Petra hands the bored teenager two tickets and tugs me toward the ramp.

"I feel I should be paying," I say, stepping onto the platform behind her. "If this is a proper date—"

"Bryce Sterling!" She whirls to face me, arms crossed. "Let go of your grip on your wallet. This is my treat. Your job is to survive without puking on me."

"That is not particularly motivating."

When was the last time someone refused to let me pay? The answer is never.

Petra hoists herself up with ease while I climb in beside her awkwardly like a penguin on stilts. The seat creaks ominously.

"Pull this down till it clicks," she instructs, locking her harness in place. "Don't worry—only three people have died so far this year."

"Real funny." *She's joking. Right?*

I glance at the semicircle of riders. We're facing each other. Excellent. Not only am I about to die—I get to make eye contact with strangers while I do it.

I fumble with my restraint, the clicking mechanism rejecting my increasingly sweaty palms. Finally, it locks securely. "Why exactly is this machine called *Rueda del Miedo*?"

"No clue. Sounds sexy, though."

"*¡Rueda del Miedo!*" chirps a tiny voice beside me. "*Es*... how you say... Wheel. Of. Fear!"

My seatmate can't be older than seven. She's sporting lopsided pigtails, light-up sneakers, and a grin so wide you'd think we were boarding a unicorn, not a death trap.

My throat closes. "I beg your pardon?"

"*Sí, sí!* Very scary *pero muy* fun! My *tío*, he cry like *bebé* when he ride!"

Her uncle cried. A grown man cried.

"Kid, you made this experience ten times cooler." Petra leans over me and high-fives her new best friend.

A man in a sweat-stained polo with a name tag that reads EMILIO does a half-ass tug on Petra's harness, then mine, then the little girl's. That's it. That's the extent of the safety protocol.

"Perhaps I should just watch—"

The opening guitar riff from "Thunderstruck" by AC/DC explodes from the speakers, and my escape plan dies. The ride lurches to life, and Petra lets out a full-body whoop.

"*¡Aquí vamos!*" the kid yells.

The platform shudders. The curved row of passengers begins to rise. The first swing is mild—a lazy pendulum stretch. Deceptive, because then it builds.

Each new arc of movement picks up more momentum. Higher. Faster.

Forward—pressure pins me to the seat, my body's organs protesting gravity itself.

Backward—my chest lifts, and I feel myself straining against the harness.

Then the semicircle spins.

*DA-NA-NA-NA-NA. S*yllables of song jibberish fill my skull as the chaos ratchets up. A teenage couple across from me starts screaming. We rotate again. We swing higher. The arc tips farther.

"Thunder!" Petra and the pigtailed girl chant in unison.

The speed intensifies, and wind rushes against my face. I can taste the sweat of my own panic.

We swing again, and, for a split second, I'm weightless. The restraints bite into my shoulders—my ass lifts clean off the chair.

Beside me, Petra laughs with untamed joy, her hair dancing in the wind, while the young girl to my left puts both hands in the air as if gravity's just a suggestion.

Vertigo sets in. The music feels faster. The lights strobe in broken rhythm—yellow, red, purple, white, nothing. My vision blurs, and I can't tell if the pounding in my ears is from the machine, the song, or my heart fighting to exit through my eardrums.

The hot dog—*Christ!*—is waging an all-out revolt against my digestive system.

And then, the contraption swings upside down.

And freezes there.

Sweet mother of God.

I'm dangling like a chandelier, white-knuckling my harness—the only thing keeping me from becoming street art on the pavement. I stare at the tiny people below, moving like ants. My stomach is in my throat. My balls? Anyone's guess.

Don't pass out. I'll have to be rescued upside down with wet pants.

"Bryce!" Petra's voice cuts through my panic. "Look at me!"

I turn my head, fighting the disorientation, and find her hanging beside me with that wild grin plastered across her face, arms dangling free.

"Let go!" she shouts over the screams.

"Absolutely not!"

"Trust me! Let go of the harness!"

"Have you lost your goddamn mind?" I grip the bar harder, my knuckles pure marble.

"*¡Sí*, let go!" the tiny terrorist beside me chimes in. "*¡Es más divertido!* More fun when you no hold!"

I'm suspended forty feet in the air. Taking life advice from a seven-year-old and a bartender.

"Bryce! Stop being a pussy. Let! Go!"

"Yeah, *señor*, no be pussy!"

God help me, I let go. My fingers fall away. And then—

I scream. Something inside me releases.

The spinning beast bucks beneath us. This time, a full, violent 360-degree spin. It whips around then loops again. I roar. But it's not panic. It's the sound of freedom.

I've never felt so fucking free in my entire life.

I'm soaring. Untethered from it all—the board meetings, the impossible expectations, the suffocating legacy of being Bryce Sterling. I scream like a maniac.

The second we touch the ground, I grab Petra's hand. "Again. We're doing that again."

She raises an eyebrow, cheeks flushed, wind-tossed hair sticking to her red lips. "Hold on, daredevil. Pace yourself. We'll come back. Each ride here gets two rounds. That's the rule."

I'm already tugging her toward the exit. "Then we better get started."

Next up? The Scrambler. We cram into the too-small seat, thighs pressed tight. The ride jerks to life, and suddenly we're a streak of spinning color. Each wild spin hurls her into me, full-body, no apology—her breath hot against my neck. She laughs like it's breathing, and I'm laughing too—loud, unfiltered, completely gone. If this is what losing control feels like... maybe I've been doing life all wrong.

I'm obsessed.

Petra is reshaping me, pulling me into her beautiful world of chaos where anything feels possible.

We finish the bumper cars, and suddenly she's handing me a golden mystery stick.

"Emergency corn dog!" Petra declares.

I chomp down and nearly sear off my taste buds. "OW—what the hell!"

"Rookie error, rich boy. That meat just took a swim in molten lava." She snatches it, blows on it, then bathes it in mustard. "Now try."

My next bite sends me into a food coma of happiness. "I can honestly say this is superior to any meal I have ever consumed."

A blob of mustard decorates her chin, and before my gentleman's education can stop me, I lean over and lick it clean.

Petra freezes.

I shrug. "You're still my favorite flavor."

Her face flushes. Then she shoves the corn dog in my mouth. "Focus, Casanova. We've got more spinning to do."

The swings ride catapults us into the air. Suspended like kites on chains, we drift in wide, unhurried arcs over the carnival lights. I throw my arms wide, allowing the cool night air to slap my face. Everything transforms into a blur of lights.

I glance over. Petra's shrieking with glee, her boots kicking like she's dancing with gravity, and something in my chest splinters.

How does she know exactly what I need when I don't even know?

She remembered an eight-year-old boy's disappointment and turned it into magic. She saw through twenty-nine years of careful conditioning to the *me* who just wanted to be a kid at a carnival, eating junk food and screaming with friends.

She sees me.

Not the man my father engineered.

Me.

For the first time in my life, I wonder. *Maybe being myself is enough.*

Thirty minutes later, I have powdered sugar in places I didn't know could get sticky. I'm not accusing Petra of lacing that funnel cake, but I've never inhaled anything so fast. Or with such a lack of decorum.

"Were there... narcotics in that?"

"Confectioner's cocaine," Petra deadpans, tearing a bite from the edge. "Highly addictive. If I let you get a second one, we'll have to add 'vomiting' to our date itinerary."

I give the food truck a final, longing glance. "You're cruel."

"I'm keeping you alive."

Apparently, that includes rushing me straight to the next death machine: The Turbo Drop.

I buckle myself into the seat so fast it squeaks. Petra's gaping as I slam my harness down shamelessly.

"Uh-oh," she says as she drops beside me. "I think I've created an adrenaline junkie."

The coaster starts its ominous climb skyward, and I fling my arms up like I'm surrendering.

"You know you're not supposed to do that until the actual drop, right?" Petra snorts.

"I want to be prepared."

"You're so fucking adorable, I might die."

"Please don't. I'm saving the best ride for last... You."

"That was always part of tonight's agenda, Moneybags. Now quit trying to control my magical evening."

The machine gears snap into position at the top. Petra flings her arms up, her eyes sparkling with excitement.

Then we drop.

HOLY MOTHER OF—

We plummet like skydivers without parachutes, screaming uncontrollably. My brain submits a formal objection to the rules of physics while my stomach relocates to my esophagus.

As we ascend for the second drop, I reach over and intertwine my fingers with hers. She lifts her eyes to mine, and we plunge once more, her face dissolving into bliss.

She's positively glowing... My heart is going to burst. This is what I have been missing my whole life.

Not the adrenaline. Not the junk food. Not the thrill of breaking social protocol.

This.

Being completely authentic with another human being. No masks, no performance, no image to maintain. Just someone to be ridiculous with—and loving every second of it.

... and apparently, also motion sick.

Moments later, I'm doubled over a trash can confessing my sins to the garbage gods.

"Okay, champ," Petra says, her hand making gentle circles on my back. "Let's pump the brakes."

She guides me to a bench and presses a water bottle into my trembling hands. "Sip. Don't chug. We're not here to waterboard your stomach."

I obey as we settle into people-watching. The carnival is a brilliant backdrop of neon lights and swirling music as locals greet each other with warm smiles. An elderly couple strolls hand in hand, sharing a churro like it's their first date. Two young lovers embrace on the Ferris wheel, eyes only for each other. I look past a group of teenage girls dancing for a TikTok, and that's when I see her—

My gap-toothed accomplice from the Wheel of Fear. She's standing near the rollercoaster with tears streaming down her cheeks. A woman who's clearly her mother crouches beside her, gesturing helplessly.

"What do you think is wrong?" I ask, nodding toward the scene.

Petra follows my gaze, her expression softening. "I have a pretty good guess."

She's moving before I can respond, heading for the small family. The mother lifts her eyes, cautious, but Petra's already handing over a thick stack of tickets—along with what appears to be every dollar in her wallet.

The child's tears transform into squeals of delight as Petra crouches down for a high-five. The mother says, "*Gracias, gracias*" as she pats Petra's arm with a gratitude that comes from unexpected kindness.

Petra returns, settling beside me like nothing happened.

"I've got a radar for single moms," she says. "You can always tell. That look—dead tired but still hell-bent on making things magical. My mom wore it too, back when she maxed out credit cards on school supplies or scraped together whatever she could to make my birthday feel special."

I watch as the young girl shows her ticket to the ride operator like it's a golden pass to Willy Wonka's factory.

"I had every financial need met," I say quietly. "And every emotional need ignored. That's why I gravitated toward Gavin. He had something I'd never experienced—a family who cared for each other."

"Your family doesn't know what they're missing," she says gently.

Petra rests her head on my shoulder, and for a brief moment, it feels normal—this parallel world. Watching this innocent child climb into her seat, arms up, grinning like she's on a personal roller-coaster to heaven.

"Is that why you want to become a lawyer? To help struggling mothers?"

Petra's eyes snap open like I just accused her of murder. "What makes you think I want that?"

"Well, your passionate speech about justice on the yacht, your tendency to correct those who are out of line, and the extensive collection of law books scattered throughout your apartment suggested as much."

She's quiet for a long moment, and I'm not sure if she's touched or concerned that I noticed all those pieces and put them together.

"Please don't tell Gavin. I'm not ready to spill that dream to him yet. But yeah, I wanna do pro bono work. Fight for the little guys who don't have anybody in their corner. And if I'm lucky, maybe take down some evil corporations while I'm at it."

I nod. "You have my word. And between us, I think you'll make a remarkable lawyer. I would, however, strongly advise you to leave your taser outside the courtroom."

"I dunno... Zapping the opposing counsel would be super effective during my opening statement."

I thought I had Petra Brinkman figured out. Sarcastic bartender with a leather jacket and a death wish for authority figures.

But I've been seeing the tip of the iceberg.

Petra's not wild for the sake of chaos—she's a storm with purpose. She doesn't start fights for fun; she stands up when someone's getting steamrolled. She refuses to let the world stay broken.

She's been underestimated her whole life. Dismissed as too loud, too messy, too tattooed, and yet she's making it her mission to fight for people who get the same treatment. All while I'm going to be trapped three thousand miles away, feeding into the very things she's fighting against.

The irony is so brutal it hurts.

"Well, if Sterling Industries ever finds itself in a lawsuit where you're representing the other side," I say, trying to keep my tone light, "I'll tell our legal team to settle immediately. We're guaranteed to lose."

"Smart man. I like a guy who knows when he's outmatched." Petra places a gentle kiss on my cheek. "Should we call it a night?" she asks, glancing toward the carnival exit, where families trickle out with exhausted kids dragging oversized plushies.

"Actually, Pip, how about a walk on the beach?"

"Yeah," she says quietly, her fingers sliding between mine. "That sounds... nice."

I have to have more time with her.

I don't just want Petra in my bed—I need her in my life. *How the hell am I supposed to walk away from her after tomorrow?*

***

"All right, B. Your turn, what's the most rebellious thing you've ever done?"

She's tucked between my legs, back snug against my chest. The salty ocean breeze nips at my skin as the two of us cuddle under a thin carnival blanket that smells like kettle corn and sea salt. My jacket's beneath us, doing its best to keep the damp beach from creeping in. Her bare toes wiggle adorably in the sand.

Off in the distance, the carnival is shutting down, with rides going dark one by one.

"I once demanded a peanut butter and jelly sandwich after seeing one on a television commercial."

"That's your rebellion origin story? A PBJ?"

"I was six. Nanny Wetherby permitted me to watch the Disney Channel after I completed my economics tutorial early, and there was this advertisement—a regular boy unwrapping a slice of happiness in his lunch." *The memory feels both silly and poignant.*

"What happened after you asked?"

"Mother referred to it as 'culinary backsliding' and promptly scheduled an emergency consultation with our family nutritionist. She was certain that processed foods would ruin my developing palate and turn me into—her words—'a McDonald's enthusiast.'"

Petra releases a full-body laugh that rattles my ribs. "Please tell me you've had a PBJ. If not, we're on a mission to find a 24-hour market this instant."

"Our chef smuggled me a sandwich the following week. White bread, creamy Jif, grape jelly—I ate it in the wine cellar like I was consuming contraband."

"You radical little anarchist."

"Okay, I have one. Are you planning to call a truce on this whole vendetta against Fiona after she becomes Mrs. Brinkman?"

"I have considered it." Petra sighs. "Gavin seems happy, so maybe I can stand her. But if she hurts him—so help me God—I'll shave her head in her sleep and donate the hair to one of her pet charities.

You know, toupees for bald eagles or birds too broke for designer nests."

"Vengeful and oddly specific."

"Conspiracy theory time," she announces. "I'm almost certain Nigel has a secret tattoo of Miss Muffy Von Cashmere the Second."

I pretend to ponder. "Hmmm. I see. Go on."

"I've given this a lot of thought... He's a gold-digging butler."

"He's trying to marry the dog?"

"Why not? People do weird shit all the time for money."

I can't help the chuckle that escapes. "We should definitely investigate. He could be slowly poisoning her kibble to inherit her billion-dollar trust fund."

"Laugh it up, B, but I think you just cracked the crime of the century. Surprise, surprise—the butler did it."

We sit quietly, comfortably, and watch the tide come in.

"Might be smart to head back before we get wet."

She tips her head and shoots me a look. "I thought you knew I like living dangerously? Makes me feel alive. You could use more of that."

"Noted. But I'd rather test *your* limits." I say, letting my tongue trace the sensitive spot behind her ear, teasing the hidden ink I know is there.

"My turn for a question," I say softly. "What does the broken heart tattoo stand for?"

She stiffens. "Ugh. It's dumb. Some guy broke my heart."

I already hate him.

"Who?"

"Pass. Next question."

The rejection stings, but I don't push.

"Okay, different question. Why did you drop out of college to go to Europe?"

She sighs. "If I answer that, you'll think less of me."

"I doubt that."

"I chose to be a walking cliché. I fled to another continent thinking maybe if I put an ocean between us, I could get over a guy who hurt me."

Something twists in my stomach—part curiosity, part dread. "And did you? Get over him?"

"Nope. Turns out you can't outrun your feelings, even with a backpack and a Eurail pass." Her laugh holds zero humor. "Guess I'm doomed to carry this torch until I kick the bucket. Hence the permanent reminder behind my ear. There, you're officially in on two of my secrets."

The air shifts. My own truth sits heavy on my chest, begging to be said.

"I'm leaving Heartvest."

She whips around. "What?"

"Gavin doesn't know yet," I murmur. "No one does. Looks like we're both hiding things from him."

"Holy shit. That's huge."

"I don't have a choice. My father is forcing my hand. I either become the heir I was born to be or watch him dismantle everything I built with Gavin."

I leave out the part about Amanda—the forced marriage, the timeline, the trap. Some truths don't belong in moments like this.

"Your father's always struck me as a sociopathic dick," Petra says bluntly, "and this cements it."

"No argument there. He cares about power. Not people. Least of all his own son. You do not get to opt out of being a Sterling. You just get to choose how miserable you want to be about it."

"That's so fucked. Bryce, I'm sorry."

"Well," I say, attempting to lighten the mood, "at least there's the consolation of hot dog carts in New York."

"Best ones are in Brooklyn. Culinary magic on the tongue. The heartburn's totally worth it."

We fall quiet again.

But this silence is heavier.

I don't voice the question burning in my throat—*would you visit me?*

Petra finally speaks, her voice surprisingly shy.

"At the carnival tonight, you mentioned waiting seven years to taste me again. That night at my graduation—when I kissed you—were you really thinking about me all this time?"

My heart stutters. I pull out my phone, fingers gliding over the screen to my hidden playlist. The glow cuts through the dark as I land on the song that's always been my emotional downfall. I press play.

The opening piano notes of "Alone" by Heart drift softly from the speaker.

Petra's breath catches. "Oh my God. That song was playing that night in my room."

"I remember."

"Bryce..." Her voice breaks. "That was the worst day. And the best. All at once."

She shifts to face me fully, her legs curling around my waist, drawing me in. A flicker of vulnerability crosses her face, flaming up a surge of emotions inside me.

The music, aching and electric, grips the air between us like it knows what we're about to do. I lift my hand and trace her jaw, committing the delicate contours of her face to memory. My pulse pounds as I lean in—

"Wait," she breathes, her palm pressing against my beating heart. "I need to confess something, and if I don't admit it now, I'll never find the courage."

Her fingers tremble as she looks away, brushing the silky strands behind her lobe to expose the delicate broken heart.

"It's you, Bryce. I've been helplessly in love with you since I was fifteen."

The earth stops spinning. Waves freeze mid-crash. Every cell in my body plunges into free fall.

"I'm not telling you so you'll say something back. It was just a stupid, over-the-top, teen girl crush that somehow never died. A few years ago, I finally worked up the courage to tell you, but you had already moved in with Amanda. I fled to Europe like a love-sick idiot."

Her laugh is hollow. My chest is caving in.

"I realize how insane this sounds, but... before we go our separate ways, I wanted to finally tell you. I'm glad we had this time and that I got to know you. The real you. It honestly made all the heartbreak worth it."

"Why me?" slips out.

She shrugs like it's obvious. "My heart says you. Always has."

I'm speechless.

"Maybe because you've always been decent to me. Or it's that you never talked down to me when everyone else did. I don't know. You're you. That's the whole reason. Love is stupid."

She's loved me since she was fifteen years old. She could've been mine this entire time?

"Okay. Enough about my unhinged teenage obsession. I promise not to stalk you in New York like a psycho. Let's go see if there's a bar still open."

She starts to rise, but I grab her waist and pull her onto my lap.

"No."

"B—"

"No," I repeat, firmer. "You can't drop that on me and leave."

"Really, Bryce, I didn't tell you to force you into anything."

"Pip, I've never felt this way about anyone before. There's *a pull* between us. I can't explain it. Can't categorize it. Can't control it. I'm drawn to you."

She tries to avert her eyes, but I cup her face, guiding her back to me.

"You're extraordinary, Petra. You see injustice, and you fight it. You help strangers. You remember details about people that matter. You're fierce and loyal and brave enough to call out people when no one else will."

Her mouth opens to speak, but I can't stop now; my thumb traces her lips as I'm lost in the sheer wonder of her.

"Jesus, you're beautiful. Outside, yeah, obviously, but it's more than that. You walk through this world like bullshit doesn't stand a chance. You make people feel like they matter. You make *me* feel like who I am is enough. Like I can finally stop holding my breath."

Tell her you love her.

The thought hits like lightning.

You love her. Of course you do. She makes you happier than you've ever been.

But the truth is cold and brutal. *How could it work?*

Don't say it. Don't give her hope. You can't be together. Don't make this harder than it is.

So instead, I kiss her.

It's deep and needy. A kiss that tastes like heartbreak and home. Her mouth meets mine with the same aching need. As if maybe we can hold the world still.

How can I let her go?

Waking up every day, painfully aware she's not mine. But she could've been.

"Bryce," she whimpers.

"I know," I rasp, placing my forehead onto hers. "Pip, I know. I need you too."

I glance out at the beach—the pitch-black stretch of sand, the endless dark water, the distant sparkle of carnival lights long since shut down. We're alone. Our song fills the air, and there's only shadows and sky.

Wordlessly, she stands, the blanket still wrapped around her shoulders. She unzips her jeans like it's nothing and peels them down along with her panties, tossing them aside.

The moonlight kisses her thighs. Her leather jacket is still on, shirt tugged up, and her bare center glistens. I can't help but groan.

She's perfection. She's rebellion. She's everything I'm not allowed to have.

And she's offering herself to me anyway.

My pants are off in seconds, kicked somewhere behind me. They can end up in the damn ocean for all I care.

She climbs onto my lap, blanket slipping as she settles against my cock. A hiss of breath before she drags her slick heat along my shaft—slow, sinfully slow—as though she's trying to set me on fire one silky glide at a time. *Jesus, I'm going to bite my own tongue off.*

My whole body's begging—for her.

"I want you bare," I grit out.

She stills. "What?"

"Raw, Pip. I need to feel all of you. I want this—*us*. Nothing in the way. So I remember this forever."

Her eyes search mine. She nods.

"I want that too."

She lifts up on her knees, and I watch her wrap her hand around my length, teasing her clit with my tip.

And then she sinks down.

Her velvety, taut pussy devours my cock.

"Petra," I groan, my hands clutching her hips, barely hanging on. "I need—fuck—I need a second."

Petra deliberately squeezes her inner walls around me, her eyes full of mischief. "So... don't do this?"

I grab her hips and growl, "You're going to pay for that."

Then I drive up into her with a force that yanks a gasp from her throat. Her fingers dig into my neck, seizing me like we're the only two souls left on Earth. Her breasts rise and fall frantically against my chest, and I can't get enough.

"Yes, Bryce. You feel—more!"

"I want to live inside you, Pip. You're my heaven."

My body races toward a release at breakneck speed. The need for insatiable pleasure rises like a fever until suddenly, my selfish thoughts grow greedy and dark—a sinister idea slithers into my brain.

No matter how incredible this moment is, she's already gone. But what if she gets pregnant?

If she did... I could take care of her. Spoil her. Make sure she and the baby want for nothing. And then at least I'd have some part of her. A reason to stay in her life when I'm being pulled so far away.

The idea is poison.

And still... it tastes like hope.

You're a bastard for thinking it.

There's no way she can survive in my world. There's equally no way I can escape into hers. The brutal truth pounds through my skull with each thrust. But a child would require us to remain in each other's lives.

The vision is shameful. But it won't leave.

She starts to tremble, breath hitching, and I move faster. She syncs with my movements—seamless, instinctual—her body clamping onto mine as though we're two parts of the same soul finally reunited.

I squeeze her ass tighter as I hear the familiar symphony of her building release—soft sighs and airy moans that I've memorized like my favorite song. I drive into her, holding nothing back, and she topples over the edge.

I feel the most incredible sensation of my life.

Petra's release crashes over her, her come coating my cock as her walls flutter and pulse around my length, milking me with decadent pressure. She cries out my name.

Without the barrier between us, every thrust makes me forget my own damn name. I pump again. And again. Chasing the edge, fighting the inevitable, until—

I break.

"Petra..." I choke out.

I empty everything I am deep inside her, my muscles locking tight, the pleasure crashing through my body in waves.

We collapse into each other, wrecked and gasping.

Our chests flush. Our heartbeats thunder. I lock my arms around her, worried if I let go, she'll vanish.

The ocean keeps whispering as my playlist drones on. I realize...

This was it.

The closest thing to forever I'll ever have with Petra Brinkman.

CHAPTER EIGHTEEN

PETRA

Group Chat : CPK Forever

Me: *Quick poll: CAN YOU DIE FROM HAPPINESS??*

Cam: *Okay, spill.*

Me: *He played it. Our song. From my graduation party. The one we kissed to.*

Katie: *That was seven years ago!*

Cam: *Casual hookups don't play meaningful songs, babe.*

Me: *Help. I think my heart's doing that dumb thing again… Hoping.*

"**Ladies and gentlemen, please** assume your respective positions. We will now begin the wedding rehearsal."

Nigel announces it as a royal decree. You'd think that would snap everyone to attention, but nope. No one's listening. We're all too busy staring at the absurdly oversized luxury circus tent we're standing in.

This tent isn't just big. It's obscene.

No joke—if a jumbo jet wanted to crash this ceremony, it could land inside and still have room to do a three-point turn. The ceiling is vaulted like a cathedral. White silk drapes billow dramatically, catching the ocean breeze. And there are fifty-two crystal chandeliers, each one the size of a Honda Civic, sparkling as if somebody captured the sun and broke it into a million pieces. I can't look directly at them without squinting.

The lavish displays of white roses and peonies are as beautiful as they are boastful, screaming: *We told you money was no object.* Behind them, industrial AC units hum away, because no one's makeup is going to melt off at tomorrow's picture-perfect outdoor wedding. Not on Fiona's watch.

Through the tent's open archway, the ocean sprawls beyond the altar, as if Mother Nature is trying to photobomb this over-the-top production.

Nigel stands in the center of it all with his clipboard in hand, commanding an army of staff as if he's directing a military operation. Which, let's be honest, he basically is.

"Nigel," I call out, "quick etiquette question: Will Miss Muffy's ceremonial cushion be in silk or velvet?"

"Miss Von Cashmere has very specific preferences, Miss Brinkman. The burgundy velvet, positioned precisely six inches from the aisle for optimal viewing."

"Right. And if someone accidentally sits in her spot?"

"I believe you Americans have an expression about 'finding out.'" The corner of his mouth twitches, and I swear I catch a glint of humor. "Now, Miss Brinkman, if you would kindly assume your position with the bridal party."

I grin, because getting Nigel to crack even a microscopic smile is a personal victory. He produces a small silver bell from his jacket pocket.

PING! PING! PING!

"Casa Cashmere has hosted precisely one hundred and twenty-seven weddings," he announces. "Each has proceeded with dignity and grace. We shall continue that tradition. First position, if you please. Mr. Echo shall stand in for Mr. Whitfield, who has yet to arrive."

Fiona's voice floats over from where she's fussing with her rehearsal dress. "Daddy should be arriving soon! He's always a little late because he's, for sure, the busiest man ever. I mean, you should see his calendar."

WHUP-WHUP-WHUP-WHUP.

A helicopter roars overhead, making the chandeliers rattle and sending rose petals flying like confetti.

"Ooh, maybe that's him!" Hana squeals, clapping her hands.

I catch Fiona glitch for the barest second. Blink and you'd miss it. But I don't miss much.

"Oh yes, probably!" she says with a beauty pageant smile.

Probably? The word triggers my internal alarm system, but I shut it down fast. New Petra no longer assumes the worst.

Nigel, unfazed by interruptions, continues, "Mr. Brinkman, Mr. Sterling, please demonstrate your entrance sequence from the eastern pavilion. That will signal the beginning of the ceremony."

I watch Bryce approach the altar behind my brother, both of them decked out in three-piece suits. Gavin looks sharp and self-assured in his charcoal gray, but Bryce outshines him in every way. Especially that navy suit, which brings his blue eyes to life.

Drown me in that ocean, please.

His jaw flexes, smiling slightly as he looks my way—like he's remembering everything we did last night in vivid, skin-on-skin detail.

Yeah. Me too, Blue Eyes.

Off to the side, a woman starts playing a grand piano, the familiar notes of Pachelbel's "Canon in D" filling the air. Then a man joins in with his cello, weaving a melody that's as serene as it is magical.

"Bridesmaids," Nigel calls out, "please begin your procession."

I smooth my hand over the lavender silk of my Prada sundress and follow Hana down the aisle, locked into the same slow-motion bridal zombie walk she's performing.

Step. Pause. Smile. Repeat.

I glance up, and he's looking at me. Not at the décor. Not at Gavin. At *me.*

And for one dizzy second, my breath catches. What if this was our wedding? What if he was waiting for me?

I'd be sobbing through winged eyeliner, overwhelmed with happiness. We'd present our own vows—real ones. I'd tell him he makes me feel like I'm worth choosing, and then he'd say he only sees the best parts of me, the ones that everybody else misses.

We'd kiss—a naughty, hungry lip-lock so hot and heavy the guests would blush and look away. Then we'd race to our luxury hotel suite and spend our entire honeymoon dining on room service and each other.

Quit torturing yourself, Petra. This will all be over soon.

I wish I could stop myself from hoping this was more than just a secret fling. *But after last night, how can I not imagine being his for real?*

Four thousand baby steps later, Hana and I position ourselves across the altar from Bryce and my brother.

Fiona appears at the top of the aisle on Echo's arm, and the staff-turned-pretend-guests rise as Nigel says, "Now we shall witness the bride's grand entrance."

Today's Echo ensemble is surprisingly toned down. Sure, the guy's wearing purple leather pants vacuum-sealed to his legs and he has enough jewelry to open a pawn shop, but there's no body glitter and his nipples are covered, so that's practically black-tie for him.

Fiona clutches his arm as if he's a status symbol. Her white rehearsal dress sparkles, and her makeup is impeccable. She's stunning.

Witnessing her glow with happiness at Gavin waiting at the altar, I feel this strange twist in my stomach.

No warning bells. No fury.

Today, I am not the suspicious sister.

I'm a girl in love.

Fiona takes her place beside my brother, and it's like they stepped right out of the pages of a wedding magazine—elegant and beaming.

The song ends, and Nigel strides to center stage, facing the audience. "And now," he says, "the officiant would begin by saying, 'We are gathered here today for a sacred celebration of unity—the joining of Gavin Brinkman and Fiona Whitfield in marriage.'"

I peer at Bryce, and he's locked on to me. His stare doesn't waver.

What if I could belong in his world?

There's nothing physically stopping me from following him to New York. I could learn to be a society woman, couldn't I? I survived being manhandled into couture by Sebastian Bellini. These fancy clothes barely even itch anymore.

And my tattoos? I mean, I love them, yeah, but I could remove a few. Play the part. For him.

Hell, I've got a blowout, been waxed from brow to bum, tried that weird bird snot soup, and even let a freaking dog tell me off! I could watch my language in public and learn to enjoy posh fundraisers, gallery openings, and weekend brunches.

I might have to kiss my law school dreams goodbye. Marrying into his world means trading personal ambition for legacy management, so I wouldn't be Petra the lawyer, I'd be Mrs. Sterling. Still, I could champion legal aid clinics, homeless shelters, and help teenagers aging out of foster care. I'd convince these billionaires to write checks bigger than their egos.

Bryce's life is drowning him in expectations. What if I was his escape hatch? His safe harbor after brutal board meetings and family manipulation. The storm he could lose himself in when the Sterling name weighed on him like an anchor.

I could be the girl he comes undone for, not just in bed but in *life*.

In a single moment, the fantasy obliterates.

"I trust we're not intruding on the festivities."

Reginald Sterling. Bryce's father.

He is a towering wall of power and intimidation—six feet of silver-haired authority wrapped in a custom Italian wool suit. His ice-blue stare twists my stomach into knots. Those eyes don't just scan the room; they calculate with ruthless precision, quickly analyzing who's an asset and who is a liability.

But it's the woman beside him who turns my blood to ice.

Amanda Tenley is sickeningly, devastatingly perfect—a genetic lottery winner, an angel among mortals, so gorgeous she makes Fiona bland in comparison. Her honey-colored hair falls in flawless waves past her shoulders, and her soft-pink Chanel suit mirrors the soft tint of her lips.

My eyes dart to Bryce. He's staring at them.

At *her*.

"Stop the run-through," Gavin says, already working his way to them. "Mr. Sterling, what an honor that you could find time to attend our nuptials."

Reginald shakes my brother's hand. "The merger of the Whitfields and the Brinkmans? Wouldn't miss it," he says. His vulture gaze goes to Bryce. "Son, come give your girlfriend a proper hello. She's traveled quite a distance to see you."

Girlfriend? I don't breathe.

Bryce's eyes flick to me for a millisecond with a clear message. Panic.

I watch, in horror, as he walks over, leans in, and kisses Amanda on the cheek. My heart doesn't just crack. It fucking implodes.

Nigel approaches with his usual diplomatic grace. "Mr. Sterling, always a pleasure to have you back at Casa Cashmere."

"Ah, Nigel. Still running the estate like a Swiss watch, I see."

"Doing what I can, sir."

Reginald faces the guests and addresses them like he's delivering a press release.

"Amanda's mother no longer needed her care, and when I mentioned the wedding, she was simply *desperate* to see Bryce again. We thought it best to surprise everyone and come together."

I stare in disbelief as her manicured hand curls around Bryce's arm. "I missed you terribly, darling."

Darling. Fucking darling.

Fiona floats over to Amanda, wrapping her in an embrace. "Oh my gosh, this is wonderful! Having you here makes things so much more special!" She pulls back with a conspiratorial giggle. "Honestly, Bryce has been *miserable* without you. Like, sulkier than usual, which I didn't think was possible. You're the only one who can get him out of his infamous moods."

Wait. She's the only one?

That's when I spot it. The tic. Bryce's whole body is rigid as a statue, and that finger of his is going absolutely berserk against his thigh—*tap-tap-tap-tap-tap...*

You should be nervous, you two-timing bastard.

"Your accommodations will be prepared post haste," Nigel says, nodding to staff members.

"Just the single room for myself," Reginald replies. "Miss Tenley will naturally be sharing Bryce's room."

Sharing Bryce's room. The words stab straight through my ribcage, like a red-hot poker. The edges of my vision blur. *Don't cry.*

"Certainly, sir. The staff will help you to your suite so you can freshen up from your travels."

The crew jump into action as Nigel, ever the unflappable professional, redirects his attention. "Apologies, Mr. Sterling, but the rehearsal must proceed."

Bryce's dad claps a heavy hand on his shoulder. "Cigar lounge, when you're finished here," he says under his breath. "We have matters to discuss." Then his expression brightens like someone flipped a switch. "What a splendid weekend this is going to be."

He extends his arm toward Amanda with old-school gallantry. "Amanda, darling, allow me to escort you to your accommodations."

Just like that, they saunter off like they own the entire fucking planet.

"Will the wedding party kindly return to their designated positions?" Nigel calls out with renewed authority. "We shall resume from where we were interrupted."

Bryce walks back to his spot without one goddamn look in my direction.

I feel wheezy and lean against the side of the ceremonial arch. I'm about to projectile vomit all over these beautiful flowers.

Bryce is a cheater. A lying, manipulative asshole. He used me.

I can't believe I fell for his poor, tortured billionaire act. All that bullshit about feeling trapped by his legacy, about never connecting with anybody before. He knew I had a soft spot for underdogs, so he played me like a fucking virgin. Made me think I was rescuing him, when really, I was his dirty fling—something spicy to sample in Mexico.

That's how these people are trained from birth—to see everyone else as pawns in their twisted games.

How could I be so fucking naive?

Hot tears threaten behind my eyes, but I don't let them fall. Not here. Not now.

"By law," Nigel says, flipping a page on his clipboard, "you are required to declare that you know of no legal impediment to your marriage..."

Hana whisper-gushes to me, "Isn't it *wonderful* that Bryce's fiancée made it after all? I literally cannot even with how perfect they are together!"

I don't answer. I'm too busy trying to vaporize the douchebag with my eyeballs. Who still. Has not. Looked. At me.

Hana's motormouth keeps going. "Although, oh my gosh, this morning I was super worried there might not be a wedding with all the crazy prenup drama!"

That snaps me out of my homicidal thoughts about creative ways to murder lying billionaires.

"What prenup drama?" I cut her off, turning sharply.

Hana's eyes light up. "Oh, well, Gavin's lawyers couldn't get all of Fiona's legal team's requests sorted out in time, so they're just going to skip the prenup paperwork until after the wedding! Isn't that romantic? I mean, in our world, that's unheard of. It's so beautifully trusting and brave!"

The world tilts sideways.

"WHAT THE FUCK?!" flies out of my mouth like a volcanic eruption, and suddenly every eye in this ridiculous tent is staring. I don't care. I'm already moving.

"You don't have a prenup? Are you fucking *kidding* me?"

My brother's face hardens. "Petra, we're not discussing this here."

"Like hell we're not! Tell me it's not true. Please tell me you're not about to marry her without any legal protection."

"It's handled," he says in his infuriatingly calm tone. "We'll execute a postnuptial agreement after the ceremony. It's a nonissue."

"I'm aware of what a postnup is. That's not romantic trust, Gavin—that's Russian roulette! You're the idiot loading the chamber!"

"Enough. You're embarrassing yourself," he says in that big brother voice.

"Bro, you built your whole life from nothing—and now you're gambling it all on someone you didn't even know last Christmas? Are you out of your goddamn mind?"

Fiona gasps. "Petra, I understand it's difficult for someone like you. But wealthy families handle these matters with more... *nuance.*"

"Someone like me? You mean the daughter of a woman who got stripped of everything by a man with a trust fund and a wandering dick?"

Gavin's face darkens. "I said enough. This outburst is unacceptable. Apologize."

"What's unacceptable is allowing my brother to make the same stupid mistake that destroyed our family!"

The air crackles with tension. Bryce decides to enter the blast zone.

"Petra's studying to become a lawyer," he says. "I'm sure she understands prenups and asset protection better than—"

I spin on him so fast he flinches.

"Don't you fucking dare! You don't get to play knight in shining armor now, you lying piece of shit!"

He looks like I slapped him. *Good.*

"Pip, please..." His voice drops to a low whisper. "Don't do this. You're—"

"No. You can't stand up for me after screwing me over."

My brother's attention jumps between us. "Hold on. Lawyer? Petra, what the hell is he talking about?"

Fiona releases a taunting laugh. "Oh my gosh, how priceless! The little dropout actually thinks she has what it takes for law school?

Petra, angel, the legal field demands just a smidge more than a rebellious attitude and whatever tragic situation is happening with your makeup."

I see red. My fists clench. My nails bite into my skin.

She takes a step toward me. "I thought we were past this, Petra. That you'd evolved beyond these destructive outbursts, but apparently you're still the same impulsive, self-centered—"

"Fi," Gavin snaps. "Stop."

"No," I say, trembling with rage. "Let her talk. Let her say what she really thinks. Because at least when she's being a bitch, she's not pretending."

Gavin steps between us. "You need to leave, Petra. Go cool off."

"Quit pretending to be my father! You've never asked what *I* want. You just see a mess to clean up."

My voice gets stronger, more defiant with every word.

"I'm done being your perpetual disappointment. I don't want your money, your charity, or your pity for how I live my life. I pity all of you. Living in this fake-ass world where *love* comes with a price tag and no one takes a shit unless it's tax-deductible."

"Out. Now, Petra." Gavin's voice has the finality of a judge's gavel. "I've had it with you wrecking everything, when I'm trying to take care of this family."

"Family? That's fucking hilarious, Gavin. You traded *family* a long time ago so you could join these billionaire assholes."

Nobody stops me when I turn on my heel. *I'm so done with these rich pricks. They think their money can buy everything, but it will never buy me.*

I walk away. Head high. And I don't fucking look back.

***

Here in the drawing room, the chandeliers shine overhead like interrogation lights, cold and unblinking. This is where it all began: me, out of my depth before I even knew it. Now it feels like a crime scene. The only thing missing is a chalk line around my heart.

I'm standing in my real clothes—ripped jeans, battered leather jacket, my combat boots still caked in beach sand—clutching the handle of my sad little taped-up suitcase like it's the last honest thing left in this palace of lies.

A tear betrays me, slipping out before I even feel it coming. I swipe it away fast. God, I hate those sneaky little bastards.

I actually thought he'd come after me. That Bryce would burst out of the tent, grab my arm, and explain that Amanda being there was some kind of mistake. That I'm not just his dirty little secret.

It's been over an hour, and the only thing that's followed me is the sound of my pathetic sniffles echoing off these fancy walls.

Stupid. So fucking stupid.

I look up at the massive oil painting that's been side-eyeing me from the moment I walked into this wealthy wasteland. Miss Muffy Von Cashmere glares down from her ornate frame, covered in pearls with that eternal, disapproving scowl.

"Enjoying the show, Lady Snootybottom?" I mutter. "You've been waiting to judge me ever since I arrived. So let's hear it. Don't hold back."

Her painted eyes seem to narrow.

"Say what everyone else is thinking. I'm the family screw-up, the chaos monster, the walking disaster who ruins other people's lives."

I press my fingers to my temples and suck in through my nose, attempting to stop the tears from flowing. It's no use; they're winning.

"A bartender with attitude and daddy issues doesn't belong in a place like this. A guy like Bryce was always going to pick the blonde socialite."

"*Ahem.*"

The noise slices into my self-pity like a guillotine.

I whirl around, nearly losing my balance. Nigel Featherwick stands in the doorway, composed as always. Miss Muffy II sits regally in his arms, her tiny black eyes sweeping over me with what feels like sympathy.

Great. Even the dog pities me. *This is what you call rock bottom.*

"Miss Brinkman, your departure arrangements are being finalized."

And even my walk of shame gets the five-star treatment. *Fucking fantastic.*

He steps into the room and closes the door behind him with a soft click, then sets the dog down on the Persian rug. She starts sniffing around as if she's conducting a security sweep.

I stay still, remembering all too well what happened the last time I was this close to the billionaire puppy heiress in this room.

From his tux pocket, Mr. Featherwick retrieves a pressed white handkerchief and extends it toward me. "For your distress."

I take it. Blow my nose into it violently. When I try to return it, he simply stares at the fabric. Then at me.

"Madam, it is now yours."

"Right," I say, tucking it into my jacket pocket.

"Casa Cashmere regrets that you are leaving."

"No, you don't."

"Yes, Miss Brinkman, I do," he replies with sincerity. "You have been a breath of fresh air that I have sorely missed in this house."

I bark out a laugh that comes out watery at the edges.

"Why do you do this? Why waste your life bowing and scraping for these people with their inherited privilege? These emotional vampires? And no offense, but a *literal* dog."

Miss Muffy is now licking herself.

"I don't do it for them," he says solemnly. "I do it for myself. And for her."

He stares up at the portrait, and his expression softens. "I am going to confide in you, Miss Brinkman, something known only to a select few. That woman in the painting was a lot like you."

"Yeah, right," I snort. "The oil heiress and I are practically twins."

"More than you know," he says gently. "She was wild, brilliant, and the love of my life. Our romance was a secret we carried for forty-two years. Similar to you and Mr. Sterling, we came from different worlds that society did not accept."

"We are not—" I start, but Nigel cuts me off with a raised hand.

"I am well aware it was you in the closet. And the entire household staff heard Mr. Sterling's rather... enthusiastic response to your company."

I groan into my hands.

"Please, do not be embarrassed. Far worse things have transpired in Casa Cashmere's auxiliary storage rooms."

I peer through my fingers. "That sounds deeply disturbing."

"Indeed."

A pained expression flickers across his face.

"Her husband was an exceedingly cruel and violent man, many decades her senior. This union was imposed upon her by her family, who urgently needed the alliance to avert financial ruin. Upon marrying into such considerable wealth, she was expected to become the epitome of propriety, but she was not a woman to be tamed. Her husband employed me specifically to keep her... in line."

"So you were hired to spy on her?

Nigel nods gently. "But I fell irrevocably in love with her from the moment we met. She inquired if the stick firmly lodged up my arse was part of the uniform, or if I had struck a bargain with the devil for such impeccable posture." His pupils twinkle at the memory. "Lord Von Cashmere never succeeded in breaking what made her extraordinary. Her spirit was too vast, too deeply rooted to be destroyed by a small man who confused ownership for affection."

"He sounds like a total dick."

"Without question. Her punishment for not conforming was banishment to Casa Cashmere, the family's summer residence, while he remained in Europe. This place became her sanctuary. I stayed by her side, maintaining my composure at all times, never exposing our love in the presence of others. If I had, he would have been informed. He would have taken her away from me and this place she held so dear."

"But why stay if you could never be together?"

"Because she needed somebody who could help her walk the line between defiance and duty. Because someone had to witness her life. All of it."

"And the dog?"

"Our plan was to wed the moment he drew his final breath," he continues. "But then she fell ill herself—as if fate was determined to deny us even that small measure of happiness."

BARK! BARK!

"There's my precious angel," he croons, gathering the Maltese in his arms. "Were you feeling neglected, dearest? Forgive me."

The dog's tongue darts out, giving his cheek a quick lick, and he buries his face into her fluffy fur.

"I gifted my love this little companion during her final months. She took one look and declared her Miss Muffy Von Cashmere the Second. She found endless joy in choosing tiny outfits, giving etiquette lessons, commissioning custom jewelry—and would spend hours teaching this puppy how to hold court."

He pauses, vulnerability fluttering across his features.

"She used to jest that Muffy was our child. She couldn't have any of her own, you see. But she would say that this little creature has our best and worst traits. Regal, feral, disobedient, and loyal to a fault."

My throat pinches.

"During that time, she devised an intricate fantasy. Elaborate scenarios in which Miss Muffy would inherit her position as mistress of the estate. I would continue my duties exactly as before, serving our 'daughter' with the same devotion I had shown her. She would say, 'Nigel, when I'm gone, Muffy will need you. Promise me you'll carry on as if I never left. Allow her to sit at the head of the table. Let her choose the wine. I want her wearing my favorite brooches.'"

He pauses for a moment, lost in thought.

"When she became bedridden, I brought her fantasy to life," he says. "She became particularly animated about teaching the puppy to dance—salsa was our secret passion. So I hired Rosita to come teach us while my beloved was entertained from her bed. Miss Muffy and I would attempt our choreography as she cheered from her quilts."

I study the portrait, and I can picture it all—this straight-laced butler and a wild-hearted oil heiress, dancing in empty ballrooms after midnight.

"This portrait was her final act of rebellion. She loathed the mask she was forced to wear for society—that cold, disapproving demeanor expected of women of her standing. Thus, she was determined to have the last laugh."

A crooked smile tugs at his lips.

"She insisted the rich would follow whatever they were told was fashionable. They would not question the absurdity of it. They would curtsy to a dog adorned in pearls if that is what was expected of them. She bet me the world would accept a pet heiress. And she was right."

I'm gaping at him like he just confessed to being an alien. "So you're telling me this whole operation is basically an elaborate prank?"

"Yes," he says simply. "One that allows me to remain in her presence. I believe she watches our little performances from whatever realm she now inhabits, and yes, I hope she is laughing at the beautiful madness she created."

And suddenly I'm not in some grand palace anymore—I'm standing inside someone's love story.

A ridiculous, eccentric, head-over-heels crazy-ass kind of love that makes you do insane things.

Who am I to judge? An hour ago, I was mentally planning my transformation into a well-mannered, tattoo-free socialite so I could stay in Bryce's orbit.

"The inheritance is mine alone. But what value does such wealth hold? She was the only treasure I ever yearned for. I would gladly trade every billion she left me for five more minutes in her arms."

A lump forms in my throat. "I'm really sorry for your loss. She sounds like she was one hell of a woman."

"She was everything. And she would want to convey to you that this world needs individuals to challenge the status quo. You are exactly the type of person Mr. Sterling needs."

"Sorry, Nigel, but I'm done. These people can't be saved from themselves, and I'm tired of trying."

"Very well. A car has been arranged to transport you to the private airfield, and from there—"

"No." The word spills out aggressively. "No more jets. No more privilege. Take me into town. I'll catch a commercial flight like a normal person."

His eyebrows lift slightly. "As you wish." He extends his white-gloved hand. "Until we meet again, Miss Brinkman."

I shake it. "I highly doubt that, given my tax bracket, but thank you."

He turns to leave.

"Nigel, wait." He pauses, looking back expectantly. "Can you please make sure my clothes get returned? The ones Sebastian Bellini picked out?"

"Of course."

I take a breath, swallowing what's left of my pride. "And on my first night here, I *may* have accidentally dropped a multi-million-dollar ruby ring outside my window. Could you find it and return it to Bryce?"

If he's surprised by this confession, he doesn't show it. "I shall see to it personally."

"Thanks for everything, Lord Britchybottom."

He bows. "My pleasure."

As his footsteps fade down the hallway, I steal one last glance at the drawing room entrance. A part of me is still hoping—stupidly, so fucking stupidly—that Bryce will come running in.

He doesn't.

My phone stays silent. No texts. No missed calls. Nothing.

Time to face the hard truth: Billionaire Boy lied to get me into bed.

I grab my duct-taped disaster of a suitcase and force myself to the door, leaving the delusions of grandeur where they belong.

He never wanted me forever. *Who would?*

CHAPTER NINETEEN

BRYCE

Stepping into the Casa Cashmere cigar lounge feels like walking into the devil's lair—dark, smoky, and laden with power. Mahogany walls climb from marble floor to vaulted ceiling, glowing under a haze of amber light. The mounted heads of long-dead exotic animals track me from the shadows—trophies from men who killed not to survive, but to dominate. Their glass eyes lock on to me, unblinking, daring me to make a wrong move.

I sink into the bloodred leather armchair across from my father, the cushions molding around me like quicksand. He takes a long pull from his Cuban cigar, the ember glowing menacingly. The smoke coils like fingers in my lungs, but I don't cough. That would be weakness. I force myself to breathe through it, one shallow inhale at a time.

He reaches for the crystal decanter beside him, pouring three fingers of scotch. He doesn't offer me a drink. The message is unmistakable: This is no social call.

"You defied me again, Bryce. I instructed you to call Amanda. You did not. Do you think this is a game?"

I keep my voice steady. "You shouldn't have ambushed me like that. I was handling it."

He swirls the scotch in his glass, watching the liquid catch the light. "From what I hear, there was only one thing you were handling."

"What's that supposed to mean?"

"Do you really believe I don't monitor your every move? You're Sterling Industries' most valuable asset, son. Every second of your life is under surveillance. I know about the closet, the midnight trysts, the carnival getaway. Don't ever think you can pull one over on me."

"You had me watched?"

"I had you protected." He puffs the cigar like it's a punctuation mark. "From catastrophic missteps. Like the one you've been making with Gavin's trashy little sister."

My spine goes cold, hands clenched into fists at my sides. When I speak, my voice comes out deadly quiet. "Don't."

"Don't what? Call out the fact that your priorities are fucked? That your dick's doing all your thinking for you? I handed you a strategic alliance, and you chose a bartender with a dirty mouth."

Heat explodes behind my ribs. "Her name is Petra. And she's not—"

"She's a distraction. She's insignificant. I'm here to stop you from pissing away everything this family has built for some working-class delusion. Snap out of it."

"It's not delusional. She's the only authentic thing in my life."

"Then why is she slinking home like a scolded dog?"

His smug satisfaction makes my stomach plummet. He's studying my face, cataloging every expression.

"Oh, you don't know," he says with fake sympathy. "She saw Amanda and made the choice for you. Commercial flight. Coach class. Back to the shitty life where she belongs."

My throat constricts. "She left?"

"Twenty-three minutes ago, to be precise. Even tattooed troublemakers recognize when they're beaten. Smart girl. Saves us both the mess of a direct conversation."

My father reaches into his jacket pocket and pulls out a small, black velvet box—a dark omen with one meaning. One message. He places it on the mahogany coffee table.

"Focus on what's important—your future with Amanda."

The ring glints, even in the low light. Thirty-five carats of flawless diamond, emerald cut, surrounded by a halo of smaller stones. It's the same ring my grandfather used to propose to my grandmother in 1924, sealing the Sterling-Vanderbilt merger that turned two fortunes into an empire.

"Tomorrow night at the wedding reception, you'll use that ring to propose to Amanda. Just like your grandfather did. Just like every Sterling man before you."

"That's... sudden. I haven't even spoken to Amanda since our breakup."

"I've handled the preliminaries." He pours himself another scotch. "Told her you've been under considerable stress, making stupid mistakes, but that you're ready to honor your commitments. She's beside herself, of course. What woman wouldn't be?"

I stare at the ring like it might grow teeth. "And if I refuse?"

"Then you'll discover what defying me costs. Not just you, but the people who depend on you. Starting with sixty million Heartvest users."

The threat is a surgeon's blade, twisting with cruel precision.

He's not just threatening me—he'll hurt every person whose financial future depends on our company going public. Every single mom working double shifts to send her kid to college, every blue-collar hero trying to build a nest egg, every hopeful soul who thought we'd help them climb the ladder to a better life.

"I'm sure the Brinkman girl was... an entertaining pastime. She looks like she'd be a hellcat in the sack. You can keep her as a sidepiece for all I care."

"Don't talk about her like that."

"Quit mistaking pussy for principles, son. Acknowledge her for what she is. The bartender you've been fucking to rebel against your birthright."

"I told you her name is Petra." My fingers dig into the armrest, rage crawling under my skin. "And this isn't rebellion. It's my life."

"Your life is property of Sterling Industries," he says, his eyes drilling into mine. "Always has been. You're not going to be the little shit who ruins my legacy. Marry Amanda, then fuck whoever you want. Now, pick up that goddamn ring."

My hand trembles. The velvet is sandpaper against my fingertips as I slip it into my jacket pocket.

He smashes the glowing end of his cigar into the ashtray. The last tendril of smoke curls into the air and dissipates.

"Knew you'd come around, son. Welcome back to reality."

I don't look at him. "Are we finished here?"

"Not quite." He straightens his jacket. "I'll be personally overseeing tomorrow's engagement. Consider it a father's pride in his son's... evolution."

KNOCK! KNOCK! KNOCK!

Gavin pokes his head through the door, his usual confident demeanor replaced by worry.

"Mr. Sterling. Bryce. Forgive the interruption, but have you seen Petra? She's gone completely off-grid. I sent her away from rehearsal, expecting her to cool down, but she's disappeared."

Reginald's mouth curves into something that would terrify demons. "Ah yes, your fiery sister. My people tell me she hightailed it to the airport twenty minutes ago."

"Airport?" Gavin's brow furrows with genuine confusion. "I know she's upset, but ditching the wedding entirely? She wouldn't do that."

Ice floods my veins. No. Please, God, no. Don't let him—

"I imagine," my father says, his tone cold and calculated, "it's because she learned my son was fucking her while he was still committed to Amanda."

The words detonate in the room like a bomb.

Gavin turns, his face a growing storm cloud—no emotion yet, just pressure.

I stand so fast the chair legs screech against the floor. "Gavin, let me explain."

Explain what? That I betrayed him? Lied to his face? Burned every ounce of his trust to the fucking ground?

"Bryce, tell me he's lying."

I want to.

But the words are too big to lie and too brutal to speak.

I lock up.

Reginald leans back, entirely too pleased with himself. "Oh, I'm afraid you're just scratching the surface, Mr. Brinkman. My boy here has been keeping quite a few secrets from you."

Gavin's jaw tightens. "What secrets?"

"Well, since we're tearing the bandage off," he says, buzzing with satisfaction. "Bryce, want to bring him up to speed on your departure, or should I?"

"Father, no—"

"My son is abandoning Heartvest the instant your IPO finalizes." Each word drops like an executioner's axe. "He's being summoned to the big leagues, where he'll take the reins of a real company."

Gavin's face is disorientation, then disbelief, then rage.

"So, while I'm busting my ass mapping out our company's future, you're planning your little escape? And screwing my sister behind my back?"

"It wasn't like that. I never meant—"

"Meant what? To get caught? To have your old man sweep in and clean up your mess?" He steps toward me. "You're exactly like him—you use people, lie, manipulate everyone around you to get what you want."

The accusation hits me like a bullet to the chest. "Gavin, please—"

My father stands, adjusting his cuffs, with the casual indifference of a man who has orchestrated another flawless takedown.

"Well, this has been enlightening." His hand clamps down on my shoulder. "I'm honoring our deal, son. Your friend keeps his little company. Heartvest lives on. But tomorrow." He doesn't blink. "You honor yours."

I nod in defeat.

"Gentlemen, you have much to discuss," he says, pausing with a smirk. "I'll leave you to it."

The door closes shut like a coffin lid.

I focus on the Persian rug beneath my feet—intricate patterns that suddenly seem less complex than the mess I've made of everything. Gavin's stare bores into me like a laser. I can't bring myself to meet his eyes.

"Look at me… I said *look* at me, you coward."

I force my gaze upward and regret it immediately. The hatred blazing in his eyes is too much.

"Tell me it's not true. Tell me you didn't use my sister."

The desperation in his voice is more pain than anger. He's pleading for me to prove his world isn't collapsing. I don't breathe. It's the kind of stillness that comes right before a crash.

"Say it! Say it's not true, Bryce!"

"I can't."

He stumbles back as if the floor has given out.

His eyes dart around the room like he's wanting to wake up from a nightmare. He starts pacing, his movements jerky and erratic.

"The ATV ride? When you both vanished off-trail and left me searching for twenty minutes? The massage room? When I walked in and you looked like you'd been caught screwing the spa staff. *Jesus Christ…* It was her, wasn't it?"

Each one hits like a slap I should have seen coming.

"You took advantage of my little sister! She always followed you around like a love-sick puppy, and you *knew* it. But I told myself, 'It's Bryce, my best friend. He would never touch the one person I'd burn the world down to protect.' No fucking wonder Petra cracked at the rehearsal. She had just found out who you really are."

His eyes find mine, and all the built-up trust I've earned combusts.

"It's not what you think."

"What I know is you're a scheming piece of garbage who's been playing everyone around you! How many lies, Bryce? How many fucking lies are there?"

"I love her, Gavin." The confession rips out of me. "I'm in love with Petra."

Gavin stops cold, then lunges toward me. His finger jabs into my chest hard enough to bruise.

"LOVE? You think what you did is LOVE?"

CRACK.

His fist connects with my jaw before I can register. The impact sends me staggering backward, my head snapping to the side as the taste of copper floods my mouth. Pain explodes across my face.

"You have no fucking idea what love is! You don't treat people you love like this!"

There's no defending myself. I don't fight back. I don't raise my hands. Don't even straighten my stance.

Because I deserve it.

He's right.

"I was trying to protect—"

"Bullshit!" he shouts, shaking his hand. "You destroyed her! You destroyed me! And then you call it love? For ten fucking years, you were my brother. I let you in my house. Near my *family.*"

"Gavin, I didn't plan it. She just—"

"Don't you dare say she just happened to you, like you're the victim. You're not some poor bastard who tripped and fell into her bed. You chose this path, so own it."

I can't speak. Can't breathe. My entire world is unraveling.

"I'll pretend you're still my best man tomorrow because I refuse to upset Fiona any further. But make no mistake, after the wedding, we're done. And if you want to keep walking this earth, you'll stay the hell away from Petra."

He heads for the door, yanks it open, and pauses in the doorway.

"Your father's right—you leaving Heartvest is the best move for this company. We don't need someone who betrays the people he claims to care about. Enjoy your new gig with your old man. You'll fill his CEO shoes perfectly."

The door slams, and the truth swallows me whole. He's right. I am my father.

***

Petra's room is warm, as if the air has yet to realize she's no longer here.

I throw the door closed and press my forehead against the cool wood, my breath coming in sharp bursts. The silence in here isn't just quiet—it's fucking *vindictive*. Like every molecule of air knows I'm a worthless coward.

What the hell am I doing here?

I should be across the hall right now, playing the dutiful soon-to-be fiancé with Amanda. Discussing wedding venues and pretending my dick doesn't go limp at the thought of touching anyone who isn't Petra fucking Brinkman.

Instead, I'm clinging to the last remnants of her presence. If I stand here long enough, maybe—just maybe—I'll hear her call me "Moneybags" one more time.

"You have no fucking idea what love is."

Gavin's words reverberate in my skull, each syllable a crushing weight on my shoulders. Maybe he's right. Maybe what's eating me alive isn't love—it's power. Control. Owning her like she's my rich fuck-boy obsession.

But if that's true, why does my chest feel like it's been hollowed out with a rusty spoon? Why does the thought of never seeing her red lips curve into a smirk again make me want to demolish this entire goddamn estate with my bare hands?

I see the closet doors cracked open and move toward them in a trance.

Every single piece Sebastian Bellini selected for her is still there. Hanging in formation like a fashion graveyard.

She didn't take any of it. Not the midnight Prada that made her look scandalous. The Valentino that hugged her curves so brazenly I nearly came in my pants. She could've sold any one of these pieces for six months' rent.

But she didn't. She walked away from it all. Because to her, this world of wealth and privilege is tainted.

She only wore these—for me. For the part I asked her to play. To try and belong in a place that did everything it could to spit her out. And worse—I let it happen. I held the door open for her transformation. Watched her wear my world's expectations like a straightjacket. Not once did I tell her the version of her I loved didn't need fixing.

My hand moves without permission, drawn to the crimson silk dress she wore that first night we made love. As it slips through my fingers, soft as sin, I swear I can feel her in it—her arched back, teasing words, hands in my hair, heartbeat against my palms.

That night she told me she preferred the man who wasn't proper when he touched her. There were no games, no coyness, when she whispered, "I want you, Bryce."

It was Petra, brave and burning, saying exactly what she wanted.

Me.

And I gave it to her.

I made her moan my name until her voice gave out. Pressed her into the mattress and worshipped every inch of her. Told her she was extraordinary, all the while knowing I was going to leave her.

Where was my spine to fight for her?

I stood there while my father called her a whore and Gavin glared like I'd just kicked his sister into traffic.

Jesus. I'm a fucking monster.

Something flutters from the dress like a dying moth—a cream-colored notecard with "SB" embossed in gold.

My hands shake as I read the venomous script:

Miss Brinkman—This dress requires serious architectural support given your... limitations. Enclosed undergarments are mandatory. Additionally, professional hair management is crucial—your current situation resembles a trash panda more than a dinner guest. Kindly do not humiliate Mr. Sterling's investment in your appearance.

—Sebastian Bellini, Wardrobe Wizard

The paper crumples in my fist so hard my knuckles go bone-white. But there are more cards scattered on the closet floor like landmines. I grab another one, then another, my horror multiplying with each poisonous line:

Your excessive tattoos are inappropriate for polite society. Concealment is mandatory.

Avoid discussing your... origin story with legitimate guests. Silence is your most flattering accessory.

The provided body shapers will create the illusion of proper birthing hips. Wear them.

Each line drips with disdain—designed to chip away at her confidence and remind her she doesn't belong.

A godforsaken pile of them.

And she read every single one.

She stood in front of this pretentious mirror, covered in chiffon and judgement, and tried to make herself smaller. More palatable. Less... her.

All for me.

I rip up the notes, stumble out of the closet, my knees buckling, and collapse onto her empty bed.

I fed her to the wolves with a fucking bow tied around her neck.

She still chose me. She still fought. Still smiled. Still wore the dress and played the part and stood beside me when the whole fucking world tried to tear her down.

Petra Brinkman loved me with her whole damn heart.

And I broke it.

Twice.

Gavin's right. I don't know what love is. Because if I loved her, I would have told everyone to go to hell in that rehearsal tent. I would have grabbed Petra's hand and walked out with her, consequences be damned.

She wanted the man behind the Sterling mask. The real me. The one who fumbled through real feelings and made unholy sounds when her mouth touched my skin. The guy who forgot what shame was when he was inside her.

And I gave her that man for a few stolen nights, then let my father slip the leash back on me like I'd never strayed.

The engagement ring is a lead weight in my jacket. Thirty-five carats of family duty that I'll slide onto Amanda's finger tomorrow while cameras flash and my soul shrivels. I'll do it because Sterlings don't break tradition. We sacrifice our hearts on the family altar and call it honorable.

Petra will be back in LA. Hopefully covering up that broken heart tattoo I gave her. If there's any justice in this cruel, fucked-up world, she'll finally realize loving me was the worst decision she ever made.

She deserves more than a weak man who treats her like a dirty secret.

She's better off without me.

The door opens abruptly.

"Ah—Mr. Sterling." Nigel's voice tightens with surprise. "Forgive the intrusion. I was under the impression the room had been vacated. I shall return and complete the packing at a more convenient time."

My voice comes out sandpaper-rough. "She's really gone?"

"Regrettably, yes sir. I arranged Miss Brinkman's departure myself." He reaches into his waistcoat pocket. "She did ask me to return this."

The ruby ring.

The one I picked because it was her in gemstone form—that exact shade of fuck-you red she paints on her lips every morning.

I hesitate, breath caught halfway up my throat as I reach for it. The center stone is enormous—bloodred and pulsing like it knows all my secrets. My fingertips trace the halo of diamonds encircling it, like stars being pulled into its irresistible orbit. Because that's what Petra does—burns so bright she makes everything else look dim by comparison.

"Apparently, it slipped from her finger while she was on the balcony. She was quite distressed."

Two rings in one day.

One I'm being forced to give. And one I chose with my heart.

The universe has a sick sense of irony.

Nigel shifts toward the doorway then stops. "Mr. Sterling, might I speak candidly?"

I give him a curt nod.

"Would you permit me to examine this momentarily?" His white-gloved fingers gesture toward the ruby.

I drop the ring into his outstretched palm. He rotates the stone beneath the warm glow of the lamp, and it transforms into liquid fire, casting crimson reflections across his lined face.

"A truly remarkable specimen—much like the lady it was meant to honor. Rare gems like this, with such richness of color and depth of character, are the kind a gentleman encounters but once in his lifetime."

My jaw locks up tight. "I understand your meaning. You act like I had a choice in letting her go."

"I have spent my life in service and watched the wealthy crush the spirits of many extraordinary individuals. That young woman should not have been added to the list. Not on my watch. Not on yours."

"You don't know what it's like to have everything and still feel powerless. You think I want to be the heir imprisoned in a boardroom?"

"The way I see it, sir, is simple. You're deliberately closing the prison door on yourself."

Anger spikes through my chest like lightning. "Don't lecture me about freedom, Nigel. You've never had to make a choice like this. Both options end in someone you love getting destroyed. You think I wanted this? You think I chose to hurt her?"

"I believe you think you're choosing honor. But all I see is a man polishing his chains and calling them a crown."

"That is too far, Nigel. You are out of line."

Nigel drops the ruby into my palm with quiet finality.

"This jewel, sir, is not merely a complement to her lipstick; it captures her very essence. Formidable. Headstrong. Spirited. That remarkable young lady offered you love, yet you chose the approval of ghosts. Legacy, after all, is nothing more than the worship of the dead. And your decision, Mr. Sterling, clearly shows you never deserved her."

He's not wrong. I was never worthy of her love. Of course I'd choose her—if my last name didn't come with the power to destroy Heartvest and sixty million people's savings. If loving the wrong woman didn't mean my father burning down everything Gavin and I built. But that's not the world Sterling heirs live in. We don't get choices. We get obligations.

Sterling men honor their commitments.

Tomorrow I will propose to Amanda because that's what the name demands.

"That's enough advice." My voice turns icy, in a way that would make my father proud.

"Certainly, Mr. Sterling. I shall return once you've concluded your... reflection."

"No, stay. I'm done here."

I get up and drop the ruby ring into my pocket. It rattles against the engagement box already hiding there. The sound shouldn't mean anything, but it does. It's Petra leaving. It's Amanda waiting.

My eyes scan the room, like a junkie chasing one last hit.

Please let there be something of hers.

A tissue stained with her red lipstick. A hair tie. A single goddamn strand of hair. Something to hold on to.

There's nothing on her nightstand, except for Echo's sketchpad.

I pick it up. The spine is warped, the cover is bent, and the pages are curling from humidity.

I flip through the disturbing images. Page after page of some old man called Marvin. Close-ups of liver spots, nose hair, wrinkles. The words: GROSS MAN are scrawled everywhere like he's documenting his own personal nightmare. And then weird sandwich diagrams.

"This belongs to Echo. Petra—um... borrowed it. See that he gets it back."

Nigel's gloved fingers hesitate before taking the sketchpad and flipping through it. The crease in his forehead deepens, lips pressing into a thin line. When he lands on the detailed sketch of a man's face, his posture stiffens.

"Mr. Sterling, might I ask why Miss Brinkman had this particular item in her possession?"

"She had a theory that Echo and Fiona were involved in some kind of nefarious scheme. She thought these sketches could prove something, but she never figured out the old man's identity."

"Dear me," he whispers.

"What?"

"She may have uncovered something quite serious."

"What the hell are you talking about?"

He shows me the sketchpad.

The page depicts a balding man with tired eyes, sagging jowls, and countless liver spots. Echo captured him in stark, unforgiving detail.

"This cannot wait until morning," Nigel says, white as a ghost. "You must come with me immediately."

"Why? What's so urgent?"

"Because I know precisely who this man is. And he may not live long enough to tell us what he knows."

***

The call goes straight to voicemail. Again.

Those three little dots popped up twenty minutes ago. She's seen my messages, she knows it's urgent, but she's not answering. Every second of silence feels like an eternity.

In order to avoid my father's surveillance, Nigel escorted me to an isolated, off-limits section of the mansion, allowing me to call Petra and reveal all that we had discovered.

I hit the FaceTime button for the twelfth time. It rings. One beat. Two.

Then, she answers... sort of.

Her camera jerks around like it's strapped to a rodeo bull. I catch glimpses: a shoulder, a bottle, what looks like a middle finger, and then her face. Blurry, shadowed. *Where the hell is she?*

"I totally hit ignore, Katie—" *hiccup* "—jus' like you said, bitch."

The camera swings like a pendulum, finally locking on to a close-up of her lips as she tips back a bottle of tequila, chugging a massive gulp.

"Girl's-s-s-s gotta have some standards, even if her—" *hiccup* "—vagina took a week-long vacation from them."

Christ! She's wasted.

I quickly place my thumb over my camera to avoid being seen. It's not the most honorable move, but I'm past caring if it helps me locate her.

"Cam-cam-CAMILAAA," she sing-songs. But I still can't see her face. "That walking dildo probably—" *hiccup* "—had to stick his dick in Amanda's boujee pussy a few times-s to scrub off my poor-people germs-s-s before calling me."

The accusation burns worse than the tequila she's drowning in.

She swigs from the bottle again. No chaser. No pause. "I bet he wants her bare too 'cause she's so fucking special to him."

That one cuts deeper. I bite my knuckle.

I haven't laid eyes on Amanda. Not since Petra vanished. Not since Echo's sketchpad became a crime scene. Not since the gut-wrenching realization that my best friend could be the next victim if we don't put a stop to it.

"Fuck, I need my girls here," Petra mumbles. "Remember our trip to Cabo? Well, I'm never coming back. Mexico can *choke* on it. Bryce can *choke* on it. Every billionaire in the world can choke on their billions and die while I laugh and key their stupid yachts."

She goes for another drink, but this time she just… folds.

One second she's upright. The next, she's curled into herself, sobbing—violent, shoulder-shaking sobs that make your ribs ache from hearing them.

The camera finally stills, and her face comes into view.

Her phone's harsh light illuminates the devastation I caused. Mascara streaks down her face like oil spills. Her eyes are swollen and bloodshot. The defiant red lipstick is smeared across her mouth. Strands of black hair stick to her tear-soaked cheeks.

"He's with her," she chokes out. "He loves her, not me. Of course he does. He's never going to love someone like me."

Another sob escapes her while I experience what it feels like to have my intestines ripped out through my throat.

"You know what makes me the biggest fucking idiot alive, girls? I always thought… I thought maybe I was the one who saw him the clearest. Saw him as him, ya know. Just… Bryce."

She wipes her nose on her sleeve. "He never looked at me like I was broken goods. When everyone else saw Gavin's screwup sister, he just saw me." Her voice dissolves into broken whispers. "Called me Pip like it was this secret between us—not Petra the disaster, just his Pip."

The tenderness in her confession shreds what's left of my heart. She's laying bare every reason she fell for me—while tearing herself apart in the process.

The sound of waves hammering the shore fills the silence, and I catch sight of our carnival's dying lights behind her.

She's still in Mexico?

I spot her battered suitcase leaning against a piece of driftwood, contents scattered along the sand.

Jesus Christ. She's planning to sleep on the beach? Drunk and alone and heartbroken because I'm a spineless piece of shit.

That's when I break.

"Pip."

Her head shoots up. "Bryce?" she calls out, her eyes searching desperately. "Where—?"

"I'm on the phone," I say quickly.

Finally, she lowers her eyes to the screen, her gaze settling on my face, lip trembling.

"Petra, I'm so—"

"NO!" she shouts, tears streaming harder. "You don't get to apologize! You don't get to fix this with your fancy words and your—"

"Please, just listen. You can't sleep on the beach."

"You don't get to tell me what to do!" she shouts, voice cracking. "Or take care of me! Nothing! Goodbye!"

"Wait, Pip! I called about Echo's sketchpad. Remember the drawings—"

"I don't care about any of you assholes!"

Panic claws up my throat. "Please, go to a hotel. I'll pay for it. Or I'll get you a car back to Casa Cashmere. Just share your location—"

"Ha! Good luck finding me, Moneybags!"

SPLASH.

The screen goes black.

She threw her phone into the ocean.

Goddammit.

CHAPTER TWENTY

PETRA

Ow. My skull pounds. *Where am I?*

There's a tiny construction crew jackhammering into my eyeballs. Everything hurts, and my mouth tastes like I licked the floor of a cantina.

Wait. Did I FaceTime Bryce? Oh hell. It's all flooding back.

Me, drunk off my ass on bottom-shelf tequila. Me tearing into him about his sleazy betrayal. And then… *Crap! My phone.*

Why didn't I simply end the call? Why did I have to go full drama queen and launch my phone into the ocean?

I try to sit up and immediately want to die. Everything is so goddamn bright. My eyelids hurt. *How is that a thing?* The bed, the walls, and carpeting are blinding. Even the stupid bathrobe I'm wearing is practically glowing.

Again it hits me—I have no idea where I am. More importantly, where are my clothes? I'm dressed in white, surrounded by beaming white walls, and there are mysterious voices calling from beyond.

The loud chatter from the other room grows to a fever pitch. Multiple conversations layer over each other like chaotic TikTok videos all playing at the same time. My hungover brain starts clawing at the walls, begging for a mute button.

Everything's too loud. Too white. Like heaven turned up to eleven.

Am I dead? Did I drink my way to the eternal happy hour in the sky?

My legs are limp noodles as I stagger out of the bedroom, leaning on the wall for support. Gravity is not my friend. I enter the main room.

Fuck. Me. Sideways. Not only am I dead... *I'm in hell.*

Because this is Sebastian Bellini's Glam Squad Headquarters.

Sunlight spills through the massive ocean-view windows. *Think, Petra, think.* I'm in a hotel. On the same beach as the carnival. *Okay, so I know where I am, but why in God's name is Sebastian here?*

The legendary stylist stands in the center of the hotel suite, the eye of a fashion storm. His model-minions flutter around him, resembling fashion-forward bats. Racks upon racks of designer outfits are being delicately zipped into garment bags as if they're newborn babies. Accessories disappear into protective cases.

Sebastian holds his ever-faithful iPad in one hand and a bottle of sparkling Perrier in the other. His piercing gaze locks onto me; his expression shifts into theatrical disapproval.

"Look what the tequila fairy dragged in," Sebastian announces. "I see you've added 'decaying zombie' to your list of fashion faux pas."

Someone put me out of my misery.

"What—where—how did I—?" I say in a voice that sounds like I've been smoking cigarettes made of sand.

He calmly sips. "Monica found you last night sprawled tragically on the beach. She insisted we rescue you."

"You were singing rock ballads to the waves," Monica says while folding scarves. "Also crying. A lot. Your luggage is in the closet, along with your empty bottle."

The word *bottle* sends my stomach into a warning spin. Tequila is now officially dead to me. Along with hope, dignity, and FaceTime.

"You are absolutely *committed* to testing the limits of my considerable talents, aren't you?" Sebastian says, handing me two tiny spoons. "Here, chill your under-eyes, and you might just pass for human again."

I'm about to tell him how far up his ass he can stick his beauty tips, when the mirror across the suite shows the truth. *Yikes.* I look like roadkill that got hit, stumbled into the next lane, and then got hit again. Puffy eyes. Streaked cheeks. And my topknot is giving *I just cried in a Walgreens parking lot, so don't ask* energy. I slap the spoons under my eyes and pray.

Sebastian sighs. "We *cannot* have the sister of the groom looking like she slept in a department store dumpster." He pivots toward his fashion army. "We have twenty minutes to clear out and descend upon Casa Cashmere. Today, we style the wealthiest individuals in the world. And most importantly, make sure this woman doesn't vomit on the mink. Chop-chop, fashionistas!"

"Thanks for the rescue," I say, "but I don't need a ride. I'm not going."

"Monica, assume control. Do not let those girls ball up my couture capes like gym socks."

She nods and starts barking orders. "Valentino goes in garment bag twenty-three. Careful with those Louboutins! Where is the nipple tape?"

His expression is unreadable as he gestures toward a closed-off sitting area. Two plush chairs face oversized windows that offer front-row seats to the ocean.

"Sit," he says as he opens a suitcase with velvet-lined compartments. Inside, there's a portable espresso machine.

"You travel with that?"

He tosses me a look. "There are two things I never trust to amateurs. Orgasms… and coffee. Espresso?"

My hungover body practically weeps with gratitude. "Please."

The grinder whirs to life, filling the space with rich, earthy promise. Sebastian moves like a high-end barista in a slow-motion commercial.

"Do you know why I ride you harder than an unpaid intern at Milan Fashion Week?"

"Because you're the style antichrist and cruelty is your kink?"

He snorts. "Because I *see* you. It seems impossible looking at me now, but I have not always possessed this level of… fabulousness."

"Sure, and next you'll say you weren't hatched from a Dior egg in Paris."

"Regrettably, my origins were mundane. Blue-collar family, off-brand cereal, parents who only provided clearance-rack fashion."

The espresso machine hisses and gurgles. Warm, nutty, roasty. My soul claws its way back into my body at the sound.

"Fashion became my path to salvation. I wanted to be a designer. So I poured every dime I had into chasing the neon trend. Glow-in-the-dark accessories. Belts, ties, suspenders, headbands—all made from *actual* glow sticks."

"You made clothes out of glow sticks? That's either genius or a fire hazard."

"Sadly, the eighties proved to be an unforgiving era for establishing one's reputation. The critics were merciless. 'Bellini's Radioactive Disaster'—that was *Harper's Bazaar*. *Cosmo* called it 'Chernobyl Meets Club Med.' And the hardest to endure was from *Vogue*: *'Glow Hard: One Man's Nuclear Meltdown on the Runway.'*"

"Ouch."

"Soul crushing but profoundly instructive. I learned that if you cannot join the sharks in their feeding frenzy, you must intimidate them into submission. I created an entirely new persona obsessed with styling, and Sebastian Bellini was reborn. And now? I am the critic. I became the fashion world's gatekeeper."

He removes the espresso from the machine with ceremonial care, then places a tiny cup before me, dark and aromatic as sin. I take a sip.

"Holy shit. You should abandon styling and open a coffee empire."

Sebastian cradles his cup. "I am aware of my many gifts. However, who has time for such pursuits when the fashion-challenged require constant saving?"

He pauses, studying me with his sharp little eyes. "I find myself in the rather unprecedented position of needing to say, I'm sorr—sarcastically aware that I may not have been fair to you."

"Wait. Are you trying to say you're sorry?"

"No. I'm Sebastian Bellini. I'm saying... I acknowledge your greatness while reminding you that I am the sun."

"Oh, thank God. For a second, I thought I'd entered an alternate dimension."

"Do not make this more insufferable than it already is," he huffs. "I've been especially hard on you because you strutted into my space with confidence and zero regard for my reputation. Your arrogance and style were... irritatingly difficult to comprehend."

"So I annoyed you into respecting me?"

"Precisely. The sassier you got, the more curious I became. I thought, *this one... this little barracuda might be bold enough to swim with the sharks.* And then there was Mr. Sterling. The way his eyes were glued on you. It was like watching a duke fall in love with a flamethrower."

"He doesn't love me, Sebastian. I don't belong in his world."

"Ridiculous! Was not a single syllable of my incredibly moving personal story absorbed? I just told you—*passionately*, I might add—that belonging isn't something *they* decide. They don't get to define your worth. *You* do. Always. And if that handsome man is the one, then for the love of Prada, don't let anyone stop you."

"I appreciate the pep talk, I really do. But Bryce made his choice, and it's not me."

He rises with signature grace, collecting our cups as he moves to the counter.

"Such a pity. You two were radiant together. And might I add, you've created quite the sensation—I have acquired several new clients thanks to your dramatic transformation! *C'est la vie!* Looks like I'll be riding the wave of your new sister-in-law's scandal instead."

"What scandal?"

"The Whitfield family's spectacular implosion, naturally. What else could I mean?"

"What the hell are you saying? And don't give me some cryptic fashion metaphor, or I'll Photoshop Crocs onto every one of your clients and run a paid ad targeting the staff at *Vogue*.

His face twitches, then illuminates with delight.

"THERE she is! My spicy little honey badger."

"Sebastian!"

"Rumor is, they're bankrupt. I had an inkling, of course. Their account has been delinquent for nearly two years, but one doesn't discuss such vulgarities. Mr. Whitfield borrowed beyond his means to keep up appearances. The estates, the properties, even the jewelry—it's all about to be seized. And according to my sources, he's looking at prison time. So naturally, he's fled the country."

The floor dissolves beneath my feet. *Oh fuck.*

Fiona's card being declined. Her desperation. The rush to move up the wedding.

It all makes sense.

"My brother has no fucking clue! Fiona convinced him to marry her without a prenup. She's gonna take everything he has."

He gasps. "No. Not that magnificent, symmetrical specimen! He's one of my most lucrative clients."

"Glad your screwed-up priorities are consistent."

My mind's doing cartwheels. I need to call my brother, but my phone is fish food, and he's still furious with me. Plus, this isn't a convo you have through a screen.

"I need to sneak into that wedding and get five minutes alone with him." I swallow hard. "Oh God. I can't believe I'm saying this."

I take a deep breath, like I'm about to jump off a cliff.

"Sebastian... will you style me?"

He responds by dramatically throwing the hotel suite doors wide.

"Code White Swan! Our lady of wrath wants revenge! Give me outfits that scream 'lethal injection.'"

Models scurry like runway rats.

"I require Chanel—the archival collection, not the influencer glam bin! GUCCI, but tastefully unhinged! Valentino with leg slits! Dior with vengeance in the hem! No Oscar de la Renta. Florals are for funerals and Fiona's lackluster soul."

Sebastian snaps his fingers. "Jewelry. I want weaponized sparkle. Give me earrings that say *back off, bitch* and a necklace that whispers *I brought receipts.*"

He turns to me with manic glee. "You, my dear, are wearing white."

"Isn't that, like, the cardinal sin of weddings?"

"Exactly. You want vengeance? Step one: upstage the bride."

"Step two?" I say as a flock of models circle me, ready to remake me from head to heel.

Sebastian's grin widens.

"Save the groom. And step three: Make Mr. Sterling rue the day he didn't choose you."

***

Turns out, infiltrating a billionaire wedding is super easy when you're disguised as one of Sebastian's lovely assistants.

I adjust my giant black sunglasses and stomp across Casa Cashmere's manicured lawn, ready to fuck shit up. My white dress is dreamy—lace bodice, flowy skirt, covered by my leather jacket and combat boots. Because yes I feel pretty, but I also like feeling powerful. My tattoos are on full display, and my red lipstick is locked and loaded.

Sebastian Bellini is a fashion god. I look fucking hot.

I slip past the security guard and make it to the back of the ceremony tent, mentally rehearsing my dramatic entrance speech, when—

WHAM.

Something hard slams into my back, and suddenly I'm being bear-hugged from behind. My arms are pinned to my sides, and whoever's got me is hauling ass toward what appears to be a service entrance.

"PUT ME DOWN, YOU LUNATIC!"

"Shhh!"

Taser! I need my taser.

I frantically paw at my leather jacket, trying to reach the pocket that's hiding my lipstick-sized weapon. This is precisely the scenario Bryce envisioned when he gave them to me.

A hand covers my mouth before I can yell for help.

I thrash wildly, sending my sunglasses flying. I'm shoved into a closet, the door slamming shut and casting me into darkness. The second the grip lets up, I pull out my taser, whirling around with my finger on the trigger.

"Hey, asshole! I'm about to tase the fuck out of you. Turn the lights on nice and slow so I can see which one of Fiona's goons you are."

The lights flip on. It's Bryce Sterling.

Of. Freaking. Course.

He stands in a black tuxedo, his bow tie perfectly straight, his golden hair styled in soft, touchable layers.

"Are you fucking kidding me?" My arm drops. But not all the way. "You have two seconds to explain, or I will light up your balls."

He glances at the taser, then back at me with a smirk. I want to slap it off his face.

"I had to subdue you to get you alone. Which meant immobilizing your arms so I could—"

"No, explain why we're here, not how you got me here, you lying, cheating jackass."

"Oh. Nigel caught sight the moment you arrived and sent me to retrieve you."

"Great. So much for my career in espionage."

"He's coming to meet us," Bryce continues, not taking his eyes off me. "You look... Christ, you're stunning."

My traitorous heart tries to soar, but I squash it like a bug.

Nope. Not falling for that shit anymore.

I point the taser at his chest. "Save the smooth talk for your next sneaky fuck. I'm not here to relive mistakes. My brother is about to marry a con artist, and somebody needs to stop him."

Bryce raises his hands slowly. "Agreed and understood. I'm also here for him."

"Then why are we playing hide-and-seek in the linen closet? Shouldn't we be dragging Gavin away from the altar?"

"There's a lot that's happened since you left—"

The closet door swings open, and Nigel appears holding Miss Muffy like she's a furry Fabergé egg, dressed in a suspiciously familiar peach dress.

"Miss Brinkman," Nigel says briskly. "What a pleasure to have you with us again. I'm afraid we haven't time for pleasantries."

I stare at the ruffly peach gown, then at the dog. "Is that... my bridesmaid's dress?"

Nigel nods, adjusting the dog's glittering tiara. "Miss Whitfield made a last-minute substitution."

The absurdity lands hard and fast. "Let me get this straight. I got replaced by a dog."

"Indeed." Nigel turns to Bryce. "How much have you told her?"

"None of it," Bryce admits. "I was waiting for you."

"Well, how *gentlemanly* of you both," I snap. "Allow me to drop the first bomb: Fiona's family is broke as hell. Her dad's accounts are frozen, he's running from the feds, and this whole wedding is an elaborate heist designed to drain my brother's bank account."

I blink. They look at me like I'm not done yet.

"Hello? No gasps? No 'oh Petra, you brilliant sexy genius, we never should've doubted you'?"

Nigel nods. "Yes. The Whitfield estate is bankrupt. This wedding is a calculated play to secure your brother's assets before the truth goes public."

Bryce steps forward. "You were right about Echo and Fiona working together. But it's worse than you thought."

"When Mr. Sterling showed me Echo's sketchpad," Nigel begins, "I instantly recognized the gentleman depicted in those rather obsessive portraits. That man is His Royal Highness, the King of Liechtenstein."

"The King of where-the-fuck? Is that a real place, or did you make that up?"

"Very real. Very small. Very rich," Bryce interjects. "The kind of country that has more money than people."

"What I failed to realize," Nigel continues, "was that Echo had been serving as the artist-in-residence at the royal palace mere days before arriving here."

"Echo poisoned him, Pip. Nearly killed the man. Those bizarre sandwich diagrams you discovered? That was his recipe book for royal assassination."

I blink. "I'm sorry—did you just say he *sandwich-poisoned* a literal king?"

"To steal the reservation," Nigel explains. "Interpol has been hunting for Echo, but they had no idea of his whereabouts until I contacted them with our suspicions."

BARK! BARK!

Miss Muffy's series of demanding barks bounce off the closet walls like furry little sirens.

"Oh, darling," Nigel coos. "What is it, my sweet girl? Are you feeling anxious?"

The dog's growing obsession toward my jacket pocket makes it clear. "Princess Fluffington wants a snack."

I pull out the napkin-wrapped cookies I snagged from Sebastian's suite, and both men immediately look at me like I'm holding a loaded weapon.

"Oh right," I laugh, the irony no longer lost on me. "We established that fancy food equals potential death." I break off a piece and pop it in my mouth. "There. Official taste test complete. Only peanut butter, no royal assassination attempts."

"Given Miss Von Cashmere's apparent determination," Nigel says, "I suppose a small portion would be acceptable."

I offer Muffy a nibble, and she scarfs it down, her little pink tongue working overtime to get every crumb.

"So," I say, "Echo poisoned the king to open up a reservation slot for Fiona? But why?"

"Because she needed to marry your brother before two things happened," Bryce explains. "Before news of her family's bankruptcy went public, and before Heartvest's IPO made your brother a billionaire. Hence her move to convince him of no prenup."

"You assholes and your money really are the root of all evil," I mutter. "Like seriously—get a fucking job."

"The authorities were only able to establish Miss Whitfield's money-laundering activities because she deviated from her usual pattern. Typically, she would extract modest amounts over extended periods from her nonprofits. However, the financial demands of this wedding required her to drain the charity accounts entirely."

"So greed made her sloppy."

"Precisely," Nigel confirms. "There are currently outstanding warrants for both Miss Fiona Whitfield and Mr. Marvin Grossman."

"Who the hell is Marvin Grossman?"

"That's Echo's real name," Bryce explains. "Marvin Grossman, age thirty-two, from Fresno, California. Turns out our mysterious European artist is actually a failed community college dropout with a Roblox gaming channel."

"Please tell me you've taken my brother aside and explained that his bride-to-be is basically a sexy Ponzi scheme."

"No," Bryce says simply.

"And we have no intention of doing so," Nigel adds.

"Are you out of your goddamn minds?" I shriek, making Miss Muffy's ears perk up in alarm. "My brother is about to legally handcuff himself to a federal fugitive! We have to warn him!"

BARK! BARK! BARK!

"Miss Brinkman," Nigel says, "perhaps another small treat for Miss Von Cashmere? She seems to find your energy rather... stimulating."

I break off another cookie chunk and feed it to her. "I guess maybe we are a little alike, Miss Muffy. We both love being loud and demanding snacks when we're stressed."

"I've consulted with the authorities," Nigel continues, "and they've requested that we proceed with the wedding ceremony as scheduled. They're concerned that we may spook Miss Whitfield or Mr. Grossman and cause them to flee."

"It's unclear how much money those two have stashed away," Bryce adds. "If they run, they could disappear permanently. We can't risk making them suspicious."

My brain chugs away, trying to process what I've just learned.

"You want justice, Petra?" Bryce's blue eyes lock on to mine. "This is how you get it."

"Can't we at least tell Gavin?" I ask.

Nigel shakes his head, regretful. "Given his emotional attachment, I do not believe that's wise. I have witnessed Miss Whitfield's powers of persuasion. It is entirely plausible he might try to assist her escape."

Shit. I can't argue with that.

My brother is Mr. Fix-It, and Fiona's got him wrapped around her manicured fingers.

God, this is so fucked up.

"All right, listen up, gentlemen. There is no way in hell I'm letting that deranged Barbie doll marry my brother. I'll go along with this undercover cop show, but only until they break out the wedding rings. If your police buddies haven't shown up by then, I'm taking the law into my own hands."

I hold up my taser. "And by law, I mean arson. I'll burn that overpriced Dream Doll Tent to the ground before I let that she-devil say 'I do.'"

Nigel processes my threat. "I find your terms entirely acceptable, Miss Brinkman. Though I believe it won't come to that. Law enforcement is scheduled to arrive momentarily."

"You better be right, Lord Britchybottom, because I'm not bluffing."

"Understood," Nigel declares. "Now, we must all execute our performances flawlessly. I shall resume my hosting duties with Miss Von Cashmere. Mr. Sterling, you should mingle amongst the guests in your customary manner. Miss Brinkman, I beg of you, stay out of sight, but stay close."

We all bob our heads together as though we're accepting assignments in a wedding heist movie.

"*Mission Save My Brother from Marrying a Felon* is officially a go."

Nigel extends his hand toward me. "The remainder of your confection, if you please. We mustn't risk another outburst from Miss Von Cashmere."

I groan and hand over what's left of the cookie. He exits, Miss Muffy perched on his forearm.

Bryce turns halfway out the door then hesitates. "I didn't treat you the way you deserved. I'm sorry for everything. My world taught me that people like you were beneath me, when actually, Petra, you're above us all."

My stupid eyes want to water, but hell if I will let him see me cry. I snap back, "You don't get to rewrite the ending to make yourself feel better. Stay the rich asshole you are, a man I can hate from across the damn country. Okay?"

He exhales. "That's fair. I guess this is goodbye, Pip."

I bite down hard then flash him a smile that feels like barbed wire. "Good luck ruling the world. I'll be expecting my monthly credit card bills from your family's bank. See you never, Moneybags."

The door clicks shut with a ferocious finality, leaving me with one soul-crushing realization. The man I love is out of my life forever.

***

There's nowhere to hide in this boujee tent. Outside was easy, but inside I'm a walking contradiction of white lace and black leather. Security guards are clocking every step I take. Servers stare like I'm a stray cat in the wrong neighborhood, and wealthy guests stop mid-mingle, as if they've never seen a leather jacket before.

I duck behind a fruit tower overflowing with velvet-skinned plums, glistening blackberries, and succulent figs. I snag a few grapes as I sweep the altar area for the best place to stake out.

Option 1: Behind the floral arrangements? Too obvious. Not with this white dress I'm wearing that screams "Wedding Crasher."

Option 2: Near those industrial AC units humming like angry wasps? Too loud. The noise would drown out the vows and I'd miss my cue.

Option 3: Sit in the back row like a civilized human? Too exposed. If Fiona sees me, she'll cram her bouquet straight down my throat.

My best bet is to hide in one of the oversized white curtains wrapped around each tent pole. If I wedge myself in just right, the folds should swallow me whole. Combat boots and all. Probably.

So that means I have to get as close to the altar as possible.

Silver trays rest on a nearby table, loaded up with on-call champagne flutes for guests. I grab one and hold it high, like a shield, as I weave between clusters of old money and new hair plugs.

"The jet was detained for *maintenance*, so we had to fly commercial. The trauma."

"Our nanny *quit*, can you imagine? I had to make my own coffee, like an animal."

"... rained the entire week in the Maldives. I *told* the staff to fix it, but you know how unreliable they are."

"We didn't even *want* to go back to the Amalfi Coast, but the yacht's a write-off, so what could we do?"

A guest grabs a flute from my tray, and I glance away to avoid eye contact.

That's when I see her.

Lois Brinkman, my beautiful, smiling mom. *I wish I could give her a hug.*

Minus the punk rock flair, I'm her mini-me—same stubborn jawline, same full lips. Her silver-streaked hair is in a no-nonsense bun, with a simple blue dress that stands out in the ostentatious crowd. She oozes maternal wisdom *(which I could really use right now).*

And she's talking to Gavin. *Shit.*

"I keep calling her, Mom," he says. "It just rings through to voicemail every time. What if she's hurt? What if—"

"She's probably nursing her pride," Mom replies. "You know how she gets when she's embarrassed."

I hold up the full tray and move closer, behind a spectacled man checking the DOW on his phone. It's risky, but I can hear better. I promise myself I'll only stay a minute.

Gavin runs a hand through his styled hair, messing it up in a way that's very unlike him. "I shouldn't have brought her to Mexico. It was a mistake. Casa Cashmere, forcing her to work with me all summer... I put too much pressure on her."

"You were trying to help her find her footing."

"Was I?" he mutters. "Because she looked at me like I was Dad."

"You are not your father, Gavin. That bastard betrayed us. You fight for the people you love."

"Then why does it feel like I've lost my sister?" His voice cracks like he's twelve again, asking why Dad didn't want us. "She should be making fun of my tux, threatening to object during the vows. It feels wrong getting married without her here."

Stop it, bro. You're going to make me cry.

"She's been my responsibility since Dad left," he says, voice thick. "I'm supposed to protect her and make sure she never feels abandoned again. But what did I do? I told her she was embarrassing and to leave."

The guilt in his voice kills me.

"You're her brother, not her father, and Petra loves you. She always comes home."

Gavin nods, letting out a deep sigh. "Fiona's dad isn't here yet either. We're both missing somebody important. I'm not big on superstitions, but maybe this wedding is cursed."

Mom laughs gently. "Okay, stop giving yourself an ulcer. Nothing is wrong. Loosen up and let yourself be happy today, son."

She pulls him into one of her trademark bear hugs, and I bite my lip to stop it from quivering.

This is going to destroy him. I was so hellbent on taking Fiona down, I forgot that the shrapnel's going to pierce Gavin's heart too.

Still, allowing him to marry a con artist is not an option.

"Esteemed guests, kindly take your seats," Nigel announces. "The ceremony shall begin momentarily."

The crowd starts shuffling to their designated zones, and I see my opening. Front-row curtains, the perfect vantage point. I ditch the tray and make my way to it while everyone's distracted. I settle in, wrapping myself in the silky fabric like a moth claiming its cocoon. As I'm tucking my boots behind the too-short curtain, a familiar voice startles me.

Reginald Sterling.

I peek through the fabric gap and see Bryce's parents locked in a heated whisper-fight right outside the tent.

"You let him dump Amanda? Do you have any idea how that looks?" his mother Judith hisses.

Whoa, hold up! Bryce really did break up with Amanda?

Judith continues, "You did remind him, didn't you, that if he doesn't make this work with Amanda, he's cut off from the family."

Reginald smooths down his tie. "I talked to him and made things crystal clear. The situation is handled."

"How exactly? The gossip mill is churning with tales of him *canoodling* with the Brinkman girl. The sister."

"It's handled, Judith. Bryce understands his responsibilities. He has the ring, and he knows he has no choice in the matter. He will propose to Amanda tonight, and then this indiscretion will be forgiven."

Holy shit, they're forcing him to get married. That's some Bridgerton-level manipulation.

Bryce is still an asshole, but at least he's not a cheating asshole.

A soft piano melody begins, joined by the warm, low hum of a cello. Through the small opening in the curtains, I see the altar. As rehearsed, Hana is the first to sashay down the aisle, eyes already shimmering with happy tears.

The crowd "oohs" and "ahhs" when Miss Muffy trots down the aisle with paws of confidence. She's wearing *my* peach bridesmaid's dress, altered to fit her pint-sized form. Her tiny tiara glitters under the chandeliers.

Damnit. She wore it better!

Finally, Echo steps into view, with Fiona gliding beside him like a bridal grim reaper, beautiful and deadly. The guests rise with murmurs of appreciation as Fiona meets my brother. Gavin stands gallantly at the altar, the personification of a romantic hero in every way.

The police should be here by now.

The ceremony is flying by. No sooner has Hana wrapped up her reading of "Love is patient, love is kind" when Gavin starts his vows.

"Fi, you hold a permanent seat on the board of my heart. And I vow to keep showing up—even when the market's down."

I need a plan! I can't reveal the truth about Fiona's crimes without tipping her off. If she smells trouble, she'll scurry away with Echo like the roaches they are.

Fiona's already reciting her vows. "You are my timeless piece, my Rolex watch. I want to be your forever plus one."

They're almost to the kiss. *Do I really have to blow this up myself? Where the hell are the cops?* There should be sirens and a raid happening. Somebody should've burst in shouting "Hands up!" already.

"We will now exchange rings," the officiant proclaims.

FUCK.

That's when I hear it—my personal soundtrack kicking in. The opening guitar riff of Joan Jett's *"Bad Reputation"* blares in my head like it did in high school, and suddenly I know exactly what to do.

I'm going to let every rich prick in this tent believe I am the reckless, chaotic screw-up they always assumed. I'm going to give them a show they'll never forget.

This is something I can't come back from. Something only I can do.

They will whisper. They will clutch their pearls. And when I'm done, there will be no doubt I don't belong here. No chance to ever be respected, much less accepted.

Bryce will see me and finally understand—we were never meant to be.

But this isn't about me.

I'm doing this for my brother.

Time to live up to my reputation.

CHAPTER TWENTY ONE

BRYCE

"Sterling? The ring?"

Gavin's voice crashes through my headspace. I've been numb the entire ceremony, too lost in thought. But his glare? Oh, I *feel* that. If it could, it would push me off the nearest cliff.

I fumble in my jacket pocket, fingers searching frantically. When my hand emerges, two rings sit in my palm—the diamond wedding band for Fiona, and the ruby ring. *Petra's* ring.

The one I've been carrying around like a complete fool.

"Quite the jewelry collection," he says with a snarl.

Oh, he definitely knows I bought it for his sister.

I jam the ring back into my pocket where ruby meets velvet, Amanda's engagement box—the one that's ticking like a time bomb.

"Apologies, Gavin."

He snatches the band without comment. The line of his back is stiff and unforgiving.

We haven't spoken since yesterday's cigar lounge blow-up. When he looked me dead in the eye and said I was just like my father. A decade of brotherhood—gone in seconds.

My tie is too tight. My collar is choking me. The sweat crawling down my spine feels like acid.

Without thinking, my eyes drift to where I know Petra's hiding.

To the side of the tent.

To the curtain.

To her combat boots.

Apparently, I'm the only one who's noticed. Maybe it's because I'm drawn to her in ways I'll never be able to understand. Ways that defy logic, social conventions, and basic self-preservation.

"See you never, Moneybags."

What she said in that closet echoes in my skull like a firing squad. *Those were her last words.* I will spend the rest of my miserable life replaying that harsh goodbye.

As the officiant drones on about love and commitment, my eyes are glued to those boots. They're drumming out a steady beat, tapping some invisible cadence. My finger starts patting on my thigh, matching her frantic pulse. *Tap-tap-tap-tap-tap!*

What is she waiting for?

She said she'd stop this. Would she actually burn the place down? She wouldn't. Would she?

I could stall. Gavin hates me, so what's one more offense on the pile? What if I fake a choking fit? Pretend I was stung by a bee? Collapse from heatstroke? *Hell, I'm pretty much on the verge of that already. Where are the goddamn police?*

"Fiona, repeat after me," the officiant says. "With this ring..."

I turn back to the boots. They're gone.

Shit.

"EEEEAAAAAAAAAYAAAAHHHHHH!"

A primal screech rips through the tent, followed by a blur of white lace, flying red lipstick, and murder in the shape of a woman.

WHAM!

She tackles Fiona with the force of a meteorite meeting a wedding cake.

CRASH!

Petra doesn't just collide—she *pounds* Fiona into the grass, taking out half the altar flowers in the process. White petals fall like snow.

A collective gasp ripples through the crowd.

"You crazy bitch! Get off me!" Fiona screeches, arms flailing. She swings her bouquet like a weapon.

THWACK! SMACK!

Petra blocks with her elbow then straddles her, white dresses billowing around them like they're wrestling in a cloud. "Stay away from my brother, you psycho!"

Gavin launches forward. "Petra! Stop this madness right—"

No time to think. My foot moves on instinct.

One quick sweep behind his knee, and—*BAM!*—he hits the ground beside me with a curse. I'm already on him, pinning his arms, locking him up. He's strong, but I'm desperate.

"Bryce, have you lost your goddamn mind?" He struggles against my grip. "What the fuck is wrong with you? My sister's having a complete breakdown!"

"You need to trust her."

He jolts harder. I tighten the hold.

At the front, the women roll through scattered petals in a flurry of flying limbs and expensive fabric.

Hair-pulling. Screaming. A loud *SLAP!*

"You wore *white* to *my* wedding?!" Fiona screams.

"Damn right I did," Petra snaps back. "And I'm not sorry I look hotter than you."

I catalog the faces in the audience—three hundred of society's elite watching their first live cage match. They're mesmerized and mortified in equal measure.

Fiona breaks free and rakes her French manicure down Petra's cheek like a savage house cat.

"Keep your claws to yourself, you fake-ass princess!" Petra jerks back, avoiding the worst of the scratching assault.

"Get your *poor-person* filth off me!" Fiona screeches.

"YAP! YAP! YAP!" Miss Muffy barks frantically.

"Oh my stars, Miss Von Cashmere!" Nigel swoops in, cradling the dog and putting his hand over her eyes. "Don't look, precious. This is most unseemly," he says, planting himself ringside.

Fiona struggles upright. "Pathetic little nobody! You're nothing but gutter scum!"

Petra stomps her combat boot down on the train of Fiona's gown—*RIPPP!* "Time to end this, you gold-digging parasite!"

She reaches into her jacket with theatrical flair, producing the lipstick-sized taser I'd given her. *Uh-oh.*

"You brought a taser to my wedding?!" Fiona gasps.

CRACK!

Fiona's stiletto flies through the air and hits its target. Petra's wrist flinches as the device goes flying.

The weapon spins and cartwheels. It bounces once off a champagne flute, ricochets off the baby grand piano, and lands between Hana's heels.

She picks the object up, giggling nervously. "Oh wow, this is... a taser? It looks just like my emergency lip gloss."

"Fiona, you glitter-brained demon!" Petra growls, nursing her wrist. "That was a gift."

"I will END you!" Fiona hurls herself forward with a scream that's part banshee, part Broadway soprano.

THUD! They collide in a flurry of slapping hands and kicking feet, falling to the ground.

BAM! Petra blocks her assault with street-smart instincts, but then Fiona, thrashing and enraged, gets the upper hand and climbs on top of Petra.

SLAM! She smashes Petra's head on the ground. "You have no idea what it takes to make a wedding like this a reality. You know nothing! You *are* nothing. I had to plan, steal, beg, and blackmail to get here."

"Boo-fucking-hoo!"

Fiona's voice spikes with hysteria. "I've worked too hard and too long to let some poor, white-trash loser ruin it! I didn't POISON A KING to be stopped by you!"

The tent falls silent.

Petra stops mid-wrestle. "Did you just confess to poisoning the King of Lick-my-dick-tenstein?"

Fiona's face drains as her brain catches up with her mouth. "I... no... that's not... Echo did it!"

WEEEE-OOOO-WEEEE-OOOO!

Sirens in the distance grow louder by the second.

Echo's head pops up from the audience. His face is pale.

He runs.

Right. Past. Me.

I reach out, hook my hand into his absurd peacock-silk scarf—and yank. The fabric goes taut like a leash, and Echo slingshots backward, hitting the ground with a bone-jarring "*YELP!*"

I release Gavin, lunging up and onto the winded artist.

"The cosmos demands my dramatic exit," Echo says.

I wrap him in a chokehold, grab his scarf, and stuff it into his mouth. "Marvin, the universe just told me to tell you to shut the hell up."

SCREECH!

Tires skid outside the tent.

"*¡POLICÍA! ¡TENEMOS UNA ORDEN DE ARRESTO!*" a voice blasts from the bullhorn across the grounds. "Everyone freeze! We have arrest warrants!"

"About damn time," I mutter, maintaining my stranglehold.

Fiona moves before anyone can react—a wild rush of satin and spite.

She barrels into Nigel, ripping Miss Muffy from his arms with both hands. The Maltese shrieks, paws scrabbling midair, as Fiona clutches her like a prize. Nigel stumbles back, eyes wide, hands still frozen in the shape of the dog. Gasps ripple through the crowd, but Fiona doesn't flinch.

"Everyone BACK OFF! This furry gold mine is worth more than all your portfolios combined!"

"Unhand Miss Von Cashmere, you deranged debutante!" Nigel growls.

"Screw yourself, Featherwick!" Fiona backs toward the altar, clutching the terrified dog. "I'm done kissing ass to a glorified rodent! You want your fuzzy ATM back? Time to negotiate!"

Petra stalks forward with the focus of a shark smelling blood. "Give me the dog. Or I swear to God, Fiona, you'll leave here with bite marks—and they won't be from her."

Fiona's eyes dart. Her grip tightens.

"Fi, baby," Gavin says, voice raw, "whatever's happening... we can fix it. Just talk to me. I love you."

She laughs. "Love? Don't kid yourself. We both know you were only interested in a family upgrade."

Gavin winces—and the whole room feels it.

Echo tries to break free, squirming like a demented octopus. I lock him down.

"Your mom scrubbed my family's toilets! Your sister's a bartender, for God's sake! You really thought a few billion dollars could make you one of us?" She snorts. "You're a knockoff in Tom Ford, Gav-Gav."

I glance at Petra, but she's locked on Hana. With a single, almost imperceptible dip of her chin, Petra signals something. Hana returns the gesture.

Whatever they cooked up, it's happening.

"The Whitfields *built* this country! We owned land when your ancestors were picking potatoes! I'm American royalty! When I rebuild my family's fortune, I'll buy this mansion, and every single person here will bow down, lick my shoes, and—"

"Oh my GOD, Fiona, shut UP!" The words explode from Hana's mouth.

Fiona whips around, blonde curls bouncing, nostrils flaring. "Hana! How dare you—"

That's when Petra moves.

Time slows. She dives for the dog, pulling Miss Muffy out of Fiona's surprised grip, shielding the animal with her own body. Petra skids across the floor, dog safely cocooned before they both roll to a stop at the altar steps. And then—

BZZZZZZT!

The taser makes contact. Fiona convulses midscream before collapsing backward into what's left of the floral display—limbs twitching, lips mumbling nonsense.

"This is for all the pets you stole from," Hana yells, taser in hand. "And also... you're just a bitch."

Jesus Christ. Sweet, innocent Hana just electrocuted the bride.

Stunned silence. Until...

The black-uniformed authorities flood in with tactical efficiency. Echo and Fiona are hauled upright, silver handcuffs click into place.

"This arrest is an illusion!" Echo wails as they take him away. "The handcuffs are merely props in my latest art piece!"

As the officers escort Fiona's still-shaky form toward the exit, Petra straightens up. Her white dress is grass-stained, her dark hair no longer styled, but she's never looked more magnificent.

"Hey Fiona!" she calls out cheerfully. "Hope you like orange! It's gonna be your new signature color for the next ten to twenty!"

Miss Muffy yips in agreement, appearing smugger than usual *(which is saying something)*. Petra places the Maltese into Nigel's waiting arms.

"I am eternally in your debt."

"Don't get all mushy on me. Somebody had to save my bridesmaid's dress."

Nigel chuckles. Then he pivots to the stunned guests, voice crisp with ceremonial command.

"Ladies and gentlemen, allow me to explain. A criminal conspiracy was just thwarted. One that included international art fraud, attempted royal homicide, and emotional manipulation of a future billionaire. We will no longer be having a wedding today. However, Casa Cashmere extends a special thanks to the bravery of Miss Petra Brinkman."

A smattering of confused applause breaks out.

Nigel turns to Gavin. "Your sister possesses remarkable courage. You are lucky to call her family."

That shy, sweet smile Petra gives her brother—it's like watching love in its most genuine form. I stand back, swallowing everything I'll never get to say about how fiercely she shines.

I'll never get to tell her I love her.

Nigel continues, "Now, if you will all adjourn to the reception ballroom, there will be a dinner and—"

"Hold on, Nigel."

The room snaps to attention. To Reginald Sterling. To my father.

Every hair on my body lifts as he rises from the audience, adjusting his Hermès tie.

"Seems wasteful to squander such an elegant gathering. Wouldn't you agree, son?"

The engagement ring box burns in my jacket. "Father, this isn't the time or place."

"On the contrary," he says, stalking toward me. "It's excellent business. Everyone's here, the arrangements are made, the officiant is standing by. Let's have the help collect a few scattered flower petals and proceed."

"We should discuss this privately, Father."

"Nonsense. Time to salvage the day. Make your announcement, Bryce."

Checkmate.

No. There must be a way out of this.

I glance at the disaster—overturned chairs, petals like snowdrifts—and then at Petra.

She's watching me with those unreadable hazel-green eyes. The kind of expression she'll weaponize in a courtroom someday. *What would she do in this situation?*

Answer: Find the weakness and attack the foundation.

"The wedding won't be legally binding without proper documentation. We'd need licenses, witnesses, official—"

He dismisses my concern with a wave. "We can handle the paperwork tomorrow. This is the celebration. The fun part."

Right. Nothing says "fun" like forced marriage.

He rotates toward the crowd with fluid confidence. "We all came here to witness a wedding, didn't we?"

The billionaires nod in agreement. Murmurs of approval ripple amongst designer gowns and thousand-dollar suits.

"Absolutely," someone calls out.

"Quite right," echoes another voice.

With a nod from my father, Amanda rises with practiced grace as he guides her into the aisle. Her rose-gold gown shimmers with every step, and her honey-blonde hair is gathered in a graceful updo.

"Then let's have a wedding!" he declares.

Polite applause fills the tent. Amanda's cornflower-blue eyes find mine, and I see resignation cloaked in pageant polish. As if pulled by gravity, my gaze shifts.

Everything fades except Petra, standing by the wreckage she caused. Her mouth is a tight line, her lip quivers, and then, with one slow blink, a tear escapes.

I feel a sudden crack in my chest. A fracture that finally splits wide open.

"Mr. Sterling," Nigel whispers at my side. "Is this… what you truly want?"

No. God, no.

But I nod. Just once.

"Yes," I say. "Please arrange a few things for me."

I bend close to the butler, detailing what needs to happen. When I straighten, there's unmistakable pity swimming in his weathered eyes.

"Of course, sir."

The staff moves like shadows, resetting chairs, smoothing linens, and brushing away the mess like it never happened. Like *she* never happened.

I take my last breath of freedom and face the crowd. *Time to lie through my teeth.*

"Many of you are probably thinking this feels rushed, but I assure you it isn't. I've been wrestling with this decision for a long time."

My fingers fumble in my jacket pocket then hone in on the velvet box. "My father drilled into me that real men don't play make-believe; they step up and take responsibility. He was right. It's time I stop making excuses and start being the man I'm meant to be."

Amanda plants her heels and smooths her dress, the posture of someone who knows exactly what's coming. My father inflates with pride, relishing every word.

The ring box emerges in my hand, and Petra's composure shatters. Fresh tears cascade down her face like a dam bursting. She spins toward the exit.

Suddenly, the pianist begins with a gentle chord, the opening note of the song I'd asked Nigel to request. The tender melody of "Alone" by Heart floats through the air like a ghost from our past, carrying the weight of that first kiss and seven years of what-ifs.

Petra stops dead in her tracks. She turns around slowly, and our eyes meet.

"I've made mistakes and followed orders. I let fear dictate my decisions. But there's one thing I have never regretted: letting her in."

Unsettled murmurs ripple through the crowd as heads swivel between Petra and me.

"She doesn't fit into my world. She spray-paints it and flips it on its head. She challenges it—challenges *me*—not to live based on others' approval, but to rebel against the norm, to do the right thing. She makes me feel alive."

I take a step toward her, then another, each step irreversible.

"So here I stand, asking the most extraordinary woman I've ever known to do the most rebellious thing she's ever done."

I flip open the ring box, revealing the ruby ring.

"Marry me, Petra. Right here. Right now."

She stares back with tear-streaked cheeks, her lips parted in silent shock. Before she gets out a single syllable, my father's voice detonates.

"Heartvest is finished!" Veins bulge in his neck as his control snaps. "You want to throw your life away, boy? I'll make sure you burn for it."

I face him, squaring my shoulders to my full height. "I refuse to inherit an empire where I have to be a carbon copy of you."

Reginald scoffs. "As if you were ever *close* to the image of the son I wanted."

"That's no secret." I take a step toward him, my fear dissolving into dangerous courage. "This is my life. My future. I'm done living for your approval. Your legacy dies with you."

His face turns purple, like he's being choked. "You go through with this idiotic choice, and you're no longer my son."

"Works for me. I'd rather build something meaningful at Heartvest than spend another second inflating your offshore accounts."

"You better savor this little act of defiance. My lawyers are gonna sue you and your shit company into oblivion. You'll be bankrupt and forgotten."

"You better think twice about lawsuits, old man." I smile smugly. "I've had a front-row seat to every dirty deal you've ever made. Lay a finger on my company, and I will make certain you share a cell with Whitfield."

Something new flickers behind his eyes—something that might actually be terror. "You don't have the spine."

"Try me." I lean in until we're nose to nose. "I can be exactly the monster you tried to mold me into. I learned from the best. This is *your* one warning."

He shoves me back with all his might. "You'd destroy everything our family built for some tattooed slut hunting for a payday."

CRUNCH!

The crack of bone and fury splits the air. Gavin's fist connects with Reginald's jaw in a perfect right cross that sends the old bastard sprawling across the aisle like discarded trash.

"Nobody disrespects my sister," Gavin says, flexing his knuckles. "She's got more honor in her pinky finger than you've had in seventy years of breathing."

He rolls his shoulders, loosening up like he's considering round two. "Here's some free advice—start praying she doesn't pass the bar exam. Because when she does, she'll strip you of every stolen dollar you've ever hoarded. Girl doesn't know the meaning of quit."

"Mr. Featherwick," I say, smoothing down my jacket. "Could you please arrange for my father's immediate departure? He's overstayed his welcome."

Reginald staggers upright, blood painting his bottom lip. "Don't touch me, or I'll arrange for your mutt of a boss to fire your ass before morning."

Nigel's face transforms into genuine amusement. "Best of luck with that endeavor, sir." He signals the security team, and two guards in black suits surround Reginald.

"Mr. Sterling," he continues, "you've confused wealth with worth, and let me assure you, you possess only one of those things. Your presence is no longer tolerated at Casa Cashmere. Miss Von Cashmere demands you be ousted with great haste."

She barks in agreement.

"Get your hands off me," Reginald bellows, spit flying, as security escorts him out. "You're a disgrace, Bryce. An embarrassment!"

I turn my back on his crumbling threats and give my full attention to Petra. "Are you okay?"

She raises an eyebrow. "You're asking me? After you just incinerated your family dynasty?"

"I'm going to explain everything, but I need to handle something first. My father blindsided everyone, including Amanda. Two minutes," I promise, lifting her hand to brush my lips across her knuckles. "Then I'm back to finish what we started."

I don't want to let go, but I do.

Amidst the wreckage of the ceremony, Amanda stands with a poise that defies the destruction around her, not a single hair out of place.

"I'm sorry you got caught in my family's crossfire," I say. "That ambush was unforgivable."

"Apology accepted." She steps closer, speaking in a conspiratorial whisper. "Honestly, it was worth the trip to see you finally put Daddy Dearest in his place. And I hate to say it, but getting dumped at the altar? Huge strategic advantage for me. I give it forty-eight hours before someone from Monaco proposes. Goodbye, Bryce, and good luck."

She glides away without a backward glance.

I turn around and catch sight of Petra approaching Gavin. Her black leather jacket is half-zipped, and dark scuffs mark the hem of a once-delicate lace dress. Her lipstick's faded, mascara smudged, and my God... She looks like a badass angel who strolled through hell in combat boots and kicked the devil right in the nuts.

I'm so far gone for this girl.

"Bro," she starts, "I'm sor—"

"Don't you dare apologize," he says. "You were right about Fiona, and I didn't trust your instincts. I never should have dated someone who was cruel to you. You tried to warn me; this is my fault, not yours."

She exhales, shoulders loosening, a flicker of warmth in her eyes.

"I got so obsessed with proving I belonged," he continues. "As if marrying a Whitfield would somehow erase the fact that I used to deliver pizzas to pay Mom's electric bill."

"You don't need some crusty old family tree to validate you. News flash, genius—you built an empire from nothing. You're the reason Mom doesn't work three jobs anymore."

From the front row, Lois Brinkman watches her children, pressing a tissue to her eyes, her face radiating with pride.

"I've spent so long trying to be your dad, I forgot to be your brother."

"I just wanted you to be proud of me," Petra whispers. "I thought if I could play the part of *reliable office girl*, I wouldn't be seen as a failure anymore."

"Let me make this clear: I'm proud of you exactly as you are—stubborn, brilliant, and a little unhinged. Whatever path you choose, I've got your back. And if you need tuition money, consider it done."

"Oh, shut up and hug me before I start ugly crying," Petra demands, throwing her arms around his neck.

He catches her and lifts her off the ground. "Love you, Wildcat."

"Love you more, big bro."

When they separate, Gavin's eyes are locked on me. His expression is something I'm all too familiar with—calculating, targeted, and ready to engage in a hostile negotiation.

"Now for you—"

"I know I lied," I say, raising my hands. "About Petra, about leaving the company. I've been living a double life, and you deserved better. But I'm not sorry I love her. She's the best thing that's ever happened to me."

His hazel-green eyes—so much like Petra's—studies my face. The gears in his mind are turning, weighing my sincerity.

Finally, he shakes his head. "Don't waste your breath on me, Sterling. She's the one holding the verdict."

He steps aside, patting my arm—a silent touch of forgiveness.

Petra stands there, arms crossed, hip cocked. "B, you cannot be serious. You just survived a Sterling family implosion, nearly got into a fistfight with your father, and proposed in the middle of a felony arrest. You *might* be concussed. Maybe we save the emotional declarations for when you're not drunk on rebellion and adrenaline?"

After everything, she's thinking I'll change my mind. That this is some temporary breakdown.

"The adrenaline didn't prompt my proposal, Pip. It simply gave me the balls to voice it out loud."

"Pump the brakes there, billionaire boy. You said it yourself—it's not even legal. There's no marriage license. No prenup. Your father's probably halfway to convincing a judge you're having a full psychotic break."

"Screw the prenup—If I hurt you ever again, you can have it all. I want to marry you, Petra. I'll do anything to make you mine. I'll crawl through broken glass to make it happen."

"So you're telling me you'd live in my sketchy-ass neighborhood? Where dudes are barbecuing over barrels and the rats have side hustles?"

My sterile mansion flashes through my mind—twenty thousand square feet of loneliness wrapped in Italian marble. Then I picture her tiny apartment with its duct-taped shower curtain blinds, cookie dough stash in the freezer, and laundry piled on the floor.

"Pip, I'd pitch a tent on your sidewalk if you were sharing it with me. Whatever it takes to earn the right to wake up next to you. I'll drive that death trap you call a car. I'll eat boxed mac and cheese every night until I die of powdered cheese poisoning. I'll fight cockroaches the size of cats. Bare-handed. Shirtless, if that helps."

A tiny laugh slips out before she locks it down again.

I reach out and cup her cheek. "If you're there, I'm home."

She exhales sharply, like I've taken the wind right out of her. Her eyes are waging war again—hope battling fear, dreams duking it out with doubt.

"Do you know why I called you Pip when we were kids?"

She huffs. "Because I was an annoying little gremlin and you couldn't remember my real name?"

I chuckle. "'Pip' means something small. And there you were, this fierce little tornado barely reaching my chest, all elbows and attitude, stomping around in those adorable boots like you were ten feet tall."

She watches me, guarded but waiting.

"Everyone else looked at you and saw trouble: a scrappy loudmouth from the wrong side of Beverly Hills. But I saw a force of nature trapped in a pocket-sized package. You'd get in the face of guys who could bench press you, tell off teachers who tried to shame you, and defend kids who couldn't defend themselves. And I'd think, *How the hell does someone that small contain so much fire?*"

Her breathing stutters, and vulnerability flickers in her gorgeous eyes.

"I fell in love with that fire. That defiance. That mouth that never stops running. Every stubborn inch of you, Petra. You're the storm I never saw coming."

"This isn't how it goes for girls like me. I'm not the princess in this story—I'm the sarcastic friend who gets the best one-liners from the sidelines. I don't get chosen."

"You're the only girl worth choosing. My life is nothing without you in it. Let me stand beside you. Love you. Support you... and sometimes piss you off a little just to keep things interesting."

Her lower lip trembles, but she's still holding back. I turn to face the three hundred witnesses and make my declaration.

"I love this woman. And if she'll have me, I choose her over every single one of you. And that includes you, Mother."

A collective gasp ripples through the crowd. Judith Sterling-Holloway's bejeweled hand flies to her mouth.

I drop to one knee, pulling out the ruby ring. The afternoon sun catches the stone, sending crimson fire dancing across Petra's stunned face.

"I love you. I realize now I always have. Ever since that first kiss you were brave enough to give me. You've always been the brave one."

A pulse ticks in my neck. My hand shakes a little as I extend the ring, my gaze fixed on her shiny eyes.

"You've loved me your whole life. Let me love you for the rest of mine. Marry me, Pip. Please."

"Yes."

I surge to my feet, ready to seal this moment with a kiss that'll knock us both sideways.

"Slow down there, B," she laughs, dodging me. "Gotta get hitched first."

She starts unzipping her jacket.

"What are you doing?"

"Looking all bridal-like in my white dress," she says, like it's obvious.

"Keep it on, and the boots," I say firmly, catching her wrist. "They're a part of you, and this is how I want to remember you in fifty years."

I'll tell her about my vivid fantasies later, the ones where she's wearing nothing but that jacket and those boots.

"Ahem." Nigel's British accent interrupts my inappropriate thoughts. "If the bride and groom would kindly assume their positions, we can proceed."

Petra whips around to face Hana. "Will you be my maid of honor?"

She gasps. "Me? Are you sure?"

"You tased a felon in stilettos and didn't flinch. I'm proud as hell to call you my friend for life."

Hana launches herself at Petra, wrapping her in a hug. "Thank you for showing me how to be a badass."

"You always were. You just needed to set her free. And now the world better watch out."

Hana pulls back, tears welling up in her eyes. "You're getting the love story. The real thing." She pauses, biting her lip. "Do you think... maybe there's one out there for me too?"

"Abso-fucking-lutely." Petra's response is immediate and fierce. They hug tightly.

Christ, watching her build people up like this—it's her superpower.

Nigel clears his throat. "Perhaps we might resume our conversation *after* the ceremony?"

"One more thing!" Petra says, dropping to her knees to face our Maltese hostess. "Miss Muffy, would you please do me the honor of being my bridesmaid?"

The fluffball barks only once—posh, dignified.

"Miss Von Cashmere accepts with great enthusiasm," Nigel translates, deadpan.

He produces a cookie from his jacket, handing it to Petra with ceremonial care. She feeds it to Miss Muffy then straightens the tiny tiara perched between the dog's ears.

Then Petra's face goes pale. "Wait. STOP. This is all wrong!"

My stomach drops.

"I can't get married without Cam and Katie! My best friends! They're supposed to be here! We promised—no matter what—we'd be at each other's weddings!" Petra spins toward Hana. "Can I borrow your phone? Emergency bride situation!"

Relief floods through me.

Hana hands over her phone without question, and Pip mutters while she types: "It's Petra. EMERGENCY BRIDESMAID SUMMONS! I'm getting married in approximately five minutes. FaceTime now, or forever hold your peace."

Seconds later, two split screens explode onto the phone. One blonde, one brunette. Both screaming.

"MARRIED?!" they shout in unison.

Petra holds the phone high and says, "No time for emotional speeches or backstories. Cam, Katie—this is Hana. She took down Fiona; she's a legend, and you're gonna adore her. Hana, meet my ride-or-die besties."

Virtual squeals. Rapid-fire hellos. Then Petra angles the phone toward me, and I find myself face-to-face with two women who've clearly been hearing about me for ages.

"Ladies, meet my future husband, Bryce Sterling. B, these girls are why I got through college without a criminal record."

"Hi, I'm Katie. Hurt her, and I have very detailed spreadsheets for hiding bodies," the blonde friend says.

"Camila Morales," the brunette adds cheerfully. "I'm a videographer who knows how to destroy somebody with a single viral video. Whatever Petra needs."

"More threats later!" Petra laughs. "Right now, I need my girls! I'm getting married!"

A collective squeal erupts—loud enough to be heard from space.

Sebastian's fashion army converges on Petra at the tent entrance—a swarm of concealer, curling wands, and emergency dress repairs. Within heartbeats, she's transformed into a vision of dangerous elegance.

The piano starts the processional, and Petra is a goddamn knockout walking toward me on Gavin's arm. She looks like holy chaos—white dress, leather jacket, combat boots, and that red-lipped smile. That lethal, *I-know-you-want-me* smile. And I do.

This is the moment I'll remember for the rest of my life. Because for the first time, I know she's mine.

"I'm putting my trust in you," Gavin says as they step up to meet me.

"I won't let her down," I promise.

"Then let's make it official, brother," he says, gently guiding her hand into my palm.

Everything after that dissolves into fragments: Petra's eyes never leaving mine as we exchange vows. Her laugh when the ring slides onto her finger—two sizes too big.

Her voice breaks slightly on the word "forever." My vision blurs when she says, "I do," finally hearing the words that make it real: "husband and wife."

... sort of, pending paperwork.

The instant my lips touch hers, every civilized instinct I possess is obliterated. I sweep Petra off her feet, her startled laugh ringing out as I sprint down the aisle clutching my prize.

I carry her past the shocked billionaires, past the scattered flower petals, through the wreckage of what was supposed to be someone else's perfect day. We burst through the tent flaps into the Mexican sunshine, and I don't stop until we're alone in a secluded corner of the villa.

I press her against the sun-warmed wall, growling into her neck. She giggles, grabs my face, and pulls me into a kiss full of joy. We're laughing, breathless, drunk on each other. I'm ready to consummate this marriage right here, right now.

"Whoa there, Moneybags. Pace yourself! We've got a whole lifetime now."

Suddenly, her eyes go huge. "Oh shit, oh fuck—your inheritance! YOU LEFT YOUR BILLIONAIRE BANK ACCOUNT FOR ME? I can't believe you did that!"

I set her down carefully, my hands on her waist. "Pip, yes, I left Sterling Industries. But I won't start our marriage with a lie, so I have a confession. I'm still a billionaire. I have trust funds. Plural. My assets have assets."

"Well, if you think you're locking me up in some Beverly Hills mansion, you've got another thing coming."

"I will only ever tie you up with your consent," I say, loving the way her pupils dilate. "We'll make our home wherever you want. But if it's your apartment, I'm buying you a proper marriage bed. Because I'm going to fuck you like it's my job."

She leaps into my arms, her lips crashing into mine, her red lipstick smearing across my face. *God, I love the way she claims me.*

"Ow! What's in your pocket, B? Is that a rocket launcher, or are you just happy to marry me?"

I burst out laughing and set her down. Digging into my pants pocket, I pull out her lipstick-sized taser, waggling it like a trophy. "Gotta keep Mrs. Sterling armed and dangerous."

Her face transforms into pure horror. "Bryce! The safety's off! Don't grab it like—"

BZZZZZAP!

Every neuron in my body throws up. My teeth chatter like wind-up toys. My balls write a formal resignation.

I collapse into the grass like an Armani-fried corndog.

"GLARBLE-WARBLE-BLITZKRIEG!"

Nigel approaches with Miss Muffy tucked under his arm. They peer down with polite concern. "Shall I arrange for the reception to commence indoors whilst Mr. Sterling regains basic motor function?"

"Nah, he'll be fine. Just give him a minute." Petra crouches beside me, patting my cheek. "This is basically foreplay for us."

"WIFE! FNNNGH-GLLLUUURRBB-BOOBIES."

"Welcome to married life, Moneybags. Better buckle up... This is just day one."

Despite my electrical fog, I'm completely smitten. Petra Sterling—my wife, my chaos, my forever.

Worth every volt.

EPILOGUE

PETRA

1 YEAR LATER

I FLIP DOWN THE mirrored visor in Bryce's Aston Martin and immediately regret it. My reflection shows smeared eyeliner, my lopsided graduation cap, and a weird sheen of post-ceremony sweat. My lipstick has gone AWOL thanks to the three-hour event and Bryce's congratulatory kisses.

Time for a refresh.

Digging into my bag, I shove aside a linty granola bar, and pull out my partner in crime: Wet n' Wild Sexpot Red. The same shade I've been wearing since I was in high school, back when a $1.99 felt like a financial commitment. Now I could buy the entire factory, but some things are sacred.

I swipe the color across my lips, watching my mouth go from sleep-deprived college grad to totally kissable.

Bryce's eyes flick to me at a red light, and a familiar, slow smile spreads across his face—the one that says, *I want to worship you against the closest solid surface.*

"You know I could launch a lipstick line just for you?" he says. "Call it 'Petra Red' and charge a fortune for your signature shade."

"And deprive the world of affordable beauty products? What kind of monster do you take me for? Besides, this little tube has gotten me through more disasters than your bank account has digits."

He chuckles. "I think I may have developed a graduation gown fetish. I'm having very inappropriate thoughts wondering about what you're wearing under there."

"Wouldn't you like to know, Moneybags."

"I would and I will, as soon as we get home, Mrs. Sterling."

"Promises, promises. You'd say I look hot in a hazmat suit if you could strip it off me."

"Should I order one?"

I burst out laughing. "I do love that you've fully embraced your dirty side."

He's adorable. And mine. *Which, yeah, still blows my mind a little.*

We're cruising down Sunset Boulevard, rolling past palm trees and twenty-dollar smoothie shops. I lean my head back and my tassel taps against the window. This stretch of Sunset feels different today. Like it's winking at me. Like it knows I finally crossed some invisible finish line.

"One degree down, Pip. One to go."

"Ugh. Don't remind me."

"Have you decided about taking that gap year before law school?"

"I'm scared if I stop, I won't start again. But also, I'm so goddamn exhausted, I could sleep for five years straight."

He reaches over, laces our fingers together, and gives my hand a squeeze that says, *I'm here for you*.

And he is. His support has never wavered through an incredibly long year of sprinting, studying, and sleepless nights.

After our *holy-shit-we-did-that* wedding, Bryce and Gavin got their asses back to L.A. in under twenty-four hours. No honeymoon—unless you count christening the bedroom on Bryce's jet *(and yeah, we did break the headboard)*.

As soon as Heartvest went public, it blew up. Stock prices shot through the roof, and suddenly everyone wanted a piece of the "rebel billionaire's" investment app. Their user base doubled, then tripled, and then I stopped counting *(because that many zeros makes my head hurt)*. Bryce and Gavin have been hiring people left and right, expanding faster than they thought possible.

It's like watching someone build a rocket ship while riding it.

The media attention has been relentless, especially after Bryce's very public middle finger to the Sterling Family empire. Turns out people prefer a good "choosing love over legacy" story, and Bryce unwittingly became the poster child for rejecting nepotism in favor of something meaningful.

The best part? Reginald Sterling has been suspiciously quiet. After his very public humiliation at our wedding, he slithered back to Manhattan and decided *not* to retire. Bryce stayed on the Sterling Industries board, if only to keep the old man in check. It's power, but subtle. Like a finger hovering over a detonate button labeled: TRY ME, BITCH.

I do still wonder if Bryce will take over his family empire... someday. Maybe transform it into something that doesn't just hoard wealth like a financial dragon. But for now, Bryce says he's perfectly happy living without a five-, ten-, or even twenty-year plan. And honestly? Watching him discover who he is without someone else's script has been better than any honeymoon.

As for Fiona... *hoo boy.*

Let's say karma didn't just knock on her door—it repossessed the mansion, torched the designer closet, and left a bag of flaming dog poop signed by *"the poor girl."*

Turns out, being "American Royalty" doesn't mean much in prison. She's learning to make her own bed, do her own laundry, and eat food that's all the same color. The girl who told me I was a "poor, white trash loser" is now literally picking up trash on the interstate.

And Marvin Grossman *(yes, we all learned Echo's real name)* was giving art lessons in prison. Unfortunately, they were forgery lessons, so he scored himself another ten years.

I'd feel bad for them if I weren't so busy enjoying the poetic justice.

Bryce lifts our joined hands to his lips and gently kisses the back of mine.

Between his insane work schedule and my class load, finding a place to live turned into a months-long nightmare. We ping-ponged between his sterile mansion and my shoebox apartment like nomadic newlyweds, living out of suitcases and pretending it was romantic *(it wasn't).*

Bryce kept pushing Beverly Hills. He'd say, "Logical commute, safe neighborhood" and I'd reply with, "Snooty, boring, and hell to the no." My stubborn ass refused to surrender to zip code snobbery until...

"Waaa! Waaah!"

Until *she* happened.

Our three-month-old baby wails to life in the back seat like a tiny but mighty airhorn. I spin around and switch to mama-bear mode. There she is, my precious little storm: black hair, red-faced, and furious in her way-too-fancy car seat *(designer, really?)*.

"Oh no, baby girl, what's wrong?" I ask, reaching back to stroke her velvet-soft cheek.

I fish around for her pacifier—a simple pink one. Bryce wanted a diamond-encrusted binky, but I can be pretty persuasive when I threaten his vajayjay privileges. Our baby glares with ice-blue eyes, but then she slowly latches on with a pouty grunt. Blessed silence fills the vehicle.

"Tell Mommy she's a superstar for finishing college, Ruby," Bryce coos in his special baby-doting voice.

I snort. "Daddy should know by now that Ruby only cares about one thing. Mommy's boobs."

"We've had in-depth discussions," he says, eyes twinkling. "And we're both heavily invested in the boobs department."

"Should Daddy drive his absurdly expensive car around the block again so Baby Empress can finish her nap?"

Ruby grunts.

"That's a yes. Make it snappy, Moneybags."

He signals left. "Already turning."

Neither of us was even *slightly* interested in protection after "I do." We got pregnant instantly *(and I mean instantly)*. Turns out a hurricane of unprotected newlywed sex was no match for my birth control. Later—after I stopped throwing up daily—Bryce admitted he secretly hoped I'd get pregnant that night we made love on the beach.

He got what he wished for. Our little Ruby.

If everyone thought our lightning-fast wedding was shocking, the pregnancy announcement made their heads explode. His mother needed smelling salts when we dropped the news.

Bryce chose our daughter's name, and honestly, I melted when he told me why. Ruby—after my ruby ring and the red shade of my lips; the color that's apparently burned into his soul.

"She's going to be twice the handful you are," he whispers.

"That'll be your fault for spoiling her."

This man doesn't mess around when it comes to his girls.

Ruby's closet rivals Nordstrom, her nursery belongs in a magazine, and she owns designer… well, everything.

And me? I'm also spoiled rotten. Not because I need it, but because he's a gift giver and he gets twitchy if he can't prove it.

He bought me a fancy espresso machine *(that I still don't know how to use)*. Surprise deliveries of lingerie and flowers. A weekend to Paris where we didn't wear pants the entire time. And oh yeah, he flew in the band *Heart—freaking Heart!*—to serenade me for my twenty-sixth birthday. I was a full-on blubbering snot-monster into my candlelit dinner.

This life? It's bananas.

But mostly, he's happy playing house like a normal husband. We do Kraft Mac & Cheese at least once a week—the good stuff—and order CPK takeout while binge-watching whatever Netflix serves up *(why yes, algorithm, we do love romcoms)*.

Not saying we don't still hit the occasional black-tie gala, where I pretend to know which one's the salad fork *(I am a billionaire's wife, after all).* But we're making up the rules as we go, answering only to each other.

Most shocking of all is how domesticated I've become. We have an actual house now, a modest three-bedroom ranch in Beverly Hills with real curtains *(not from a shower)* and an actual bed instead of just a mattress. I'll tolerate the 90210 zip code if it means more family time.

"B, between finals and night feeds, I haven't taken a full breath since Easter. If I don't get some sleep, I'm hopping on the next flight to Europe and you're raising our adorable tyrant alone."

"Oh, no. I'll hire private investigators. There's no escape clause now, Mrs. Sterling. But I *will* take night duty so you can get a full eight hours."

"That deal will get you full-body access. Partially clothed, or tied up naked—your choice."

His grip on the steering wheel tightens. "Keep talking like that, and you can sleep until Tuesday."

Bryce pulls into our driveway and puts the car in park. That's when I spot it—my beautiful disaster of a car parked on the street like a middle finger to the neighborhood's HOA.

"Um, why is my Lexus out of the garage?"

"I needed the space to build Ruby's activity center."

"She's basically a smiling potato. She just discovered her toes last week. She won't need a gym for, like, a year."

"If you want it built properly, it requires extensive planning."

"Fine, you beautiful control maniac. Build away. But when I get slapped with a parking violation, you'll be chasing down all the paperwork."

"Agreed."

Bryce gingerly pulls the carrier from the back seat with both hands. Ruby is sleeping like pampered royalty, looking adorable in her lavender Dolce & Gabbana dress.

"The wildflowers on her outfit," I whisper, tracing the delicate patterns. "They match my ink."

"Noticed that, did you?"

I brush my lips against his. "I love you."

"I love you too."

"But I love sleep just a *little* bit more right now," I mumble.

He laughs. "Fair."

We step up to the front door, and I fish out my keys. "Also, thanks for keeping it low-key tonight. CPK, stretchy pants, and hopefully no diaper explosions."

"You deserve it."

"I was thinking *you* deserve to finally see what's under this ugly graduation gown."

I unlock the front door and reach for the zipper at my neck, letting the gown fall to the ground.

Bryce gulps audibly.

"Jesus, Petra. You wore the red dress?"

"What, this old thing?" I throw him a mock-innocent look. "You remember what I was wearing the first time you got me naked?"

Ruby shifts in her carrier, still blissfully asleep. I drop my voice to a whisper, then hook my thumb under one strap.

"Thought I'd remind you what this dress does to your self-control."

My gaze drops deliberately to his pants, where evidence of my success is already showing. He lowers the baby carrier over his bulge. *Cute. Like that'll hide it.*

I smirk. "Guess I still got it. Now be a good daddy," I purr, brushing a kiss against his cheek. "Put her down for a nap, and I'll help you take care of that. Then you can work me over until *I* sleep like a baby."

As I turn the doorknob, I slide the strap off my left shoulder, ready to let my dress fall to the floor.

"Pip, hold on—"

The door swings wide.

"SURPRISE!!!"

"Waaahhhhh!"

I scramble to cover myself while Bryce magically calms our baby with his daddy superpowers.

"Surprise?" he says sheepishly as he bounces her.

I pause in the doorway, soaking it all in. The living room is half designer showroom, half indie music festival. Bryce brought the symmetry and muted tones, I brought the vintage flair, framed concert posters, and my record player, which has finally graduated from milk crate slumlord to walnut cabinet royalty—summa cum loud-a. Together, it's a magical mess. It's our home.

But tonight, the whole place has been transformed into graduation central. A massive CONGRATS PETRA, YOU GLORIOUS BADASS! banner stretches across the living room wall in bold silver letters. Balloons in UCLA blue and gold bob from every surface. There's a cake the size of a suitcase covered in edible glitter—three tiers with PETRA STERLING, COLLEGE GRADUATE scrolled across the top in elegant script.

But the decorations aren't what make my throat tight with emotion.

It's the faces.

My living room is packed wall-to-wall with people, all here to celebrate... me.

I gape at the twinkling lights, the presents, the crowd—then at Bryce, who just shrugs like this isn't the most romantic thing he's ever done.

My throat goes tight. "You threw me a graduation party?"

"You deserved better than the one you got in high school. This is your do-over. And if I did it right, it will end with your lips all over me again."

A runaway tear escapes down my cheek before I can stop it. I grab his face and kiss him hard, like I'm eighteen again. We don't break free until Ruby squawks in protest.

"B, tonight you're going to get the kind of thank-you that requires soundproofing."

"Don't ruin my magical evening with spoilers. Go greet your guests and take our little troublemaker with you."

He transfers our baby into my arms, and she grabs a fistful of my hair like she's claiming territory.

We step into the crowd, Ruby serving as a total conversation magnet. Everyone loses their collective shit over her genetic jackpot—my wild black hair paired with Bryce's knockout blue eyes.

I stop dead when I spot Nigel standing at military attention near our bookshelf, Miss Muffy nestled in his arms. Fluffy, fabulous, and wearing the *exact same* Dolce & Gabbana wildflower dress as my kid.

"Oh my God, are you freaking kidding me?" I burst out laughing. "Miss Muffy, on behalf of my adorable offspring, I must formally ask that you remove that outfit immediately."

Miss Von Cashmere II releases an indignant little bark, her tiny diamond collar catching the light.

"Just joking, Your Highness," I tease. "And no worries. I'm sure my daughter will blow chunks on hers and be changed out by dinner."

Ruby gurgles and kicks her leg out, ruffles bouncing. Miss Muffy gives her a once-over and—*swear to God*—nods. Just once. Like the queen acknowledging her smallest subject.

"Might I hold the little princess?" Nigel asks.

Ruby lands in the stone-faced butler's arms, and he instantly melts into mush.

"Oh, aren't you an angel sent from heaven!" he coos in the most ridiculous baby voice imaginable. "You're going to come visit Uncle Nigel at the big beautiful castle, aren't you? And then Miss Muffy will teach you how to have proper tea parties."

"I'll bring her after she's mobile enough to destroy your priceless antiques," I promise.

Sebastian Bellini appears out of nowhere, one hand pressed to his chest in mock horror.

"I know what you're gonna say," I cut him off. "They're matching, and it's a travesty."

"Ruby was supposed to be in the cerulean blue to complement those devastating eyes," he says indignantly, "not this ghastly lavender! This fashion crime will get her banned from babybrunch."

"Sebastian, she's three months old. Her biggest crime today was a blowout in the car seat."

He waves me off like the drama queen he is. "Bring her by next week. The *new* Baby Dior collection needs to be on that cherub's face immediately. And I swear to Donatella, if you put her in something from Target again—"

"You will personally burn my entire wardrobe?" I offer sweetly.

"Exactly."

Hana squeals, "OH MY GOSH! I missed you so much!"

I'm about to return the sentiment when I realize she's talking to Ruby, not me.

"Hello to you too, Hana," I laugh.

She launches into baby talk, pulling out an adorable stuffed elephant from her purse. "I brought presents from Africa! The food there was incredible. I tried mopane worms. Crunchy. Earthy. Slightly nutty. You'd love them!"

"I'd rather eat my diploma. So, are you staying in L.A. long?" I ask.

"Not a chance! I'm a woman of the world now, and I'm just getting started," she says. "I've decided not to wait for love to find me—I'm going out to hunt it down. Who knows where my Mr. Right is hiding. London? Paris? Brazil? Greenland? I'll check 'em all off my list until I find him."

"Sooo... since you broke off the engagement, have things gotten any better with your parents?"

"They're still livid, and they're already plotting another arranged marriage. But I'm standing my ground. It's true love or nothing."

My phone buzzes at my hip, and just seeing the notification makes me smile.

Group Chat : CPK Forever

Katie: *Eating pizza in your honor! Sorry Matteo and I couldn't get off work. Summer tours = chaos.*
Me: *No worries. Bryce told me he's gonna bring us to you.*
Cam: *WHERE is our niece?? I require my daily dose of cheeks.*

I pivot, strike a pose with Ruby—her tiny fist gripping my necklace, drool artfully decorating her chin—and snap a selfie. Sent.

Cam: *¡Dios mío! Are her eyes even bluer than last week?*
Katie: *Stop making me jealous! Auntie Katie is stuck in Italy while you get all the baby snuggles.*
Cam: *A Ruby sleepover is happening with Auntie Cam the moment Reece and I get back. Mark your calendars for sexy time.*
Katie: *When I'm home for Christmas, full-on CPK reunion! Matching pajamas and chocolate chip peppermint cookies!*
Me: *I'm adding matcha to mine, but definitely! Wouldn't miss it.*

I can't wait for the day we're all on the same continent again. Who would've guessed over one hot mess summer, we'd each find our happily-ever-afters. We may be in different cities and different time zones, but our friendship is the kind that distance can't touch.

I spot Bryce across the room deep in conversation with both our mothers. He and Judith have been slowly reconstructing their relationship. She learned real quick that her son wasn't messing around about accepting his new stance on life.

Ruby fast-tracked the peace talks, no question. But nothing prepared me for the day Judith—yes, *that* Judith—turned into a babbling, baby-talking idiot over my daughter. It nearly broke my brain. My mom, meanwhile, has gone into full-time grandma mode. She lives five minutes away and doubles as our emergency childcare.

There's heavy knocking at the front door, so I hand Ruby to Bryce and wade through the partygoers to answer. My face breaks into genuine happiness when I see the familiar figure waiting on my doorstep.

Jim. Still wearing his well-worn army jacket, but his silver hair is freshly cut, and his face looks healthier and more rested than I've ever seen it.

"I was told there'd be cake," he deadpans.

"Jim! You showed up," I say, hugging him.

"Your husband delivered a personal invitation. Couldn't ignore such fancy correspondence."

"Come inside! There's enough food to—"

He hands me a small wrapped package, and I tear it open to reveal a beautiful leather journal with initials embossed on the cover: P.S.

Petra Sterling.

"For when you start writing closing arguments that make grown men's balls duck and cover."

My throat clogs. "I love it. Thank you. Now, go grab a plate. Bryce got enough catering to feed half the neighborhood. You'd be helping me out by making a serious dent in it."

Jim smiles, the corners of his eyes crinkling. "Anything for a friend."

I slip back inside and search for my husband and daughter. Ruby's now perched like a princess on my brother's forearm—her baby fist gripping his tie in a total power move.

Bryce is stuck near the bookshelf, giving polite "uh-huhs" while next-door-neighbor Steve deep-dives into crypto again *(it's all the dude ever talks about).*

His body is there, but his soul? Long since tapped out. Literally. *Tap-tap-tap.* His index finger raps a rhythm against his thigh—the Bryce Sterling equivalent of an SOS.

Time to mess with him.

I pull out my phone, fingers dancing across the screen.

Me: *I want to recreate the first night I wore this red dress. I'm getting wet just thinking about how you tied me up.*

He checks his phone, perks right up, then searches the room. When his eyes find mine, the corner of his mouth twitches.

Moneybags: *You're evil. I'm trapped discussing Bitcoin while imagining the taste of you on my tongue.*

My thighs read the text first and clench.

Me: *Poor little billionaire, pretending to care about digital wallets. Bet you wish you could excuse yourself and fuck me senseless.*

Me: *Also, I'm not wearing panties… thought you should know.*

His jaw ticks—another tell. Dave keeps rambling, unaware that his audience is mentally undressing his wife.

Moneybags: *Keep texting me filth and I'll throw you over my shoulder caveman-style in front of everyone.*

Me: *You wouldn't dare. You're too polite to cause a scene at my graduation party.*

Moneybags: *Try me, Pip.*

The challenge in those three words makes my pulse spike. This is dangerous territory—the space where polite Bryce is replaced by the man who ruins my body on a regular basis. The man I fell in love with.

Me: *Ruby's nursery. You have sixty seconds or I'm starting without you.*

I don't wait for his response. I navigate through clusters of well-wishers, slipping down our hallway toward the back of the house.

The nursery is a dream of soft whites and pale yellows. I picked this room because our bedroom has been hijacked by guests and their handbags. I'm fussing with the curtains when the door creaks open.

Bryce steps inside, already working his tie loose. "Sixty seconds? I made it in forty-three."

"Show-off."

I gasp-laugh as he presses me into the wall, lips dragging down my neck. His hands are already exploring, roaming over satin.

"This dress," he murmurs, "has been driving me insane all evening."

"That was the point." I thread my fingers through his flawless hair, messing it up on purpose. "We've got fifteen minutes tops before someone sends a search party," I whisper.

"Then don't waste a second."

He kisses me—hot, deep, addictive. It's the kind of kiss that tells you even after rings and diapers and middle-of-the-night feedings, this man *wants* me bad.

His hands slide to my thighs, hitching the dress just enough to feel skin. I'm ready to move this to the floor when—

Footsteps. Heavy ones. Moving toward us.

"Shit," I say, glancing down at the door handle. "B, where the hell is the lock?"

"Safety hazard," he whispers back, still pressed against me. "What if Ruby gets locked in and we can't reach her?"

"She's three months old! She can't even roll over!"

"PETRA! BRYCE!" Gavin's voice booms down the hallway, getting closer.

Dammit.

I yank open the nursery closet and shove Bryce inside among the designer onesies and receiving blankets.

"We gotta make this fast," I whisper, crowding into the small space. "Are you up for the challenge?"

His hands immediately find my waist, pulling me flush against him. "Pip, please. You know I am."

The closet is narrow enough that every inch of our bodies is pressed together, and I can feel exactly how ready he is through his dress pants.

"Vell, vell," I purr in my deliberately awful Russian accent. "Is wery good zing you are rich boy. Zey alvays have quick trigger, dah? Pop off faster than champagne cork."

"Keep challenging me and I'll stay in here until I break my record. What number are we up to now? Seven climaxes in one night?" The possessive edge in his voice makes my vagina growl. "I'll take my time licking that sweet little pussy until you sing for me."

I crash my mouth against his, moaning into the kiss. "God, B, are you trying to make me so wet I have to change my dress?"

I'm frantically undoing his belt when...

The closet door swings open.

Gavin's standing there with Ruby in one arm, eyes going wide.

He whirls her around so fast it's a miracle she doesn't go flying.

"Oh, for the love of—" he groans, fake-gagging. "Don't look, sweetie. Uncle Gavin needs to have a deeply uncomfortable chat with your parents about appropriate party behavior."

Bryce clears his throat. "We'll be there in five minutes."

"Ten," I say, wiping lipstick off my chin.

Gavin sighs. "Once again, you're violating the Overshare Treaty we established. Happy for you. Deeply disturbed. Never want to talk about this again."

Bryce moves to close the closet door, but Gavin stops him and points. "Not so fast, Sterling. I'm here because the princess puked on her dress. That's above my pay grade."

"Oh, baby girl," I coo, taking her from him and holding her at eye level. "Daddy's about to have the worst case of blue balls in Beverly Hills, and it's all your fault."

Ruby responds with a perfectly timed burp.

Gavin claps Bryce on the back. "You've got two women in your life now pulling the strings. God help you."

The bitter edge in his voice hits me hard. It's been a year since Fiona was dragged away in handcuffs during what was supposed to be their "I do" moment. Now Gavin treats love like it's a pyramid scheme designed to separate fools from their dignity. He's thrown himself into Heartvest with the intensity of a man trying to escape his every thought, working eighteen-hour days and treating every business deal like personal vindication.

The worst part? He's convinced himself he's better off alone. Claims romantic relationships are just elaborate cons waiting to happen. I want to shake him until he snaps out of it, tell him that not every woman is a sociopathic, money-laundering con artist. But when Gavin's in full defensive mode like this, it's like hugging a porcupine—painful for everyone.

I hope he'll find his way back to love. Because giving my heart to Bryce? Having Ruby? It rewired my soul, and I want that for my brother.

Hours later...

Party stragglers have claimed our driveway, setting up camp in a semicircle of mismatched chairs, surrounded by half-eaten food. As the sun dips below the horizon, the streetlights flicker on, their light slowly replacing the natural glow of dusk.

I'm curled up in Bryce's lap, his arms around me like a security blanket. Across from us, Hana cradles a zonked-out Ruby in one arm while gesturing wildly with the other mid-story—she's sharing an animated tale of her solo travel adventures.

"Last month, I spent two weeks in Bali," she continues. "I stayed at this incredible resort where they bring you breakfast on a silver tray every morning, and the infinity pool overlooked the most gorgeous rice terraces..."

I bite back a smile. Hana's version of "adventure" involves room service and spa treatments, which is way different than my college days of hostels and questionable street food. But I'm not bursting her bubble. She's happy, she's free, and she's figuring out who she is. That's worth celebrating, even if it comes with a five-star price tag.

"Gavin, you simply must try solo travel," she gushes. "It's life-changing."

"Not a chance. The last thing I need is to end up alone in some foreign country with a beautiful stranger who sees me as a walking ATM. Been there, done that. I don't repeat my mistakes."

His response only fuels Hana's determination, and I lean back, happily settling in for the show. Their verbal sparring is like watching a black hole try to devour the sun.

I glance around at the aftermath—tipsy balloons, murdered cake, and the smell of celebration still clinging to the air. My heart is obnoxiously full. Like stupid-happy, can't-believe-this-is-my-life full.

"Thank you for my do-over graduation party," I say, gently kissing Bryce's lips.

His arms tighten around me, pulling me closer. "Love you, Pip."

"Hey, Wildcat?" Gavin's voice cuts through my post-kiss haze.

"Yeah, bro?"

"Your car's being towed."

WHAM.

I shoot up so fast, I headbutt Bryce under the chin.

"OW, Pip!" he groans, hand flying to his jaw.

"Sorry, Moneybags."

I whip around—and yep. There she is. My busted beauty. Dangling mid-air like she just lost a bar fight.

"Hana, watch Ruby," I announce, scrambling to my feet. "Her virgin ears cannot be exposed to the profanity parade I'm about to unleash."

I storm down the sidewalk, my red dress billowing like the cape of a very pissed-off superhero.

"HANDS OFF MY RIDE, JACKASS!"

And there he is. The gnome from my nightmares. Officer. Freaking. Cockburn—radiating the energy of a man whose wife left him for someone with a bigger... badge.

"Overnight parking is prohibited seven p.m. to five a.m. in residential zones." He points at the street sign. "It's seven-oh-two, sweetheart. You can read, can't you?"

"Are you shitting me, Cockburn? You're committing grand theft auto over TWO MINUTES?" I plant my hands on my hips. "This is harassment disguised as enforcement, and you know it."

"You can slap on heels and marry into money, but I see you. Still the same spoiled brat who thinks the rules don't apply. I know your type well—hell, I *married* it. She smiled like that too. Right up until she took the house, the car, and my hairline."

Bryce materializes at my elbow, slightly winded. "Need reinforcements?"

"From you? Always and forever. For this glorified traffic goblin? I eat dickweasels like him for breakfast."

Cockburn turns to Bryce like he's handing down divine wisdom. "Pro tip—women like this will steamroll your existence if you don't establish dominance early. Otherwise, you *think* you've set the rules, until suddenly you're sleeping in your truck. Meanwhile, your ex is remodeling your kitchen and renaming your dog."

Bryce's face goes stone-cold serious. "Oof. You just said that. Out loud. To my wife." He shakes his head. "Yeah, man... You're about to lose your ego *and* your pension. Buckle up."

I step into Cockburn's personal space, channeling every law textbook I've ever cracked.

"Selective enforcement is discrimination. You've targeted this address before, and I've got the citations to prove it. Two-minute grace periods are standard, and you're about to become my first *official* law school project."

I rip the citation from his stubby fingers with dramatic flourish. "See you in court, Officer Fuckface."

Spinning on my heel, I stride back toward our house, riding high.

Bryce jogs to catch up, grinning. "So… no gap year?"

"Hell no. I've got a war to wage and a list of assholes to annihilate."

Without warning, Bryce sweeps me off my feet, breaking into a full sprint toward our front door. "GAVIN! HANA!" he shouts. "Childcare emergency! My wife just verbally destroyed a man, and I need to show her how hot that was!"

"Boundaries! Seriously!" Gavin shouts back.

"True love is so beautiful!" Hana sighs dreamily.

I crash my lips against Bryce's as he bulldozes through our front door, tasting promises and the kind of forever I never felt I deserved.

I was the girl everyone wrote off—the family screw-up, the troublemaker, the one who'd never amount to anything. I thought I had to change everything about myself to be worthy of love, success, or belonging.

Turns out, I had it backwards.

This is what happily ever after actually looks like—not changing who you are, but embracing your most unapologetic self with a partner who welcomes your chaos as something beautiful. Wealth didn't polish my rough edges. Marriage didn't make me behave. Motherhood didn't quiet my rebellion.

I'm still the girl who spray-painted a dick on her car trunk, calls out bullshit when I see it, and fights for the underdog with everything I've got.

Turns out the girl who never belonged anywhere was exactly who she was supposed to be the whole time.

And that's more fucking beautiful than anything money could buy.

***

Want more hilarious enemies to lovers romance? Read the vacation love stories of Petra's best friends (Katie and Cam) in the **HOT MESS SUMMER SERIES.**

melisaryun.com/shop

BONUS EPILOGUE

hey there, hot stuff ;-)

Paradise. Privacy. Passion—maybe?! Petra & Bryce escape to Casa Cashmere for alone time... but a tiny Sterling and a pampered Maltese have other plans.

Don't miss the hilarious chaos in this hot and heavy□
FREE BONUS EPILOGUE!

HOT MESS SUMMER SERIES CONTINUES!

You demanded more disaster. More steam. More laughs!
And we listened.

The mayhem is just getting started... Bleach-blond hair? √
Fire-breathing gremlin riding a pizza tattoo? √√
No filter & even less common sense? √√√

Blake "Blaze" Tate is as brawny as he is brainless, and he can't read a room to save his life. He's also totally falling in love... he just doesn't know it yet.

Blaze's story delivers the heat in 2026!

AUTHORS' NOTE

Hey Lovelies!

Okay, real talk: we may have gone a little feral with this book. A billionaire Maltese with her own butler? Superyachts with glass bottoms? A salsa dancing dog? Not as over-the-top as you might think—these are all surprisingly real. We dare you to Google it.

But what about Bryce, a billionaire attracted to a troublemaker who challenges him in every way? And Petra, a firecracker who tases first and asks questions later?

We actually know a little something about this dynamic. Before you roll your eyes, here's some behind-the-scenes for you.

Petra and Bryce are basically us in fictional form. MéLisa's always been the rebel, trying to corrupt Ryun's soul since high school—tempting "Mr. Good Student" to skip class *(spoiler: he never did)* and racking up a long list of scandalous offenses. But what she didn't expect?

That her "good boy" had a secret naughty side and dared her right back. He challenged her to ride on the back of his motorcycle in the snow, climb rooftops, camp on picnic tables, and even go skinny dipping at midnight in a freezing lake. *(Sure every horror movie says don't do it, but we don't back down from a challenge).*

That's the heart of this book. Two people who fall for each other, not *in spite of* their differences, but *because* of them. We're living proof that not only do opposites attract—they drive each other lovingly nuts forever.

We dare. We tease. We push.

And no matter how long we've been together, we still look at each other like: *"What wildly unexpected stunt is this maniac about to pull now?"* And that delicious unpredictability is what keeps the fire burning.

Whether you've found your person, or you're out there dodging red flags and questionable dating app profiles, we hope this book can be a reminder: The right kind of love doesn't tame you. It pushes you to grow bigger and dream bolder. It even, as Bryce says, "pisses you off a little every now and then... just to keep life interesting."

So if you laughed, swooned, or are now considering your fur baby's trust fund, please **LEAVE A REVIEW** and help us prove that opposites don't just attract, they ignite the whole damn world.

We're off to demolish some mac and cheese *(don't judge our writing snacks)* while we debate who's the real bad influence.

MéLisa & Ryun
www.melisaryun.com

Review Here

ACKNOWLEDGMENTS

To our readers—thank you for crashing this wedding, dodging scandals, and surviving the drama (and humidity) with us in Mexico. You're the reason we keep writing these wild, laugh-so-hard-you-snort love stories. Every review, social share, and "OMG, I need a Petra in my life" keeps our hearts salsa dancing.

To the incredible people who've hyped us up, talked us down, and reminded us to eat something—you're the real MVPs. We're so lucky to have you in our corner.

- Joquena Lomelino
- Happily Booked PR
- Literary Media Tours
- AuthorEverAfter

To the brilliant and bonkers Pippa Grant: your books inspire us to embrace our biggest, silliest, and weirdest ideas without apology. Mr. McHottie is beyond a comedic work of art—universities should offer entire seminars on its laugh-out-loud genius. Thank you for proving that romance can be ridiculously funny and deeply moving at the same time. We'll never stop preaching the gospel of Pippa to unsuspecting strangers in checkout lines and Instagram comment threads.

AUTOGRAPHED BOOKS NOW AVAILABLE!

Want us to ruin a perfectly good book with our questionable penmanship? You're in luck! Our brand-new online store:

MELISARYUN.COM/SHOP

now offers personalized, signed copies of all our books. Tell us who to make it out to, and we'll add our signatures plus a little extra love *(and probably a dirty joke).*

ABOUT THE AUTHORS

MéLisa Ryun is our combined pen name, and we're a husband-wife duo who've been finishing each other's sentences (and steamy scenes) for nearly 30 years. We left the glitz of Hollywood for the glitter of Vegas. Despite calling Sin City home, we say what happens in Vegas should definitely not stay in Vegas—not with our scorching hot romcoms.

We spend our days in a death match of yoga and joke-writing. Living out our happily-ever-after while making silly social media videos together. **Snark. Swoon. Spice!**

VISIT MELISARYUN.COM

FIND US ON SOCIAL MEDIA @MELISARYUN

www.ingramcontent.com/pod-product-compliance
Lightning Source LLC
Chambersburg PA
CBHW061537190726
48289CB00004B/1074

* 9 7 8 1 9 4 7 7 7 5 1 7 6 *